Praise for *Trace of Magic*

"Best book of the year! Best new character of the year! Best new series all year! I. Loved. This. Book. You gotta read it."
—Faith Hunter, *New York Times* bestselling author of the Jane Yellowrock series

"*Trace of Magic* caught me up fast and pulled me in tight for a fun, action-and-sass adventure full of deadly magic and dangerous romance. Diana Pharaoh Francis delivers a downright terrific read."
—Devon Monk, nationally bestselling author of *Hell Bent*

"A vividly written world of magic and kick-ass action."
—D.B. Reynolds, author of the Vampires in America series

"Wonderfully fun read! The perfect mix of magic, sleuthing, action, and romance—with a likeable, wise-cracking heroine in a dangerous, well-developed world. I couldn't put it down."
—Barb Hendee, co-author of the Noble Dead Saga

Other Bell Bridge Book Titles
by
Diana Pharaoh Francis

The Crosspointe Chronicles (fantasy)

The Cipher

The Black Ship

The Turning Tide
(coming soon)

The Hollow Crown
(coming soon)

The Diamond City Magic Novels

Trace of Magic

Edge of Dreams
(*Coming soon*)

Trace of Magic

Book 1 of The Diamond City Magic Novels

by

Diana Pharaoh Francis

Bell Bridge Books

This is a work of fiction. Names, characters, places and incidents are either the products of the author's imagination or are used fictitiously. Any resemblance to actual persons (living or dead), events or locations is entirely coincidental.

Bell Bridge Books
PO BOX 300921
Memphis, TN 38130
Print ISBN: 978-1-61194-514-0

Bell Bridge Books is an Imprint of BelleBooks, Inc.

Printed and bound in the United States of America.

We at BelleBooks enjoy hearing from readers.
Visit our websites
BelleBooks.com
BellBridgeBooks.com
ImaJinnBooks.com

10 9 8 7 6 5 4 3 2 1

Cover design: Debra Dixon
Interior design: Hank Smith
Photo/Art credits:
Background (manipulated) © Unholyvault | Dreamstime.com
Woman (manipulated) © Avgustino | Dreamstime.com

:Lmth:01:

Dedication

For Tony, for all you do, especially making me laugh

Chapter 1

EVERYBODY LEAVES a magical trail of sorts, like an indelible ribbon unrolling behind them. It isn't actually on this plane, but in a sort of other dimension that only tracers like me can see.

It fades pretty quick for most tracers, disappearing in a matter of hours or maybe a week or two if they are really strong. It never fades for me. I can even see dead trace. It can be tricky to follow, and doing it can leave you vulnerable to the spirit world. I try not to follow dead trace if I can help it. Altogether, those talents make me a unicorn, the tooth fairy, the Easter Bunny, and the Loch Ness Monster all rolled into one. In a word, I am unique. A very special snowflake.

I grimaced. It makes for an interesting life, in the Chinese curse sense of the word. I spend most of my time figuring out ways to hide out and stay below the radar of every Tyet faction, crew, and boss. I make a living tracking cheating spouses, missing employees (they usually took money with them), missing persons in general, and the occasional thief or housebreaker. It isn't a lot of money, but then I don't need much.

On the side, anonymously, I track down stolen kids. Nine out of ten times, some sadist in the Tyet is responsible. About half the time I find the kids alive. If I didn't look for them, the odds would be about perfect that they'd be found dead. I'm that good. I wish I was better.

I swallowed, my teeth grinding together, thinking of little Philip Johns. He'd never seen his first birthday. His kidnappers had suffocated him with a plastic bag before tossing him into a dumpster. So help me, Nancy Jane Squires was not going to die. Not on my watch.

Nancy Jane and her mother went missing on the second day of January. It was a Tuesday and Nancy Jane's birthday. She was seven. From the moment I heard about it, I knew it was one of my cases—the ones that either I solved or the victims died. Sometimes they died anyway.

Patti had texted me with the news. She's my best friend and part owner of the Diamond City Diner, where I hold my office hours, such as they are. She didn't say much, just: *Another one. Check the news.* I got the message at eight in the morning as I was on my way to pick up groceries. I never go near my house with my phone on in case I'm being tracked. I had powered it up when I got to the central metro station this morning. By then, Nancy Jane and her mom had been missing more than twelve hours.

I didn't have a lot of time. This kidnapping stunk of yet another damned Tyet tug-of-war, which meant Nancy Jane and her mother were entirely dispensable. The only good news was they hadn't been killed on site; that meant the kidnappers hadn't just wanted to make a bloody statement. They wanted something and needed the girl and her mother alive to get it.

It wasn't hard to find coverage. The story was plastered all over the place along with an Amber Alert. There weren't a lot of details. The two had been taken outside a shoe store in Midtown about six thirty the night before. It was out on the south side, where Tyet turf wars seemed to explode every other day. There weren't any witnesses or video. The kidnappers had used nulls to shut down the magic in the area and vanish all trace.

Basically, they'd disappeared into thin air.

I missed my train as I checked the underground rumor sites, and certain social networks. It's amazing how many Tyet crews post online, either bragging about jobs, setting them up, or threatening people.

In the last decade or so, Diamond City had reverted to something of an Old West/mafia war zone. Way back when diamonds were first discovered here, there'd been a huge rush followed by massive territory wars. Eventually the Tyet had emerged—basically a united consortium of very bad people who ran the diamond trade and the town. Our most lauded town hero, Zachary Kensington, had brokered that pact somehow, bringing order from chaos. But then something happened about ten years ago and all hell broke loose. A lot of it had to do with a changing idea of what the Tyet could or should do and various factions wanting more money, more power, more, more, more. A drug trade had entered the scene as well—Sparkle Dust, or SD.

It was made from minerals found only in the Diamond City Caldera, minerals infused with the magic of their violent birth. It lent normal people small random magic talents for a short time, plus made users feel twenty feet tall and orgasmically good. Supposedly if you already had talent, you could do extra special spells while on it. I'd never tried. It wasn't worth it. Sparkle Dust was seriously addictive and sold for a pretty penny. For makers and dealers, they could make almost as much as diamond miners. For addicts, it turned them into wraiths. Literally.

The point is that ten years ago, the shit hit the fan, and now there were dozens and dozens of Tyet crews trying to grab a piece of the pie, while the bigger syndicates made and broke alliances trying to control the entire pie.

The old Chicago and New York mob families used to have the one unbreakable rule: don't go after the women and children. The Diamond City Tyet factions have one too: don't fuck up the diamonds and drug trade. Everything else is on the table, including seven-year-old girls and their mothers.

I hate the Tyet more than I can begin to say. They killed my mother, and if they knew what I could do, they'd hunt me down and repeat the favor on me or take me captive. I'd rather be a corpse than a slave, and I'd rather be free than either. The rest of my family thinks I should get the hell out of the city and go live on the other side of the world. Maybe I will. Before I do, I'm going to find out who killed my mom and what happened to my dad. Then I'm going to make someone pay. After that—I could see myself living in Tahiti. Maybe Venice or Barcelona, or better yet, the Greek coast.

Until then, I planned to do all I could to very quietly make their lives hell. Like finding a way to spike their plans for Nancy Jane and her mom.

I scrolled through the posts I'd pulled up on my phone. Nobody online was claiming responsibility for the Squires kidnapping. Most were pointing fingers at each other, calling names and condemning such heinous acts. Blah-blah-blah. It was nothing more than pots calling the kettles black and made me want to drop them all down the deepest mine shaft I could find.

My next stop was the police feeds. Most cops were dirty. At least, it was safer to assume they were. I hadn't found one yet who wasn't, though I liked to think they existed. There was one I trusted more than the others—Detective-Asshole Clay Price. He was a jerk. Arrogant, prickly, and impatient, he worked for Gregg Touray, who was one of the top Tyet bosses in the city. Everybody knew Price was one of Touray's cop enforcers. He made sure things went Touray's way when the police were called into a situation, and he passed on whatever information he got. The only reason I trusted him more than other cops is that most of the time, he also actually tended to do his job. He also didn't like it when innocents got pulled into a Tyet fight, especially kids.

This case wasn't in his jurisdiction—he worked out of the Downtown—but I was sure he'd have his hand in it. I almost always saw notes from him in these kidnap files.

Accessing case notes on my own was next to impossible. Luckily, I had a tinker friend who was an elite hacker and had given me the keys to the cop feeds in exchange for a top-end null. I didn't hand those out very often—I was supposed to be a crap tracer with minimal talent. Sean was in the same boat as I was. He wasn't going to let my secret out, not if he expected me to protect his.

Price had only written a few lines. Nancy Jane's mother was Tess Squires. The girl's father, Abe, was a low-level tinker working as a mechanic at the Lazarus mine. No one had seen or heard from him since before the kidnapping. The cops had set up checkpoints at every Diamond City exit and at the airport. Price also noted the family's address.

I backed out of the system and shut off my phone before I triggered an alarm. I had a place to start. I fished in the inside pocket of my jacket and pulled out a red glass marble. It was a null, one that targeted my own trace rather than voiding the magic around me. I'd activated one on leaving the house, but as planned, it depleted by the time I reached the metro station.

The only time trace vanished for me was when it was nulled. Depending on who made the null and what they told it to do, the trace would reappear after a while. Good nulls, the kind I made, kept a person from leaving any trace at all for as long as the null lasted. They cost a lot more than the others. I had a feeling that Nancy Jane's kidnappers had gone the cheap route at the shoe store and that their trace would reappear. I was hoping so, anyway.

I'd find out soon enough, but first I wanted to check out the Squire's house and get a clear trace signature for each. I also wanted to see who else had been there recently, particularly the missing father.

I caught the train—half subway/half train really—to the south side of the Downtown shelf. Diamond City is built inside an ancient volcanic caldera in the middle of Colorado, fifty miles south of Gunnison. The crater is more than a hundred miles across and cut in half by the Buffalo River. The river drops in a series of falls on one side, then widens into a big lake near the middle of the caldera before draining out through a network of lava tubes on the other side. The west side is empty lowland meadows that like to flood every spring. Mines make the entire basin and opposite side of the caldera look like it has been bombed, though there have been a few projects to restore the vegetation and prevent erosion and landslides.

Diamond City clings like barnacles to a series of wide basalt shelves on the east side of the river, starting on a broad table of rock at the bottom and rising in steps to the rim of the caldera. The lower part of town houses people who can't afford the rents higher up. Most of them are either living off the diamond dole, or they're too new in town to qualify for it. In the summer, the mosquitoes are nasty down in the Bottoms, and in the winter, the ice and snow turns the place into a cold hell.

Right above the Bottoms is the ledge known as Downtown. It's the city's widest shelf. It covers a good fifty or sixty square miles all told, with the business district in the heart of it and dozens of little neighborhoods, shopping malls, and industrial parks spreading out from there. There is also a healthy share of smaller diamond mines, though many of those have been closed or are getting so regulated they can't hardly dig anymore. I live on the north side of Downtown in an old Tyet hideout created more than a century ago and long forgotten by most people.

The next ledge holds Midtown, where people with any money at all live. The neighborhoods on the north side are ritzier than on the south side. They get more sun and are farther from the falls and the noise of the mines. It's prettier up there, with a lot of parks and trees, a couple of art colonies, and an assortment of glitzy shops and restaurants. The upper rim of the city is Uptown, where you have to have a few million dollars just to buy a dog house. Up there are hundred-acre estates and even a few castles.

I don't like enclosed spaces, and riding the train underground made me sweat fire-hose style. By the time I reached my stop, my tee shirt was clinging to my back and sides, and my deodorant had probably exhausted itself. I put my jacket back on and pulled up the hood. The wind cut right through me. The temperatures were hanging right around five degrees. We hadn't had snow since November, and that had all melted off within a few weeks.

I didn't mind. Winter lasted far too long this high in the Rocky Mountains, and I was never eager for it to arrive. Once the snow started falling, it would pile to the eaves of the houses, and to get in and out, people would have to use their second-and third-floor doors that now exited onto empty air.

I hunched against the wind and fell into a long, ground-eating walk. Traffic was heavy with bicycles zooming past on the sidewalk. The scent of hot bread lured me into a bakery, where I grabbed a cup of hot chocolate and a breakfast sandwich to eat as I went.

The Squires's place was in a fourplex pinched between the back of a laundry mat and a little Mexican taqueria. Cop cars lined the road, the lights flashing. Orange-and-white sawhorses kept the road clear of traffic. Clusters of people stood on the sidewalk, rubbernecking and gossiping. I sidled up close to one group.

"What's going on?"

People love to talk about disasters. It's human nature. A grizzled man with a yellowing beard and a Vietnam vet baseball cap eyed me.

"What's it to ya?"

People love to talk about disasters, except when those disasters come at the hands of the Tyet. Then they get nervous and closemouthed.

I shrugged. "Nothing. Just wondering how long they're going to have the street blocked."

One of his companions, a younger guy with a barely there mustache and a receding hairline, pulled a cigarette from his mouth. "Why? Need to get your car through?"

He laughed as if he'd said something funny. The other men in the little group joined him, then abruptly quieted.

I smiled. "My mom's getting a new bed today from Barrows." I named a furniture store down in the Downtown where the prices were reasonable and a lot of working people shopped. "I'm hoping if we tear apart her old bed, she'll have the new one in time to sleep tonight. She lives a little ways farther by Eaglesdale Church."

I make a habit of knowing what's where in Diamond City. At least in Downtown and Midtown. I'll pick an area and walk it until I remember street names and landmarks. It helps in my line of work. I stay out of Uptown. I look suspicious there, like I'm casing the houses.

Yellow-beard softened. A fictitious mom in need tended to have that sort of effect.

"There's a route up Calloway, if the truck keeps going past Horton Mines and turns up Mason Lane. It dead-ends into Calloway, and that will take 'em right back to Glasspell."

We were standing on Glasspell Avenue.

"Thanks," I said. "I'll call and make sure they know not to come this way." I yawned and started up the street toward the Squires's residence. "You gentlemen take care."

They forgot me before I'd gone three steps. I kept to the other side of the street from the fourplex, keeping my head down and trudging like I had a long way to go, peering sideways at it from under my hood.

The Squires lived on the end. The living space was upstairs, with a garage underneath. White metal steps rose to the second-floor landing overlooked by a picture window and a white door. Dusky blue paint looked pretty recent. The Squires still had Christmas lights twining around the balcony railing and looping around the window. All in all, the place looked cared for, if a little worn at the elbows and knees.

Cops milled around the yard and went up and down the stairs into the apartment. A uniformed tracer paced back and forth on the sidewalk in front of the house, the green stripes on his sleeves giving his talent away. Detective-Asshole Clay Price stood on the postage-stamp lawn, arms crossed, watching, his expression coldly furious.

He had the silky black hair, pale skin, and blue eyes of the black Irish who'd first come to Diamond City to work the mines. A shadow scruff of beard heightened the angles and hollows of his square jaw and obstinate chin. Above them, his sharply wedged nose was asking to be punched. His lips were firm and straight. He had no laugh lines, like he hadn't so much as smiled more than once or twice in his entire life.

In a word, he was gorgeous. And also, he was totally and completely off-limits.

Here's *my* one rule: I try very hard not to be stupid. I don't take the same path home every night, I sleep with a gun under my pillow, I reinforce my nulls every day, I stay out of the spotlight, and I avoid the cops and the Tyet whenever humanly possible. Given that Price was both, he had extra big *no-no* written all over him. Didn't make him ugly though. The bad thing was when the pretty scenery noticed me and stomped across the street to stop me.

"Riley Hollis," he said, glaring down at me. His dark sapphire eyes were intelligent and far too penetrating. "What are you doing here?"

I hated that he knew my name. Not unexpected, given that my cases brought me into his orbit more than I liked, and given that I kept my office hours at the Diamond City Diner, less than two blocks away from his precinct. I still didn't like him knowing who I was. I really didn't like him seeing me here. I should have been more careful.

"Detective Price," I said, pushing my hood back and blinking innocently. "What's happened?"

"Don't play games, Miss Hollis. You're here because you know exactly what's going on. I want to know who's paying you and exactly how your client is connected to the Squires."

I had to admire him. He was a skilled cop. Smart as hell and clearly frustrated. From the expression on his face, it looked like he was bouncing off a dead end. The police tracer must not have been able to pick up anything.

"Sorry, Detective. I saw the lights and decided to see what the fuss was about. I'm on my way to an emergency meeting. Got a lady whose cat went missing."

At his look of pure disbelief, I shrugged and smiled wryly, playing the part to the hilt. "She's kind of a shut-in and her family wants her happy. I told them I doubted I could help since animal trace is nearly impossible for me to pick up, but they're desperate. Seems no one else will even talk to them."

He tipped his head, eyes narrowed. He didn't believe me, but he couldn't exactly hold me for walking down the sidewalk. He reached into his jacket and took out a pen and a notebook, flipping the latter open. "What's the name of your potential client?"

"I can't tell you that," I said. "It's confidential."

"You don't have a confidentiality veil in your line of work."

I did my best to look sorrowful. I was enjoying his irritation far more than I should have been, especially since every second we spent together made me more memorable. "I'm afraid you're going to have to get a warrant. I can't let clients think that I just spew information whenever the police ask for it."

"This is a kidnapping case," he ground out, snapping the notebook shut. "A mother and her seven-year-old daughter. So you can damned well cough up your client's name or you can go to the precinct and wait for me to come question you. Which do you want?"

I chewed my lip. How was I going to get out of this? "I suppose I could help you," I said. "See if I can see any trace."

He snorted. "You're a hack, Miss Hollis. If a department tracer can't find anything, you sure as hell aren't going to."

Just then the man in question shouted Price's name. He glanced down at me and then across the street. As fast as he'd arrived, he strode away.

"This conversation is not over, Miss Hollis," he called over his shoulder. "Expect to hear from me again."

Chapter 2

I HURRIED UP the sidewalk and around a corner out of sight. I hadn't a snowball's chance in hell of going out of Price's mind. I wanted to kick myself. Worst part was, I hadn't got what I needed, and Nancy Jane and her mom were running out of time. Twenty-four hours was the best window for getting them back alive. After that, well, most times either the victims stayed disappeared or turned up dead.

My only option was to sneak back to the fourplex in order to pick up trace from each of the Squires. I could do that from the alley behind. I didn't need line of sight, I just had to get close enough. I looped around a couple of blocks to come around behind the apartments.

There was no alley. A row of houses with postage-stamp backyards nestled right up to the property line. I gritted my teeth. Of course. Why would it be easy? I considered knocking on doors until someone let me in to their backyard, but given how the men on the sidewalk had reacted to me, I doubted I'd make much headway. There was a narrow slot between the back fences of the houses and the taqueria and fourplex. The dry cleaner had blocked it off on one end. Yellow crime-scene tape hung across the other, but no one guarded it. It was almost like they wanted me to go in.

I smiled to myself and slouched down the sidewalk along the fence. The sun was shining, and I did my best to look like I belonged there. I ducked under the yellow tape and squeezed into the narrow space. I edged along until shadows disguised my presence, then opened myself to the trace.

The Squires were easy enough to pick up, even with all the cop traffic to confuse the issue. Like I said before, everybody leaves behind a trace trail, unless it's nulled out in some fashion. I'm betting the police tracer was having a hard time because the Squires's trace was fading on him. Or rather, his ability to see it made it look like it was fading away. That's an assumption most people make—that trace fades over time. It doesn't. The tracer just hasn't got the power to keep seeing it as it ages.

Anyhow, the apartment was full of the family's trace. It was easy to find Nancy Jane's. She had her own room and spent a lot of time in it. Her mother's trace was all over the house in the kitchen and the bedrooms. The father's went to the refrigerator—for beer after work or maybe before—then to what I imagined were the table and the couch, then a bedroom and bathroom. He'd gone into the laundry room maybe once.

Nancy Jane's trace was a ribbon of golden orange. Her mother's was a dark pink, and her father's was gray. The man was dead.

Not good. That meant Nancy Jane and her mom were being used as leverage against someone else. I'd been hoping the father was the kidnapper so I could use him to track them. I had no idea how to find out who was actually involved, at least not in the next day or so. Price had the juice to uncover more, but he wasn't going to give me a heart-to-heart, and I couldn't wait for him to load notes into the computer system. I needed the trace to reappear at the kidnapping site. If it didn't . . .

I thought of little Philip Johns. *No.* I would figure something out.

I inched back down to the entrance and peered out. No one was looking my way. I ducked back under the tape and strode down to the next street and turned out of sight. Next stop, the parking lot where Nancy Jane and her mother had been stolen. I couldn't help but wonder who'd got the ransom note. Maybe the father's body had been the proof of commitment and Nancy Jane and her mother were the treasure to be retrieved. In that case, whoever was on the receiving end of the ransom demand might already have paid it or more likely, be in the middle of their own rescue attempt. Or revenge crusade. Maybe they'd already given the two up for dead.

Fuck, but I hated the Tyet. I hated the politics and the trade in bodies that came with it, and the way everybody ran scared of every shadow. They could all burn in hell, and I wouldn't miss a single one.

I caught the train to Midtown after looking up the shoe store address. It wasn't that far from where my sister's ex-fiancé lived. I grimaced. Ex-fiancé, but not ex-out-of-her-life. I didn't judge, but it was clear that Josh and Taylor were still involved, even if they weren't planning a marriage. Whatever. Not my problem and not my concern. If Taylor was happy, so was I. Unless making her happy meant annoying the fuck out of me, which happened with irritating regularity.

Encanto wasn't your ordinary, run-of-the-mill sort of store. It carried designer shoes and high-end name-brand stuff. Nancy Jane's mother shouldn't have had the money to shop there.

I wandered into a frozen yogurt shop a couple doors down and took my cup to a table in the window. There were two cop cars still parked in front of the store and a crime-scene van parked nearby. Several men and women collected evidence from around the deserted car, using magic and prosaic tools of the trade. I wasn't interested in them. I was waiting for the trace to come back. I'd give it another couple or three hours before I gave up. It had been fourteen since the kidnapping, and a null that lasted longer than that would cost a hell of a lot of money. Since most tracers weren't strong enough to pick up the returning trace, or maybe they just didn't bother to look for it, I figured it would appear soon if it was going to come back at all.

I'd eaten another yogurt and switched to a cafe for hot cider and a sandwich when the trace returned. There was a tangle left behind by five or more people, including Nancy Jane and her mother. I got up and left money on the table for the tip before wandering down the sidewalk. I only needed a trail. A casual walk-by would give me that.

There were three kidnappers and the two victims. Everybody's trace was still colorful and very alive. The getaway vehicle had gone out the east exit of the shopping village and headed east toward the escarpment leading up to Uptown. That surprised me. I thought for sure they'd head for Downtown. The kidnappers didn't strike me as particularly well-funded. Otherwise, they'd have used better nulls. On the other hand, well-funded criminals weren't necessarily smart, and many were cheap enough to pass for stupid.

I followed on foot, wishing I had my mountain bike. I'd wrecked it in October and hadn't gotten around to making the necessary repairs.

They never went to Uptown. They hit the Midtown Pearl District, and turned off the main avenue to zigzag through several neighborhoods. I followed down a long wooded drive to a cul-de-sac with only one driveway leading off. The trail disappeared behind a set of wrought-iron gates attached to tall stone walls. Within was an estate with tall, sweeping trees. I could see the blue-slate roof of the house, but that was about it. A quaint-looking stone guard shack stood just inside the gates. A mat of winter-dried vines covered it over.

The guard noticed me immediately. He stepped out, wearing a puffy down parka and a ball cap with gold braid on it. He wore a gun holstered on his hip and had a radio speaker clipped to his collar at the edge of his hood.

I hesitated, then decided that running was not a good option. There was nothing to indicate that Nancy Jane and her mother had left after they arrived. If I took off now that I was seen, I might spook the kidnappers. They could easily kill Tess Squires and her daughter and get rid of the bodies before I could call in the cavalry.

"What do you want?" the guard demanded. He had a deep voice and skin the color of day-old coffee. He rested his hand on his weapon. Like I would be able to attack him through the gates.

I shuffled up closer and wrapped my hands around the iron bars. "Hey, man, it's really cold out. This place is really a whoop-de-doo, you know what I mean? Like money on the half shell. I don't need cash. Places like this always have stuff to give away, stuff they don't want anymore. Maybe something I could sell? Maybe shoes or clothes? I can get good money for those. I'm really struggling. I got kids. The old man died in a rock fall in the mines and left us with nothing. I can't find a job. I gotta get some food on the table."

The moment I started talking, a look of pity and disgust shadowed the guard's features. His eyes slid away from me like I was suddenly invisible. He dropped his hand from his gun.

"Lady, you need to get out of here. Go beg somewhere else. What the hell you doing here anyway? Go to a church or a soup kitchen or something."

"I will, I will," I said. "Can't you just give me a little something? Maybe a watch? Or a couple dollars? I got another few months before I can get on the diamond dole. Just gotta get there. Kids are sick, you know. Haven't had anything to eat since yesterday. You understand, I know it. You've seen down times. I'll pay everything back. I promise."

I let the panic and desperation ratchet up in my voice, even as I piled more problems on. He didn't believe me; but he wanted to get rid of me, and I had to make my act believable if he wasn't going to get suspicious about me being here.

"Look lady, you've gotta leave. I don't know what made you pick this place—"

"The Lord led me here," I claimed. "He lit the path for me because he knew I'd find help here." I really hoped I wasn't going to burn in hell for using the Lord's name in vain. Not that anybody in heaven knew my name.

"Well, he was wrong. Get lost."

Just then his radio crackled, and a voice barked, "What's going on, Randall?"

The guard gave me a furious look and pressed the button on the speaker. "It's nothing. Just a vagrant, sir. She's leaving."

"She'd better be," the voice snapped back. "Get rid of her now or it's your head."

That wasn't actually a euphemism or an idle threat. I shuddered, but continued to look beseechingly at Randall. He swore and pulled out his wallet and shoved a couple of twenties into my hand.

"That's it, lady," he growled. "You go and don't ever come back. You do and you'll have reason to regret it."

I instantly started to retreat, calling blessings down on him and thanking him. I wanted my exit to look like I was afraid he'd change his mind, but really I just wanted to get out of the line of sight of the security cameras and the chance of him noticing I wasn't quite what I seemed. I'm a jeans and tee-shirt girl. I don't go for designer wear, and I like hiking boots or running shoes. I wear clothes I can move in and that won't get shredded when I have to climb over fences or crawl under a hedge. I do those kinds of things more frequently than I like. So it wasn't that I wasn't looking the role of the beggar—at least for this kind of neighborhood—but that I was awfully clean and neither my shoes nor my jacket were cheap. If anybody stopped to consider, they'd know I wasn't what I claimed to be.

I hustled up the roadway. The trees marching along the sides of the road beyond the drainage culvert gave the estate seclusion, and also protected potential witnesses from watching me get murdered.

A sound alerted me to pursuit. I glanced back. The gates had slid open far enough to let Randall out. He was jogging after me, his hat pulled low.

Fear forked through me, and I broke into a jog. I was fit. I walked or biked most everywhere I went, and Randall was carrying a spare tire around his gut. He also had a gun. I wanted distance between us, as much as I could get.

"Hey!" he called. "I got something else for you! The lady of the house wants to meet you!"

He tried to sound enticing. I wasn't buying. I accelerated. Just over the rise was a four-way stop. After that was about a quarter of a mile with just one or two other houses set well off the road before I got anywhere near population.

Randall swore, and his pace quickened into a long run. Damn, but he was a lot faster than he looked. I started to sprint, hoping he ran out of juice before I did. Not that it would matter. He'd have friends along in a minute. I needed to come up with an escape plan and quick.

I scanned the sides of the road. Tall iron fences threaded behind the trees. Ahead was a driveway with a gate. I wasn't going to take a chance that Randall would catch up with me while I tried to convince another guard to let me in. Tires squealed behind me. Fuck.

The ground to the right exploded, sending rocks and bits of wood and dirt into the air. I swerved left and something splatted down where I would have been and again exploded. Terrific. Randall didn't just have a gun, he had magical explosives and good aim. I'd assumed he didn't have any magical talents—you didn't end up a security guard if you did. That didn't mean he didn't have tricks up his sleeve.

As hard as I try not to be stupid, I'd followed trace into a dead-end trap and then made a ridiculous assumption. I'd been too focused on finding my prey, and now I was paying the price. I deserved to get dead. Not that I was going to go down easy.

I reached into my pocket and fingered the various glass and metal balls I carried. I gripped a steel bearing, about the size of a good-sized grape. I activated it with a pulse of power, feeling the ripple of magic roll through me and out. A null field surrounded me. Nothing magic could penetrate the field until the null's power zeroed out. If any of Randall's bombs hit inside the null's radius, they would be snuffed out.

Bullets, however, were an entirely different story.

I zigzagged back and forth in case he decided to stop and shoot. Given how accurate his bomb-throwing skills were, I expected he was a decent shot as well. The rumble of the car came closer, and I knew I was just about out of time.

I couldn't see a damned thing that would help me. I was stuck in a narrow chute, with fences to the sides of me and trouble crawling up my ass. I couldn't outrun a car or a bullet. Stopping would only lead to them killing me faster. They seemed to be in a shoot-first-ask-questions-later sort of mood.

I blew through the intersection without looking for traffic. I was on a slight downhill grade now and gaining a little bit of speed. My legs were just getting warmed up, and despite my having to zig and zag, I was keeping ahead of Randall, who'd begun to lose steam. Up ahead I could see brick buildings where the trees thinned. There was a little shopping area there, I remembered. A neighborhood gathering place, with a common area, a family grocery store, an Italian restaurant, a little movie theater, a donut shop, and I forgot what else. Most importantly, there were people there.

I wasn't going to make it unless I got rid of the goons chasing me in the car. Behind me the engine revved and tires squealed again. I glanced back over my shoulder. A green car sat in the middle of the intersection. A big SUV had swerved to miss it and had turned down the opposite direction. It was working furiously on getting turned around on the narrow road, but the deep drainage culverts on either side were slowing it down. Men leaned out the window swearing and yelling, and several shots popped off into the air.

Randall was still after me. Only now he'd pulled his gun and was setting up to shoot. My heart thudding, I jumped into high gear, jerking back and forth and hoping he wouldn't hit me.

A bullet struck the ground ten feet ahead of me on the right. My brain went white. An adrenaline bomb exploded in my chest and panic took over. I dove into the nearest culvert, skidding down on my ass and back to the bottom. Roots and tough branches tore my jacket and shredded my hands. The steel null went bouncing off into nowhere.

I landed on tumbled rocks the size of my head. I scrambled up despite the pain blossoming in my left ankle and knee. I clambered over the uneven rocks, gripping weeds on either side for balance. I could hear footsteps above as Randall ran to catch up with me. That's when I finally got lucky.

On the left, under the road, was a pipe big enough to walk through bent over. It emptied into another culvert. That one ran fifteen or twenty feet down to another drain covered by a steel grate. On my right was a runoff gully from the estate above. Fence bars blocked it, but there was room at the bottom to scooch under, if I sucked in my gut.

I scrabbled at some rocks and pulled them out of the way, then lay on my back to pull myself up under the bottom of the gate. I wasn't going to make it. I unzipped my coat, sure that at any moment Randall would look down and see me. He was about twenty-five feet back, looking down into the steep ditch. Weeds and scrub bushes blocked his view. The SUV roared up behind him.

"Where's the bitch?" a woman demanded. "Did you get her?"

"She went to ground in the ditch," Randall said.

I shoved my coat through the bars and then started to wriggle under. The bars were rusty and rubbed red on my skin and clothes. Rocks cut into my back. I ignored them, shoving with my heels and elbows as my chest cleared the fence. I'm curvy. That means I have boobs. Luckily, they mashed enough to let me through. After that, I squirmed and dragged myself the rest of the way in, pulling my coat back on. I still wasn't out of the woods. Randall could still see me if he looked in the right spot. I need to find cover.

"You'd better find her." A male voice threatened this time.

"I get paid to keep people out, not hunt them down," Randall said, glaring at his companions.

Someone got out of the car. I didn't waste time looking back. The runoff gully made me a sitting duck. The sides were soft dirt covered in dry pine needles from the trees growing above. I had no handholds, and my knee and ankle screamed every time I tried to crawl up.

"You get paid to do what we tell you to do. If you don't, you'll find yourself snacking on my bullets, you understand me, *security guard*? Find the girl and kill her."

I chanced a look back. I could only see Randall's legs and the shoulders and waist of the guy threatening him. It looked like he was prodding his handgun into Randall's chest.

Randall slapped the gun aside and shoved the smaller man back. "Don't threaten me, Burke. I'll cut your balls off and wear them for earrings."

I had to smile. I was almost beginning to like Randall. Sure, he was trying to kill me, but he had style. I went back to crawling up the gully. I put my back against the steep slant and started walking myself up, bracing my feet on the other side. I dug my hands deep into the soil to find traction, and soon developed a rhythm.

I climbed as quietly as I could. Luckily, the soft soil and the loud voices covered for me. Unfortunately, my pursuers couldn't fight forever.

"Would the two of you shut the fuck up and get back to finding the girl? We're screwed if she gets away." It was the woman again.

"Like she knows anything," Randall's attacker said. "She's a beggar."

"Or she's not and someone's on to us. You want to take the chance?"

There was no reply to that.

"Check the other side," Randall said. "There's a storm drain under the road. She probably went through. I'll keep going on this side."

I was about level with the road and near the top of the bank inside the fence when he stopped to look down right across from me. I froze. I was in the dappled shadows beneath the trees and my coat was a dusty green. My jeans were covered in dirt. I couldn't have been better camouflaged. All the same, I knew that if Randall looked up, he'd see me.

"Any sign of her?" the woman hollered from across the road.

I could see her now. She had short brown hair and a stocky body. She carried an Uzi, or something like it, with a sling strap over her shoulder. One man sat in the driver's seat of the SUV, which was slowly rolling along. The man who'd threatened Randall must have jumped down into the culvert on the other side of the road. Thank goodness I'd climbed out of view; otherwise, he'd have seen me through the pipe.

"Not down here," he answered. His voice echoed.

"What about you, Randall?" She swung around to look at him.

He stood with his back to her, his gun at his side, looking straight at me. My heart stopped, and I didn't breathe. He turned away. "Nothing here. We'd better step quick. She might be on her way into town."

"Shit." The woman broke into a jog, and the group moved on.

I struggled the rest of the way up to the top and flung myself backward, my legs dangling over the edge of the bank. I felt like throwing up. Why had Randall let me go?

I didn't have a clue, but I was going to have to pay him back, because

I was pretty sure he was going to catch hell for this, if they didn't kill him.

I fumbled in my pants pocket for my cell phone. It came out with a handful of dirt and pine needles. I shook it off and keyed in my passcode. I had one ghosting call left. Sean had set them up for me, no charge, when he found out what I used them for. His contribution to saving kids. The spell allowed me to call Price directly without him being able trace the call back to me.

I activated the spell and waited for him to come on the line. He answered on the second ring.

"Price," he growled.

"Look for the Squires at the end of Sienna Avenue in Midtown," I said. The ghosting spell disguised my voice for me. "The mansion at the dead end. Hurry."

I hung up. I wanted to curl up on my side and just sleep, but I wasn't out of the woods yet—figuratively or literally. I was trespassing. I had to get out of here before whoever owned the place discovered me and decided to tear me limb from limb. Welcome to Diamond City, where private property means stay out or get dead.

I ended up following in the same direction Randall and his companions had gone. I climbed higher into the trees so I couldn't be seen from the road. Going the other way would take me back to the guardhouse I'd passed. I wasn't in the mood to chance that.

I climbed up a low hill and eventually found myself facing another fence. On the other side was someone's backyard. Beyond that was the shopping area I'd been aiming for. The curtains on the back windows of the two-story house were open, and I could hear piano music. A golden retriever poked his head out of a doghouse on the deck, warm breath pluming in the air. Not a good place to escape my prison.

I still hadn't seen or heard any alarms or signs of imminent attack, so I decided to risk waiting out Price. I went down the fence, ignoring the retriever, who finally noticed me and bounded across the yard, barking furiously.

I passed three more houses and found myself at the corner of the property. On the other side was a foot or two of flat land before a twenty-foot straight drop into the culvert. I sighed. Getting out of here was going to be just about as difficult as getting in had been.

I examined the fence. Glyphs had been etched into the undersides of the crossbars. Fuck me. I'm not sure what they'd do if I touched the fence. It depended on what sort of talent had infused them with magic, but no matter what, I wasn't getting over without nulling it. The magic where I'd come under must have been disrupted by years of running water and the rust on the fence. I had to go back there.

I hadn't gone far when a line of black-and-whites whizzed by on the road below. Their lights flashed, but they had no sirens. The third car was one of the new black Camaros. The windows were tinted dark, but I was sure Price was at the wheel. I broke into a jog. Getting down the gully where I'd climbed up was much easier than getting up.

I slid down on my butt, the deep bed of needles protecting me. Landing was more painful, with my twisted ankle and banged-up knee.

Once again I took off my coat to get under the fence, after digging out a few more rocks to make the process easier. Once underneath, I hunch-walked through the storm drain to the other side of the road. I was tempted to follow the cop cars and see what happened, but I didn't want Price to notice me. He was far from stupid. He'd know I'd found Nancy Jane and her mom, and he'd want to know how.

I couldn't let him or anyone else know how powerful I really was. I had no doubt his boss, Gregg Touray, would snatch me up in a minute. He had a decent-sized syndicate and was working hard to shut down the rampant violence and reunite the fragmented Tyet factions. Touray tended to protect his own and the hell with everyone else. Don't get me wrong—he wasn't the bloodiest of the Tyet bosses, but he sure as hell was no angel. I wasn't interested in becoming anybody's puppet, and as long as I was a relative nobody on the Tyet food chain, I had free rein to find out who'd killed my mother and what had happened to my father. Not that I was making any headway. I had zero clues.

My mother was murdered when I was four. One day she was there, the next she wasn't. Like me, she was a tracer. Unlike me, she wasn't crazy powerful. At least, not that I'm aware of. All I know about her is what I remember. After she died, Dad boxed up everything that belonged to her and put it into storage. It was all ruined in a fire that burned the place down a few years later. Dad never talked about her. It was like she didn't exist—except a year or so later, he married my stepmom, Mel, and she could have been my mother's sister. Same red hair and green eyes, same joy, same warm heart. After my dad went missing on my sixteenth birthday, Mel and my half-sister Taylor and my stepbrothers are all I have left. We're family—as tight as blood—but I wake every morning wondering who killed my mother. And then there's the mystery of my father. His trace had simply vanished the day he disappeared. I don't mean he nulled out and stopped leaving a trail, I mean that there was no trace of him left. Like he'd never even existed. What the hell had happened?

That question drove me. He had so many answers to so many questions about my mom and about me. When I was growing up and I asked anything he didn't want to tell me, he always put me off, saying I wasn't ready.

I'd never been ready enough for him.

I realized I was clenching my teeth. Sometimes I wondered if I wanted my dad to have disappeared of his own free will or if I'd rather that he'd been kidnapped. I was torn between missing him with all my heart and a bottomless anger that he'd left me, and not only that, but he'd never bothered to tell me what happened to my mom or why someone would kill her. I always knew it had something to do with me. I don't know why, but I know it's a fact. Like water being wet and fire being hot. No doubts.

I never did get groceries. I was too sore, and I looked like I'd been dragged behind a car for a few blocks. I texted Patti to tell her I was okay and that I was on my way home. She ordered me to come to the diner for dinner, but I told her I'd come in for breakfast, then shut my phone down. I needed to be alone. I'd watch the news and make sure Price had found Nancy Jane and her mother. *Alive*, I thought. He was going to find them alive. After that, I'd soak away the day's soreness and bruises in my bathtub. I'd had some close calls, and I knew that pretty soon it was going to hit me. I could have died. Randall could have shot me—twice. That didn't take into account the bombs he'd been throwing. I'd been lucky. The trouble was, luck had a tendency to run out. I had a feeling mine was running on empty, and I really didn't want to know what was coming around the bend.

Chapter 3

A WEEK LATER, I walked into the Diamond City Diner a little after two in the afternoon. I'd spent the night before following a carpet cleaner who was stealing supplies from his boss. I'd slept a few hours after tracking him to his storage unit, then turned in my report and collected my fee. I hadn't eaten since lunch the day before, and I was starving.

Patti glared at me when I walked in. "You look like shit."

I had no grounds to argue. I hadn't been sleeping well the last week. Nancy Jane and her mother had been rescued alive. I should have been over the moon. Instead, I couldn't shake the feeling that something was very wrong. I spent hours reinforcing my nulls, and I'd taken to carrying my gun everywhere I went, along with the Chinese baton I hid in my sleeve. I usually kept one or the other on me, but tended to leave them behind when I went shopping or to visit my family. Not anymore.

"Thanks. I spent hours on this look." I was wearing my hair in a ponytail, with my usual uniform of jeans, hiking boots, a long-sleeved shirt, a heavy jacket, a hat, and gloves.

"It's cold out there. Got anything to eat?" I asked, unzipping my coat and stuffing my gloves and hat into a pocket before hanging it on a hook fastened to the bench of my usual booth. A snowstorm had moved in, the first of several to come, all piled up like cars stuck on an LA freeway. By the time they were done with Diamond City, we'd be buried.

"Hold your horses, Laraby." Patti glared at the dentist who was waving a check at her. "I'll be there in a second." She grabbed a clean coffee cup off the counter and set it down in front of me and filled it. "I'll get you something to eat."

Ten minutes later, she returned carrying a white oval plate mounded with an omelet, hashbrowns, pancakes, and a half-dozen slices of bacon. I didn't want an omelet, but Patti tended to get me what she thought I needed, not what I wanted. It was loaded with vegetables and cheese. Tasty, but not the burger and fries I was craving. Arguing wasn't going to do me any good. I'd eat what I was given and try to look happy about it.

"Give me a few minutes," she said. "We should slow down soon and I'll join you. People are trying to get home before the weather gets too heavy."

I glanced through the front window. Snow was falling in a thick curtain of fat flakes. Already the ground was white. I was willing to bet there'd be an inch or two on the ground by the time I finished eating. Giving lie to her promise, the door jingled and half a dozen people came in, stomping their feet and dusting the snow off their clothing.

Patti zipped off to help them. I cleared my plate and immediately wanted a nap. I considered heading upstairs. Patti kept a room for me in her apartment. I spent two or three nights a week at the diner, sometimes more, depending on the jobs I had. Right now I didn't have anything lined up. I was planning to hit the grocery store and go home and hole up until the storms blew themselves out.

I took my dishes to the bus tub, waving at Ben, Patti's partner in the diner, through the kitchen window. I grabbed a pot of coffee and filled my empty cup before sliding back into my seat. I didn't bother looking up when the bell on the door rang again. I was checking the weather radar on my phone.

A shape loomed over me suddenly, and Clay Price slid into the seat opposite me. My mouth dropped open. As far as I knew, he'd never even set foot in the diner before.

"What do you want?"

He slid my coffee out of my hand and took a sip, then eyed it in surprise. "That's good," he said.

"Not to mention it's mine," I said, eyeing him balefully. It was the best coffee in town, though I'd not yet creamed and sugared it to suit my taste buds. He seemed to like his black.

He set the cup down, then ran his fingers through his hair. He was the carefully controlled type, so his gesture startled me. I examined him. He didn't look any better than I did. His eyes were sunken, and grooves cut deeply around his nose and mouth.

"You know, if you're hungry, there are other tables. Empty tables," I pointed out.

He sipped my coffee again. "But you're not sitting at the other tables."

A frisson of foreboding rippled through me. I shivered. It had nothing to do with cold. "You came looking for me?"

"I knew you were a smart woman."

"Why?"

He pulled a manila file from inside his leather jacket and set it on the table. "I want you to do a trace for me."

Like I said before, my cardinal rule is not to be stupid. Taking a case working for Price—a cop *and* a Tyet enforcer—was the dictionary definition of stupid. Insane even. I didn't even think before I said, "No."

Price didn't seem to notice. He shoved the file across the gray Formica.

I looked at it and then back at him. "Maybe you have a hearing problem," I said. "I'll speak slower. No. I'm *busy*. If you want me on a trace, you're going to have to wait your turn. Give me your card. I'll call you in a few days." Like hell I would. I wouldn't call him if I was buried alive and he owned the only shovel on the entire planet.

I started to get up. He grabbed my arm and yanked me back down. "You don't seem to understand, Miss Hollis. You're working for me until I find what I'm looking for. Unless, of course, you want me crawling over you like stink on shit. In that case, I'll make your life so interesting you won't have time to sleep."

Interesting was code for he would dog my ass all the way to hell if necessary. He would, too. Detective Clay Price was a pit bull. He didn't know the meaning of "back off." Once he got his teeth into you, you'd be dragging him around like a ball and chain until you gave in or died.

I stared at him. How did I get out of this? He watched me back with a look of cold calculation, the way a snake watches a cornered mouse.

I had a feeling he saw a lot more than I wanted him to see. "Wait a second. Working for *you*?" I asked, his words finally eating their way into my brain. "This is personal?" What was so important about this trace that he came looking for me rather than use someone on the Tyet's payroll? I mean, it's obvious why he didn't use a cop tracer. They were mediocre. The Tyet owned the best. Well, except for me, and they don't have a clue how good I am.

His upper lip twitched—almost into a snarl—but then his face smoothed into an unreadable mask. He said nothing.

"You don't want anyone to know about this," I mused out loud, sure I was right.

A flicker of something cold and black ran across his face. If I hadn't been trying to catch a reaction I would have missed it.

"That's right," he said, and I shivered at the stony ruthlessness in his tone.

"Why?"

"None of your business."

"Exactly. Since we're in agreement, I'll be hitting the bricks now."

I began to stand up, but he grabbed my arm so tight his knuckles turned white. It *hurt*. I twisted to get away, and he only tightened his grip.

That did it. I slid my telescoping baton out of my sleeve into my palm and flicked it open. I snapped it down on the back of his wrist. I was careful not to hit hard enough to break bone. That would have been a fatal mistake. He jerked away with a yelp.

Everyone in the diner turned to look. Good. He wouldn't want a scene. I stood and started past him for the door. Before I'd gone two steps, he had ahold of my arm again. He hauled me down into the booth beside him and held me tight to his side, keeping me from using my baton again. With his free hand, he pressed something burning cold against my neck. Shock made me go stiff. Did the fucker tab me?

I elbowed him hard in the ribs. He grunted, but didn't let me go.

"Listen, you cat," he said roughly against my ear. "If you don't settle down, I'm going to drag you across the street to the precinct and book you for assaulting an officer."

For a second I considered calling his bluff, but I doubted it would get me out from under his thumb. With the tab, he could follow me anywhere. Unless, of course, I broke its magic, and if I did that, he'd know I wasn't as weak as I pretended to be. Which meant the Tyet would know. *That* would be epically stupid. I stopped fighting.

"Good girl," he said like I was a dog and eased his hold, still keeping a firm arm around me. "Now, have a look at the file." He shoved it toward me again.

The low hum of conversation had resumed, along with the clatter of plates and the click of Patti's heels as she hurried back and forth behind the counter topping off coffees. Through the window into the kitchen, I could see Ben scowling at me. He was holding a boning knife and looked like he was ready to come over the counter and gut Price. I gave him a little shake of my head.

"Smart," Price said, watching the exchange.

I shook him off and compressed my baton before sliding it back up into my sleeve. Heat poured off his body like a stove, and he smelled delicious. I bet that's what rats thought about the cheese right before the trap snapped their necks.

I shoved the thought away and opened the file. There wasn't much in it. Just a single picture with a name on the bottom: Corbin Nader. He was blond, with a rounded jaw and a white smile. He was dressed in a gray suit and tie, and he had a hundred-dollar haircut.

"What's he done?" I asked, knowing full well I wasn't going to get a straight answer.

"He's got information I want," Price said, proving me right. "I need him found, and now."

I turned the picture over. I needed something personal, something this Corbin Nader had touched, to pick up the trace. "Is this all you've got?"

"I've got his apartment," Price said. He nudged me with his hip. "We can be there in a half hour."

I shook my head. "Not before we settle on what you're paying me."

His eyes narrowed. "What do you have in mind?"

I had in mind tripling my daily rate. "Six hundred a day."

"That's ridiculous. You're a hack. You work out of a diner."

I shrugged. "I told you to find someone else. But if you want me, you pay me."

He grimaced. "All right. But this is your only case until you find him."

Holy shit. He must be desperate. "Oh, and another two hundred a day for the tabbing." I rubbed my neck, but the spell wouldn't be wiped away so easily. Given how strongly the magic radiated, I'd have to pay through the nose to have the spell broken. Might as well get paid for being lojacked.

"Don't push it," he growled.

"Who's pushing?" I demanded. "You're forcing me to work for you, and you tabbed me so you can follow me anywhere I go. Call it a privacy tax. Take off the tab, and you don't have to pay it."

"Not a chance," he said, baring his teeth in what might have been a smile. If it was, he needed practice. "All right. Eight hundred a day. Let's go." He scooted against me, shoving me to the end of the bench.

"I want three days up front," I said.

He glared at me, and I swear there was steam coming out of his ears. "You think it's going to take you three days?"

"Might. Don't worry. I'll give you a refund if it doesn't—except for your privacy tax. I'll be keeping that. But you haven't given me a lot of reason to trust you." I touched the spot on my neck where he'd stuck the tab. "I'd just as soon be sure I get paid."

His mouth twisted, and his hand clenched on the gray Formica tabletop. For a second I was sure he was going to blow up. Then he just reached into his leather jacket and pulled out his phone. He called up his bank and asked me for my account. I gave him the number. He typed it in and shoved his phone back in his pocket. "Done."

I thumbed the screen on my phone. Twenty-four hundred bucks had been added to my account total. The weight of that payment crushed the last of my excuses not to work for him. "Good enough," I sighed and then got up, grabbing my coat off its hook.

I'm not short. I stand at around five foot ten in my bare feet. My boots put me at almost six feet. Even so, the top of my forehead barely came to the bottom of his nose.

"Leaving?" Patti asked, coming around to stand between Price and the door.

She stood only about five foot nothing, wearing knee-high boots with four-inch heels. She wore a jean miniskirt with fishnets and a tightfitting black shirt. She held two full pots of coffee and she was ready to dump them on Price. She looked like a Chihuahua facing off against a pit bull. I'd put my money on her.

"I've got a job," I told her.

She looked at Price and then back at me. "Are you drunk?"

I wished. "Not yet."

Patti was older than me by about five years, but we were as close as sisters. Check that. Closer, because my sister Taylor is kind of an alien. Or maybe I am. I love her to death, but we really don't get each other very well. Anyway, Patti and I are two peas.

"Friends don't let friends walk blindly off cliffs," she said. "How much is he paying you?"

"Too much," Price said, starting to push past her.

She gave him her patented stand-still-or-I'll-kill-you look, and as usual, it worked. She turned her attention back to me. "Are you okay with this?"

I shrugged. "Not really, but he made me an offer I couldn't refuse," I said sourly. "At least the pay is good."

"Call me later," she ordered after a considering moment. She glared at Price. "You hurt her in any way, and I'll make sure you don't survive to your next birthday."

He snorted softly. "I'll remember."

"You'd better." She stepped aside. I gave her a quick hug before leading the way out.

The Diamond City Diner sat on the corner of Atlantic and Sod streets. Its tables were rarely empty. Down the block and across the street was the 4th Precinct and beside it, Firehouse 11. The weatherman had promised a good two feet of snow, and already there were a couple of inches on the ground. I zipped up my coat but didn't bother with my hat and gloves, figuring Price would have a car close by.

He gripped my elbow and turned me up the sidewalk away from the precinct. We'd covered a couple of blocks before I began to wonder if he had any plans to stop. My hair was wet and his head had a mound of white capping it.

"Are we walking there?" I asked in annoyance as I skidded on a patch of ice.

He looked down, almost like he'd forgotten me. "No."

He glanced over his shoulder. The heavy snow swirled in the air and hid most of the street. Price pulled me suddenly into a doorway between Riker's clothing store and Roadkill Bikes. Before I could protest, he pushed me behind him.

"Company," he warned.

Lovely. Somebody was following us, and Price didn't expect them to be friendly. Nice of him to shield me. 'Course, I wouldn't have needed it if he hadn't blackmailed me into working for him. I shoved the thought aside. Shit happens and all that, but trouble was here and now. I opened myself to the trace.

Strings of light flickered out over the pavement and sidewalks. They melded into thick cables—too many strands to differentiate between them. I focused on the brightest threads, the ones belonging to people here now. On a busy street like this, most tracers couldn't pick out a live person's trace from one left behind an hour before. I could.

A half-dozen people strode up the sidewalk behind us. Price's bulk prevented me from seeing them. He seemed to think one or all were threats. He wasn't the nervous type, so in the name of preparation, I pulled my Ruger out of my coat pocket.

"Try not to shoot me in the ass with that, would you?" Price said, glancing back at me.

"Don't get in my way and I won't. Maybe."

The corner of his mouth curved up. It was almost a smile. I wondered if it hurt.

"I'm beginning to regret paying you up front."

Then his attention was back on the sidewalk. I edged to the left, trying to get a view. He grabbed me and shoved me back behind him. I was getting really tired of him manhandling me. Then again, if he wanted to take the heat so I could walk away free, who was I to argue?

Three pedestrians passed by, never pausing. That left three more. From what I could tell, they were walking slowly, spread out across the sidewalk. The one in the middle was flanked by two others trailing a couple of steps behind. Not good. That seemed too organized for casual strollers.

I waited, wondering what Price would do. Not a lot of people would be willing to take him on. Whoever was after him was risking a lot. Price was a known asset for one of the biggest Tyet organizations. Going after him would earn some serious retaliation. The trio was totally insane, if you asked me.

The three followers slowed and started to bunch together. Damn. No way they could see us, so that meant they had to have a tracer with them. I touched one of my nulls in my pocket. It was short-term and weak. If I'd known there was a chance we were going to trap ourselves in a doorway with three goons hunting us down, I'd have nulled us out.

Suddenly I had an idea. I turned and checked the door. It was locked, but with an old-fashioned key lock. I smiled and shoved my gun back into my outer coat pocket. I slipped my lockpicks from the coat's breast pocket and went to work. It took me less than ten seconds. It was a crappy lock.

I twisted the knob and slipped inside, pulling Price after me. His eyes widened, but he followed. I turned the deadbolt, and then pulled two nulls out of my pocket. They were cat-eye marbles, the kind that come in quarterbags at the toy store. I put one in his hand and invoked it, then did the same to mine. If we were lucky, we could escape the building before the goons caught sight of us.

"Come on," Price said.

He dashed up the narrow stairs as someone rattled the door behind us. Gunshots sounded. Wood splintered in the door and stairs. I stumbled, bashing my shin as I missed the step.

Price grabbed my hand and hauled me up after him. "Do you want to get dead?"

He didn't let me go as he pulled me down the hall. I was still wrestling with my panic and clung to him like a child. He tested the knobs of each door. None gave. He finally stopped at the end. "Pick it," he hissed as someone crashed against the door downstairs. He stepped past me and drew his gun. He carried a .44 Desert Eagle. A hand cannon. I could have made a joke about a man overcompensating, but decided it wasn't the time. Occasionally, I have moments of reason.

I went to work with my picks, trusting I wasn't going to get shot in the back. If there was one thing I could trust about Price, his aim was good and he wasn't afraid to kill. And the faster I opened the door, the faster we'd be hidden. I was hoping we'd have time to figure out an escape that didn't involve bullets and bodies.

The lock gave, and I opened the door. There were no lights on. I gave a quick, low whistle, but Price was already shoving in after me. The man had to have eyes in his ass.

He locked the knob and the dead bolt behind us. The curtains were closed, and there was precious little light. I jammed my knee into the corner of something hard and sharp as I went across the room to open the drape. I clamped my teeth to keep from swearing.

"What now?" I whispered. Now that I had a moment to take everything in, my hands shook with adrenaline and fear.

Price toured the apartment before coming to look out the window. We were on the corner of the building above the bike shop. Outside, a fire ladder was bolted just below the window. There was no landing. Price slid open the window and motioned for me to climb out, then went back to the front door. I assumed he was watching for our pursuers out the peephole.

I hoisted myself up on the sill and slid out feet first. The steel was frigid and slippery, and I had to twist myself around onto my stomach. At last I was facing inward again with one foot securely on a rung. I started down. About halfway to the ground, the ladder ended. I looked over my shoulder and groaned. It was another fifteen feet to the pavement.

I squatted on the ladder and gripped the bottom rung tightly, then let my feet go. My weight hit my arms with a jolt. I dangled a moment, then dropped.

I flexed my knees to absorb the shock, and then scooted up against the building as Price followed me down. I opened my mouth to ask who was after us, but I didn't want to waste time and give them a chance to find us. So I kept silent and motioned him on. That startled Price. He gave me an appraising look, then grabbed my hand and pulled me through the thickening curtain of snow. I gritted my teeth and fought the urge to twist myself away. I was a tracer, for crap's sake. I wasn't going to *lose* him. And given that the fucker had tabbed me, he wasn't in any danger of losing me, either.

We hadn't gone far up the alley when my phone buzzed against my thigh. I pulled it out and checked the display. It was a text from my sister, Taylor. I opened it, then stopped dead, yanking out of Price's grasp. All it said was: *911*.

In our entire lives, no matter what was going on, she'd never sent an emergency message. She had told me more than once that she wanted it to count, so that if I got one, I'd know it was real, and not just a hangnail or a stubbed toe.

I held my hand out flat as Price started to say something. He must have read the violent fear in my face because he shut up and waited as I hit the speed dial for Taylor. She picked up almost before it rang.

"Oh God! Oh God! You have to come now, Riley!" She was screaming and crying, and I was pretty sure Price could hear her.

"What's wrong? Where are you?" I asked, forgetting we were trying to make a quiet escape. My heart pounded. What was happening? Was someone breaking in? Trying to attack her?

She gasped and choked on sobs, then she caught herself enough to answer. "I'm at Josh's. Oh God, Riley. There's so much blood!"

Chapter 4

I COULDN'T GET any more out of Taylor, except that Josh was missing and there was a lot of blood. I told her to sit tight and I'd be there as soon as I could. I hung up and looked at Price. "Our deal's off for now. My sister's in trouble. I'm going to help her."

I didn't wait for an answer, more than halfway expecting him to try to cuff me. To my shock, he simply fell in beside me as I headed for the nearest hotel and a taxi stand. I wasn't going to waste time on the subway. I was grabbing a cab, though in this weather, that might take longer.

"My car's not far," he said. "I'll drive you. It'll be faster." At my doubtful look, his brows winged down and his mouth twisted. "I'm not going to stop you. She's your sister. I may be able to help. I *am* a cop, and a pretty good one."

I was surprised and oddly grateful. I nodded and he started off. We'd only gone a few feet when the apartment we'd just fled exploded. Glass and bricks flew through the air like shrapnel.

Price shoved me down behind a dumpster, sheltering me with his body. My ears rang and my body reverberated with the shockwave. Snow soaked through my jeans. Price braced himself over me, his chest and thighs wedging me tight to the dumpster.

When everything had settled, he pulled me up again. "You all right?"

I glanced down at myself. I curled my fingers into fists to hide the fact they were shaking. "Fine. What the hell happened?"

"A lesson. It doesn't pay to come after me."

I glared at him, and part of me couldn't help but feel a stab of disappointment. For a second I'd forgotten he was a Tyet man and a killer. A stupid mistake. I couldn't let my guard down ever. "You did that? What the hell is wrong with you? Did you even think about who else could get hurt? Or were you only worried about your own skin and your revenge? Your enemies get killed and so do all the Nancy Jane Squires and their families in the whole building?" The words tumbled out in a torrent, partly emotional reaction to the blast and partly fury that he could be so brutally cold-blooded.

"Relax," he said. "I shaped the charge to blow out the window wall and make a mess of the place. I'd be surprised if the men chasing us got more than a few scratches. Nobody else was in the line of fire."

The relief I felt had less to do with the safety of the apartment dwellers and more to do with the fact that he wasn't the monster I'd momentarily imagined him to be. I closed my eyes and bent over, catching myself on my knees. *Don't go there*, I warned myself. *Don't let yourself think he's anything but dangerous.* Maybe he didn't kill anyone this time, but he had before and he would again.

"Are you okay?" He put a hand on my back.

I shook it off and straightened. "I'm fine. Perfect even. It's almost like nobody tried to shoot at me or blow me up." I resisted the urge to shove him away. "We should go."

Price gave me a frowning look, then turned and led the way to the Luna Hotel. It was a small, ritzy place standing only about twenty stories tall. It was one of the first buildings in Diamond City and had been completely renovated a few years back. A night's stay in a regular room cost five grand. The suites were quadruple that. But it had tight security, luxuries to give even a well-heeled mogul a hard-on, and it was discreet. If you stayed there, no one got into your business. It was owned by Barry Ostrander, a pretty high member of the Thaler coalition—allied with Price's boss Touray—and working his way to the top, if rumor was correct.

Price led me up past the valet stand. I felt the two nulls I'd activated for Price and me snuff out as the hotel binding ring killed them. It didn't permit any unauthorized active magic to cross it. My other nulls were fine. Unless they were activated, Ostrander's suckers couldn't touch them. Beefy guards in navy blue trimmed in gold stood at careful attention around the doors. There were more than a dozen of them, and they were all armed, and not just with guns. Three of them moved to intercept us as we turned up the sidewalk.

I kept my head down and hunched my shoulders. It wasn't that hard to look inconspicuous in the snow. It was coming down so heavy now that they probably couldn't make out much detail anyway. I doubt any of them could have picked me out of a lineup if they tried. Not that they'd need to, but it pays to be careful. You never know when someone is going to decide you're interesting enough to check out. As a rule, I do my best to fade into the wallpaper in every situation.

"Can I help you?" one of them asked Price in a tone that said "you don't belong here, get the fuck out."

One of them got a look at Price's face. "I got this, Wings," he told the other man and waited for his two companions to retreat.

The burly guard motioned for us to follow him up under the awning. He fished a set of keys out of his pocket and passed them to a valet, who ran off to fetch the car. He gave me a searching look and then turned his attention to Price. "You need anything else?"

"Might be some characters looking around for me. They shouldn't head this way, but if they do, I wasn't here."

"You got it. That it?"

"For now. Thanks, Ed."

"Anytime." I could feel him looking at me again and then he turned and returned to his post. A couple of minutes later, Price's black Camaro emerged from the parking garage beneath the hotel.

The valet held the door open for Price and then came around and opened mine. I stamped my feet and shook off whatever snow I could before sliding into the buttery soft leather seat. I ignored my seat belt and so did Price. Cop habit, that one. You never knew if you might have to jump out and chase someone. Plus, it made it hard to draw a gun. I just liked having a quick escape ready.

Price tossed a bill at the valet and pulled out to the street. "Where are we going?"

"Midtown," I said. "North side."

He made a left and navigated his way carefully through the already-drifting snow, staying off the main drag, where traffic was knotting up. We took the Prockney Tunnel up to the Midtown shelf. It took a good half hour to get through the traffic to the other side. I was getting twitchy as hell.

"Who is Josh?"

Price's question made me jump. I pushed my hair back over my ear. For a second I debated telling him a lie, just on principle. But he was about to find out anyhow. "He's my sister's ex-fiancé. They broke it off about six months ago."

"Ex-fiancé?" He sounded like he was interviewing a witness. Maybe he was. I kept myself from squirming like a first-time nude figure model in a classroom of artists.

"Yeah. My sister is still in love with him."

"Why did they break up?"

I shrugged. "Josh got cold feet or something. He wanted to see other people." I snorted. "I'm not sure he actually ever did. Taylor was a wreck. She lost about twenty pounds and looked like she'd just been raised from the dead."

"But they stayed in touch?"

"Josh kept calling and talking to her. He didn't want to marry her, but he didn't want to let her go either." I shook my head. I'd thought my sister should lose his number and cut him off completely, but despite her anguish, she was too much in love to do that. "I know he was worried about how she was taking the breakup. Maybe he was afraid she'd do something stupid. Or maybe he's just a selfish bastard."

The trouble was, I liked him. I always had. Up until the point he broke my sister's heart, I thought he was about perfect.

"Was he mixed up in anything illegal? Maybe drugs?"

Yep, Price was doing his cop thing. For Taylor's sake, I chose not to mind. But accepting his help meant he was going to get a lot more access to my family and to *me*, to things I didn't want him to know. I was going to have to be extra careful.

Before I could answer, the phone rang. It was Taylor.

"Where are you?" she wailed. My sister was not a wailer. She did not lose control. Usually she had ice water running through her veins.

"Just coming out of Prockney Tunnel," I said in a soothing voice. "The snow has slowed everything down. I should be there in ten minutes." It would be closer to twenty, but she didn't need to know that.

"Ten?" she said, and she started crying in great gulping sobs. "Can't you come faster?"

"Taylor," I said sharply. "Go somewhere away from the blood. Make yourself some tea." I didn't think she'd drink it, but it would give her something to do. I considered telling her to leave the apartment and go down to the building lobby, but I doubted she'd go.

"Tea?" she repeated stupidly. "I don't want tea. How can I make tea when Josh is probably—" She started crying again, and she sounded like she was on the verge of hyperventilating.

I was shocked when Price pulled the phone from my hand. "Hello?" he said before I could grab it back. I could hear the startled silence from Taylor. "This is Detective Clay Price. I need you to take a deep breath and hold it for the count of six. Ready? One-two-three-four-five-six," he counted off slowly. He sounded like he was talking to a child. "Good. Now again. One-two-three-four-five-six. That's very good. Once more."

He did that about ten times. I tapped his knee and pointed where I wanted him to turn. He was keeping her busy, and that's what Taylor needed—something else to concentrate on. When she had stopped her hysterical crying, he tried to focus her in another direction.

"Now, Miss Hollis, I want you to get up and go in the kitchen. Find the tea." She didn't object because he didn't have to ask again. I don't know if she was hypnotized by his voice or what, but she simply obeyed.

"Have you found it? Get the kettle and fill it." A minute later he said,

"Now get out the teapot and sugar. Put at least five spoonfuls in."

I winced. Taylor hated sweet tea. She apparently told him so.

"That's okay. It's for me," he told her. Good call. Taylor would do things for other people she wouldn't do for herself. "Your sister is pretty wet from the snow," he said with a glance at me. "Maybe you could round up a couple of towels. You know, I bet she could use some coffee. Maybe you could brew a cup when you're done with that tea."

He kept her talking until we were on Josh's street. He lived in a condo up near the top of one of those steel and glass buildings that look like they ought to be in outer space. I pointed and he parked, still talking to Taylor. I have to admit, he impressed me. He wasn't dead inside like I'd always assumed he was. Or if so, he faked human kindness well.

The doorman for the building was nowhere to be seen, nor was there anyone in the lobby. My skin prickled warning. I led the way up the stairs. I don't like elevators, and if I can avoid them, I do. The door to Josh's apartment was ajar. Josh had enough money to pay for good wards, and he had. He kept them charged, too, so either he'd let his attackers in, or they'd had a null or an unbinding charm. A strong one to eat the magic of those wards. I heard Price calling out a warning to let Taylor know we'd arrived as I pushed inside.

The place was in shambles, and those are the kind words. The furniture was turned over, the cushions ripped apart, and a bunch of holes knocked into the sheetrock. The bookshelves lay topsy-turvy, and the wall of glass overlooking the city was covered with spiderweb cracks. That was all I had time to notice before Taylor slammed into me. She clutched me around the neck in a death grip. I hugged her back.

Price slipped past us and prowled through the rubble of the room, going down the hallway to investigate the bedrooms and the den. He returned, his face that inscrutable mask except for a furrowed line between his brows, like his brain was in overdrive.

I stroked Taylor's back. "Easy," I whispered. "I'm here. We're going to find Josh. But I need you to get it together so we can figure out what happened, okay?"

My sister nodded against my ear. She gathered herself and stepped away. I kept hold of her hand.

Taylor is about my height, with the same narrow face as mine. Her cheekbones and chin are rounder, and her eyes are blue. Mine are green. Her hair is a rich dark auburn streaked with dyed sunshine. I've always envied her her hair. Mine is the color of burnished copper. It gets a little more red in the winter, and in the summer it turns brassy blond. I also get freckles, though I tan better than she does. Her skin is porcelain. She also has long, polished nails and dresses in the height of fashion. I cut my nails short and wear whatever happens to still be reasonably clean. I don't think I've ever ironed anything in my life. Taylor shudders in horror at wrinkles.

But now she looked anything but neat and put together. Her mascara had smeared over her cheeks, and her eyes were swollen. Her nose was red, and her face was blotchy.

"Hey," I said. "Go wash your face, okay?" It would make her feel better and give me a chance to look around.

She gave me a stricken look and nodded. As she went up the hall, I joined Price.

"There was definitely a struggle," he said. "It's certain they were looking for something and I don't think they found it.

I agreed. Why take Josh if they had?

"Come here," he said and led me down the hall to Josh's den.

The room was even more of a mess than the rest of the condo. His desk and bookshelves had all been cut apart with a saw. The only thing still upright was an armless chair. Blood smeared the seat and ran down the legs to pool on the floor beneath it. I stared. It was a lot of blood. This hadn't just been a beating.

"They cut him pretty good," Price confirmed, looking over everything clinically. "They must have had a tinker to seal the wounds so he wouldn't bleed out and die before they got what they were looking for. Presupposing it's his blood." He looked at me. "Did he have another girlfriend?"

"I don't know," I said, my lips wooden. My stomach churned as I thought of Taylor. What if she'd been here? Would they have cut her? Killed her? My hand clenched.

"What can you see?" he asked me.

I gave him a confused look and then opened myself to the trace. I could have kicked myself. I should have begun scanning the minute I walked into the condo. Being personally involved was totally throwing me off my game. I couldn't afford it. I had to focus. For Josh, for Taylor, and for me.

I could see a weaving of old trace. Most were Josh and Taylor, though it looked like she didn't come in here all that often. I had a feeling the bedroom would tell a different story.

There were three new tracks overlaid on the old. I crouched and reached through the dimensional plane to touch them. I hissed and jerked erect.

"What is it?"

I didn't hesitate to lie. Well, not so much lie as withhold some important truth. "There's no trace of anyone but Josh, Taylor, and three others. One of them is a tinker," I said, since he'd already figured that out.

The other two were haunters. Haunters were rare enough that most of them worked for one of the Tyet factions. If I told Price they'd been here, he'd be just as likely to protect them than not, and block me from finding Josh. But why the hell had they come after my almost brother-in-law in the first place? I couldn't begin to imagine what had been worth sending a tinker and two haunters.

Tinkers weren't as versatile or powerful in the world of magic as the main five abilities—tracer, traveller, maker, dreamer, and binder. But they could be nasty all the same. They, as their name implied, tinkered with things. They had the ability to make small things move. Not exactly teleportation, more like bending, breaking, mending, and so on. A lot of them were doctors. My bet is this one had been responsible for torturing Josh and making sure he didn't bleed to death. His track said he was strong.

The haunters were another story. They were a little like dreamers, in that they could mess around in your mind. But mostly they picked up on emotions and could amplify them. They could find your nightmares and make you live them like they were real. They could trap you in a nightmare for a little while. The good thing was that their magic wore off faster than most. Haunters weren't that powerful, but with two of them keeping a regular vigil, they could've driven Josh to insanity pretty damned quick.

"One tinker? The other two weren't magic users?" Price asked.

"Not that I could tell," I said, and the lie rolled off my tongue easily.

"And there was no one else?"

"That's what I said." It annoyed me that he seemed to doubt me. I know I was pretending to be a hack, but I wasn't supposed to be that bad.

He nodded thoughtfully. "So they don't have a second hostage. That's good. If he can hold off talking, it will give us time to find him."

Taylor could have been here. She could have walked right into it, and they'd have used her to make him tell them what they wanted to know. Then they'd have killed her.

I turned away so that Price wouldn't see my reaction. A second later I felt his hand on my back. He turned me to face him.

"Are you okay?"

His dark sapphire eyes roamed over my face, and there was a gentleness to them that warmed the ice running through my veins. But it wasn't about me. It was habit. He was a cop, and he was just reassuring the witness. Okay, I wasn't a witness, but close enough.

I stepped away. "Taylor could have been here."

He nodded understanding.

I heard the bathroom door open and went to find my sister. She stood in the hallway, arms wrapped around herself, and I could see her starting to shake. I took her to the kitchen. It was as much a disaster as the rest of the condo. She'd found the tea, coffee, and sugar and had made hot water. The teapot was insulated metal and hadn't broken, and the French press was plastic. I cleaned off one of the barstools and sat her down, then poured her a cup of the sweet tea. She sipped it and then made a face at the syrupy taste.

"Drink it," Price said, coming in behind me. He picked his way through the mess on the floor, opening cupboards and drawers, exploring. "You need the heat and the sugar or you'll go into shock."

To my surprise, Taylor drank without another protest.

He poured coffee into a cup that had lost its handle and spiked it with a heaping spoonful of sugar. "You too," he said, holding the drink out.

"Thanks, dad," I said with a grimace. Luckily I do like my coffee sweet and with cream, but I wasn't going hunting in the refrigerator for any. Talk about insensitive. Instead, I sipped the bittersweet brew, glowering at Price all the while. *I* didn't need him bossing me around.

I took my coffee and went to the front door and out into the hallway. I was betting the kidnappers had used a null to keep anyone from following. I was right. There was no incoming trail for the tinker and haunters and no track for Josh leaving. I had a feeling they'd used a better one than Nancy Jane Squires's kidnappers. I doubted the trace would be coming back.

I picked my way uneasily through the living room, looking for any clues. The null wards were completely drained. I walked back down the hall past the kitchen, giving a little shake of my head at Price's questioning look.

There hadn't been any other women in Josh's bedroom. Taylor was the only one. She'd been there today, no doubt looking for Josh. But she'd also been there repeatedly for a long time. I could have unraveled back years, but I didn't need to. It was clear that though they'd broken up, she was still sleeping with him.

I shrugged one shoulder. None of my business.

There wasn't much else to see in the room except the wreckage of Josh's very neat life. If he survived whatever had happened to him, he was going to have a hell of a time putting it all back together.

Price propped himself in the doorway behind me. It felt like he was standing in the doorway of a jail cell and I was trapped inside.

"Got any idea what they wanted?"

I shook my head. "None."

"Your sister says she doesn't either."

"You think she's lying?" I asked without heat. He was a cop, after all, and witnesses did lie.

"Probably not. But I'll bet she knows more than she thinks she does."

I thought the same.

"I need to talk to her some more. But not here. She needs to go somewhere she feels safe, where she can open up."

"Are you making this an official investigation?" I'll admit I was surprised, though I'm not sure why. He was a good cop, when he wasn't enforcing for Touray.

"Any reason I shouldn't?"

I could hear the suspicion in his voice. "Not as far as I know," I lied. "But you have this other case. The one that almost got us killed tonight. I didn't get the feeling you wanted to be working on anything else."

"I don't. But I can see I'm not peeling you off this, so I might as well speed things up. I'm going to call in the crime-scene guys to see what they can find."

I did my best to look like that was good news. They'd have a tracer, and he'd figure out pretty damned quick that there'd been two haunters here and that I'd lied about them. He wasn't going to take that well. And if this did turn out to be one of his boss's jobs or an ally's, Price was not only going to stop helping, he was going to do everything he could to get me out of the way. Hell, even if an enemy gang was responsible, he could shut me down just to keep peace.

My jaw knotted. Let him try. I wasn't going to be so easy to kill, and that's what he'd have to do to keep me from finding Josh.

Chapter 5

I FOLLOWED PRICE back into the kitchen. Taylor was sitting at the island, clutching her cup, staring blindly at nothing. She was shivering. I took the cup out of her hand, and she jumped and yelped. It would have been funny if she wasn't so scared. You'd think from the way she acted with Josh that my sister was weak. But she's not. She's made out of steel most of the time. She's a pilot and has no fear. She flies charters out of Diamond City. She learned to fly before she could drive and worked private military service when she got out of college. She flew a lot in Afghanistan, Iraq, and a few other places we weren't supposed to be. She does not scare easy. Nothing knocks her off balance except Josh. He's always been her own personal kryptonite.

"It's okay," I said. "We're going to figure out what happened. I promise." Well, *I* was, anyway.

Price started punching numbers into his cell, and after a couple of seconds, he gave Josh's address to someone on the other end, saying something about a possible homicide. Taylor heard the words and shuddered; the tears that had momentarily stopped starting to flow again.

I put an arm around her, half expecting her to shake me off. Taylor didn't go in for a lot of touching and feeling. Neither did I, for that matter. But she clearly needed it, because she leaned into me, pressing her face against my stomach.

"They should be here in a little while," Price said as he hung up. "Depending on the roads and visibility."

He'd want to wait for them. I went to where the linen closet had been emptied onto the floor and found a soft blanket. I put it around Taylor's shoulders.

"When was the last time you heard from Josh?" Price asked gently, pouring more tea into her cup.

"Last night. We talked before bed," she said in a hiccupy voice.

"Is that something you usually did?"

She nodded. "When I didn't—" She broke off and looked at me, flushing.

"When you didn't come over and spend the night," I finished

matter-of-factly.

"Things were getting better between us," she said defensively. "He was talking about getting a place together."

That was a step down. He'd talked about marriage before. He'd actually bought her a ring and started planning the wedding. Then he'd dumped her. I didn't say it. Taylor didn't need me chewing on her about that at the moment. Besides, maybe he *had* changed. I hadn't seen him to know one way or another.

"Did he seem worried when you talked to him?" Price pursued. "Did he say or do anything unusual?"

Taylor started to shake her head and then stopped. "I didn't think anything of it at the time, but he told me he loved me. He told me never to forget it, no matter what happened. I thought it meant he was starting to think about getting married again." She bit her lip. "He knew something bad was going to happen to him, didn't he?"

Price ignored the question. "Can you think of anything else that might have seemed unusual or different about his behavior or anything he might have said that would indicate who might have come after him?"

She shook her head. "I don't know. I didn't—" She covered her mouth with her hand.

"Didn't?" I prodded.

"I didn't want to upset him. He was busy and things at work were really complicated. I didn't want to give him any reason to—" She broke off again with a helpless wave of her hand.

I filled in the blanks. She had no idea why he'd broken off their engagement and didn't want to do anything that would make him do it again. I sighed inwardly. This wasn't Taylor. She was outspoken, assertive, and totally in control of her life. This woman—she was needy and pathetic.

She read my expression before I could mask it. "Don't look at me that way," she said sharply, almost sounding back to normal. "You've never been in love your entire life. You have no idea how it feels or what you'll do to keep it."

"He dumped you," I said. "How is that love?"

"He had his reasons and he never dated anyone else. Whatever made him break off our engagement, it wasn't about us," she declared.

Except she was clearly afraid that it was. I kept my mouth shut.

"Could what happened here today be related to your breakup?" Price asked suddenly.

Both Taylor and I stared at him.

"It was six months ago," she said warily.

"But you said he didn't date anyone else and clearly you both are still very close. You have a key to his condo, right? How many ex-fiancées still have one of those?"

Taylor nodded. I was trying to wrap my head around the possibility that Josh had broken up with her to possibly protect her from whatever trouble he was in. It sounded like something out of a soap opera. It also sounded all too possible, given the current circumstances.

"Think back. Was he acting strange? Was there anything going on that seems suspicious now? Maybe something to do with his job? Or maybe he gambled?"

Taylor started to shake her head and then stiffened. "Wait. There *was* something. He seemed kind of nervous and sometimes I'd catch him up in the middle of the night in his office. I just thought it was work stress, or the wedding. But then he ended things and I thought that's why he'd been so strange. He'd been trying to figure out how to break up with me."

She looked at Price. "What's going on?" There was a measure of hope mixed in with her fear. That maybe Josh hadn't *wanted* to break things off, but that he'd had to. That maybe she and he could still have their lived-happily-ever-after future. If he turned up alive, of course.

"Wait a minute. You're suggesting that this all started six months ago. But if he did end the engagement to protect Taylor, why would he keep seeing her?" I asked.

"Don't sound so surprised. Maybe it wasn't that easy to let go of me," Taylor said with a glare.

I winced. I wasn't being a very supportive sister. "Of course it wasn't," I said. "This makes better sense than him suddenly falling out of love." Maybe it did, but it would have been a lot better for Josh if he had just fallen out of love. Now he was in serious trouble.

Price drummed his fingers on the countertop. "I need to do some digging," he said.

"Looking for what?"

He looked at me. "I wouldn't have to hunt if I knew what I was going to find," he said like I was five years old. Asshole. "I want to check into his financials. Phone records. Talk to people where he works and do a general background check. It also wouldn't hurt for you to do a trace on him. See where he's been recently."

I'd already thought the same thing. If I didn't have to worry about getting Taylor home and taken care of, I'd probably be out doing it instead of letting him insult me. Not that I would be able to follow Josh and his captors. Their nulls prevented that. But I could track his backtrail and find out where he'd been for every second of every day since he was born. Not that I could ever let Price in on that particular talent.

"This storm is going to shut everything down for the next twenty-four hours or so," he said. "But I can at least get an analyst to run down his dossier."

The ding of the elevator in the hallway made all of us jump. Price palmed his Desert Eagle and pressed a finger over his lips to tell us both to be quiet. No shit, Sherlock. I grabbed Taylor and pulled her down behind the kitchen island, pulling my own gun as I did. Price went to stand against the wall, out of sight of the front door.

Whoever they were, they weren't trying to be quiet. There was a rumble of low voices and the thud of feet. I counted four people. Suddenly they went quiet, seeing the open door. They pushed inside, kicking aside debris.

"What the fuck?" said one and there were hisses at him to be quiet.

Before they could go farther, Price stepped out. "Diamond City PD. Drop your weapons."

"FBI. Put your weapon down," came one booming voice.

There was a tense moment, and then Price said quietly. "Show me your ID."

There was a rustle of fabric.

"Now show us yours," came the first voice, low and angry.

Another slide of fabric, and I felt the tension drop, but only a tiny bit.

"It's all right," Price called. "Come on out. They're legit."

I tucked my gun back into my coat pocket and rose slowly. Taylor did the same. She grasped my hand tightly.

Three men and a woman stood in a semicircle inside the door. The men were your basic clean-cut high-and-tight soldier types with bad suits and wrinkled trench coats. The woman had long blond hair pulled back into a sleek ponytail. It emphasized the sharp ridges of her face and her slightly upturned eyes. She looked like she she'd eaten a rotten egg. She glanced around speculatively, ignoring the pissing contest among the four men.

"Where is Joshua Reist?" She asked, her gaze stabbing first at Price, then at me, and settling finally on Taylor. "You're Taylor Hollis, correct? Where is your boyfriend?"

"I don't know," Taylor said coldly, her chin rising as she let go of my hand.

My gut clenched. If they knew Taylor's name, then they'd been watching Josh for a while.

"Miss Hollis, if you know what's good for you, you won't try hiding him."

"She isn't hiding him," I said. "And what business is it of yours?"

There was something about the female agent that set my teeth on edge. She was predatory, in a sly, secretive way. I didn't trust her at all. I got the impression she didn't care much about the people she protected; she just wanted to get the bad guys. The victims were only interesting because they made it possible for her to attack.

The woman reached into an inside pocket and pulled out a folded paper. "We have a warrant for his arrest."

"What for?" Price asked.

She eyed him coolly, tucking the paper away. "That's FBI business. Now produce Mr. Reist."

I had to wonder if she was even the slightest bit curious about the mess in the condo or why we were there. If so, she wasn't asking. She also didn't seem a whole lot interested in interagency cooperation. Not that I could blame her, really, since most cops were corrupt, Price being one of them. All the same, maybe someone should tell her she could catch more flies with sugar than salt.

"He's not here," Price said.

"I see," she said, sounding like she didn't believe him. "Where is he?"

"No idea. There appears to have been a struggle."

She glanced at two of her men. "Martin and Josephson, go take a look."

Two of the agents strode down the hall. It was all of ten seconds later that one returned. "You're going to want to see this," he said to the woman.

She looked at the three of us. "Stay put," she said. "Watch them, Cranford," she told the last of the agents and strode down the hall. She was wearing a tailored dress and high heels, which looked soaking wet. They looked expensive, too. No wonder she was pissed.

Price had holstered his gun and now came to stand with Taylor and me.

"Don't say a word to them," he said beneath his breath. Fury lit his sapphire eyes. I didn't blame him. The agents were treating us like suspects.

On the other hand, he was an enforcer for the Tyet. Maybe he was really saying: *Don't talk or else*. None of the Tyet factions wanted the FBI in their business, and they considered everything and everyone in Diamond City their business. I drew slow breath and blew it out. I should have stayed in bed this morning.

"Hey. Keep quiet," Cranford said. He had a bull neck and a round head, and his hair bristled from his head like a porcupine.

"We'll talk if we damned well please," Price snarled.

That caught Cranford up short. He wasn't quite sure what to say to that. We weren't suspects really, and Price was a cop. I suppressed the urge to clap.

The woman agent came striding back into the kitchen. "What's going on here?" she demanded, leveling a steely-eyed glare at Price. "Where's Reist?"

"That is the question of the hour, isn't it?" he drawled, clearly deciding that he wasn't going to be any more polite or helpful than she was.

"He's missing?"

"Can't say."

She swore. "Is that his blood? Is he dead?"

"No idea."

Her face flushed. "What are you doing here?" She demanded, her frustration practically crackling through the air.

"I called him," Taylor said, sounding impressively haughty and collected. You wouldn't know that five minutes ago she'd been a puddle of anguish. "I found the condo in shambles and the blood."

The agent looked at me. "Who are you?"

"Innocent bystander," I said.

The corners of her mouth twisted downward. "Is that so?" she said. "The way I see it, you're a witness. I might have to take you into protective custody. It could be weeks or months before we get to the bottom of this. The accommodations will not be all that comfortable."

"Not your jurisdiction," Price countered, folding his arms over his chest. "It's a possible homicide or kidnapping. Maybe a missing person. FBI has no business here."

"We have business with Reist," she declared.

"You can take it up with him once we find him. Until then, it's my case." He smiled in a most unfriendly way, like a hyena to a wildebeest. "Don't let the door hit you in the ass on the way out."

A vein in her forehead throbbed. She was pissed, but apparently she was standing in quicksand and sinking fast.

She drew a sharp breath and blew it out, then twitched a card out of her pocket and handed it to Price. "I'd appreciate it if you kept me updated," she said stiffly. "Cranford, Martin, Josephson! We're leaving." She marched out of the room and punched the elevator button several times. The three men followed her.

Price examined the card.

"Who is she?"

"Special Agent Sandra Arnow," he read.

"What do they want Josh for?" Taylor said. She'd pulled her composure up and around herself like armor. She stood tall, her jaw thrust out, her lips stiff.

"I don't know. I'll see what I can find out. In the meantime, let's get you two out to the car. The crime-scene guys will be here soon. I don't want you in the way."

He handed me his keys, and the warning in his eyes told me that I'd better not run. He had me tabbed, and he'd be pissed if he had to waste his time running me down.

I guided Taylor down to his car, started it up, and flipped the heater to high, then climbed into the backseat with her.

"What are you doing with a cop?" she asked. "Are you insane?"

"He hired me for a job. It was an offer I couldn't refuse," I said. "Trust me, I tried. And he isn't just a cop. He works for the Tyet."

"Jesus, Riley. What are you going to do?"

"Do the trace. Not much else I can do. Then I'm going to bury myself in a deep hole until he forgets me. Are you telling us everything about Josh?"

Taylor's mouth pinched together. She gave a little shake of her head. "He's been on edge for months. Some weeks are fine, and then suddenly—he gets uptight. He snaps at everything I say and wants to be alone. A few days pass and then he's calling me again like nothing happened. He's lost weight and he's been drinking. He barely sleeps."

"He's never told you why?"

She averted her head. "I didn't want to ask."

Meaning she didn't want to take the chance of pushing him away and losing him altogether. Then my sister did something completely unselfish and made me feel about two inches tall.

"You should go," Taylor said. "I'll be all right. I'll call Leo and Jamie."

Here's the thing. After my mom was murdered, my dad got remarried. I was five. Taylor came along less than a year later.

We got along fine. No big half-sister hatred or anything. But Dad had always treated me different. Special, in the way that the smallpox virus is special. I always knew I needed to hide and that if the Tyet or anyone like them found me, I'd be in trouble. He made sure that the rest of the family knew it, too. They did everything in their power to keep me under the radar.

Now Taylor was going to sacrifice her heart to let me off the hook. Leo and Jamie weren't going to be any help. They were my stepbrothers. Leo was four years older and Jamie was my age. After both had gone and got engineering degrees, they had completely changed career direction and gone into business together making high-end jewelry. Their designs were expensive and popular. The kinds of pieces stars begged to wear to the Oscars and Grammys.

Anyhow, the point is they couldn't help with Josh. I could. I sure as hell wasn't going to let my sister bleed to death when I might be able to help. Especially not to just keep my own hide intact.

"I told you. I'm stuck with Price until I do his trace." I grimaced. "He tabbed me. As long as I have to be under his thumb, I might as well use him to help me find Josh. Besides, you're my sister. I'm not going to go hide while the love of your life is missing."

"It's too dangerous for you. Break the tab," she urged, and she actually meant it. As much as she loved Josh, she was willing to let me off the hook rather than risk myself. My entire family would do the same. For that, I'd walk into hell for them.

"If I do, it will make him suspicious. Don't forget he's a Tyet enforcer," I said, my throat tight with emotion. Dad always said family was the most important thing in the world. You stick together, and you always have someone to lean on. He'd always meant that I was the one that was supposed to do the leaning, letting them hide me and protect me. Not this time. For once, I was going to be the one to help.

"So?" she countered. "Break it and run."

"He won't give up. He'll be too curious." I shook my head. "It's better if I just play the part he expects and then drift away when it's over."

She bit her lip. "Are you sure? I don't want to risk you, too."

"I'm sure. I'm going to find Josh for you."

"Thanks," she said, and tears trickled down her face again. Suddenly she put her arms around me and hugged me hard. "Thanks so much. I know you're the best. If anyone can find him, it's you."

I hugged her back, and then she pulled away, wiping her eyes with the backs of her hands.

"I'm a fucking mess," she said. "I didn't cry this much when I broke my leg in first grade."

"Maybe you're pregnant."

"Bite me," she retorted. "I'm totally protected and so is Josh."

Just then the driver's door opened and the overhead light popped on, making me squint. Price slid into the seat. He brushed away the snow on his arms and shoulders.

"We'd better get going. Snow's almost too deep to drive in." He looked over his shoulder. "Where to?"

"You're not taking us to the precinct?"

He frowned and shook his head. "In this weather? No. I'll get you home and we can start working the case from there where there's food and beds. You've got a decent computer setup, right?"

He looked at me, but it was Taylor who answered. She knew I'd rather skinny-dip in lava than let Price anywhere near my house. "I do. I don't live far. Take Porter Avenue up to Excellsior."

He nodded and then turned on the windshield wipers. It didn't help much with the thick blanket of snow that had fallen over the car. He jumped out and knocked the snow from all the windows, then hopped back in again. "Damn, it's cold," he said, rubbing his hands in front of the heater vent.

He looked back at us. Something moved across his expression as the overhead light faded slowly. He deliberately set his gun on the center console, leaving one hand on it. The threat was clear.

"One more thing. I want to know what you aren't telling me. Right now." But he looked at me, not at Taylor.

I didn't blink. "I don't know what you're talking about." I didn't either. I mean, I was hiding everything I could from him. How was I supposed to know what exactly had set off his radar?

"The haunters."

"Haunters?" I echoed, pretending I had no idea what he was talking about and scrambling to figure out what to say next. I'd hoped he wouldn't figure it out so soon.

He sighed and his jaw knotted. "The crime-scene unit has a tracer. I know there were two haunters. The question is, why didn't you tell me?" He pointed at me. "If I'm going to help you, you can't lie to me."

"Who says you're going to help me?" I tossed back, then reminded myself I should just shut the fuck up before he put a bomb in my shoes. Don't get me wrong. I mostly believed that he hadn't killed the guys that were after us, and if he had, they'd have got what they probably deserved. But to Price they were as disposable as Kleenex. I knew I was, too.

"I did help you," he snapped.

"You're a Tyet man. Now that you know there are haunters involved, your incentive for finding Josh disappears," I accused, sudden anger getting the better of me. Taylor clutched my arm warningly. I ignored her. "Since someone in the Tyet is clearly behind his kidnapping, there are decent odds you'll jump in to help cover it up, or do whatever dirty work your boss—Gregg Touray—needs you to do. You know Josh cares about Taylor; I'm guessing that whoever took him will want her for leverage to make him cooperate. You know the drill: cut her, make her hurt, make him behave. Maybe your boss has Josh and will want to use her himself, or maybe he'll sell her to the kidnappers. Either way, we'll be lucky if anybody finds our bodies."

Taylor gasped, and I put my arm around her, my stomach clenching. I hadn't meant to put it so baldly, but here we were in the backseat of an enforcer's car with nowhere to go and a gun aimed in our general direction. Mincing words seemed pointless. My chin jutted. "Am I wrong?"

His face worked. "There is at least one other possibility," he said. "Has it occurred to you that I might just help you?"

"No," I said bluntly. "Why would you?"

"I'm a cop. It's my job." His teeth clipped each word off sharply.

"Now you're asking us to believe in fairy tales." I leaned forward. "I know you're a decent cop. I've paid attention. But the fact of the matter is that you work for the Tyet, so you'll have to forgive me if I don't trust you."

He met my gaze for a long moment. His eyes were turbulent and hot. I resisted the urge to look away.

Finally he spoke. "I might surprise you," he said, before he twisted around and slammed the car into gear. The wheels spun and the rear fishtailed as he jumped on the gas. I had no idea if he was going to take us to Taylor's or if he was going to turn us over to the bad guys. I silently jeered at myself. If I really didn't trust him as much as I said, I'd have broken the tab and run when he sent us out to his car. The truth was, I did trust him, as stupid as it was. At least I wanted to. I hoped I wasn't going to regret that.

Chapter 6

THE CAR SLID around a corner and nearly skidded into a street light. Price straightened out just in time and jammed the accelerator to the floor. I held onto Taylor, who had a death grip on the arm of the door and my thigh. Neither of us spoke, except when Price asked for directions.

Taylor's place was one of the picturesque postcard sorts of places that tend to end up on the covers of magazines. It was three stories tall with a broad porch running all the way around it. Built back in the late eighteen hundreds, it had lovely gables and two squared-off turrets in the front. By the time Taylor got ahold of it, the previous owners had let it fall to pieces. She'd bought it for a song and gutted the place, restoring it to splendor, but adding in every modern convenience. After that, she'd turned the three-acre garden into her own private Eden.

Price pulled into the long, looped driveway and stopped beside the front steps. The snow was more than a foot deep and his car chugged and died. He jerked the keys out of the ignition and flung open his door, snatching up his gun as he got out. He jammed it into his shoulder holster and yanked open the back door.

I slid out first, tugging Taylor after me. I'd been rethinking my decision not to break the tab and run. I'd be better off looking for Josh on my own.

"You can just stop thinking about it," he said as we went up the steps.

"Thinking about what?"

"Getting away from me. I'm not letting you out of my sight."

"That will make peeing interesting," I said.

His brows rose, and then he flashed an unexpected grin. "Won't it?"

The smile startled me. So did the innuendo. It was like he was a real human man, not to mention it smelled a lot like flirting. The idea did things to my insides that it had no business doing.

"I mean for you," I explained, deciding to needle him. It was definitely *not* flirting. "I've heard it's hard to pee when someone's watching. If I've got to be there for it, I might as well check out the equipment. I hope you're not shy. Or embarrassed. I mean—" I waggled my pinky in the air. "I've heard some men can be really sensitive about that."

"I'm not worried in the least." His gaze ran down me and lingered at my crotch. "I admit it will be interesting to see if the carpet matches the drapes. Not to mention if the hedges are trimmed or if they grow wild. *Hmmm.* Wonder if there are any hedges at all?"

I blushed. I couldn't help it. If I could have hit him and gotten away with it, I would have. As it was, I grabbed a handful of snow from where it had drifted up onto the porch and squashed it into his neck.

He yelped and spun around, grabbing my arm in a hard grip. "What the hell was that for?"

"You seemed hot. I thought I'd help cool you down."

"How old are the two of you, anyway?" Taylor demanded as she thrust open the door. "Josh has been tortured and kidnapped. Try to remember that, would you? Take your shoes off in the mudroom. I don't want snow all over the house. I'll turn the fire on in the back living room. My laptop is in there. You can get started looking for Josh."

Josh. I pushed my hair out of my face. It was wet. Icy water trickled down my neck. I shivered as I kicked out of my boots. My socks were only slightly damp so I left them on. I pulled off my coat and hung it up. Price did the same. He motioned for me to lead the way, so I did, all too aware that he had a good view of my ass. After his comments about my pubic hair, I couldn't help but wonder what he was thinking. I mean, I've had men compliment me on my ass before, but all of a sudden, I was paranoid about whether it was too big or too flat or too wide—

Shit! Who cares? This was Detective-Asshole Clay Price! He was an enforcer for the Tyet and I was pretty sure he was going to kill me or get me killed before the end of the week, if not the day. So why on this side of hell did I care what he thought of my ass?

But I did. I'm sick. Really, really sick.

Taylor had the gas fire crackling and had turned on her laptop.

"Want something to eat?" she asked, and disappeared into the kitchen before either of us could answer.

"She cooks when she's upset," I said.

"I could eat," Price said, sitting down in front of the computer. He glanced at me. "What do you do when you're upset?"

A whole cascade of smartass answers ran through my head, from "masturbate" to "kill people." "Drink," I said and went in search of some wine.

I don't actually drink much, but we were about to be snowed in and I didn't have any place to be. There wasn't much I could do to find Josh without following his trace, which would mean returning to the scene of the crime. For now, all I could do was wait and see what Price found out.

Drinking seemed a fine way to fill the time.

I went into the kitchen and pulled a bottle of Riesling out of the wine cooler. I like sweet wines. Taylor eyed me, then fetched three glasses. I pulled the cork and poured. I raised my glass in toast. "To finding Josh. Sooner than soon."

Taylor's mouth twisted. She clinked my glass and took several gulps. Good. Maybe I could get her drunk enough to pass out. She could use the sleep.

I filled the last glass and carried it out to Price, setting it down on a coaster. Not using coasters could get you killed in Taylor's house.

"What's your sister's password?" he asked.

"I'll go ask."

She turned red when I asked and marched out into the living room and typed it in herself. Probably something sappy involving Josh. I couldn't possibly hope it would be racy. Not Taylor's MO.

She vanished into the kitchen.

"I hope you're hungry," I said to Price. "She found a hunk of prime rib or something in the fridge. We'll be having a five-or six-course meal before she's through."

"I do love a woman who cooks," Price said absently as he brought up the police portal.

For the record, I do not cook. Well, that's not entirely accurate. I can make fettuccine Alfredo to die for, and I can make the best cheesecake you ever want to taste. Otherwise, what I eat comes off a menu or out of a box. It's one of the reasons I work out of the diner. Patti makes sure I'm fed.

Price looked over his shoulder at me. "You can go help your sister, if you want."

"She doesn't need me," I said innocently, totally ignoring the hint. "Besides, you didn't want me out of your sight, remember?"

"Then go have a seat on the couch. I don't need you breathing down my neck."

Whatever. I did as told, stretching out and pulling a plush throw down over me.

"What can you tell me about Josh?" Price asked as he typed out something on the keyboard.

"He's a suit. Uptight. Likes to rock climb and bike in his spare time. He works at—" I wrinkled my nose up, trying to remember the company's name. "The Franklin Watley Group. He's been there something like a decade. He's apparently a wizard at his job. From the way he tells it, his bosses think the sun shines out his ass."

"What does he do?"

"Hell if I know. Makes money. Gobs of it. Breaks my sister's heart and then keeps screwing her on the side. So pretty much he's a douchebag."

"Please, don't hold back. Tell me how you really feel," Price said dryly.

I turned on my side to look at him. "I don't like liars and cheats."

"I don't know that he's done either. He's broke his engagement with your sister—"

"And her heart."

"And her heart. But he didn't lie or cheat that we know of."

"Yet. But that's not the point. The point is he's been leading her on, using her for sex because she's still so in love with him she'd do anything to hold on to him."

"That's not the nicest portrait of your sister."

I shrugged. "Love makes people stupid."

I didn't know why I was saying all this. I wasn't sure I even believed it. Josh could be the sweetest guy on the planet. Before he ended the engagement, I thought he was. But now? How does a guy do that to the woman he loves? I couldn't help but feel that whatever Josh had gotten into, it was his fault and the fallout was going to splash onto Taylor and hurt her too. It already had.

"You don't believe in love?"

"Are you serious?"

He shrugged. "Sure."

"Do you?"

He looked at me and then back down at the screen. "I believe it happens for some people."

"But not you."

He shook his head. "I'm too selfish. I can't give that much of myself. I won't."

I considered. "I suppose I'm the same way. My parents were crazy about each other. So were my dad and my stepmother. They'd have done anything for each other. It's a nice thought, but not very practical when you get down to it." I barely paused before the question that was bugging me most of the night popped out.

"Why'd you hire me?"

He didn't even blink at the change of subject. "I thought we covered that. I needed a tracer and you fit the bill."

"But not a cop or Tyet tracer."

"Sometimes I like to keep my business private," he said.

"Fair enough. What about those men who were chasing us? The ones you blew up. Who were they and what did they want?"

"I didn't blow them up. They walked out alive. As for what they wanted, some people don't like me much," was Price's unhelpful answer. "Sometimes they try to get in my way; sometimes they want revenge."

"I don't like you; doesn't mean I'm going to try to kill you," I muttered.

"Good to know."

"Doesn't mean I won't, either," I said, sipping my wine.

He smiled. "You aren't a killer. You don't have it in you."

"You don't have to make that sound so much like an insult. Besides, I don't have to kill you; just hurt you."

"Except you know I'd be after you when I healed up. If there's one thing I've learned in my life, you don't want to leave trouble behind you to hunt you down."

I didn't have an argument against that. It was the main reason I hadn't broken the tab and tried to vanish. Even if I gave his money back, I knew he'd keep after me just to figure out how I'd gotten away.

After a while, the smell of cooking food filled the air and my stomach cramped. I wanted to nap, but I couldn't. Every time I closed my eyes I saw blood, and I kept wondering what was happening to Josh. I opened myself to the trace. His lines were all over the house. I breathed a sigh of relief. They still glowed with a vitality that said he was still alive.

I stood, suddenly feeling like I needed to move. Price glanced up, sharp gaze pinning me in place.

"Where are you going?"

"I thought I'd go wander out into the blizzard." I rolled my eyes at him.

"I wouldn't put it past you."

"It's not like you know a damned thing about me," I said. "Except possibly that I'm smelling a little ripe and I need a shower. So I'm going to go take one. Upstairs. I promise I won't crawl out the window. Consider Taylor your hostage against my good behavior."

With that I trotted up the stairs.

The nice thing about having money is being able to buy luxury. Taylor had done just that. Her bathroom wasn't much smaller than her bedroom, which took up the entire third floor. She had a closet the size of a garage. I swear I sank up to my knees when I walked across the carpet.

The bathroom was a spa. The jetted tub was big enough to hold me and Price without touching. The unexpected image of bubbles sliding over his warm bare skin made my breath catch.

"Don't even think about it," I told myself out loud. "That is one act of stupidity you will never survive."

Oh, great. I was talking to myself. I really needed more wine. Too bad

I left the bottle downstairs.

Confronted by the enormous tub and the array of bubble bath and scented soaps on the shelf, I decided that I had plenty of time to soak. It wasn't like anyone was going to miss me.

I lit a bunch of candles for ambience. The tub faced a wall of windows with sliding glass doors that led out onto a broad deck. The glass was treated with magic to see out without anyone seeing in. Not that anyone could. The snow whirled in a thick curtain outside.

I let the tub fill with steaming water, dribbling in some bubble bath that smelled of cloves and oranges. When it was about half full, I got out of my clothes and sank down into the water. Heaven.

I'm not sure how long I was in the tub before Taylor came to get me, but I was way past the pruny stage. She walked in and sat down on the vanity chair. Her eyes were red and swollen, and her voice sounded stuffed up.

"If you're hungry, there's food," she said. Her voice sounded listless and empty. "Price is still on the computer. He's had a couple of phone calls, too. He won't tell me anything."

Her eyes snapped to mine. "Do you really think he's going to help whoever took Josh?"

I didn't want to think so. "I don't know. Maybe. Probably." I couldn't lie. Not over this.

"You're wrong," came Price's voice from the doorway. He leaned on the jamb, his sapphire eyes glittering.

I sank down as low as I could into the tub, hoping the few remaining bubbles and the dim candlelight would hide me. Unlikely. I didn't have enough bubbles left to hide a flea. My stomach clenched at the idea of being naked in the same room with him and my entire body flushed red.

"Well, crap on a cracker. Why don't you just bring the whole neighborhood to my bath? Maybe a marching band while you're at it? Can't I get any privacy at all?"

"Just checking to make sure you haven't escaped."

He grinned and holy crap, but he was handsome. My thighs about melted. *Don't be stupid, don't be stupid, don't be stupid . . .*

"Like you wouldn't have known. You tabbed me, remember?"

"Oh, that's right. How could I have forgotten?" He didn't move. "I have some news for both of you about Josh."

"Can it wait til I get out?" I said, and at the same time Taylor practically shouted, "What?"

"Feel free to get out anytime," Price said to me as he went to lean against the counter near Taylor. "I won't mind. Nice tattoo, by the way."

"What did you find out?" Taylor demanded before I could call him an asshole.

At least he couldn't see me blush. The only tattoo I had was around my belly button in the shape of calla lily drawn in shades of violet and purple. At least—it was my only visible one. I had another done in white ink up on my scalp. Both were nulls. It wasn't all that smart to make part of your body a null—someone might cut it out. But I liked the idea of having one around when I was stark naked. The scalp one was a backup in case the stomach one didn't work, for whatever reason.

If he saw my tattoo, then—

Well, now he knew the carpet matched the drapes and I had been known to wax a little. Oh hell. Twenty-four hours ago Tyet-enforcer and Detective Clay Price had barely known who I was. Now he'd tabbed me *and* seen me naked. Could the day get any worse?

Famous last words. Of course it could.

"I talked to one of my friends in the FBI," Price said. "Seems Josh is wanted for several counts of embezzling, fraud, and money laundering. Plus there seems to be some connection to the Sparkle Dust trade."

Sparkle Dust? That didn't make sense at all. Josh despised the stuff. I rubbed my forehead. This didn't feel right at all. Then the implications hit me. Oh fuck. He was a dead man.

"What? That's not possible! He'd never do anything like that!" Taylor said. She must have realized that I'd gone deathly quiet. She looked at me. "What does it mean?" she demanded.

"It means that he's as good as dead. The Tyet won't put up with anyone bringing the FBI down on their territory, and if he's involved in Sparkle Dust, he's in way over his head." I looked at Price. "And it means that you can't help us get him back. The Tyet will have your balls in a jelly jar."

Taylor looked at me and then him. "Is that true?"

He nodded. "Except they'd not take my balls; they'd put all of me in a jar."

"But—you said Riley was wrong. You said you were going to help us get him back."

That's my sister. She's doesn't give up easy on what she wants. Tenacious as a pit bull when she wants to be. Probably why she was still with Josh when I'd have kicked him to Timbuktu and been done with him.

"I am going to help you get him back."

I sat upright, furious. "Why would you lie straight to our faces? That's just downright cruel. My sister doesn't need that kind of crap. Can't you see how bad she's hurting?"

I'd hit the point where I was too mad too care who got a look at my pubic hair or any other part of me. I stood up and sloshed out of the tub, grabbing a terry cloth robe off the back of the door and wrapping it around myself. I tied the belt like I was tying a knot in a safety line. I'd probably have to cut myself out of it later.

I put my hands on my hips, already thinking of ways to take him out. I could hit him over the head with one of the many vases Taylor kept around the house. Maybe she had drugs that would put him to sleep. I could put those in his mashed potatoes or pudding or whatever was for dinner. If he could stomach eating after that pack of lies he just spewed out.

"I'm not lying," he said, beginning to look annoyed.

"Really? You're going to help us get back Josh, thereby getting yourself killed, if not tortured and killed? Why do I find that just a tiny bit hard to believe?"

Taylor had begun to cry. The sound sent my blood pressure rocketing. I did not like it when my family was hurt.

"I've got my reasons, and I don't intend to get killed or tortured. There's a way out of this for everyone."

"Like hell there is."

He smiled, and there was menace in every line of his face. This man was more than dangerous; he was walking death. "Trust me. I'm good at this sort of thing. It's what I do. I will help you get Josh back, then all you have to do is help me with my little problem and then we can forget we ever met."

I shook my head. "No way we can trust you."

"Do you have a choice?"

"Riley—please?" Taylor looked at me, blue eyes pleading.

The truth was, I could find Josh, but not rescue him, not without help. Someone like Price was the best kind of help, if he didn't throw me to the wolves first. But there was a better than decent chance he was going to find out what I was, what I could do. If he did—

There wasn't a snowball's chance in hell he was ever going to forget me. I'd never be free of him or the Tyet.

"Fine," I said. Look at that. I thought signing my own death warrant would be harder.

"Thank you!" Taylor threw herself into my arms and hugged me tight. She drew back and wiped her face with the back of her hands. "I'll be downstairs. My closet is yours. Wear anything you want."

She ran off, leaving me with Price.

"There's something else wrong. Something you aren't telling me," he said, all too accurately.

"Yep."

I pushed past him and headed for the closet. I hoped my sister would have something decent to wear, but she didn't really believe in anything that wasn't designer.

My mistake was in hoping that Price wouldn't follow me. His filled the doorway, trapping me inside. I swear he could be a football player with those shoulders. I ignored him, or tried to. He wasn't making it easy. He drifted inside to the dresser that was also an island (what kind of closet needs a freaking island, anyhow?) and pulled open a drawer. He fished out a pair of lacy thong underwear, holding them up between two fingers.

"Perhaps I can help?"

I stomped around in front of him and grabbed the pair of panties. "Really? You're flirting? You don't even like me. Stop it. It's confusing and weird and I hate it when men lie to me."

I threw the panties back into the drawer and shoved it closed with a bang, then instantly thought better of it. I was going to have to wear *something* under my clothes. I wasn't going commando. *Please, God, let Taylor have at least one pair of underwear that wouldn't end up flossing my ass.* I yanked the drawer back open and began searching. Price was standing so close I could feel the heat of him through my robe. I glared at him, but he was staring down at me with a curious look.

"How am I lying if I flirt with you?"

"Don't act stupid. You don't like me. You aren't attracted to me. Therefore, flirting with me is a lie of action."

He folded his arms and propped his hip against the island, watching me intently. "And what if I am attracted you?"

I scowled at him. "What is the point of even going there? You aren't. End of story." I couldn't imagine he was. I was pretty sure I was the equivalent of nails on a chalkboard to him.

I found a pair of underwear and went around to the other side of the closet to flip through the jeans dangling from hangers. I found a pair that could fit and probably cost a good five hundred dollars on sale. There wasn't a tee shirt of any variety to be found, but Taylor had some long-sleeved Patagonia shirts that weren't too bad. I picked out a dark green one that would set off my hair—

Oh, hell, was I losing it or what? Josh had been tortured and kidnapped, and I was thinking about looking good? For *Price*?

Sometime in the day, I must have gotten a concussion. Brain damage. There was no other explanation.

Having collected my wardrobe, I faced Price again. He hadn't moved.

He was watching me like I was dinner.

"What?"

He stepped forward until there wasn't much between us but my robe and his clothes. I shivered all the way down to my heels.

He bent so that his lips were a millimeter from mine. He held himself there, unmoving, until I thought I'd have to kick him in the shins. Given I was barefoot, I'm pretty sure which one of us would regret it most. Then quietly, he said, "I like your hair."

He straightened and flashed a wicked grin at me before disappearing out of the bedroom. I stared after him, my stomach melting into ribbons of hot taffy.

He liked my hair.

He wasn't talking about the stuff on my head.

Oh fuckity fuck fuck fuck. I would not, *could* not, be stupid enough to even contemplate getting into bed with Detective-Asshole Clay Price.

If only my idiot body agreed, but it definitely had other ideas, and they all involved getting sweaty with Price.

I was so screwed.

Chapter 7

BY MORNING I'D managed to get my libido under control. Or so I told myself firmly as I rolled out of bed.

I looked out the window. The world was white. A few flakes of snow still floated down over what looked like a German fairytale setting. Buildings were frosted thick, their edges soft and rounded. The streets hadn't been cleared. Everything looked still and silent.

We had to get out there, through this snow somehow, and find Josh. Who knew how long they'd keep him alive? He might already be dead. The thought spurred me.

I yanked off my borrowed nightgown and pulled on my borrowed clothes. I ran downstairs to find Price drinking a mug of coffee while flipping through pages on the computer.

"That smells good," I said. "Where's Taylor?"

"Still asleep, which is good. You and I need to talk."

"Are we breaking up so soon?" I asked, putting a hand over my heart. "Oh no! Whatever shall I do? My heart is shattered."

"You're an idiot," he said, leading the way into the kitchen and filling a mug with coffee. "Sugar? Cream?"

"Both," I said. "Plenty of them."

He made a face at the mixture. I sipped it with a grateful groan. "Oh, my sweet, sweet delicious coffee. How I've missed you."

He watched me lick my lips. *Oh, there you are little libido*, I thought as heat zinged through my belly. *I thought I told you to stop this.*

"We need to go back to the apartment and see if you can trace Josh," Price said, jumping right to business.

I could live with that. Much better than imagining me and him wrestling around in bed.

Heat spiraled up from my toes to the crown of my head. *Hell.* Focus.

"We aren't going to find him that way," I said, pointing out what he already should have known. "Whoever took him knocked out Josh's house wards and hid their trace on the way out."

"Then we'll follow him backward and try to figure out who might have taken him. We know he's involved with something."

"Do we? Just because the FBI thinks so, doesn't make it true."

"We do because he's been tortured and kidnapped, and because he broke his engagement with your sister even though he was still in love with her."

"He might just be using her. A convenient sex buddy." I didn't believe it, but I had to see what Price would say. After all, he was a detective; reading suspects, reading people, was what he did.

"He had pictures of her all over his apartment, including his bedroom," Price said, as if that settled the matter.

Maybe it did. What sort of player kept pictures of his ex-fiancée everywhere if he wasn't still in love with her?

"All right. I'm in. One small problem, how do we get there?"

"Snowmobiles."

I lifted a brow. "Keep a pair of those in your pocket, do you? Or maybe you've got them stashed in your trunk."

"I called the precinct. There are a couple sleds registered nearby. We'll go borrow one on police authority."

"The owners will be thrilled, I'm sure."

"I don't particularly care how they feel. The faster we find Josh, the faster you can get back on my case. Don't think, by the way, that this diversion will come off my bill."

Ah, back to practical matters. Thank whatever gods might have a hand in it. This Price made it a lot easier not to want to screw him senseless. "I wouldn't dream of it."

I wrote a note for Taylor, who wasn't awake when we left. I'd managed to get a fair amount of wine into her last night. I laced on my now-dry boots. At some point Taylor—ever the good hostess—had slid them onto a pair of dryers. I was more than grateful. Nothing worse than stuffing your feet into wet boots. I thought of the blood splashed around Josh's floor. Okay, there was a lot worse. Perspective is a useful thing.

I dug my jacket out of the coat closet—one of those light as air things that will keep you warm on Everest—a gift from Taylor. I checked my pockets, taking inventory. I had nulls tucked into various pockets, along with my lockpicks, some lip balm, sunglasses, my house keys, my wallet, my pocketknife, and my phone. I took my baton off the hall table and shoved it up my sleeve before tucking my holstered gun in my rear waistband.

Price led the way out the door and down the steps. We slogged through the snow. In some places it had drifted over my head. That's the way it snows here. One day it's bare ground, the next you're drowning in the stuff. Before I'd gone fifty yards, I was panting.

"You could come back and pick me up," I suggested to Price, who was ahead. Even with him breaking the trail, I wasn't keeping up. "I don't mind waiting."

He looked over his shoulder, then reached back and grabbed my hand, towing me along. He didn't slow down. Pretty soon my arm felt like it was going to fall off. I didn't complain. If Josh was alive, hurrying was imperative.

Price was following the GPS on his phone. It took us up a few blocks and then had us zigzagging through various odd-sized lots to find the right house. It was a take on a log cabin, if Paul Bunyan had built a house for his entire giant family and maybe half a town besides. It was anchored by one central building that reminded me of a church, with three or four wings prodding outward. Wood smoke curled from at least five chimneys pricking from a slate roof.

I sucked in a deep breath. "I love that smell. Gas fireplaces seem so pointless."

Price looked at me. "The point is that they put out heat."

I gave him a disgusted look. "Some people just don't get it."

Someone had attacked the sidewalks and driveway with a snow-blower, but another four or five inches had fallen since to ruin their hard work.

Price finally let go of me and marched up to the front door. He stabbed the doorbell a couple of times and then banged the knocker. After a few minutes, a stout redheaded man carrying a mug of coffee opened the door.

"I'm Detective Clay Price from Diamond City PD." Price flashed his badge and ID. "Are you Barney Peltier?" The man nodded, looking worried. "There's been an emergency and I need to requisition two of your snowmobiles. They'll be returned to you."

"You're kidding me, right?" Peltier stepped into the doorway and glanced at me and then around the yard. "Kelvin put you up to this, didn't he? Where is the bastard?"

"It's not a prank, sir," Price said, his voice turning cool and hard. It was his don't-fuck-with-me cop voice, and enough to make Peltier jerk to attention. "Please show me where you keep them."

"Uh—you're really serious? But—you're just going to take them?"

"Yes, sir. It's an emergency. Federal, state, and local law all grant that in an emergency, an officer of the law may requisition civilian goods, subject to return or reimbursement." He rattled off some code numbers.

Peltier wilted. "Gimme a minute." He set his mug down inside and disappeared. He came back a minute later. He'd grabbed a jacket and shoved his feet into a pair of boots. He stomped down the walk, protesting all the while. But the words bounced off Price like he was teflon.

Outside the garage, Peltier typed in a code on an electronic pad, and the door rolled up. Inside was a candy store of boy toys. Quads, snowmobiles, boats—you name it and he had it. Price looked a little glassy-eyed as he took inventory.

"They're over here," Peltier said, pressing a button.

A rack rotated downward. He actually had seven snowmobiles. I couldn't tell one from another, but apparently Price could. He let the rack rotate around until he could offload one he wanted. The key was in the ignition. He started it and guided it down the runners built into the floor and out onto the snow.

He looked at me. "You can ride one of these, can't you?"

Not even. "Sure, why not? Just like riding a bicycle, right?"

I think it took every ounce of strength he had not to roll his eyes. He turned back to Peltier. "We'll just need the one then." He pulled a pad of paper and a pen out of his pocket and scribbled out a quick note. "This is a receipt. Take it to the impound lot on Sixth and Dutch in a couple of days. It will be gassed up and waiting for you."

He grabbed a couple helmets off another rack and jammed one on my head before pulling his on. Mine was pink. Seriously, sparkly pink. I looked like a Barbie matchstick. His was a midnight blue. On the rack were a wide variety of helmets in dark colors. Mine was the only ridiculous one.

Jerk.

He climbed on and beckoned me to get on behind. Snuggle up with him? Crap. I should have pretended harder that I could drive one of these things. On the other hand, I didn't like the idea of accidentally driving off the edge of the crater, and as deep as the snow was, the guardrails weren't going to be much help in preventing my accidental suicide.

With a sigh, I flung my leg over the seat and slid on behind him.

"Hold on," Price said, and gunned the motor.

The snowmobile leaped forward, and I lurched back. I snatched wildly at his coat, pulling myself back up and locking my arms around his waist. His chest jerked like he was laughing. I resisted the urge to bite him. Hard.

He took us back out to the road. Cold air and snowflakes nipped my skin. After a few minutes I was forced to tuck down behind his shoulder to keep my face from freezing off.

We got to Josh's place way too fast. I itched to try driving. I know, we were on a dangerous mission that was likely to get me killed, but it was a hell of a fun way to go. I was sorry when Price started to pull up in front of

Josh's, but then he sped up again and went by.

"Where are you going?" I shouted over the engine.

"FBI," was his only reply.

I twisted to look back. I didn't see a damned thing.

He drove down a couple of streets and turned and turned again, coming back along the back of Josh's building. I sat there a moment until I figured out I was the one who was supposed to get off first. I dismounted and instantly regretted it. My thighs and chest missed his heat.

He set his helmet on the back rack and I did the same. He deposited the key into his pocket and slogged across the street. The snow came up over my knees, higher where it drifted. I should have taken some of Taylor's ski pants to keep me dry. The building's back door was locked. It opened out anyhow. We would have needed a shovel to get it open.

We went around front. I finally figured out what had tipped Price off. A guy in an overcoat, soaked loafers, and a bad suit stood outside under the awning. He was smoking a cigarette. Price didn't acknowledge him, but simply walked in. I followed, ducking my head to avoid FBI guy's curious gaze.

We both headed for the stairs. Nobody got in our way until we got to Josh's apartment. The door was open, and two goons stood outside. Really, goons. As in, ape arms, bull necks, thighs like trees. Both wore sunglasses—because it was so bright, what with the lead skies and snow. The wall window on the side of the stairwell might as well have been made of concrete for all the light that came through. They each had earpieces with little coily wires that disappeared into their collars, plus matching shaved heads and blue suits. They could have been brothers. Goon brothers.

Price made to push between them while I hung back where I could run like hell. I don't trust Price; I trust the FBI less. Price will stab you in the chest so at least you can see him coming. He's honest about it. The FBI has someone else slip you some poison at your favorite restaurant so you never know it was them. You don't even know you're dead until you're standing at the pearly gates. Or the doors to hell, whatever they are called. I'm guessing I should figure that out, since that's where I'm likely to end up.

"I'm DCPD. This is my crime scene," Price said, flashing his ID again. "Let me through."

"Can't do that, sir," said goon one. "It's FBI jurisdiction now."

Goon two was saying something to his wrist.

"Since when?" Price demanded.

"Since early this morning," came a crisp female voice from inside. I recognized it. Special Agent Sandra Arnow.

The sound of her shoes heralded her arrival. The two goons parted to let her through. She stopped in the doorway, looking smug. Her hair was pulled up in a smooth chignon. She wore a charcoal pencil skirt with a tailored blazer and a cream-colored blouse. Her shoes were stiletto platforms that gave her another five or six inches in height. She looked Price in the eyes. Overcompensating much? Next to her, I felt a lot like a wadded-up piece of paper someone had tossed in the gutter.

"Judge Moralez of the forty-second district court kindly granted it."

"On what grounds?"

She handed a piece of paper to Price. He glanced at it, his face turning to stone. "This is crap."

"You said yourself it was a kidnapping."

"Not across state lines."

She smiled, her full red lips looking like she'd been drinking blood. I bet she had raw meat for breakfast. If she ate. She looked like she wore about a size negative four. "You have no way of knowing that."

"The case should be ours until there's proof he was taken out of state."

"Take it up with the judge." She turned to pin me in place with her pale blue stare. "You're back. The innocent bystander, if I recall. However, you are also Taylor Hollis's sister, are you not? Riley Hollis? I have some questions for you and your sister."

Oh crap. She knew my name. The fucking FBI knew my name. I opened my mouth. I had no idea what I was going to say. Probably "fuck off and die," but it's possible I would have been polite. Before I could speak, Price reached out and took my arm, pushing me down the stairs ahead of him.

"She's got nothing to say."

"I'll be the judge of that," Special Agent Sandra Arnow said, following after us.

Clippity-clop, clippity-clop. Like a horse. How could she even walk in those stilts? Yeah, I'm about to be hauled into an FBI interrogation room, and I'm thinking about her shoes.

"She's got rights, and she doesn't want to talk to you. She saw nothing; she knows nothing. Any questions you have can go through her lawyer."

Wasn't that contradictory? I mean, if I have rights and don't have to talk to her, then why would it matter that I don't know anything? And then why would my lawyer need to answer any questions? Not that I have a lawyer. I don't even have a mailman.

Price dragged me down the stairs away from Arnow. She watched us with narrowed eyes, tapping crimson fingernails on her thigh. She didn't look like she planned to give up.

We went back outside into the snow. The smoking goon was still there, but now he gave us a glowering look like he'd like to cuff us. I waved as we went around the corner, returning to the snowmobile.

Price pulled on his helmet and brushed the seat clean. I put the pink bowling ball back on my head.

"What now?"

"Can you find his trace?"

I'd been looking the moment we walked up to the door. "Yeah. He's still alive."

Price gave me a narrowed look. "How long before it fades out for you?"

Shit. If I was as weak as I pretended to be, I probably wouldn't still be seeing it.

I shrugged. "Never can tell."

He gave me another of those penetrating looks. I stared back wide-eyed, even as my stomach plummeted. I could tell I was becoming a puzzle to him. I didn't have a choice, not if I wanted to find Josh. But moving to Tahiti was beginning to look better and better.

Chapter 8

WE CLIMBED BACK on the snowmobile and took off up the street. I didn't know where we were going, but I was just happy that Price wanted to put some distance between us and Arnow in case she decided she wanted to snatch me up after all.

It was eerily quiet in the city. The snow hushed everything, and most everything was closed. I could hear plows running to clear the main streets, but there was a hell of a lot of snow to move and I was betting it would be close to a week before they got the streets cleared.

After a while it became clear that Price was actually heading somewhere. He went back down into Downtown through the Prockney Tunnel. That was jarring. A fair bit of snow had drifted down inside, so that helped, but we had to slow down to nothing when the road went dry. I expected Peltier would be shitting bricks if he were here and saw what we were doing to his machine.

Once through, Price headed for the center part of the rim where the Buffalo River dropped down into the caldera. My fingers were getting cold inside my gloves. The rest of me was plenty warm—either Price was made of some serious hot stuff, or he was getting me all hot and bothered. I didn't want to even think about it.

The wind picked up, and the snow was starting to whirl drunkenly. If it kept up, we were going to have a blizzard. Often-Wrong, the weather guy on the news this morning, had been disgustingly excited about this storm and the two or three that were following in. It was an official snow emergency. He kept nattering on about how he hoped everyone had emergency supplies and they should hunker down and stay in place.

"We aren't going to run out of gas, are we?" I shouted.

He shook his head. I think. It was hard to say.

I was beginning to consider shoving my hands up under his coat when he finally slowed down. We were in a canyon of skyscrapers. Snow-mounded cars lumped up along the roadway. He navigated up onto the sidewalk and pulled up outside the Franklin Watley building. Josh's employer. A red closed sign blinked brightly over the subway entrance at the end of the block.

Price killed the engine and I got off, putting my helmet on the seat. The building was made of a blue-gray granite polished to a high sheen. The front had a portico with columns and two-story glass windows. Price had parked under the portico.

"It's not open," I said. "Nothing is."

Actually, the diner would be open. Patti and Ben didn't close except for a few holidays. People counted on them. Especially in bad weather. My stomach growled. I could really use one of Ben's giant hamburgers with bacon, bleu cheese, and sautéed onions and mushrooms, plus a huge mound of crispy fries and a chocolate shake. My mouth watered just thinking about it.

"Doesn't mean we can't get in," Price said.

I eyed him. "How?"

He didn't answer. He went to the door and pulled on it. Locked up tight, and not just with ordinary locks. There was magical security here, too. I didn't bother telling him. He was a cop; if he didn't expect there to be magical locks, then he was an idiot. He'd never struck me as particularly stupid. All I knew was that these far exceeded my paltry picking skills.

He fished in his pocket and pulled out the little flip-open wallet containing his badge and ID. He pressed it against the seam between the doors. Yellow tentacles flowed out of it in every direction. They wriggled across the glass and through the cracks surrounding the doors. More and more poured out until the doors were covered in solid yellow. It shimmered a moment, then faded. The glass vanished with it.

"Come on."

Price reached out and pulled me through the doorway. I turned to look back and the glass was back. I blinked, impressed. That wasn't your basic police department-issued magic. Nice being supplied by the Tyet.

A shadow swept over me. It was all too easy to forget his connection to the Tyet. Too easy to forget he didn't wear a white hat. At best, it was gray. The worst part was that I was starting to like him.

"What's wrong?" he asked, noting my sudden chill.

"Nothing," I said, pulling out of his grip.

He watched me a moment longer as if debating whether or not to push. "Do you know where Josh's office is?"

I shook my head. "Taylor does." I pulled out my phone, but he shook his head.

"Don't. FBI is probably listening in. I don't want Agent Arnow to know we're here."

"I'm getting really tired of Agent Bitch," I said, glad I'd never turned my phone on yesterday.

The corner of his mouth quirked. "Look for the building directory."

I wandered around. The reception area was a museum full of expensive artwork. A sculptured glass chandelier the size of a buffalo lit the space. Or would have, if it was on. I checked by the left bank of elevators, circling around the lobby back to the reception desk. I shook my head at Price.

He went behind the desk. "Computers are probably password protected. Use the landline. Call your sister."

"You don't think her phone is tapped?"

"Might be, but I doubt they'll be listening to her in real time. You, on the other hand, have caught Arnow's interest. She'll be paying close attention."

It was almost reasonable, and I didn't really have any other options, so I did as told. Taylor sounded groggy. "What time is it?" she mumbled.

I checked the massive clock embedded into the far wall. "Just after noon." We hadn't gone to bed until four in the morning, and Price and I had left the house around nine. "We're at Franklin Watley. Where is Josh's office?"

Silence met my question, then in a choked voice she answered, "Twenty-fifth floor. Room 2562."

"Go back to sleep," I said, knowing full well she wouldn't. I dropped the phone back into the cradle before she could ask any questions and relayed the information to Price.

"Why aren't there any security guards?" I asked, following him to the elevators. I hated riding in them, but walking up twenty-five floors didn't seem like a good option either. Especially with Price. At least our time trapped in a small box would be short. I hoped, anyhow.

"Even guards have to follow snow emergency protocol. Everyone has to go home so they don't get stranded and starve or freeze to death if the power goes down."

Made sense. He hit the elevator button. Nothing happened. He hit it again. And again. Because if once doesn't work once, more times will make it happen. I smirked. He didn't see.

"What's wrong?" I asked, keeping the laughter from my voice.

"They must have locked the elevators down as a precaution. Stairs it is. Let's go," he said, striding off down the hallway to the stairs' entrance.

Price was breathing a little rough by the time we reached the tenth floor. I was just getting warmed up. I've been known to take the stairs down to the Bottoms and back. Work takes a girl where it takes her. And she's got to follow. I don't have a car, and the train doesn't run down there.

I'd left him two floors behind by the twentieth landing, and I don't know where he was when I got to twenty-five. I pushed through the fire door into a long, plush hallway. Every sixth light was on. It was like walking into a mausoleum. Not that I'd ever been in one, but this place seemed like dead people ought to be stacked up to the rafters.

A sign said Room 2562 was off to the left. I headed that way, turning through a maze of gloomy corridors until I found his office. I reached out to try the handle and stopped. The door wasn't latched. I pushed it wider. The space inside was brighter than the hallway. His outer wall was all glass and gave an excellent view of the crater. Or would have, if it wasn't totally white outside. The snow had increased since we came in.

I switched on the light. His office looked like you might expect: piles of papers, ledgers, notebooks, and folders littering most surfaces. He had a big mahogany L-shaped desk and one of those leather chairs with little rivets making a diamond pattern all over it. Bookshelves lined one wall with a little seating area with a table and chairs off to the right. As offices went, it was huge.

It had already been searched.

Josh was nothing if not a clean freak. You could move a magazine sideways on his coffee table and he'd have to come straighten it, usually in less than a minute. He had radar for that kind of thing. Even though things looked neat enough for an ordinary person, the lopsided stacks of papers and disorganized tchotchkes would have sent Josh around the bend.

I went to his desk. I had no idea what I was looking for. I checked out the trace. He'd been here within the last twenty-four hours. It was probably the last place he'd been before he'd gone home and been attacked. Others had followed, but I didn't recognize their trace.

"Do you have bionic legs or something?" Price asked as he strode in. "Remind me not to try to run you down on foot."

I would do no such thing. Hopefully when I started running, he'd never catch me. "The door was open," I said. "The place has been searched. Josh would never leave his office like this."

Price's attention sharpened, and he went into cop mode. "What makes you say that?"

"Let's just say he could walk through a mud bog without getting a drop on him," I said. "He doesn't *do* untidy." I gestured around me. "This is downright messy. He'd go into convulsions before he left it like this."

He surveyed the room. "The FBI would have seized everything. I'm a little surprised they haven't cleaned him out already."

"Maybe Franklin Watley was looking for evidence or sensitive documents. They had to know he was being investigated. If he was embezzling, presumably it was through work."

"The question is, did they find what they were looking for?"

"Actually, the question is, what are *we* looking for?" I asked. "And don't go all Velma on me and say clues. 'Cause *duh*. What constitutes a clue?"

"We'll know it when we see it," he said, most unhelpfully.

"Gee, thanks, Velma." I sat down at the desk. I was looking for whatever hadn't been found. Josh has always been a straight arrow and not particularly imaginative, but he apparently had another side, which meant I should be looking for good hiding places.

I pulled out all the drawers and turned them over, then felt around the drawer cavities for hidden compartments or documents taped inside. I decided I needed to be thorough and I got down on the floor and looked inside.

I didn't find any secret writing or codes or hidden compartments, but I was beginning to sense a distinct pulse of magic. Except it seemed to come and go. At first I thought I was imagining things, but it kept happening. I stood up and blinked into trace mode, but didn't see anything except the usual—trails of people coming and going, and a couple of knickknacks holding charm spells. I could usually see evidence of magic in trace mode. There was a safe behind a picture on the wall with a magical lock, but Price and his badge made quick work of that. There wasn't much inside; some folders, cash, and a velvet box with a diamond and emerald necklace. I'm pretty sure that was destined for Taylor's neck.

Price left the necklace and cash, and shoved the papers into a satchel he found in the small coat closet. Josh even had a private bathroom. Price disappeared in there to check for anything hidden in the toilet or behind the sink. I doubted he'd find anything. That's where cops always look. Crooks, too. We all watch the same movies.

That sense of subtle magic kept chewing at me. I paced slowly around the room. The further from the desk I got, the weaker it got. I frowned. There weren't a lot of tracers who'd even feel it. He must have paid a lot for whatever it was. Nobody else knew it was here, either. If he'd done it—whatever it was—with company consent, they'd have already popped it open. Probably. I was pretty sure the company had done the search. Nothing was damaged. Someone breaking in wouldn't have cared what sort of mess they left.

I zigzagged back toward the desk, trying to get a better sense of the source of magic.

"What are you doing?" Price asked from the bathroom doorway.

I held up a hand and kept moving. I stopped each time the pulse faded and then inched forward when it returned. The closer I got, the more it quieted. Curiouser and curiouser. Not to mention fucking impressive.

I worked my way to a spot just about where his chair would be if he decided to prop his feet up and look out the window. Not that Josh ever did. He never slowed down enough to just look at the scenery.

The magic quieted. I stepped away from the spot, and it began again. I stepped back on. Stopped.

"Are you going to tell me what the hell you're doing?" Price demanded. He'd come up to stand on the other side of the desk.

"There's something in the floor," I said. I fished in my pocket for my knife. I flicked it open and kneeled down. The rug fought back against the cutting. As soon as I stuck my blade through it, I got stuck. It was like someone had grabbed it in a vise. Magic tingled in my fingers, heating the knife to red-hot. I yanked my hand away and shook it.

"What's wrong?"

"Nothing I can't fix," I said and dug out one of my nulls. It was a marble, just like the two I'd used when we'd run from the goons, but this one was a hell of a lot stronger.

I set it down in the middle of the dead spot and activated it. There was nothing to see, but I could feel my magic spread out like a sponge and suck up the other spell until it was all gone. I kept a finger on the null, palming another in my other hand. The absorbed magic sizzled up through me and I channeled it back into the second marble. Most tracers couldn't do that, either. Like I said, I'm special. I grimaced inwardly. Sort of like meat in the supermarket that's about to go rancid and they put it on sale to get rid of it. Having the power I did hadn't been much of a blessing, to say the least. It hadn't helped me find out who killed my mother or what happened to my father. I pushed the thought away. Those were old problems.

When it was done, I put the spent null back into my pocket and started slicing the carpet again. This time it separated easily. I pulled a flap back and cut through the padding. Underneath was a flat panel. It had no handle. Probably opening it with the proper magic would have popped it up. I pried it up with the tip of my blade. By this time, Price had come around the desk to squat beside me. Way too close for comfort.

I'm not sure what I was expecting to be inside. The compartment was only about eight inches deep and about a foot square. A navy-blue canvas bag fit neatly inside.

Price pulled it out. "We'll take it with us. Let's get out of here."

I didn't argue. I was ready to be out of the building. I was not really cut out to be a burglar. I'm too nervous to steal.

I put the carpet back together as well as I could and rolled the chair on top of it. Anybody making a search of the place was sure to find it, but it wouldn't be obvious to someone just looking in.

Price shut the door behind us, and the lock clicked. It was reinforced with magic that activated as soon as the lock snicked shut.

We wandered back toward the stairs, taking two different wrong turns and ending up near the elevators. We had just gone past them when one of them dinged. I looked at Price.

"I thought they were shut down?"

He pushed me toward the staircase, handing me the bag of stuff we'd collected from the office and the one from the floor safe. "Get going. I'll catch up." He turned and drew his gun.

I didn't know if I should stay or go. Not that Price couldn't take care of himself. With my hands full, I couldn't grab my gun, so I started running.

I had only made it halfway down the hallway when a man and a woman came out of the stairwell. I dug to a halt. Magic vibrated off them. I didn't know if it was shielding or weapons, but I knew for certain they were Tyet. There's a look, cold and snakelike, that a lot of them get. Like they are cold-blooded and don't care who they kill. These two had it in spades.

They saw me about the same time I saw them. "Stay where you are," the woman said.

Unlike Special Agent Sandra Arnow, this woman was dressed for snow. She wore tall boots over tightfitting ski pants, and a matching gray ski jacket with neon green striping. Her hair was a short cap of brown. She only stood about five foot two, but I didn't make the mistake of thinking that made her an easy target. Her companion was about as tall as Price, but had a shaved head and shoulders that seemed to brush both walls at once. There was no way I was getting around the two of them.

That left me with staying there and waiting for them to grab me, or hauling ass back to Price. I chose Price. Hard to believe he is actually the safer choice in any version of reality.

I turned the corner to the elevators and stopped just in time to not barrel into Price. He stooped over an unconscious man, rifling his pockets. He looked up at me.

"Company," I said and leaped for the elevator. It was still open, thanks to the fact that the door kept bouncing off the unconscious guy's foot.

I was in before Price. He's the size of a bull and came through the doorway just when the other two started shooting. So how the hell was I the one to get shot?

The bullet seared my left side and knocked me against the wall. Price shoved me down to the floor and the door finally closed. I'd already punched the lobby button. We lurched downward. I hoped to hell there wasn't anybody waiting for us when we got there.

Price dropped down beside me. I was hyperventilating. My body had seized so tight that it was turning into one big cramp. I could hardly think. All I could do was feel the spreading heat of my blood as it leaked out of my skin, and pain. Whoa fuck, the pain was beyond words.

"Let me look."

He pulled my hand from my side. Apparently I was trying to stop the bleeding. Or maybe I was hoping to stop the bullet, long after it hit me. Brains can be stupid.

Before I knew what else he was going to do, he pushed me onto my side. I squeaked and let out a cry that sounded like a raccoon caught in a trap.

"It's through and through," he said. "We can't do much now. We have to get out of the building. Can you walk?"

Well, duh. It's not like riding the elevator up and down was an option. It's not like I wanted to get shot again.

"Help me up." I sounded like I had a bad cold. That's when I realized I was crying. I couldn't stop it either, any more than I could stop bleeding.

Price put his arm around me. I grabbed his shoulder to steady myself. The bags were still looped over my arms. As the elevator reached the lobby, he maneuvered me off to the side to make me less of a target. Like that helped before. Maybe this time it would work.

I didn't dare leave blood behind. I reached into my pocket and pulled out a blood null. Magic flooded outward in a scalding wave. Price about jumped out of his skin.

"What the hell?"

"I'm burning my blood trace. We should go. It might cook us too." The spell might think the stuff in our bodies needed frying, too.

Another thing a lot of tracers can't do. It's actually a tinker trick. I didn't like having to rely on a tinker, though, so I figured out how to do it for myself. The only problem was that it was pretty obvious when I used it, and there wasn't much finesse to it. What blood it found, it liked to cook, whether or not a person was still using it.

Price pulled us out into the empty lobby. He dragged me toward the doors. I was already drenched with sweat and could barely catch a breath. My head was spinning and it took all my concentration to control the null. I had no idea what my feet were doing.

I vaguely noticed the doors were still closed. I guess the Tyet goons didn't want anyone to notice they'd broken in either. If they had broken in.

Maybe they had a key. Price didn't waste time using his badge to open them up, but popped off six or eight shots. I expected a hail of glass, but the doors held, the bullet holes pocking the right one in a long oval. Price kicked out the glass and it folded down like crumpled paper. He swung me up in his arms and carried me out to the snowmobile. He knocked the helmets off and settled me on the back, then swung aboard, and we roared off. I hoped he'd managed to keep the two bags, otherwise I'd gotten shot for nothing.

I slumped against him, deactivating the null. I was pretty sure it had scabbed up the bullet's entry and exit wounds. My clothes were stuck to my side and felt crusty. I made myself put it into my pocket.

I don't remember a lot after that. Price took a corner sharp, and I slid off. At least the snow was deep and soft. I couldn't even feel the cold. He said something that sounded like Charlie Brown's teacher—*mawawaw wawa mawawa.*

He put me back on snowmobile, this time in the front. I flopped forward like a rag doll. The bullet holes had cracked open, and I could feel blood seeping. The ride seemed to go on forever. It didn't even thrill me to have Price all wrapped around me. Apparently if you get shot, you don't care much about sex. Who knew?

At some point it turned abruptly dark and the growl of the motor died. I was vaguely aware of Price lifting me again. Pain lanced through my gut. He talked to me, I guess. It didn't make much sense. He was probably telling me to pull up my big-girl panties. I started to giggle, only it came out like I was choking. I couldn't pull up my big-girl panties; I was wearing Taylor's boy shorts underwear. I know, it wasn't funny.

We went inside a building, and Price laid me down on something soft. A couch? A bed? Where were we, anyway? He disappeared, and I sank down into gray. The next thing I knew, I heard scissors and then something tugged against my side. Fire seared my skin. I yelped and twisted away. Something heavy landed on my shoulder and pain exploded in my side. I'm pretty sure I screamed. I know I cried like a baby.

I've heard that when you're in a lot of pain, after a while it just gets monotonous and it doesn't seem that bad. Fuck that. I don't know what Price was doing to me, but it felt like he was kneading dough—I was the dough in that metaphor. It hurt on a level I don't even have words for. I passed out sometime in the middle of his ministrations.

When I woke up, my mouth was sticky and my teeth felt furry. My eyelids gritted like sandpaper over my eyes when I opened them. Otherwise, I didn't move, the memory of pain holding me still.

The room was dim. Overhead was a white ceiling. Way overhead. The room must be a cavern. I took an inventory of myself. I felt . . . okay. The pain was gone. I was tired though. And really hungry. Tired won out though. I closed my eyes.

The next time I woke up, I was both starving and I had to pee. Bad. Well, nothing to do about that but find a bathroom. And then a kitchen. Hopefully stocked better than mine, which had some ramen noodles, peanut butter, microwave popcorn, and some frozen dinners.

I pushed myself up. I was sitting in the middle of a king-sized bed, wearing a tee shirt and pair of sweats, neither of which were mine. Also, I was not wearing them when I was shot. This I was certain of. As I started to scoot to the edge of the bed, I realized I was also not wearing underwear. This gave me pause. A girl doesn't just lose her underwear. Someone had taken it and the rest of my clothes as well. Presumably that was Price.

I didn't look at my bullet hole. Holes, since it went in and out. I wasn't ready for that. Dizziness swept over me as I stood. I grabbed hold of the tall post at the foot of the bed and hung on for dear life. Didn't work. My legs sagged, and I slid down to the floor. The good news was that across the room was an open door. I could see a sink inside. Where there was a sink must also be a toilet. All I had to do was get there.

Since walking seemed out of the question, and since I didn't want to pee on the floor, I eased onto my hands and knees. I had got about halfway across when Price swooped in out of nowhere.

"What the hell are you doing on the floor?"

He sounded furious. What would his reaction have been if I'd pissed all over the rug? It was a nice one. I imagine I would have ruined it.

Before I could answer, he lifted me to my feet, holding me against him when I instantly started to melt back down to the carpet. Man, he was hot. Or I was really, really cold.

"You are hot."

"Thanks for noticing," he said.

I blushed. That came out well. True, but still embarrassing.

"Why were you on the floor?"

"I wanted to go to the bathroom."

"You didn't want to walk?"

"I did, but my legs had other ideas. It seemed safer to crawl."

"Very logical."

"Thank you. I still have to go."

He grinned. Shit, he was pretty. I sighed.

"What's wrong? Do you hurt?" He frowned and his hair fell across his eyes.

So, so pretty.

"I'm hungry, too." For him. I managed not to say it.

"Good. Food will help you recover."

"Recover?" I repeated stupidly as he helped me to the bathroom.

"You were shot. Don't you remember?" He sounded worried.

"Of course I do. They hit my side, not my brain."

That brought out the smile again. "That's my Riley," he murmured. "Feisty."

His Riley?

I didn't have a chance to ask, because we were in the bathroom beside the toilet.

"Do you need help?"

"I don't think so," I said, even though I probably did.

"I'll be right outside the door."

Yay. Because him listening to me pee is guaranteed to stop me up like a cork. "I'll be fine."

He just gave me a long look and stepped out, pulling the door closed behind him.

I pulled the tie on the sweats loose with one hand, holding onto the towel rack with the other. The pants fell around my ankles. I sat down with a sigh of relief. It was about that time that I noticed that my thighs were smeared with dried blood. Clearly someone—Price no doubt—had done his best to clean me up, but hadn't been able to get all of it. My stomach lurched, and bile burned my tongue.

It's not that I am afraid of blood, or even that I freak out at the sight of it in general. But this was mine, and it came out of a bullet hole. Two bullet holes. An innie and an outie. That makes a big difference in the way I look at it.

I bent down and tried to breathe. My side hitched and felt tight, but otherwise there was only an ache. I straightened and finished my business, suddenly needing to see what had happened to me. I didn't bother pulling up the sweats. I left them in a puddle in front of the toilet. A full-length mirror hung on the back of the door. I stared at myself for a long moment.

My skin is usually pale with freckles. I'm a ginger, after all. But at this moment, I was pasty white. My eyes were bruised looking and my lips had no color at all, like I'd been sucked dry by a vampire. My left thigh had smears of blood on it, and of course, I wasn't wearing underwear.

Biting my lips, I pulled up my—Price's—shirt. It was your basic black V-neck, with a pocket on the left breast.

The bullet had gone through my left side below my ribs and above my hip. Apparently it hadn't hit my kidney or liver or spleen. Not that I had a clue where they were except inside my stomach. Where it had gone in was puckered red. I touched my fingertip to it. It was slightly numb. No pain, but an ache inside, like freezer burn. I twisted, but couldn't see the exit hole. Instead I traced it with my fingers. It was bigger, somehow, like the bullet had grown inside me.

"Are you okay in there?" Price asked just outside.

I started. "Where are my clothes?"

"I cut your shirt off. Your pants and underwear are in the dryer."

"I want to shower." Suddenly I really, really wanted it, like dying of thirst want.

"Are you sure you're strong enough?" he asked doubtfully.

"Most definitely. Do you have a razor?"

The knob of the door twisted, and before I could protest, he came in. Luckily his shirt covered my rug, as it were, which he'd already seen more than once. Why I should possibly be embarrassed to let him see it again, I don't know, but there you are.

He stopped just inside and looked me over. His expression was brooding. Impatient even. Look, it's not like I planned to get shot, right? Sorry I'm taking so long, but I am not of fan of wearing my own blood.

"Are you all right?"

What kind of question is that? I've been shot and apparently healed up. How did he manage that, by the way? A question I'd be asking soon, once I was clean. Maybe after I'd had a sandwich.

"What happened to my blood?" I asked.

Let me explain something. Blood can be used to find people, plus do magic against them. 'Course they have to be decently strong, and the blood has to be super fresh. The longer it sits, the more powerful the person's magical ability has to be. I've done some testing of my own limits. About two hours max is what I've got. Josh's blood was too old by the time we found it for me to find him with it.

"I burned it," he said.

I nodded, and I wondered if he really had. Not that he had any real use for it. He didn't seem to have any magic talent. If he did, he was hiding it well.

"Hey." Price snapped his fingers in front of my face.

I blinked and focused on him. "What?"

"How about I get you something to eat first? Then you can shower. You'll be stronger. You won't fall down while washing."

He continued to stare at me. I shifted and swayed, leaning back against the wall. He was right. Plus I was very, very hungry.

"Okay."

He helped me back to the bed and sat me down. "Stay here."

With that he vanished. I pulled a soft throw over my bare legs and snuggled into his pillows. His smell was a delicious drug.

I was asleep by the time he returned with a sandwich. He woke me with a gentle hand on my shoulder.

"Come on. Let's get some food into you."

Price helped me sit up against the pillows. The sandwich was ham and pepper jack cheese with lettuce and tomato on sourdough. I devoured it and guzzled the milk that came with it. He sat on the foot of the bed and watched me.

I set my glass down. "That was good. Thank you." Already I felt a lot better. Still weak and tired, but not as shaky, and I thought I could stand. "It's time for my shower."

Price looked doubtful. "You'll collapse. You can't even stand without help."

"I'll be fine. Besides, if necessary, I'll sit. I need to get clean."

He considered and then gave a little nod. "Then I'll stay and help."

He had that bulldog look, the same one he'd gotten when he first hired me. I wasn't going to win this argument. Neither was I going to forgo the shower. It wasn't just the blood. I felt dirty and I smelled ripe, like I'd run a marathon. Maybe shock does that to a person. I sighed. What the hell? He'd already seen me naked. What was one more time?

Crazy how I could have a barely healed bullet wound and be dizzy as hell, and yet the idea of having Price helping me shower made fireworks go off in my stomach. I sucked in a sharp breath.

"What's wrong? Are you in pain?" He put a hand under my elbow.

"Can we just get on with this, please?" I tried not to sound eager.

HE KICKED ASIDE my abandoned sweats and closed the toilet before sitting me down on it. I still had the throw wrapped around my lower half. From the closet behind the door he pulled out a big basket of froufrou-looking stuff. He set it on the counter and started pulling out bottles.

"That doesn't exactly look like your style." I sat slumped over with my elbows on my thighs and my chin on my hands. "I thought you'd go in for something more masculine than—" I lifted my head to get a look at one of the labels. "What's a plumeria, anyhow?"

"A flower from Hawaii."

"You don't strike me as a flowery shampoo sort of guy." More like woodsmoke and leather.

"I like to keep it around just in case." He took a couple of towels out of the cupboard, along with a washcloth.

Just in case he had feminine company. Why did that bother me? I have to admit it did. I really didn't want to think about other women taking showers in his bathroom. Or doing other naked things in his house.

Oh crap. Please, *please* do not let me even think about being stupid enough to fall for Price. *No, no, no, no, no!*

I looked down at the floor while he started the water and adjusted it. A minute later, a pair of bare feet showed up in my vision and then a hand. I straightened and put my hand in his before I realized he wasn't wearing a shirt. *Oh my.* Price's body was lovely. Sculpted muscles with a line of dark silky hair arrowing down his chest to vanish into the waistband of his jeans. I averted my gaze and bit the inside of my lip. I tensed myself against the urge to touch him, to feel the hot satin of his skin.

He let me go and reached for the shirt I was wearing. "Raise your arms."

I drew in a breath and held it and lifted my arms. He pulled the shirt over my head and dropped it on the floor. I am proud to say I didn't blush. I'm pretty certain I couldn't, what with all my blood loss. Never thought I'd be grateful to get shot.

The shower was big enough to hold a half-dozen people. Glass tiles shimmered on the walls and floor. There were sprayers in the walls and several on the ceiling. It was like stepping into a carwash. A steamy one. There was a seat in each of the three corners and a glass door, which Price closed behind us.

Us.

He'd kept his jeans on, which only made me imagine peeling them down his legs and licking my way back up.

I groaned and twisted away to face the wall.

"What is it? Are you hurting?"

As nice as this shower was, I just wanted to hurry up and get out before I humiliated myself. "Hand me some shampoo."

I grabbed the bottle out of his hand, squirted some into my palm, and scrubbed it into my hair. I may have scraped off some skin. I was a little vigorous. Because he didn't need to see my boobs jiggling, I kept my back to him. I rinsed out my hair and reached blindly behind me. "Conditioner?"

He put it in my hand. I closed my fingers on it, but I had a bad grip. I dropped it. Without thinking I bent to retrieve it, and was swept with a gray wave of dizziness. I keeled sideways against the wall, hitting it hard with my shoulder and the side of my head. My ears rang and spots kaleidoscoped across my brain.

Strong hands caught me. Price pulled me upright against his chest. My nipples rubbed his skin and hardened. My stomach went molten, and my knees turned wobbly again. I stared straight at his throat, unwilling to meet his eyes.

"Riley? Are you okay? You hit your head."

His fingers ran slightly over my head, looking for a concussion, I suppose. Or maybe another blood fountain. The way I was reacting to his touch, I felt like I had a concussion. My hands were pressed against the flat planes of his pecs. Steel and velvet.

"I'll be fine," I said, and I sounded like I'd eaten a handful of gravel. "Let's just get this over with."

I made myself lower my hands, but his hand remained on my hip while the other trailed down the side of my face. I was still pressed up hard against him, and I could feel his hard length inside his wet jeans.

That was when I made the mistake of looking up into those sapphire eyes. He looked down at me with smoldering intensity. His jaw knotted and then he slowly slid his hand around the back of my head and pulled me into the hottest kiss I've ever experienced in my life.

Chapter 9

HIS LIPS SLANTED over mine. From the ferocity of his look, I was expecting something rough, but he was gentle. Worshipful even. He took his time, sliding the tip of his tongue along my lips. He pulled away and so our lips barely touched, and our breathing mingled, then came back like a starving man, deepening the kiss.

Heat ribboned through me, sending sparks dancing along my nerves and turning my stomach to hot gold. I skimmed my hands up his arms to his shoulders. I bit his lip gently. He groaned and his hands contracted on me.

That did me in. I leaned into him and pushed up on my tiptoes. His left arm slid around my back to hold me like an iron bar. His tongue danced with mine, clever and wet. The taste of him was indescribably delicious. I couldn't get enough. My arms locked around his neck. I was barely standing on my own.

I can't tell you how long that moment went on. Neither one of us wanted to be the one to stop. The shower kept pouring on the hot water. We weren't going to be saved by a cold dousing.

In the end it was me that put a stop to the best kiss of my life. Or rather, blood loss and maybe shock catching up to me. I felt myself starting to shake. I thought at first it was reaction to Price. But it increased until I was shivering enough for him to notice. He pulled away.

"Riley?"

I tried to say something, but I couldn't even make words. Everything was starting to go blurry.

"Shit."

He swung me up into his arms and carried me out of the shower, standing me on the rug. He grabbed a towel with one hand and rubbed me down. He had to hold me up. I couldn't stand. A couple seconds later he carried me back to the bed and laid me in it. He pulled the blankets up to my chin. If anything, I was shivering harder. Weirdly, I didn't feel cold. I felt more numb.

Price vanished and then the covers were pulled away and he slid in beside me. He'd dried off and changed his wet jeans for a pair of dry sweats. He pulled me into his arms and rubbed his hands over my back and arms. He was murmuring something. I couldn't make out a single word over my chattering teeth.

After a while, you'd probably think I'd start getting warm. But I didn't. All of a sudden Price jumped out of bed. I made a protesting sound, but he totally ignored me. I curled up into the fetal position, wrapping my arms around my knees, and I say this without any pride at all, whimpered in self-pity because my knight in shiny armor had abandoned me. Knight or Detective-Asshole Clay Price. The same guy who'd tabbed me and forced me to work for him. Oh, how low I'd fallen. Disgusting really.

At some point, to my ridiculous delight, Price came back. Of course. I mean, he couldn't leave a wreck like me in his bed. Plus the kiss said he kind of liked me.

He pulled the covers back and tried to make me sit up. I gripped my knees tighter and wriggled further down into the covers.

"Come on, Riley. You can't stay this way. Just sit up for me. I promise you'll feel better. Come on, baby."

Baby? Did he really call me *baby*? Some women would be insulted by that. Normally I would. But with it coming from Price, I felt my chest go all gooey. At that moment I'd probably have done just about anything for him.

I let go of my knees and let him pull me up to a sitting position.

"That's my girl," he said and put his arm around me. He put a glass to my lips. "Drink now."

I obediently drank. It was whiskey with lemon and it was warm. Yuck. I tried to pull away, but he held me firm.

"Drink it all, Riley."

I didn't really have a choice, and I sure as hell didn't have the wherewithal to fight him. So I drank. Probably six ounces or so of straight whiskey. Fire hit the pit of my stomach and exploded. I swear I was drunk in less than ten seconds. I was more than ready to go back to the fetal position, but Price wasn't done with me. He held another cup to my lips. I twisted away. No more whiskey. He persisted, and in my weakness, I gave in.

This time the cup was full of warm chocolate milk. After the first sip, I put my hands over his and gulped it down. Chocolate milk and whiskey don't really mix, but at this moment, I didn't really care.

He set the cup down on the nightstand and pulled me back down under the covers with him. He rubbed my back again and his warmth seeped into me as the whiskey and chocolate milk did their magic. After a few minutes, I went from shivering hard enough to crack my teeth to cozy comfortable. Sometime after that, I'm not sure how long he held me, I began to feel like myself again.

"What happened to me?" I murmured against Price's chest. Bare chest. I wanted to lick it.

"You got shot, you got healed, and you got kissed. You don't seem to have liked one or three of them."

"Definitely didn't like getting shot." I realized my arm was around his waist and I was rubbing the velvet skin along his ribs. I probably should have stopped. I didn't. "The healing was good—I never like to bleed to death."

Price chuckled and his arms tightened a fraction. "And getting kissed?"

"I don't remember that."

He lifted his head and looked down at me. Flames flickered in his eyes, and I remembered that a) I was naked, b) we were lying in bed, and c) I wanted him worse than I had ever wanted another man. I'm not really good with self-denial, either.

"I could remind you."

I licked my lips, and his gaze fastened on them. "It's probably not a good idea."

"It's a fucking lousy idea," he said, and then rolled me onto my back and slid on top of me.

He straddled my hips, his weight braced on his elbows on either side of me. He looked down at me, gaze running over my wet hair, down my face to my neck and then to my bare breasts. His breath caught. I smiled in wonder. It was difficult to wrap my brain around the fact that I could have that effect on this diamond-hard man.

He saw me smile, and his mouth quirked wickedly in response before he lowered himself down. Once against he kissed me.

I nearly went up in smoke.

He took his time, tasting and nibbling. My breasts ached for his touch, and the rest of me throbbed with an equal desire for attention. I swear, he could have licked my toes, and I'd have orgasmed.

He moved to my ears, biting delicately, then kissed his way down my neck. I couldn't stay still. I started to wriggle, and I reached up to pull him down on top of me.

"No, no," he said and grabbed my wrists, holding them down on either side of my head.

"Bastard."

"Trust me. I won't hurt you." He grinned tauntingly, and returned to his slow exploration. First he licked the pulses in both wrists, then returned to my neck. He kissed across the hollows of my collarbone and back up to my other ear. I started making sounds that didn't quite sound human. My hips shifted, and I ground them up against his. He gasped. He gave me a searing kiss. If that was supposed to be punishment, it wasn't working.

I lifted my head, needing more of him. He wrenched back. He was panting. Before I could argue or beg, he bent down and licked my right nipple. Lightning flashed through me. I bucked. He chuckled and did it again, then moved to the left and tortured me there. Exquisite torture. He did it over and over, blowing lightly on the tight, hard nipples until I wanted to scream in frustration and pleasure.

Finally, he sucked one between his lips, his tongue licking as he drew on me. I swear I went blind for a minute. Sounds came out of me that made no sense at all. He gave my other breast the same treatment. By this time, I was alternating between lifting my hips to grind against him and beating my heels against the mattress. I tried to wiggle out from between his thighs so I could wrap my legs around him, but he wasn't about to let me.

He kissed and licked over my ribs and down to my belly button. I waited, agonizing need pooling lower. But he moved back up to my breasts. Over and over he teased me, kissing my breasts, my belly, my lips, my neck. I was thrashing and first begging then swearing at him. I fought to free my hands, but he wouldn't let go.

Finally he took pity on me and eased down lower and lower still. Right past the heart of my need to my knees. He kissed me along the inside of one thigh and then the other, moving back and forth and higher. He blew on my clit and I moaned. Finally, finally! He let go of my wrists to slip his hands under my hips. I grabbed handfuls of the sheets as he gently licked me. I couldn't make a sound. They were bottled up in my chest. Sensations crashed into me, and my mind evaporated. All I knew was I had never, ever, felt this good.

I tipped my hips, letting my thighs fall open as he licked me. He gently scraped his teeth over my clit, and my brain exploded, along with the rest of me. I shuddered and bucked, my orgasm sweeping from my head to my feet and back again. Price didn't stop his ministrations, but kept sucking and licking until the last tremor left me.

He pushed himself up, and I pulled him back on top of me and kissed him. Hard. I ran my hands over his back, delighting in the curves and planes of his muscles. It wasn't enough. I wanted more. I wanted him. Inside me. Thrusting against me.

I pushed at the waistband of his pants. He lifted his head.

"Are you sure? You've been shot and then . . ."

"Take your pants off," I ordered. "Now."

He still hesitated. I slid my hands under his sweats and gripped his ass. At the same time, I wrapped my legs around him and rocked up against his cock. "Now."

His face contorted, and he groaned. "You make it hard to do the right thing."

"What's wrong with feeling this good?" I thrust again, and he didn't need any more convincing.

He kicked off his sweats along with most of the covers. He was long and hard. I stroked his velvet length and cupped his balls and massaged them. He moaned and bent down and licked my breasts in return.

I couldn't wait long. He might have just given me a mind-blowing orgasm, but it had barely taken the edge off my need. I guided him to me. He didn't take the hint. He propped himself on his elbows above me.

"You're sure?"

"You have to ask?"

"I should get a condom."

"I'm in no danger of getting pregnant and there are always tinkers for diseases. Now please, don't make me wait anymore to have you inside me."

He wasn't gentle. I didn't want gentle. He thrust in deep, and I met him with equal fervor. He stayed buried in me for a long minute without moving.

"You feel damned good," he whispered, his forehead resting against mine. "I could stay like this forever."

I jerked my hips against his. He gasped.

"It can feel better," I whispered.

After that, he took over. He pulled out so slow I thought I would scream. He slid back in with equal slowness. Over and over and over. I felt the tension in my stomach tightening. My nerves were screaming with anticipation of the pleasure to come.

He sucked one of my breasts, his mouth hot and demanding. As he pulled away, he bit down.

I went nova.

I twisted and convulsed. He was right there with me. His hips pistoned against me. His muscles corded under my fingers. He grabbed my hands and tangled his fingers in mine, pulling my arms above my head. He licked and bit my breasts, and the explosions kept coming. All I could do was feel.

"Come on, baby. Feel good. Feel as good as I do. Give in to me, Riley." He whispered against my ear. I felt his cock twitch, and he thrust deep into me and came, his face a tortured mask of absolute ecstasy.

I did that. I made him feel like that. I made him lose his control.

I practically purred.

He melted down over me, his breath rasping against my ear. A second later, he rolled off onto his back. Instantly I missed his heat. He pulled me against him, stroking the hair off my forehead. "Are you okay? You're not hurt?"

"I'm wonderful." My stomach growled, despite the earlier sandwich and the chocolate milk. I made a face. "Maybe a little hungry."

He just about leaped out of the bed, grabbing up his sweats and taking a shirt out of the dresser. "I'll fix something. Wait here. I'll bring it to you."

He left, pretty much at a dead run. I scowled at the door for a long minute. What the fuck? I really didn't expect cuddle time, but neither did I expect a vanishing act. Had he run for the hills because he didn't want to face me? Or because he had a crazy, desperate urge to make me another ham sandwich? Either way, mind-blowing sex like that deserved better closure.

Even if he thought it was a mistake.

Even if it *was* a terrible, terrible mistake.

I didn't regret it, whatever it was. I had never felt like that before, and I didn't imagine I ever would again.

His departure was enough to put me in a seriously bad mood. I decided I wasn't going to wait for him to come back. I didn't want to be in Price's bed anymore.

I found another shirt in the same drawer he'd taken his out of. The sweats I'd been wearing were soaked, having been dripped on after my shower, so after cleaning myself up, I put on a robe I found in his closet. It was made of dark blue fleece. I wondered if he'd bought it for himself or if someone had given it to him. A girlfriend maybe.

Jealousy clawed inside me. Oh hell. I didn't want to feel this way. He worked for the Tyet, I reminded myself sternly. And he'd tabbed me.

I must have really been out of it earlier, because as soon as I thought of the tab, I realized it was gone. After a moment, I realized the blood null must have cooked it off.

Not that it really did me any good. I wasn't going to try to escape Price; I needed his help to find Josh. I remembered the stuff we'd taken from his office. Had there been any clues to his whereabouts or who'd taken him in there?

I glanced around the room, looking for a clock. The room was big enough to fit four king-sized beds in comfortably. The dressers were made of mahogany wood. The bed had four tall posts, and a fireplace dominated the wall between the closet and the bathroom. Windows lined one wall.

They were smothered in dark curtains, and I couldn't tell what time of day it was. The clock on the mantle said four o'clock. I hadn't been out all that long, then.

I looked outside. I could see faint shapes like buildings, but mostly all there was to be seen was snow and more snow. I let the curtain fall back into place and followed after Price, my stomach twisting nervously.

I didn't really want to know he regretted having sex with me. But did I want him to care about me? The idea was almost as unnerving as working for him in the first place. If the man cared about me, he'd not let me disappear when our business was done. Sooner or later, he'd have to choose between me and the Tyet. I'd like to say he'd choose me. But I had no illusions about being special enough that Price would break ties to keep me safe. Besides, I'd seen what the Tyet could do, what they demanded once they had you. Even if he wanted to, they wouldn't let him.

Chapter 10

I WAS ON THE second floor of Price's condo. His bedroom suite took up half of it. The other half was divided between a posh entertainment room with a Bowflex in one corner, a pool table in the middle, and a comfortable TV nook with a leather corner couch and flat screen I could have parked a car on, plus a wet bar. It pays to be a Tyet man.

Next door was another full bathroom and next to it, an office. The dark wine curtains were pulled all the way open. A wood desk faced the windows, with bookcases behind it and a couch and some chairs to the left. There were some lovely landscapes on the walls, and a fountain bubbled on a marble table in front of one window. Price had a collection of rocks and minerals, with a six-foot-tall amethyst geode in the corner. Stacks of papers and files littered the couch and desk.

I ducked out and found the stairs. I could hear him moving around in the kitchen, and the smell of bacon began to permeate the air. My stomach cramped hard.

I held hard to the railing going down. My head was spinning again. Blood loss, I supposed. Or maybe the mind-blowing sex.

At the bottom of the stairs, the apartment opened up into a living room. It was definitely masculine, but tasteful, with antiques mixed with more modern pieces. Gorgeous art—a mix of prints, photographs, and textiles—sprinkled the walls. I don't know what I expected—posters from the Gun of the Month Club maybe. Most of the outer walls were windows. The floors were a scraped wood with plush rugs strategically scattered around.

Instead of turning right to the kitchen, I went left up the hallway. I found another bathroom and a guest bedroom, plus a big storage closet that could have been a small bedroom, but contained a gun safe, several mountain bikes, and who knows what in the floor to ceiling cupboards along two walls. There was also a washer and dryer. Neither were running. I took a chance and opened the dryer. My clothes were inside and dry. Neither my underwear nor pants showed any hint that I'd bled all over them.

Once dressed, I shut the door and wandered back toward the kitchen.

Time to beard the lion in his den.

Even Taylor would have approved of Price's kitchen. It looked vaguely Italian, with exposed brick on the back wall. It had stainless steel appliances, espresso-colored cupboards, and white granite counters.

Price had his back to me as he flipped bacon on the stove. I slid onto a barstool at the counter. It took him a minute or two to figure out I was there. I just waited.

Finally, he turned around. "You're supposed to be in bed."

I couldn't tell what he was thinking. "I didn't feel like it."

His jaw tightened. "You need rest. You were shot and you lost a lot of blood."

"I'm better now. Got anything I can snack on? And coffee. I could really use some coffee."

He blew out an annoyed sigh and put some bacon on a plate and poured me coffee, putting a carton of cream and some sugar up on the bar.

Price went back to cooking and ignoring me. My head throbbed. I rubbed the spot and remembered I'd hit my head in the shower.

The silence continued through my omelet with toast and more bacon. Price let me have another cup of coffee, but then forced me to drink orange juice.

"You don't need more caffeine. You won't get any sleep," he growled.

I was getting tired of the fact that he was avoiding talking about us in his bed, but neither did I want to push it. From his behavior, he was interested in forgetting it happened. Even though that hurt more than I cared to admit, he was probably right. Definitely right. So I decided to ignore the elephant in the room, too.

"Sleep is overrated. Did you look at the stuff from Josh's safe? Is there something that will help us find him?

He was still standing, leaning back against the opposite counter while he ate. "I think you need to stay out of this and let me handle it."

Suspicion trickled through my heart. I set my fork down and shoved my plate aside. I wasn't hungry anymore. "Why?"

"You got shot. You're a penny-ante tracer, and you're way out of your league. Leave this investigation to someone who's better suited for it."

"That's what I was afraid of all along. You're Tyet through and through. They don't want me to find Josh, so you're supposed to pat me on the head and send me home to wait for whenever his body turns up." I pushed up off my chair. "You do whatever you want, Detective Price. But I am not quitting until I find him."

I sagged and had to grab the counter to stay upright.

He watched me, the skin just beneath his right eye twitching. "I'm sure you'll be a great help to him. Maybe you can faint and distract his captors. Of course you'll only get yourself killed for your trouble. But you could be right. Bleeding all over their floors could free your sister's boyfriend."

"It's better than just letting them kill him without bothering to try to get him back," I retorted.

"But you don't need to. I told you I would help you."

"The stunning thing is that you just expect me to believe that because what, you're a cop? That's a second job. You are an enforcer for Gregg Touray. He owns you, body and soul."

He slammed his plate into the sink. It shattered, the fork flying across the kitchen. "No one owns me."

I snorted. "Who are you trying to kid? You had a price tag. I don't know what it was, but Touray paid it a long time ago. You've been on his payroll ever since, and no one gets to break the rules or walk away."

"There's a flaw to your logic. The people attacking us yesterday worked for the Tyet, too. I'll remind you that you weren't the only one they were shooting at. I am in this with you."

"On the other hand, *you* didn't get hit. You're a bigger physical target and you were between them and me. Don't you find that odd?"

His mouth thinned. "Are you suggesting I was working with them? That I wanted you shot?"

I wasn't, really. But it was a possibility. I said so.

"Why would I bother healing you, then? Why would I sit up for more than twenty-four hours holding your hand and worrying that I'd got you killed? I could have just let you die."

He'd held my hand? "Twenty-four hours?" I repeated. Twenty-four? That meant Josh had been missing for nearly forty-eight.

"You lost a lot of blood. If you hadn't had that blood null, I don't know if you'd have made it. As it was, it slowed the bleeding enough to keep you alive. The bullet was a through and through, but I think it nicked something inside. I keep heal-alls on hand, just in case. You used up four of them. Lucky they worked. There was no way to fetch a tinker to help."

I ran a hand through my hair. It shook. I'd come *that* close to actually dying. I didn't quite meet his gaze. "Thanks."

"You can trust me," he said quietly. "You shouldn't be part of this. I'll get it figured out. You just need to stay safe."

My dad had said that to me a lot. I was tired of letting other people look after me, though it warmed me more than it should have that Price wanted to. And the truth was, even though I wanted to, I couldn't trust him. Not with Josh's life. I shook my head. "I can't and you know it. I'd like to, but you have loyalties to people who are willing to kill me. You can't deny it. I believe you want to help me, for now, and I'm grateful for all you've done. But a leopard doesn't change its spots." And I had secrets that would win him a lot of points with the Tyet.

He looked away, then back at me, his expression unreadable. "Let's have a look at the stuff from Josh's safe," was all he said.

He stalked out of the kitchen and up the stairs, leaving me to follow. I drew a breath and let it out slowly before heading after him. By the time I got upstairs, he was sitting on the couch in his office. He'd pulled the coffee table close and emptied the bag of stuff he'd collected from the office. The other was still zipped up. I sat down on the chair on the opposite side of the table.

He glanced up from the papers he'd picked up. "These look like they are mostly investment papers. They look aboveboard."

I was grateful he was sticking to the subject at hand. "How can you tell?"

"Nothing seems shorted and no odd overages. That doesn't mean they aren't there. Someone good with finances could hide stuff pretty well. What we really need is a forensic accountant." He tossed the papers aside. "I grabbed a pile of letters." He waved to indicate the stack of papers on the edge of the table. "They may tell us more. But first let's see what's in the bag that he worked so hard to keep hidden."

I nodded, and he reached out to unzip it. I picked up one of the letters and scanned it. I went cold.

"What was the name of that guy you wanted me to trace for you?"

Price looked up at me. "Corbin Nader. Why?"

I tossed the page at him. "He knew Josh."

He scowled and snatched up the letter and read it, and then read it again. He stood and paced down in front of the windows, deep in thought. What did the guy he wanted me to find have to do with Josh? Clearly it had surprised Price.

The letter had been pretty innocuous. A confirmation of an account setup and a request for an appointment to discuss Nader's holdings in more detail.

Price came to stand by my chair and thrust the letter at me. "Can you get Nader's trace off this?"

No, not if I wanted to keep him thinking that I was a hack. "Will this help us find Josh?"

Something flickered in his eyes. "I don't know. Maybe."

"Why are you looking for Nader?"

"He's got a connection to a missing woman."

"Who?"

He hesitated.

"So I'm supposed to trust you, but you don't trust me?"

"I don't want you involved. I don't want to see you get any more hurt."

I wanted to believe him, but he was lying. He was hiding something. I figured I didn't have a choice. Josh had been in the hands of the haunters for two days now. Between what they might be doing to his mind and what the tinker had already done to his body, he needed help now.

I opened myself to the trace. Power sluiced into me and ribbons of light fluttered through the air. I clutched the arm of the chair, trying to make the room slow down, but it tilted and started to spin.

The next thing I know, I'm sitting on Price's lap on the couch. He's got a cold washcloth, and he's sponging it over my face. I pushed his hand away and tried to sit up. He held me still as he searched my face.

"What happened?" My head throbbed like someone had punched me.

"You passed out."

"Oh."

"Oh? Care to explain why?" He sounded angry again.

"No idea. I opened up to the trace and got overloaded."

"Has that ever happened to you before?"

I shook my head, holding myself stiff so I wouldn't curl up like a kitten on his chest. "I probably overdid it. Using the blood null took a lot of energy and then getting shot . . . I probably just need some sleep."

"Haven't I been telling you so?" He stood up, holding me easily in his arms. He carried me down the hall and laid me on his bed, pulling the covers up to my chin. "Sleep. We can't go anywhere until the storm lets up early tomorrow. We'll have a little window before the next one."

He spun around and shut the door behind him.

I stared at the door. My body was stiff as a board. I could smell him on the sheets; I could smell *us* on the sheets. I wasn't sleeping in his bed. I didn't belong there.

I slid out of the sheets and went back downstairs to his spare room. I crawled into the queen-sized bed and closed my eyes.

I'M NOT SURE how long I slept. It was still dark when I woke up. I was on my side. A weight lay across my side and something nestled warm against my back. My head was pillowed on Price's arm. I blinked, feeling his breath against the back of my neck. My heart thudded against my ribs as something like elation swept through me. For a second I felt drunk.

I lay there, breathing in his scent and reveling in the feel of him. It couldn't have been more than a minute before I felt tension return to his body. He was awake.

"What are you doing here?" I asked.

"You're here," he said, as if that was a perfectly reasonable explanation. He groaned and turned onto his back, pulling me around to snuggle against his side. "My bed is bigger and a lot more comfortable. You should have stayed there."

I put my head on his chest. He held my hand, toying with my fingers.

"Why did you follow me?"

"My bed was cold."

"Don't play games. I'm not good at games."

He didn't say anything for a while. I stayed silent, enjoying the feel of him beneath my cheek, the smell of him filling my lungs, and the touch of his fingers on mine.

"I had to," he said finally.

I let that seep in. I had no idea what he meant. There was a crazy, vast satisfaction in having captured his attention and interest. He was the sort of man that didn't usually look twice at a woman like me. I would have thought Taylor was more his style.

At the same time, terror curled hard talons in my gut. He was a Tyet man. That in itself was enough reason for me to run and hide as far from him as I could get. Being a cop made it worse. My father had made it very clear from the moment I could first understand—there was no possible happily-ever-after moment for me. I would always have to be on guard; everyone would want a piece of me.

Believing that had kept me safe my entire life. A traitorous voice whispered, *but what if Price is different?* Could I risk it? Taking a risk had left Taylor with a broken heart. That same risk could leave me enslaved or dead. I couldn't afford to be stupid. Yet here I was all snuggled up and happily being stupid.

"What was in the case from the safe?" I asked, needing a change of subject.

"I didn't look. Figured I'd wait for you." He paused. "You aren't going to let this go. Balls to the wall to find Josh, is that about right?"

"I promised Taylor."

He sighed. "I thought so." He tipped me onto my back and looked down at me. In the gloom, I could barely make out the angles of his face or the slight shine of his eyes. He leaned down and kissed me, slow and hard. My toes curled. I gripped his arms, clenching tight. He lifted up. "I'm not letting you get away," he said and kissed me again. At the same time, I felt the frigid cold of a tab on my neck. I stiffened and he pulled away before I could bite his tongue off.

I clenched my teeth, fury spinning through me.

"Riley?"

"You're an asshole."

"I won't argue."

"You didn't have to do that. I agreed to work for you. I'm not running out on you. You could have trusted me."

"Maybe we both need to work on that," he said, sliding down beside me and propping his head on his elbow. He ran his fingers over my cheek and across my lips. "Maybe I did it to protect you."

I snorted. "How is it going to do that?"

"If someone takes you, I'll come find you. I promise." He bent and kissed me again. "Trust me."

"Said the spider to the fly," I murmured, fighting to hold onto my anger.

He went still. "I mean it, Riley. No matter what happens, or whatever else you think, believe that. I will come find you. Do not burn this one off."

I shivered. "I'm not planning to get taken. At least, not by someone else." I put my arms around his neck and pulled him to me. Pretty cheesy, I know. But I was feeling reckless, and something in his intensity made my insides turn to liquid. I wanted him again. Bad.

He didn't hold back. His hands moved over me with an eagerness that set me on fire. I could never trust him, but that didn't mean I couldn't call him mine for a few hours.

Chapter 11

SEVERAL HOURS LATER, we got out of bed and showered and had a steak breakfast before we tackled the contents of Josh's safe. This time I sat on the couch, tucked firmly against Price's side. I wouldn't have pegged him for a touchy-feely type. I didn't tend to be either, but this was pretty damned nice. If I were a cat, I'd have been purring.

"Corbin Nader works for Westchester Bank," Price announced suddenly as he unzipped the case. Inside was a metal box. He pulled it out of the sack. It was locked.

"Why are you looking for him?" I asked, when it seemed like he wasn't going to say any more. "You said there was a missing woman."

He nodded and got up to fetch a pair of pliers, a lockpick kit, and a pocketknife from his desk drawer. "She went missing nearly six weeks ago. She told her friends and family she was going on vacation to an island in the South Seas where she wouldn't have cell service and not to worry if they didn't hear from her."

"But they did worry."

"Her ex-fiancé started asking questions. He thinks there might have been foul play." He sat down and started tinkering with the lock.

"What do you think?"

"I think he's right. There's no record she ever left the States. I found her passport in her apartment. She did take clothes and toiletries, so if she was kidnapped, they meant for her to be comfortable. If she did a vanishing act on her own, the question is why. She's an heiress and the senior financial officer at Westchester Bank. She has a great life and every reason to live it. Her family isn't saying much. I think maybe there might have been a ransom demand, but if so, they haven't paid, or the kidnappers want more than just money."

"What does Nader have to do with it?"

"His name was in her datebook. He was one of the last people she met with before she vanished. But when I went to look for him, he'd cleared out, too. Fast, like he was seriously spooked. That was about a week ago. I was hoping you could trace him, but I don't know that you can find anything now."

The letter from Nader to Josh was sitting on his desk. I hadn't touched it again. It was enough for me to get a trace from. I couldn't tell Price that. "Wait. Why would he go to Josh for financial advice if he worked for a bank?"

Price shrugged. "I wondered that myself, though maybe he preferred to keep his personal business separate from the job."

It sounded reasonable enough. "You said this woman had an ex-fiancé. When did that happen? Maybe she's just licking her wounds, getting over a broken heart."

"She ended the relationship. I doubt her heart was even involved," he said, scowling at the lock.

"And yet he is still in love with her. Poor guy."

He glanced at me. "What makes you say that?"

"He's worried about her. He's aware she's gone missing. I mean, he reported her, not her family. That says he's still got it bad for her."

Price shrugged dismissively. "Maybe he's just a good guy."

"How long were they together?"

"A year, give or take."

"He's so not over her."

"Sure he is. He's seeing someone else."

I snorted. "That doesn't mean anything. I bet he's nursing some serious hurt for her, hoping she'll come back to him. He's still in love with her. The girl he's dating is just for comfort."

"I don't think so." He slapped the box down hard on the table. "Dammit."

"Let me try." I pulled the box onto my lap with his lockpick set. It wasn't very heavy. I shook it. Several somethings moved inside. I examined the locking mechanism. It wasn't like anything I'd ever seen before. The opening looked like two crisscrossed lightning bolts surrounded by a circle. "That's a hell of a key."

Price had slouched against the back of the couch, watching me from beneath lowered lids. He looked pissed. "We might have to cut it open. I've got a Sawzall in the garage."

"Give me a few minutes. Got a paperclip?"

He fetched one from his desk. I unbent it, then took a pair of needle nose pliers and bent a circle into one end. When it sat flat on the table, the long end stuck straight up in the air. I pushed it into the outer ring of the lock, adjusting it a little bit bigger before it fit.

"Hold this for me," I said.

Price leaned against me. He smelled good. I resisted the urge to nibble his ear, but my heart started thumping and heat pooled in my belly. I really had a bad case for him. Nothing I couldn't cure with a bottle of whiskey and a few pounds of chocolate, I told myself firmly.

He held the wire ring in place. I took the picks and started feeling around inside the lock. There weren't any pins, at least what I expect pins to be like. Instead, there seemed to be a smooshy surface inside. I wasn't sure if I was going to need one, two, or four tension wrenches. I studied the lock some more, and then I got a really stupid idea.

"Just a minute," I said and handed him the box. I unplugged a floor lamp and cut the cord off at the base.

"What are you doing?" Price demanded.

I peeled back the insulation of the cord, exposing the wires. I twisted them together, plugged the cord back into the wall, and then grabbed the box from him and set it on his desk. "You still need to hold the ring inside. Hold it with the pliers so I don't electrocute you."

"This is not safe," he said, grabbing the pliers and coming around to insert the paperclip ring in place. He laid a throw pillow on the box and gripped it.

"Safety is overrated. Ready?"

I didn't wait for the answer. I jammed the exposed wire into the center of the two lightning bolts.

The box vibrated, and I felt a surge of magic. I didn't have a chance to warn Price before a shockwave slammed into me. It tossed me against the window. My feet left the floor and my back and head smashed against the glass as I dropped to the floor like a sack of dog kibble.

My vision went spotty and then black. I opened my mouth, but my lungs wouldn't inflate. I fought against panic. After what seemed like eternity, I sucked in a sobbing breath. Pain radiated from the back of my head down my back. My elbows hurt. I rolled onto my knees, holding my head between my forearms like I was bowing to Mecca.

"Riley?"

Price sounded like he was underwater. Or maybe it was me.

"Huh?" That was about all I could muster. I heard thumping sounds of him moving.

"Are you okay?"

"Uh-huh." In order to make that convincing, I pushed myself up to my hands and knees. Something tickled my nose, and I swiped it with the back of my arm. It came away smeared red. I had a nosebleed. I grabbed the windowsill and hoisted myself upright.

My vision was starting to clear. Or rather, color came back but everything else was blurry. A yellow light pulsed brightly to the side, making my head hurt worse. "Can you turn the light down?" I raised a hand to block it.

"You're bleeding again." Price caught my upper arms and guided me to his desk chair. "You really can't afford to be losing so much blood."

"I didn't actually *want* to get shot or have a nosebleed," I said.

He peeled his shirt over his head and handed it to me. "Press this to your nose. I'll be right back."

He disappeared and returned with a warm washcloth. He rubbed it over my ears and down the sides of my neck. He pulled away. Rusty pink colored the pale green terry cloth.

"Let me see your nose."

I lowered my hands and let him finish cleaning me up. He tipped my chin up and examined me. His expression was grim. More like smoking angry. I glanced over my shoulder at the windows. I hadn't broken anything. I looked back at him, raising one brow. "I'll buy you a new shirt, if that's what's bugging you."

"You could have gone through the window. You'd have been cut to ribbons. If that didn't kill you, the fall would have."

"I didn't and I wasn't," I said. Either I was beginning to get used to this almost dying thing, or my brain was tired of reacting to it. "Anyhow, it paid off," I said, gesturing at the box and the source of the yellow light filling the room. "We can find out what Josh was protecting."

"This is exactly why you should stay out of this. I can't protect you."

"I didn't ask you to."

He made a disgusted sound, and ran his fingers through his hair. "Dammit, Riley. You don't belong in this mess."

"Doesn't matter," I said. "I have to do this. I promised Taylor."

"How did I know you'd say that?" He sat on the edge of the desk. "Fine. But do me a favor and stop getting hurt." He bent to lean over the box, careful not to touch anything. I rolled the chair forward and peered inside.

On top, hiding the rest of the contents, was a square envelope with my name on it written in Josh's handwriting. I frowned in shock. What the fuck?

Of all the possibilities I'd envisioned, a letter addressed to *me* of all people had never occurred to me. I reached for it without thinking.

Price grabbed my wrist. "Wait."

"For what?"

He grimaced. "You see any trace?"

He was asking about potential spells, not evidence of who'd handled it. Given that that sort of trace should already have faded for me.

I opened up to it, despite the fact that I could barely focus through my headache. Ribbons of Josh laced the box, with a few fainter lines of two or three other people. Probably from whomever he bought it from or whoever had set the magic spells inside. Josh had no abilities of his own. There was no sign of any magic besides the light that shone out of it like a beacon. I wonder how long it would be before that died, if ever.

"I don't see anything but the magic of that light. That doesn't mean anything, because if the spell isn't activated, I can't see it anyhow."

"Comforting," he said dryly.

"Can I read my letter now?" I asked, tugging out of his grip.

"It could blow up in your face."

"Paper doesn't hold magic. You ought to know that."

"Maybe." His mouth twisted. "Just be careful."

"I'll try not to get a paper cut." I took out the letter. Underneath was a lumpy brown burlap sack.

I sat back and lifted the flap of the envelope, holding my breath. Price had infected me with his groundless caution. Nothing happened. Inside was a folded card. The cover had a tracery of pearl in one corner. Very refined and stylish. I flipped it open.

Josh's writing was tight, like he tried to scrunch all he had to say into as tiny a space as possible. Price stood back, folding his arms over his chest and letting me read it privately.

Riley:

If you've found this box, then it means that I'm dead or captured and Taylor's asked you to look into it. I'm sorry. I wish I could have warned you to stay away, but I couldn't. Now it's too late.

Just then Price's cell phone gave of a sharp beeping sound. He looked at the screen and his face turned glacial. He raised it to his ear. "Price," he said as he walked out the door.

I had wondered how long it would be before his Tyet connections caught up to us. Or maybe Price had already been talking to them, keeping them updated.

My hands tightened on the card, crushing it. I took a breath, trying to slow my heart. They weren't knocking the door down yet. So far Price hadn't turned me over to them. That reminded me of the tab. I touched it. The magic burst from the box hadn't destroyed it. I wiped a hand over my forehead. My life depended on Price right now, and I wasn't at all sure he was planning to keep me safe, despite his promises. Or even if he could.

I drew in a shaky breath and let it out slow and returned to Josh's note.

> *The FBI approached me almost a year ago. Someone had been embezzling money from several banks and funneling it through investment firms to launder it, Franklin Watley being one. I was asked to perform forensic accounting to see what sort of trail I could pick up. They didn't give me or my bank a lot of choice, so with the blessing FW's CEO, I took on the job.*
>
> *At first it was simple enough. I found what I expected—laundering, skimming, credit card mining, and fraud. But then a few months ago the FBI gave me keys to some safety deposit boxes around town. They got them in a raid and told me to check them out. Most contained drugs, money, jewelry, and that sort of thing. But there were a few that had other things. I don't even know what they are. All I know is that ever since the moment I found them, I've been hunted by the Tyet. Whatever they are, they are too dangerous to keep, yet I can't give them to the FBI. My contact is Special Agent Sandra Arnow. She would do anything to snap the Sparkle Dust trade and break Tyet control of Diamond City, including sacrificing innocents. She thinks any means is justified by the ends. Right now, the only thing I can do is keep digging and hope I don't end up buried in my own hole.*
>
> *This box contains everything I've discovered. These are little better than jigsaw pieces. It isn't much, but if anyone can find out about them, it's you. Sorry. I know I'm not supposed to know.*
>
> *I know I don't have to tell you, but I'll say it anyway. Don't trust anyone. Watch your back. I've just put a target on you, and everybody will be coming for you. Tell Taylor I love her, even though I don't deserve her.*

It was signed with just a J. I turned the page over. Nothing on the back. I read it again. My stomach sank down in my shoes. Josh knew what I could do. Taylor wouldn't have told him, but he'd figured it out. We'd probably left clues we didn't even know about, and he wasn't stupid. Not even a little bit. Luckily someone reading the note could just assume he thought I was better than I was. At least I hoped so. I had no hope of hiding the letter from Price.

I pulled the box onto my lap. As soon as I touched it, the light went out.

"Curiouser and curiouser," I muttered. I wondered where Josh had hidden the key. Or maybe he hadn't had the chance.

I untied the little burlap sack and pulled out a tin cylinder. I set it on the desk. It was followed by a wooden box about six inches long and three inches square on the ends. Next I pulled out an opaque purple glass bulb.

I set it down, feeling myself starting to shake. I recognized it. It belonged to my mother. She'd hung it from a ribbon in our kitchen window. I remember watching the light hit it and wondering what it hid inside. I once got it down, rattling it near my ear to figure out what the shadowy shape was under the glass. My mother had caught me and taken it away. I remember she'd had a look like I'd been playing with a rattlesnake. I never saw it again after that. Not until now.

I turned it in my fingers, then set it down, taking a deep breath, collecting myself. There was more to see. But deep in my heart, a spark of excitement flickered into a tiny flame. Was I finally on to something that could tell me who killed my mother?

Next were a half-dozen ziplock bags. Four contained napkins or Kleenexes. One held a button, and inside the last was a piece of gum. On the outside of the bags were written different names in black Sharpie. I felt the air vanish from my lungs as I read them: Ostrander, Drummond, Briandi, Morrell, Pajarien, and Touray. All of them were known to be major players in the Tyet.

Without thinking, I grabbed them in a handful and stuffed them into my pocket. Price didn't need to know who was involved, especially since Touray was his boss.

"What did the letter say?" Price walked back in without any warning.

My head jerked up. Had he seen? He didn't say anything about the baggies, so maybe not. Or maybe he was waiting to see what I would do. Once again my hands started to shake. See what I mean? Not cut out to be a burglar or a criminal at all. Too fucking jumpy. I took another breath to steady myself, then shoved the note toward him. "See for yourself."

While he read, I looked into the bag again. At the bottom was a blue velvet pouch and another paper folded in half. I pulled the latter out. It was another list of names and numbers with arrows and circles connecting them. On one side and underlined twice was Corbin Nader. An arrow pointed from him to Barney Stills to Caroline Moretenson to Barry Klein to Shana Darlington to a circle with three question marks in it. I passed the page to Price.

"Recognize anybody?"

He scanned it and frowned. "Shana Darlington is my missing woman."

"Looks like her fiancé is right. She didn't vanish on her own."

"Ex-fiancé," he corrected absently. "Or she did. Maybe she was part of the fraud and was spooked by Josh's investigation. What did he mean that he knows about you?"

The last question thrust quiet and swift, like a knife blade between the ribs. I'd been expecting it. "Maybe Taylor made me sound a lot better than I am. Who knows?"

Price didn't look like he bought it, but he didn't push. Now. He wasn't the type to give up before he got his answers.

"Clearly we need to find Nader, and hope he leads us to Shana Darlington. She may just know where Josh is. Anything else in the box?"

"Just this." I pulled out the pouch and set it on the desk with the other items, then put the box and the burlap bag on the floor.

He picked up the four objects one by one and turned them over in his fingers. "What do you think they are?"

"Only one way to find out."

"He booby-trapped that box. Probably did the same to these. For a guy who wants your help, he seemed to be making a point of killing you."

"My fault. I should have activated a null just in case."

He snorted, his eyes narrowing at me. I could see his mind clicking behind the sapphire. "You aren't strong enough to have nullified that spell."

"I'd have softened the blow. No pain, no gain, right?"

He rubbed his chin and came around the front of the desk. He pulled open the bottom left drawer, his hip brushing against my arm. I scooted away. I could not trust Price, and I was in serious danger of letting myself forget that.

Inside the drawer were several boxes, all upended in neat rows and labeled. He drew one out and flipped it open. It contained a variety of what looked like blown glass paperweights. He pulled one out and slid the box back into its drawer slot. He held it in his fist, and after a moment I felt the null activate.

"Handy. Working for the Tyet must be nice."

A muscle in the side of his jaw jumped as he thunked the null down on top of the desk. It made a dent in the wood. "Don't get high and mighty all of a sudden. It comes with certain perks. One of which healed that bullet wound of yours."

"Tell them thanks for me," I said acidly. "You know, since they are also responsible for shooting me in the first place. Speaking of the Tyet, are you going to tell me what that phone call was about?"

"Nothing to do with you."

"Of course not," I said. "Why ever would you lie about that?" I couldn't turn off the sarcasm or the hurt I felt. He was right. I knew exactly who and what he was, and I'd jumped into bed with him anyway. I only had myself to blame if I couldn't keep a handle on my feelings. I just needed to stop thinking about it. "All right then, let's unwrap the presents, shall we?"

I reached for the blue pouch first. I untied it and felt a swell of magic that dissolved as fast as it formed. The green swirl center of the paper-weight glowed as it absorbed the power. Flashy. Then again I suppose it was useful for someone who couldn't feel magic to know a spell had been absorbed.

"I don't know that Josh liked you much," Price said, watching me with folded arms. He looked like he wanted to punch someone. Probably me. "He sure seems to be intent on frying your ass."

I didn't bother answering. After loosening the tie on the pouch, I upended the contents into my hand. A vial of red liquid fell into my hand. Blood. It had to be. But whose? And what was I supposed to do with it?"

"What the hell?" Price said, leaning over to get a better look.

I held up the little bottle, turning it in my fingers. There was no label. It was made of an old-fashioned bubbled glass wrapped in copper filigree and was stoppered with a cork and a red coating of sealing wax. The copper was tarnished green with age.

"Who's blood is this and how did Josh get it?" I wondered. "It looks really ancient."

"A lot of powerful magic can be worked with blood."

"True, but the person who made this has to be dead. I mean, the bottle's got to be a hundred years old or more." I squinted at the wax. "There's an impression on the top. Like a letter, but unintelligible." I passed it to Price to see if he could make it out.

He put it under the lamp, then shook his head. "I can't tell what it is." He set it aside. "Let's look at the other stuff. See if they tell us anything."

"Be my guest," I said, waving at the three containers.

He picked up the tin cylinder and unscrewed the end. Once again, the null flared. A silent whine ran through my bones. The null was rapidly reaching capacity. Price tipped the cylinder over and slid the contents out onto the desk.

It looked like an ugly piece of abstract art. It was about five inches long and carved from a big hunk of turquoise. It was dully rounded on one end with what appeared to be a flat flower on the other end, if the flower's petals were nails. Connecting the two ends were three interwoven strips carved in varying shapes. One looked like a teetering stack of cubes, the second looked like knotted string, and the third was knobby.

"Don't have a clue," Price said, bending down to examine it more closely, but careful not to touch. He shook his head. "Let's see what else there is."

The top of the wooden box slid back as Price opened it. Magic surged, and the null flared and cracked in half. He dropped the box and shook his hand. "Shit. That hurt."

"You're going to need another null."

"Thank you, Miss Obvious."

"Always glad to be helpful. Lucky you have plenty." My voice was carefully neutral.

He gave me a sharp look and then finished removing the lid. Nestled inside was a long, thin piece of metal covered in silver whiskers. They shifted and moved like they were underwater.

Though I knew better, I couldn't resist brushing the fringe softly with my finger. The fine strands combed through my skin and blood welled and dripped. The metal piece convulsed and strands of silver shot out to capture my hand. I jerked back, barely in time. The box shook violently. Price grabbed the lid and pressed it down, holding it in place until the shaking stopped. Quickly he slid it back into the grooves and clicked it closed.

Blood was running pretty freely down my finger. I grabbed the washcloth he'd used to clean me up earlier and pressed it hard against my finger.

"That was unexpected," I said. "Wonder what would have happened if it grabbed me?"

"I expect it would have torn you up like a wood chipper," Price said. "I was wondering why you kept a blood null with you. Now I'm wondering why you don't have more of them." His eyes were hooded and grooves dug deep into the side of his nose and lips.

I ignored the jibe. "What do you think it's for?" I asked, jerking my chin at the box.

"I wish I knew."

Him and me both. I had to wonder if he knew more than he was saying, but it wasn't like he had his finger on the pulse of the Tyet big shots. He was an enforcer, making him the middle-class of the Tyet. The truth was that it would be more surprising if he *did* know something. "What about that last one?"

He spun the purple bulb around on the desktop. "There's no lid. We'll have to break the glass. That could trigger something unpleasant."

"You've got more nulls." My throat closed on the words as I watched the bulb. It was the only thing I'd ever had of my mom. The idea of breaking it hurt more than I can say. At the same time, it was a clue for finding Josh, and maybe for finding who'd killed my mother. I steeled myself.

Price pulled another paperweight null out of his collection. This one was orange with little blue bubbles throughout. I reached for the purple bulb.

"Oh, no you don't. You've bled enough today." He snatched the purple bulb out of reach when I tried to take it, then picked up the pliers and gently tapped the glass. Nothing happened. He hit harder, and there was a cracking sound. Magic flared and dissolved. The blue bubbles in the null glowed neon. Pretty. Someone was artistic. I couldn't have done that. I could make a hell of a null, but I didn't know how to light it up. Maybe the tracer who'd made it had some help. A binder maybe.

Price continued breaking away the glass until a tarnished brass object was revealed. It looked a lot like an oversized wing nut, except instead of mouse ears, it had butterfly wings and in the middle it wasn't a nut, but a hollow cylinder. I thought it was hollow, but when Price picked it up with the pliers and twisted and turned it in the air, I realized the tube was filled with shimmering crystals.

"Let me see." I held out my hand for the pliers, but Price waved me away, moving closer so I could better examine it.

I turned on the desk lamp and looked closer. "What's in the tube?" I asked finally. It was almost like they were only half there, ghosting in and out of being.

"I don't know. They look like diamonds. Maybe opals."

"What do you make of the way they keep fading and rippling in and out?"

His brows winged down. "What do you mean?"

"You can't see it, can you?"

He eyed me speculatively. "No. Is it some sort of trace?"

I shook my head. He couldn't pin this on me being a brilliant tracer. "I'm not looking for trace." I shook my head in real bewilderment. I don't usually see magic. I can feel it, but not see it unless I open myself to the trace. I rubbed my forehead. I was finding more questions and no answers in Josh's box.

"Does your head hurt? I could get you something for it. You whacked it pretty hard on the window."

In fact it did hurt like hell. "That would be great. Maybe a Band-Aid, too," I said with weak smile, holding up my washcloth-wrapped finger.

He left and soon returned with a bottle of water, two ibuprofen, and a Band-Aid. I swallowed the pills and let him apply the Band-Aid. Neither one of us spoke. My mind was spinning. The next obvious step was to go look for Nader. But I still had the six baggies in my pocket. What should I do with them? Did I track them down? When? I was stuck with Price. And if I did want to, their trace wouldn't be simple to pick up. They all probably used personal nulls with regularity. I needed to go a traditional route, which meant relying on Price, the professional detective.

I stared down at my lap, thinking hard. Did I dare trust him? God, I was so far up the creek, I'd left the planet. Everything in me said don't risk it.

But if I didn't find Josh, Taylor would be heartbroken. I'd never forgive myself. My only choices were to escape from Price, somehow track down Josh, and try to free him, which, after the Nancy Jane incident, didn't seem too easy. Or I could lean on Price and hope to hell he would do what he said and help me rescue Josh and not just turn me over to his boss.

I reached out and touched the letter Josh had written to me. I opened to the trace. A ribbon of silvery red light fell in coils and spun away through the wall. It pulsed with a vibrancy that said he was alive.

I couldn't rescue him alone.

I reached into my pocket and pulled out the baggies, laying them out on the desk so he could read their names. I locked gazes with him. "Josh put these in the box, too. The question is, now that you know who's involved, what are you going to do?"

Chapter 12

PRICE LOOKED AT the baggies. You know that metaphor about people turning to stone? I swear he actually did it. I couldn't tell if he was pissed, scared, or both. Hard to imagine him being afraid of anything. 'Course I could have been reading him the wrong way. Maybe he was just shocked I'd handed him all my evidence. I was sure the kidnappers had taken Josh to get this box back. Now that I'd handed it to Price on a silver platter, his captors could kill Josh, Price could kill me and Taylor, and *voilà*! No more witnesses or evidence. End of problem.

I probably should have considered that a minute or two ago, but it wouldn't have changed my decision. I still needed help to rescue Josh. Price was that help. I had to trust him.

He picked up each of the baggies and examined them, setting them carefully back down. He turned around and paced back to the wall, thrusting his hands into his pockets as he stared at it.

As the moments ticked past, my heart stuttered and then shriveled. Fuck, but I was an idiot. I pushed back the chair and stood up, gathering up the baggies and the other contents of the box. I packed them back inside the burlap sack and tied the top shut.

"What are you doing?"

Price was looking at me, his eyes nearly black. He looked like—an enemy.

"I'm going to look for Josh," I said, and my throat tightened up. "Since you aren't going to help me." I couldn't believe it. I was starting to get teary. How stupid. Should I really be surprised that he didn't catch my Hail Mary pass? So we'd had sex. It was physical. He didn't care about me. At least not enough to risk his life going up against the Tyet. It was too much to hope for. "Where are my things? Coat? Phone? Boots?"

He didn't say answer.

I paused. "Unless you're holding me prisoner until you can turn me over to your boss."

He snarled. "I'm not holding you prisoner."

"Then where's my stuff?"

"Laundry room."

I hadn't seen anything when I found my pants and underwear, not that I'd been searching.

"Great." I grabbed the sack and stalked past and ran down the stairs.

Inside the laundry room I found a basket on top of the dryer containing everything I'd had on me, including my gun. I looked around for my coat. It was still wet, hanging on a rack behind the door. A dark hole burrowed through the front. My stomach lurched and I swallowed hard.

"I don't suppose you'll lend me a coat," I said to Price, who leaned in the doorway. If he wanted to appear relaxed, he failed. His were fisted tight in his pockets, and a muscle twitched in his jaw.

He swung around wordlessly and left. I pulled on my boots and laced them up, then started distributing my things in my pockets.

Price filled the doorway again. He handed me a gray down jacket.

"Thanks."

He went back to leaning and watching. The coat was too big and smelled of him, but it had enough pockets for all my gear, including my gun. I stuck it in a roomy outer pocket. I rolled the sleeves back and put my gloves on. When I was zipped up and had the burlap sack again, I stopped in front of him.

"You make a crappy door," I noted.

"What do you think you're going to do?"

"Trace Josh. Break him out."

"How?"

"Which one?"

He scowled. "Pick."

"I'll figure it out when the time comes." Which was exactly true. I hadn't a clue what I was going to do or how, just that I had to try. "Want to let me take the snowmobile?"

He looked down at the floor and shook his head. "You're certifiable, do you know that?"

"I do know," I said. "But I don't see that I have much choice."

"You go alone, and you'll get killed."

"What other choice is there? I've known all along you're a Tyet man. You were never going to go up against them. Just let me have a head start." I gave a weak smile. "I don't want to have to hurt you."

He grinned back. As if I could hurt him. The worst I'd done so far was smack him with my baton and bleed all over him. Scary shit, that.

"I should get going," I hinted, looking past him down the hall. "I could seriously use the snowmobile."

He didn't budge. "You don't know how to drive it."

"I'm a quick learner."

He dragged his fingers through his hair. I had a flashback to doing the same thing while he was making me feel crazy good. I flushed. Concentrate, I told myself. He's the enemy now. Always was, I corrected myself, pushing away all thoughts of him tangled up with me in bed.

"You've gotta let me go now," I said. My voice had turned husky.

He flinched. Before I knew what he was going to do, he snatched my hand and pulled me into the kitchen. He pushed me down onto a barstool and poured me some coffee.

"Stay put," he said and vanished upstairs.

I stared after him, then to the door. He'd catch me before I got far. I sighed and set the burlap sack down. I took off my gloves and got the carton of cream from the fridge, pouring some into my coffee. I stirred the sugar a little overzealously, splashing coffee onto the counter. I didn't know what to think or feel. I wanted to be hopeful, but doubts continued to claw at me. I glanced again toward the door. I should try to run. Maybe I couldn't drive the snowmobile, but I could disable it and go on foot.

In this snow, it wouldn't take long for Price to catch up with me. I sipped my coffee. That brought me to the next problem. How was I going to get around if he didn't let me have the snowmobile? I'm a decent skier. In Colorado, it's pretty much required. Did I want to go home and get a pair? Or break in someplace and steal some? On the surface that sounded like a better option, but really, what was the likelihood I'd find a place with the right sized boots or even something close enough to make it work?

Details. I bet Price had skis. Or better, snowshoes. I didn't need those to fit.

I didn't have any more time to contemplate my escape. He thudded down the stairs and back into the kitchen. He was dressed for going outside, with a black turtleneck and a thick coat. He carried a backpack in one hand and a roll of black fabric in the other.

"Take off your jacket," he ordered.

I was going to make a joke, something about how I didn't have time to fool around, but there was a strained look on his face that said he might go ballistic if I pushed him. I unzipped the coat and dropped it onto my chair.

He unrolled the fabric and pulled it down over my head before velcroing it tightly.

"A bulletproof vest?" I asked, looking down at myself. He was wearing one too.

"We aren't going in unprepared this time," he said. "It won't help much against magic, but at least you won't end up Swiss cheese."

"We?"

"I told you I'd help you get him back." He went to a cupboard and pulled out a handful of protein bars. "Eat a couple of these. Hurry, we don't have much time."

That sounded ominous. What did he know that I didn't? "We don't have much time? Why not?"

"They figured out I was with you at Josh's office. I'm supposed to bring you in."

Cold slithered down my spine. I set my protein bar on the counter. If I tried to swallow now, I'd either choke or vomit. "When were you going to tell me?"

"I was working it out."

Hysterical laughter bubbled in my throat. "Working it out?" I repeated.

"I bought some time. I told him you were shot, that I needed some time. He trusts me."

"Who?" But I knew. His boss. Gregg Touray. Head of one of the biggest Tyet syndicates in the city.

"Touray," he confirmed, looking only slightly guilty.

"So you were planning to drop me in his lap, and now you've changed your mind?" I asked, acid dripping from my voice. My knight in shining armor. I should have stabbed him in his sleep.

"No, I haven't. I'm not taking you in. I never was."

I blinked, and my mouth fell open. "Excuse me. What did you say?"

"I said I'm not bringing you in and I never was." He looked like he meant it.

I snorted. "Right. Because putting yourself sideways of one of the most powerful and dangerous men in the Tyet is a sure ticket to the bottom of a deep, dark hole. Why wouldn't you do that?"

He sighed, aggravated. "It's the truth. I wasn't turning you in to him. When you got all high and mighty upstairs and decided to go off on your own, I had every intention of letting you while I tracked Josh by myself. I didn't want you in the line of fire. But then I realized that you'd end up in the middle of the mess anyway. You find trouble like a moth finds a flame. So we'll do it together, and I'll take care of Touray."

My brows knitted together. "Why? I never expected you to keep your promise. I always knew you had a conflict of interest and I wasn't on the winning side."

He gave a short bark of laughter. "You're wrong about that. Right now, you're about all I can think about. God, I could use a drink."

"My eldest brother says I could drive anyone to drink," I said, my head reeling from his confession.

"He's right."

"Are you sure? Because Touray isn't known for forgiving disloyalty." I was pretty sure I'd gone insane. I was arguing for him to take me in. Somehow he'd become important to me. *You're about all I can think about.* Even the memory of his words made me catch my breath.

"Let me worry about that. Let's go."

He gathered up the bars I'd left on the counter and stuffed them in his pack before heading out the garage door. I pulled on my jacket and followed.

It took awhile to get the garage door open. A lot of snow had drifted up against it. Price smashed a ramp down for the snowmobile, waving me out of his way when I tried to help.

"Where are we going?" I asked when he told me to get on. Our helmets were long gone, left at the Franklin Watley building. Our pursuers had probably used them to trace us. Which meant that Touray's people had shot at us. I frowned. Had they not recognized Price?

"We'll start at Nader's place."

"I should warn my family the Tyet's looking for me," I said and waited for Price to nod. Not that I needed his permission, but I was trying to show that I trusted him. Or at least that I believed him. I dug my phone out of my pocket. I had only a sliver of green left on my battery icon. Taylor had left several messages for me, but I didn't bother checking them. Instead I popped open a text message and put her, my brothers, and my stepmother into the recipient list. I hesitated. What did I tell them?

Tyet. Get out of Diamond City. Hide.

I hit SEND and powered off the phone. I hoped they'd take me at my word. I hoped it wasn't already too late.

Chapter 13

A GOOD THREE or four feet of snow had fallen since the storm first began. A few flakes spun through the gray air, but mostly it had stopped, for now. Thick clouds built up against the mountains to the north and west. It wouldn't be long before the next storm rolled in. A few people were trying to dig out. Smoke rose from chimneys, and here and there the Christmas lights of those houses slow to take them down glowed cheerily in the gloom.

Price's apartment was on the south side of the crater on a small singular shelf called, with a great deal of creativity, the Ledge. It was connected to Downtown by a long bridge. A zigzagging road on the side of the crater led up over the rim in case the bridge was ever to collapse. It should have been an exclusive and expensive area, but it was too far from the rest of the city to attract people like Taylor, and too low—on the same level as Downtown—to attract the über-rich. So a person could get a reasonably cheap place if he was willing to make the drive and didn't mind that the bridge over to the Ledge was a suspension bridge that swayed wildly when the wind spun down in the crater like it tended to do.

Luckily this morning it was decently calm. I still got a little seasick going over. The snow was piled so high the side rails had vanished. I ducked my head down behind Price and squeezed my eyes shut. If we were going to slide off, I didn't want to see it coming.

We made the other side without any problem, and I heaved a relieved sigh. Price headed for the suburbs on the south end of Downtown, a few miles from the Squires's place. A snowplow had been down the main drag relatively recently. Price pulled into a gas station that was miraculously open. A man wandered out of the building. He wore a wool hat with the flaps tied down, a heavy green jacket, and high laced-up boots. His beard was frosted with snow.

"Wasn't sure I was going to be seeing any business today," he said by way of a greeting as he approached. "Turns out, a lot of folks been needing fuel for the heaters, snowmobiles, snowblowers—been running pretty brisk. Guess nobody else got open yet. How much you want?"

"Fill it up," Price said, taking off the gas cap.

The man inserted the nozzle and started to pump. "Name's Garen. We don't usually do full service, but I've hardly seen a soul in days. Keep an apartment on the back of the shop." He motioned at the small convenience store. "Live alone with the cats. Lucky the cable's been working or I'd have gone stir-crazy. Where you folks from?"

"Over on the Ledge," Price said.

"Bridge is good then?"

"Got a lot of snow on it."

Garen shook his head. "That's bad. Hope they get it off before the next storm. Hate to see it collapse."

"It's built to withstand a lot."

"Sure, but haven't had snow like this since the 1920s. Damned wet and heavy. Almost broke my back just scooping out the sidewalk to get the blower outta the shed."

"The plows will get to it soon, I'm sure."

"I expect so. Hope folks are stocked up on enough food. Don't think we're going to see any grocery deliveries this week. Maybe not next, either. Nothing on the freeways is moving and neither are the trains or planes. Everything's shut down from here to Omaha and Salt Lake. It's a mess."

Lead settled in my belly. That meant my family hadn't left—couldn't leave. They had the means to hide. Dad had insisted that everyone had a safe house to run to. I wasn't sure they could even get to those.

Garen finished pumping gas and took the proffered money.

"Keep the change," Price said, climbing back aboard.

"Thanks and drive careful. Ain't a fit day out for man nor beast." He smiled and waved and returned to his store.

We pulled back out on to the road. We went a few more miles and turned off, then wove in and out of the streets to find the place we were looking for. It was a little house set right on top of the sidewalk. It had no garage. Snow heaped halfway up the front door and only about the upper third of the windows was exposed.

Price pulled the snowmobile up outside a side window. "Let me have your baton," he said, holding out his hand.

I gave it to him. He smashed the glass and used it to scrape away the sharp shards clinging to the pane. He grabbed the upper part of the frame and held on while he put one foot then the other onto the sill. He lowered himself inside, then turned to reach for me.

I was not nearly so graceful as he was. I ended up waist deep in snow. By the time I got inside, I my jeans were soaked through.

Price flipped on the lights. Luckily, the power was still up. The place wasn't much to look at. A couple of sagging couches, a TV, some pictures of wild animals, and a whole lot of ashtrays. I wrinkled my nose at the stench. Price wandered away into another room. I picked up some envelopes that were stacked on a couch cushion. Bills and advertisements. I tossed them back down.

I opened to the trace. The ribbon of light that belonged to Nader was dark orange shot through with brown streaks. It looped every which way in the house and in and out the door. The most recent trail led out but not in. Don't ask me how I know directionality; I just do. I can also tell gradations in time from most recent to oldest. It's like tasting the difference between coffee brewed in the morning and left to sit all day, and fresh stuff. It just tastes different.

There were other traces there too. Some of them as old as the house. Some of the people were dead. I noticed that there was a pretty teal ribbon that had come in fairly recently and only once. Whoever it was hadn't gone any farther than the living room. It looked like the visitor had come in, stayed a little while, then left.

I walked over to the bright trace and squatted down. Traces aren't actually left on the surface of things. There's another dimension, I guess you'd call it. Usually I just open up enough to see into it, but I was curious about this ribbon. After taking a quick look over my shoulder to see if Price was watching, I reached my hand into the trace dimension. It closed over my hand like cool water. Energies rubbed against me. I was never sure if they were spirits or something else. I'm not sure I wanted to know.

I took hold of the teal trace. Crackling energy zapped my hand. It felt a little bit like holding on to an electrical cord. After that initial flare, it settled into a buzzing sensation. I closed my eyes, concentrating on what I felt.

The trace belonged to a woman. She was most definitely alive, though I'd known that before I ever touched her trace. Just at the moment she was angry and a little scared.

"Did you find something?"

I jumped as Price stepped up behind me. I pulled my hand back out of the trace, hoping he hadn't noticed. I didn't really know what other people saw when I crossed dimensions. I didn't know if my hand disappeared or glowed or did something equally bizarre. Maybe it just looked normal.

I straightened up. "He's been gone for eight days," I said. "A woman visited him the same day he disappeared. It was the only time she was here."

Price studied me a moment. I knew what he was thinking. I shouldn't be able to read trace that old. I shouldn't be able to pinpoint time like that, not if I was the hack I claimed to be. Something shifted in his eyes, but he didn't say anything about it.

"Are you sure?"

I nodded. "Did you find anything?"

He shook his head. "Nothing that connects him to Josh or Shana Darlington, or the Tyet, for that matter," he added quietly.

"Do you think the woman's trace I found could have been Shana Darlington's?"

He shook his head. "It's possible."

"If it is, then she's alive."

"Good. If we can find her and Nader, she can answer some questions. Let's follow them." He headed for the window.

I hadn't had a chance to touch Nader's trace. I probably should have tried, even with Price looking on. He started climbing out the window, then pulled back in when I gave a little squawk.

"What?"

"He's dead," I whispered, watching all the bright orange and brown trace fade to gray. "Just like that."

Price scowled. "What about the woman? Is she still alive?"

I opened to the trace. "Yeah. She is."

He wiped a hand over his mouth. "Let's go find out if she's our missing woman."

"Or if it would be more help, we could follow Nader's trace and see where he went last." I opened my mouth and let the words out before I could let self-preservation stop me.

He froze, then twisted around. "What did you say?"

"Do you want to see where Nader went last?" My tongue felt like wood.

"That's not possible. The trace disappears when someone dies."

"I've heard that, too," I said.

"You can follow dead trace," he said slowly, as if he was having a hard time understanding.

I shrugged.

"All right. Tell me where to go."

I climbed back on board. The cold cut through my wet jeans. I ignored it. "Left, back the way we came."

Price pulled back out onto the unplowed street. I directed him, telling him which way to go. I didn't pay attention to where we were. Even though I can follow trace from people who've been dead a long time, I was afraid I'd lose Nader's.

We crossed up through Midtown, then to Uptown. Here were glitzy, high-end apartment towers with solid gold toilets next to sprawling estates with dozens of pools and a matching bathroom for every bedroom, eccentric wonderlands that were totally off the grid, and every kind of luxury place in between. It was like Dubai and Paris had had a love child.

The roads here had been cleared, at least enough for one car to drive down them. I directed Price down a wide avenue that ended in a circle at the rimrock wall. I pointed left, down a branch street. Another left, a right, and another right brought us to the back side of a small high-rise maybe four or five stories tall. An underground garage was guarded by sliding iron gates and a security guard in a shack. He eyed us when we stopped, then reached for the microphone on his shoulder and started talking to someone.

"I don't think we're welcome here," I said, leaning up against Price's ear.

"I think you're right," I thought I heard him say, and then he revved the engine and rounded the corner, leaving a rooster tail of snow in our wake.

He wove between buildings and then shot up a plowed street before careening through an unplowed alley.

"Where are we going now?" I shouted.

"To get lost," he shouted back, and he drove onto a wide tractor track and then found a place where a lot of snowmobiles had looped and run. He settled into a trail and followed it, then shot off across a pristine snowfield in a park and caught another trail. After about fifteen minutes, he pulled back out onto the plowed road and exited into a treed park. He parked under a big spruce with broad limbs that hung down to the ground.

As he did, snow fell onto both of us. I yelped as it went down my neck. Price switched off the key and pocketed it before sliding off.

"Come on," he said, grabbing my hand.

He pulled me along. We kept under the line of trees until we reached the edge of the park. It was easy footing, since the snow couldn't get under the thick mat of branches. He guided me out onto the roadway. There wasn't any traffic, and when we heard anybody coming, we ducked behind snowcapped bushes and cars.

It took almost an hour to get back to the high-rise. At least I thought I'd found where he'd been last. I didn't see a trail leaving, but he could have gone out the front. I mentioned it to Price. He nodded, and we made a broad circuit around to see if we would cross his trail. Nothing.

"So he died there. No more trace," I said as we hunched behind a car and watched the house. We didn't try going up the alley. The security guard was still there. A loud motor sounded and a black snowmobile cruised up the road from the opposite direction and vanished behind the building. A few minutes later it emerged. The woman driving was dressed in the same gray uniform as the security guard in back.

She zoomed off, and just as quick, another snowmobile arrived, this time from the other direction. Just like the other, it went behind the high-rise apartment building and then drove off in the opposite direction. They were patrolling.

"What now?" I asked. My teeth were starting to chatter. I couldn't feel my legs. "Got any idea who lives there?"

He shook his head. "None." He took his phone out of his pocket and brought up the police website. He typed in a code and a password, and then input the address. When it came up, he made a growling sound.

"What?"

He tipped the screen so I could see.

The building was owned by the Diamond City Development Corporation. But that wasn't what caught my attention. The list of people owning apartments in the building included Shana Darlington, Price's missing woman.

"Did you know that?"

"If I had, I would've been here already. This makes no sense. I *couldn't* have overlooked it in my background check."

"Unless someone wanted you to miss it."

"Yeah," Price said, fury cutting grooves around his nose and lips.

Price was too good to have missed something like this. Someone had set him up to fail. Realization hit me. Price had figured that out already. That's why he'd come to me in the first place. Someone on the force or in Touray's organization was rotten. He'd come to me because I worked for neither.

"Why is she listed now and not before?" I asked the obvious. Had someone wanted to lure Price here?

"I don't know. All right, so Nader came to see Darlington and now he's dead. How long was he here?"

Price had gone into cop mode again. All robot and business.

"We went by too fast. I couldn't tell."

He looked at me as if trying to decide if he could believe me. *Goes both ways. You don't tell me everything either.* I didn't say it. Why bother? We both knew it. Though in this case, I'd gotten distracted by the guard, so I wasn't lying.

"Let's backtrack and see what you can find out further up the trail."

"Fine."

By the time we got back to the snowmobile, I could barely walk, I was so cold. The temperatures were in the upper teens, but my legs were soaked through and the snow that had fallen down my neck earlier had melted, adding to my misery. No point in complaining. It's not like we had time to curl up in front of a warm fire.

I forced my leg over the seat and plopped down. I pressed up against Price, hoping his warmth would permeate through to me.

He pulled out from under the trees and took a circuitous route to pick up Nader's trace.

"Riley? What do you see?"

I rubbed away the moisture that had crusted my eyes. I found Nader's trace pretty quickly. Now that I'd followed Nader's trace, it was easy to sort from the trace lattice crisscrossing the avenue. Price slowed. I uncurled my fingers and sank them into the spirit dimension like I was trailing them in water. I summoned Nader's ribbon into my hand.

I thought I'd been cold before. Ice crept up into the marrow of my bones, followed by a deep hurt, sort of like an ice-cream headache, except all over my body. I couldn't feel myself. I couldn't tell if my other hand was still holding on to Price's coat; I couldn't feel the press of the seat or the pegs under my feet.

"Can you tell anything?" Price asked over his shoulder.

I dropped the trace. "He was here five days. He got here last Tuesday." My tongue and lips were stiff, and I slurred the words. I wanted to ask what we were going to do next. It was too much effort.

Price gunned the motor, and I did my best to hold on, closing my eyes and imagining sleep.

Chapter 14

"RILEY! WAKE UP!"

Something shook me. "Leave me alone." Well, that's what I wanted to say, but mostly it came out like a sick cat sound.

"Riley!"

The voice was sharp and demanding. Price. Detective-Asshole Clay Price. What did he want from me now? Couldn't he see how tired I was?

"Dammit, Riley. Move!"

A tight band wrapped my waist and lifted me to my feet. My knees buckled, and the band tightened.

"You need to get your blood moving, Riley. Try to walk. We're going to warm you up. Why the fuck didn't you tell me you were so cold?"

Price sounded pissed. I mumbled something. I think I said I was trying.

"What? What did you say? Come on, talk to me, Riley. Wake up, baby. Come on, sweetheart. You don't want to sleep. Not now."

What did he know? I wanted nothing more than to sleep.

Pricks of pain needled up my shins and around my toes. I lurched, trying to get away from them.

"There you go. That's a good girl."

What was I? A dog?

He kept pulling me along, and it slowly occurred to me that the band around my waist was his arm and he had pulled my right arm over his shoulder. He was marching me up and down a small room.

The needling pain soon turned into saw blades chewing into my muscles. I started to shake. My teeth clacked so hard I thought they were going to crack. Somewhere in there I realized I'd lost my pants again. You'd think that pants would be harder to lose. I still had a shirt on, but no underwear or socks. I was wrapped in a blanket, and the beige shag carpet felt like sandpaper on my feet.

"Where are we?" I sounded like I'd eaten razor blades with a bottle of rotgut for a chaser.

"Somewhere safe."

"Right. Like the Tyet doesn't have tracers on us right now."

"I took care of that. I used a null."

"Where did you get that? Oh, right, your desk drawer magic stash. I don't think I can stand up anymore." I was shivering hard enough to give me whiplash.

"Let's get you into bed."

He eased me down onto the sheets and pulled the covers up over me. I thought maybe he'd climb in with me to help warm me up, but instead he disappeared into the bathroom. I heard the sound of water running.

"I'm going to put you into a warm bath," he said.

I want to tell you that I was too freaking cold to even think about the last time Price and I were in the bathroom with hot water, but no, I wasn't that cold. I'd probably have to be dead to not make that connection.

"I can't get in the bath now," I said, pushing the covers back. "I'll be fine. We need to find Josh."

Price ignored me, dragging me into the bathroom. Price helped me pull off my shirt and bra, and then held me while I stepped into the water.

Fire wrapped my foot, and I jerked it out. "How hot is it?"

"Tepid," he said, his mouth twisting down.

Because he wasn't going to let me off the hook, I planted my foot in the tub and then the other, then lowered myself down. The sensation of saw blades was back, as were the needles. They pulsed back and forth. I swallowed a moan. I didn't need an "I told you so" from Price.

I leaned back and let the water rise over me, holding my breath until the feeling that my skin was being peeled away grew more bearable. After about ten minutes of that, I realized the shivering was easing up and I was actually feeling cold. I sat up and turned the spigot to hotter. Price had seated himself on the toilet and was watching me. He was pissed.

"Why didn't you tell me you were wet? Do you get off on flirting with death?"

"We didn't have time for me to be a baby, and besides, it wasn't the wet that made me so cold. At least, I would have been fine if I hadn't touched Nader's trace."

He went still. "Touched?"

I blew out a breath. He knew most everything about me already, what was one more? "Touch it. When I do, I can learn a lot about the person who left the trace. I've never touched dead trace before. It kind of sucked all the heat out of me."

Before he could respond, his phone rang. He lifted it to his ear. "What?"

Pause.

"No, sir. Family emergency." His gaze fell on me and then he looked away. He didn't seem that excited to have a naked woman at his mercy. "A few days. What?" His expression flattened and his teeth bared. "Yes, sir. I did." Another pause. "A case I've been looking into. Thought I might have a new lead. Didn't go anywhere." Pause. "Yes, sir. I will."

He hung up and his hand clenched around his phone. For a second I thought he was going to throw it.

"Who was that?"

"My captain."

"And?" I prodded when he just stared blankly at the towel rack on the opposite wall. "What did he want?"

He flinched like he'd forgotten about me. "He was curious, since I'd taken a few days off for a family emergency, why I was accessing the police database." He thrust himself to his feet and slammed his fist against the wall. "Son of a bitch!"

I sloshed to my feet. "Breaking your hand isn't going to do anybody any good," I said.

He glared at me, then walked out. I grabbed a towel and dried off. I wriggled into my bra and shirt and wrapped a dry towel around my waist before joining him.

Aside from the bed, the wood-paneled room contained two night-stands, a dresser and a mirror, an overstuffed brown and yellow striped chair, and some pictures on the wall of ducks on ponds. A popcorn ceiling and a white louvered double closet on the wall completed the décor. My pants and underwear hung over a wooden chair by a wall heater.

Price paced by the window. I sat down on the bed and pulled the covers over me, watching him. I got that he was pissed that his captain was having him monitored, but I didn't get why. Everybody knew he worked for Touray, just like most of the other guys on the force worked for a Tyet faction. I'd have thought they all expected to be watched.

My stomach rumbled. I like to eat—and with regularity. I'm not one of those twiggy girls who eats a half a grapefruit and a yogurt for breakfast and then is full for the rest of the day. I like food and plenty of it.

"This place got anything to eat?"

He went to the dresser where he'd left his bag and pulled out one of the protein bars. He tossed it to me. "Here."

Beggars can't be choosers. It actually wasn't all that bad. It had chocolate and fruit and nuts, along with whatever healthy crap that accidentally fell into it. Didn't do much for my taste buds, but I felt better. The remnants of my shakiness evaporated with the addition of calories.

I tossed the wrapper on the nightstand. "What time is it?"

"Somewhere around two o'clock. The next storm starts moving in tomorrow."

"What next?"

"We need to get inside those apartments and talk to Shana Darlington."

"How do you propose we do that?" Sounded about as easy as getting into the White House.

"I know a dreamer. She'll get us by the guards. We'll use nulls to kill any security. We get in and out before anyone realizes we were ever there."

A simple plan. It could even work, though it depended on a whole lot of ifs. Neither of us had any real idea what the magical security was like. Getting past could easily be more than we could handle. "Can you trust this dreamer? Is she any good?"

"One of the best I've ever met. Once bought, she stays bought."

"So she's a freelancer?" I asked doubtfully, envy spiraling through me. "If she's so good, how come she doesn't belong to the Tyet?"

"Cass isn't—" He smiled a crocodile smile. "You don't want to mess with a dreamer like her. She can send you to hell in your mind. She's very, very inventive."

And here I thought I was the only unicorn in the city. "I'm surprised they didn't kill her, since they couldn't control her."

He shook his head. "She's too good. And like I said, she can be bought. Not everybody is owned by the Tyet. It doesn't hurt she can protect herself. Plus she has powerful friends."

Could I do the same thing? I tucked the impossible notion away to consider later.

"How will she make a connection to the guards? She'll have to touch them. There's no way she can get close enough. She'll get shot first."

"She'll have you."

I frowned. "What do you mean?"

He gave me an intent look. "You can give her their trace. That's all she needs to get us in safely."

I crossed my arms, shielding myself from what I knew he was asking. "A dreamer can't touch trace."

"No, but she doesn't have to. You just let her into your mind, then after you pick up the trace, she'll do the rest."

Haunters were a lot like dreamers, the way they could mess with your head. The difference was that they had to touch you while they were twisting your mind around, and mostly you were aware of what they were doing the whole time. It made it possible to resist. Not dreamers. They had a lot more finesse. They could go right into your mind and make you think anything they wanted. They didn't need to touch you. All they really had to do was connect to your soul through a piece of you—toenails, blood, shed hair. Letting her touch me would be giving her the keys to my sanity.

"No way. She's not getting into my mind."

"I thought you wanted to rescue Josh."

"I do," I snapped, starting to feel cornered. I pushed up off the bed and went to stand by the wall, as far away from him as I could get.

"Then we need to know what Shana Darlington knows. We can't wait."

We. I wondered if his *we* included Touray and the rest of his Tyet buddies. "We have the baggies. Seven names."

He shook his head. "We don't know if and how any of those are actually involved."

"I don't want a dreamer in my head."

"What sane person would? Hell, I don't want to go into the place at all. I like to keep my skin in one piece. But we don't have a lot of choices. Unless you've got another plan. I'm all ears. Spit it out."

I would have given anything to wipe that look off his face with a brilliant plan that wouldn't put us in any danger and yet would give us all the answers, rescue Josh, and save us from the Tyet. Unfortunately, I had nothing.

"Damn you," I said at last.

He didn't smile like I thought he might. If he had, I would have had to knee him in the balls.

"When do we go?"

"Soon as we can. We don't want to get caught in the dark. But first you need dry clothes and a hot meal."

"I also need a couple bottles of Xanax and a one-way ticket to Timbuktu. I don't see them happening either."

I grabbed my still-damp pants and underwear and went back into the bathroom to relieve myself and put them on. They were cold and clammy, and I had to wrestle the jeans up over my ass. Instantly I felt chilled again. I opened the door, looking over my shoulder at the sink for an elastic band or clip to put up my hair with, and ran right into Price's chest. He grabbed my arms when I started to fall backward, and pulled me close against him. Heat instantly enveloped me and I forgot how uncomfortable my pants were.

I looked up at him. His sapphire eyes were hard as marbles.

"If you start getting into trouble again, I want to hear about it, understand?" he said. "I don't care what it is—cold, tired, hungry, or something worse. You aren't Wonder Woman."

"I never claimed to be." I pulled out of his grip and pushed past him into the room. I hadn't been trying to be Wonder Woman. I was just trying to keep up with him.

He gave an exasperated sigh. "Look, if you really don't want to do this, we'll find another way."

Part of me jumped at the notion, but unfortunately for me, another way would take too much time and that was one thing Josh didn't have. Who knew what they were doing to him.

"I'll do it."

"Good. Then the next thing I need to know is where you live."

I stiffened and faced him, the words coming out before I even thought about it. "That's none of your business."

"Jesus Christ, Riley. I'm not your enemy. I'm just trying to help you. You need dry clothes. There are some at your house. To get them, I need to drive you there. It is, therefore, my business."

"Tell me something. How come you do the cop thing? Why not just be strictly Tyet?"

His eyes narrowed in confusion at my sudden shift in topic. "What does that matter right now?"

"Humor me."

"Fine. I always wanted to be a cop, but things got complicated. Touray and I go way back. He came to me and I couldn't turn him down."

I nodded. "And if—when—he says you have to choose between him and me?" I wasn't looking for declarations of love and undying commitment. In fact, I was expecting exactly the opposite.

"I'm not going to betray you, Riley."

I think he believed it. "Sometimes you don't get to choose," I said. "Just because you don't want to, doesn't mean you won't. It doesn't mean they won't force you. Touray has access to the best dreamers there are, if he's feeling kind. If not—there's torture."

Price held my gaze a moment, then something shifted in his eyes, and he nodded. "If that's what you want. You know you risk dying of pneumonia, going out in those damp clothes."

I snorted. "Not before someone kills me, I'm sure."

FIFTEEN MINUTES later we were back on the snowmobile. Our hideout was a little motel in Downtown not far from the diner and Price's precinct house. There were more signs of life now. The sounds of truck motors and snowblowers rumbled through the air, and lights gleamed from windows. I was surprised when Price pulled up on the sidewalk outside the diner.

He got off the snowmobile. I didn't move. "What are we doing here?"

"You use this place as an office. Stands to reason you've got clothes stashed here. Plus we need to eat." He held up two fingers and folded one down. "Two birds, one stone."

I shook my head, even as my stomach growled. I would die for one of Ben's bacon fire cheeseburgers. "I don't want them involved in this mess. If we're being traced, that will put them in danger."

"Not if we eat fast and get out. As far as the Tyet knows, it's just a place for us to eat. Besides, you didn't leave me with another choice, so get off your ass and move it."

I hid my smile. Fucking know-it-all. As a matter of fact, I did keep clothes here, plus some other supplies that might come in handy.

He pulled me inside, where the scents of burgers, fries, and apple pie embraced me. The bell over the door rang a warning that someone had entered. A few booths were full and four people sat at the counter. Ben looked up as we came in. He waved his spatula at me, a grin of relief and welcome splitting his ruddy cheeks wide before he scowled past me at Price. Patti was pouring coffee with her back to us.

Price guided me down to a booth in the corner by the window and pushed me down onto the seat. He sat down opposite, facing the door. About a second later, Patti came stomping down the aisle. It's hard to stomp in platform heels. Patti has talent.

She tossed a couple of menus down on the table and slid into the booth beside me, pulling me into a tight hug.

"Are you okay? I've been trying to call you. Taylor is a hot mess. Called me hollering about a text you sent telling the family to clear out of town. I thought she was going pop out a hedgehog the way she was going on." She flicked an accusing glance across the table at Price, then looked back at me. "What's going on?"

"Riley needs some food," he said before I could answer. "We're in a hurry, so make it sooner rather than later. And some dry clothes. She won't let me take her home. She's got some here, right?"

"I don't take orders from you," she said with a sniff and raised painted black brows at me. "Riley?"

"I'll tell you everything," I said. "But Price is right." She and I both smirked at that. "We need food, I need clothes, and we have to get going quick." I looked at him. "When and where are we meeting this friend of yours?"

"I called her. She'll meet us in an hour."

Patti glared at him and then me, then stood up. "I'll put your order in." She *clip-clopped* away.

"She didn't ask what we wanted."

"She doesn't really care," I said. "You'll get what you get and you'll be happy. Or else. But go ahead and argue with her. Free entertainment."

A minute later, Patti returned with a pot of coffee and three mugs. She set them down on the table, making it clear she'd be joining us. "Ben will have your food up in a couple minutes. Let's go upstairs and get you some clothes, Riley. You can stay here," she told Price, sloshing coffee into his cup.

Price started to get up. "I'm coming with you."

"I'm not going anywhere. I want to find Josh, remember? Besides, even if I was going to run, you have me tabbed."

He closed his hand around mine again. His eyes glittered. "First of all, you and I both know you can snap that tab any moment. Second, have you ever stopped to think that maybe I'm worried something might happen to you?"

I made a face. "I doubt Patti is going to stab me with one of her shoes."

He scowled. "You've come to the attention of some bad people. Hell, the FBI isn't even a good guy in this. You have to watch your back constantly. You don't know when or where someone will come for you. Even here."

Which meant if they were upstairs, Patti was in danger. I yanked free and hustled after her, taking the stairs three at a time. She was just opening the door to her apartment. I grabbed the door and went inside first. I'm not sure what I intended to do. She was far more prepared to stop an attacker than I was. I suppose I figured if a bomb was going to go off, I'd take the blast. I should have just dragged her back downstairs. I try not to be stupid, but sometimes I'm just overcome with the urge.

"What the hell is going on?" Patti demanded, coming inside and shutting the door.

A booted foot stopped it from closing. Price pushed inside. Patti whirled on him.

"Get out. You are not welcome in my home. I may have to let you waltz into the diner and manhandle my best girl, but I don't have to let you in here. So take it outside or I swear I will drop you like a sack of potatoes."

She was serious. Patti's a tiny little thing, but she's got two surprises for anyone who thinks she's helpless. First, she's a black belt in about four or five different kinds of martial arts. Second, she's a binder. She didn't have a lot of power, but if you were smart, you could make a lot out of a little. Patti's brilliant.

Price shut the door and leaned on it. "I'm not going anywhere without Riley."

"I think you are, even if I have to drag you out unconscious."

It's amazing how fast and light she can move in those shoes. She went at him in a blur. She kicked him in the thighs and ribs, jabbing him in the chest, every move fast as lightning. He raised his arms to protect himself, but didn't return the attack. He grunted as she struck. I had to snicker. No one ever expected Patti to have that kind of impact. I've let her hit me a couple of times. Even with her pulling punches, it hurt like hell. I don't recommend it for anyone.

She stood back. "How do you like me now, asshole?" Her eyes gleamed with feral light.

Price tried to move. He was stuck like a mosquito in amber. Like I said, Patti's not that great a binder, but if she can touch you, she can put you in a world of hurt. She'd hit him in a half-dozen or more spots, each one pinning him in place. They weren't strong ties. They'd wear off in five minutes, but by then she'd have no trouble turning him into pulp. When she said she was going to drag him out unconscious, she wasn't joking.

Time to rescue him.

"Enough, Patti. Believe it or not, he's on my side. At least for now."

That last earned me a cutting look from him.

"For what?" Patti demanded. "Just what the hell is going on?"

"Josh has been kidnapped by the Tyet." As if it were all one entity. Maybe like a thousand-headed hydra. "Detective Price is helping me to get him back."

She goggled. "You have got to be kidding me. Did you fall off a turnip truck today and get brain damaged? You know as well as I do that he's an enforcer for the god-damned Tyet! He's not going to help you; he's leading you to the slaughter."

"Probably," I agreed. "But right now, he's all the help I've got and I can't do it by myself."

She started to say something, and I held up my hand to cut her off. "You're not getting involved in this. If I get myself killed, that's my fault. I'd never get over it if anything happened to you."

"That's the dumbest crock of horseshit I've ever heard in my life," she retorted. "I am already involved. I'm your friend. That pretty much puts me right in the middle of it as far as I'm concerned."

God, I love her.

"I'm not arguing about it," she said. "I'm in and that's that. Now let's get you the clothes you came for."

She ignored Price and went into the spare bedroom where I slept about as often as not.

"Uh, Patti? You want to let him go?" I asked, following her.

"He can wait."

I looked back at him with a little shrug. "Sorry. You pissed her off."

In the bedroom, I pulled clothes out of the battered dresser in the corner and changed, all the while explaining what had happened since I'd left the diner with Price. I kept the details to a minimum to speed things up, but I couldn't leave out everything. Patti's my best friend, after all.

"Wait! Wait! Wait! You did what? You slept with *Price*?"

I flushed and nodded. "Yeah."

Her eyes rounded, and she let out a low whistle. "He's the enemy, but he is definitely very *hot*. Was he good?"

"What do you think?" I buttoned my jeans and pulled on a fresh bra, followed by a tank and a long-sleeved shirt. I sat on the bed and pulled on a double layer of socks.

"I think you are playing with fire."

"Tell me something I don't know."

"I mean, working with him to find Josh—I get it. But screwing him. Are you sure you didn't hit your head? Maybe getting shot short-circuited your brain." She shifted mood fast as a hummingbird. "You got *shot*, Riley. This is way past serious. You're going up against the Tyet with a Tyet enforcer. It's crazy."

"Got any better suggestions?"

I slid off the bed and reached under it for the plastic box I kept there. Inside was a bunch of what appeared to be mostly junk. All of them were nulls of one kind or another. A lot of them were marbles. Glass holds magic well. So do rocks. I like polished rocks best, for the smooth feel of them in my hands, but really any old rock will do. Metal does well, too. Textiles like cloth, yarn, and leather have to be renewed every time they get wet, so I tend to avoid them. Paper and wood don't hold magic at all. I like using objects that people overlook as too silly to be valuable. I have Lego nulls in the tub, along with bottle caps, matchcars, and some plastic jewelry I'd experimented with. Plastic holds magic for a while, but you can't reinforce it to make it stronger the way you can metal, glass, and stone. It's kind of a one-hit wonder in that respect.

I picked out what I wanted: four blood nulls, a dozen trace nulls, and one stupidly powerful magic null. That one would suck the magic out of anyone and everything in a fifty-foot radius. I thought so, anyhow. I hadn't really had a chance to try it out. I'd experimented with weaker versions, but trying out one this strong would have put the Tyet on my tail faster than I could blink.

I put the lid back on the tub and shoved it back under the bed, just as Price thundered into the room.

"Oh, look, King Kong got loose," Patti said. "Be still my beating heart."

Price ignored her. "Are you ready?" he demanded, looking at me.

I shoved nulls into my pockets and tucked the solid silver quarter that was the magic null into the shallow watch pocket inside the right front pocket of my jeans. I didn't usually use money for nulls, but if I was captured, chances were that no one would think to take it away from me.

Downstairs our food was waiting for us. Ben had known exactly what I wanted. Deep fried jalapenos covered a thick hamburger with pepper jack cheese, chipotle sauce, and a side of beer-battered onion rings. Price got the same thing. Patti had a BLT with fries.

I ate like I hadn't eaten in weeks. It felt like it. Before I knew it, my plate was empty and I was stealing fries from Patti.

"What is your plan to get Josh back?" she asked.

Price leaned back and sipped his coffee, his eyes sleepy looking. I wasn't fooled. He was on edge and angry with me, though I wasn't all that certain why.

"I take it Riley's filled you in?"

She nodded. "Mostly."

"I'm hoping Shana Darlington knows who is involved. We'll question her and see if she knows who's holding Josh."

"What if she doesn't know?"

"Then we'll start knocking on doors," I said. I traced an invisible shape on the table. "Why do you think Josh left me those baggies?" I asked Price. "Those people are probably paranoid. They'll have nulls around their houses and workplaces, in their cars—the trace would be nothing more than intermittent bits of confetti. I wouldn't be able to trace any one of them if I wanted to. There must have been another reason."

"Maybe he had another way for you to use them," Price said softly. "It's time to put your cards on the table. What can you do?"

"Maybe it's none of your business," Patti said, slapping her hand on the table. She didn't know what I could do, really. She never asked and I never said.

He didn't look away from me. "I can't help her if I don't know all the facts."

"The fact is that you're a Tyet man and that's all that matters," she declared.

My tongue clung to the roof of my mouth. An idea had occurred to me. I'd toyed with it before, but I'd never actually tried to create that kind of null. But now—

Old ideas spun through my brain. Ideas I'd considered and dismissed as too dangerous to try. But I'd always wondered . . . Could it be done? Could I target a null at someone in particular? Tie a fragment of their trace to it so it would only go after that person and no one else? I could use the stuff in the baggies to locate the trace. The fact that it was confetti wouldn't matter for that. Everybody thought tracer magic was mostly passive, but what if it didn't have to be?

"Riley?" Price prompted, interrupting my train of thought.

I blinked, coming back to the moment. "What?"

"You haven't answered me. What can you do with those baggies?"

His eyes were dark blue velvet, and they promised he wouldn't betray me. I wanted it, that feeling of having someone watching my back, someone to lean on when I was tired and cold and shot. Patti would do it for me, but it wasn't the same. This wasn't her kind of life. But Price—he was scary, and when scary is on your side, it's awfully comforting. Not to mention he was sexy as hell.

I averted my face. Maybe if mine was the only life on the line I could risk it. Still, he needed an answer. It was the truth, even if it wasn't the whole truth, or even the best truth.

"I can maybe kill them," I whispered.

Chapter 15

"YOU CAN WHAT?"

It was nice to know I could surprise him. Patti didn't seem particularly shocked, though I'm pretty sure she wondered if I *would* kill anyone. Big difference between *can* and *will.*

"I might be able to kill them," I repeated.

"How?"

Most of my brain was still spinning with piecing together the how, but I was becoming more and more certain I could do it. If my theory proved correct. A big *if.*

"With a null," I told him.

He swore under his breath, something about strangling and infuriating women. He took control of himself and breathed out slowly. "Nulls don't kill."

"The blood null I made came awfully close. If I could target it to an enemy—"

"Holy hell." He wiped his hands over his face. He dropped them to the table and leveled that piercing cop look at me. "What makes you so special?"

Hurt drilled unexpectedly through my chest. I knew he was referring to my tracer abilities, not to me as the woman he slept with last night, but knowing it didn't make any difference. The truth was I wasn't particularly special: I wasn't beautiful; I wasn't a genius; I wasn't super sexy; I wasn't particularly brave or talented or anything else. I was damned average, except for being a strong tracer, which wasn't a recipe for making a guy fall in love with me.

I rocked back in my seat. What the hell? Why would I want him to fall in love with me? But I did. The realization was like a punch in the gut. Oh hell. I wanted to bang my head on the table. I was falling for him. I'd already fallen for him. How could I let myself be that stupid?

"Nothing makes me special," I said, putting my arms around myself and hunching in my seat. I felt like I was sixteen years old again and my boyfriend was explaining how he needed to start seeing other girls. It was ridiculous. I barely knew Price. How could I have fallen for him? "You've been around me long enough to know that by now."

"Wow, do you go around kicking kittens, too?" Patti said, scooting over to put her arms around me.

I felt the tears starting to come and pressed my head into her shoulder so that Price wouldn't see. Totally humiliating.

"What are you talking—I didn't mean I didn't think she's not—" He sounded vaguely panicked.

Crying women had that sort of effect on men. I smiled into Patti's shoulder, fighting to get myself under control. Maybe I was getting my period. That had to be it. Hormones were at work here. Get me some chocolate and some Midol. I'll be fine.

"Riley—" Price began just as the door jingled at the arrival of new customers.

I felt Price go taut as the temperature in the room dropped.

"I'm going to take care of this," Price said, sliding out of his seat. "Riley go out the back. Use a null. Now." He laid the key to the snowmobile on the table. "If I don't meet you out front, then get out of here."

He didn't look at us. His attention was fixed on whoever had come in. I pushed away from Patti and twisted to look over the back of the seat. Two men stood there. The black one had a scar across his nose and one of his front teeth gleamed gold. The white one was shorter and looked like he was as wide as he was tall. Neither looked friendly.

Price walked down the aisle to meet them. He'd pulled his gun and carried it behind his thigh. Patti grabbed my wrist and scrambled out of the booth, pulling me after her. I snatched up the key as she dragged me toward the back.

"I can't leave him," I said, trying to turn back and digging for my own gun in my coat pocket.

She tightened her grip and pulled harder. "Do you remember how I'm supposed to tell you when you're about to do something stupid? This is one of those times. He's a cop and a Tyet enforcer. He's going to eat those two for lunch. You'll only get in his way."

"But what if they are too much for him to handle?" I'd reluctantly begun to follow after her.

"Well, you could always bleed all over them. Let them beat the crap out of you until they get tired."

"You aren't making me feel any better about letting Price take them on alone."

"If I didn't know better, I'd start thinking you like that guy more than you let on," she said, grabbing a jacket off the hook by the back door. "But then, that would be terminally crazy. Since I know you don't have a death wish and you aren't insane, I must be wrong."

I didn't answer, concentrating on zipping my coat up.

"Riley?" Patti said. "You aren't saying—? Oh, hell, you *do* like him," she said. "I don't suppose I can slap you out of it?"

I shrugged and gave a cracked smile. "Please try. It can't go anywhere, even if he were interested. Which he's not."

"Which only goes to show he's a moron," she said, taking off her heels and stomping into a pair of knee-high snowboots.

"What are you doing?" I asked.

"Coming with you. Now shut up and do the nulls." She pulled her hood up and yanked open the door. "Do the nulls now."

I wasn't going to win the argument, so I didn't try. I grabbed two of the marbles and activated them, handing one to her. These would last a day at least. I'd give one to Price, too. I didn't want us to be tracked from here on out.

Ben had cleared a walkway to the dumpster and plowed out the small parking lot, pushing a mountain of snow into the alley. He made a little extra money plowing in the winter and kept a snowblade on the front of his one-ton pickup. Since the alley was blocked, we had to go the other way around to the end of the block and back to the main street. It wasn't far, but we had to walk out into the road. The snow was at least five feet deep against the building. Someone—Ben or the city—had plowed a strip down the middle of the road to allow for traffic.

Patti and I trotted out into the roadway. A shot rang out. I sprinted around the building with Patti hard on my heels. Price was standing outside the diner, wiping blood off his chin with the back of his hand. Someone had hit him and left behind a cut.

I skidded to a stop in front of him. "What happened? Who were they? I heard a gun go off." The words tumbled from me as I looked him over for a bullet wound. I won't say I was frantic, but my blood pressure was so high that I thought I might stroke out.

He grimaced at the blood on his hand and wiped it on his pants. "They wanted me to know they didn't like that bomb I set the other night for their buddies," he said. "I let them know I didn't care to be followed and shot at. They won't be back." He looked up the street toward the precinct house. "We should go. Someone probably called it in. I don't want to be stuck here explaining myself. Got the key?" He held out his hand.

I dropped the snowmobile key into it without a word. I felt like I'd been hit by a Taser. Fear and relief bounced around inside me, leaving traces of hurt in their wake. That endless moment between hearing the shot and not knowing whether he'd been killed or not had shown me just how much in love with him I was. Completely and hopelessly. The fact that we were little more than strangers and he worked for the Tyet didn't seem to make much difference to my heart.

"Wait," Patti said, pulling me into a hug. "Be careful. Call me if you need me. You don't have to do this alone. I mean it. Whatever you need, I'm here."

"I know. Thanks."

Price was already revving up the snowmobile. I climbed on behind him and he took off almost before I had my butt on the seat. I waved at Patti, then activated a null for him and dropped it into his pocket.

It took almost a half hour to get back to Uptown. Price took us back to the tree in the park. There was more traffic out now as people hustled to do whatever they had to do before the next storm moved in. Already the sky was dark pewter. It wouldn't be long before snow flew again.

I swung off and waited for Price. He seemed lost in thought, staring down at the snowmobile.

"I'd like to check Josh's trace before we go in. I need to get into the compartment under the seat."

On the drive up from Downtown, I'd made a decision to keep our relationship impersonal. No more sex and kissing; no more flirting at all. Just business. I couldn't risk him finding out that I was in love with him. Bad enough that it was true. Having him find out would kill me. He'd be all sympathetic and pitying, or worse, desperate to escape before I made a scene. No, thanks. I'd like to keep my humiliation to myself.

He twisted his head to look at me. It was a measuring look. "You aren't doing this alone," he said.

I must have looked as confused as I felt.

"Patti said you didn't have to do this alone. But you're not."

Oh. That. I sighed. "As far as she's concerned, you're the enemy. She's never going to believe you won't stab me in the back at some point."

"What do you believe?"

I shrugged. "What does it matter? It's not like I have a choice either way."

"It matters to me."

He swung his leg over the seat so he was facing me. He fixed his gaze on me. Its intensity sent tingles all the way down to my toes. No. No more of him and me. I stepped back, crossing my arms so that I wouldn't accidentally grab him and try to kiss him.

"Now who's wasting time?" I asked.

He gritted his teeth. "Just answer the question."

"Fine. Sure. I trust you," I lied. "Can we go now?"

He stared at me another long moment. His eyes went flat and his mouth twisted down as he stood up. "By all means."

I flipped the compartment open and touched the burlap sack, opening to the trace at the same time. I closed my eyes and breathed a quiet sigh of relief. "He's alive." But for how much longer?

I dropped the seat back down and clicked it into place. I was starting to get nervous and wishing I hadn't eaten. The hamburger would taste a lot worse coming up than going down. I shoved my hands into my pockets, clenching them into fists where Price couldn't see. "Where to now?"

"This way." He took off along the same track we'd followed before, but when we got to the corner of the park, instead of crossing the street as we had the first time, he turned in the opposite direction. I trailed a little behind to keep from having to talk to him. My head was a mess. Part of me was tangled up in my feelings for Price, and the other was considering how to target nulls to individuals to kill them. Just thinking about killing made me want to crawl into a hole and pull the dirt in on top of me.

Most people thought trace magic was defensive. Mostly it was for finding people and nulling out harmful magic. My father had always told me I couldn't afford to rely on my defenses. Sooner or later, someone would figure out what I was and come looking for me. If I wasn't ready to fight back, I'd be a goner. I knew he was talking about my mom. His eyes would get this faraway look, and he'd look bitter and sad.

Some of my earliest memories are of me sitting in his lap as he explained that I had to master my magic and learn to use it to protect myself and the people I loved. After he vanished, I tried all kinds of things. I was like a kid playing with a stack of matches. I got burned more than once. One time I ended up in the hospital with a concussion after my stepmom had to club me over the head when I got magic-locked and I couldn't get myself free.

I'd learned to attempt things I shouldn't be able to do—like make blood nulls. Since tracers are considered the weakest of the five big abilities, if I could figure out how to make weapons, I'd have the advantage of surprise.

Lost in thought, I wasn't paying much attention to where we were going. All of a sudden Price twisted around and scooped me up, lifting me over a berm of snow. I squawked and grabbed him. He set me on my feet and started off again, grabbing my hand as he did. He laced his fingers through mine, pulling me close.

I couldn't help but revel in his touch.

He went around a corner and up a covered walkway to an imposing brick house. With the snow frosting the roof and the cedar trees, the place looked like something off a calendar. Price tapped lightly on the door, and it instantly swung open.

"Hurry up. We don't need to be seen." A reedy woman waved us inside.

We obeyed, and I managed to untangle my hand from Price's for about a half a second before he enveloped it again, holding firmly.

"Cass, meet Riley. Riley, Cass," he said.

Cass looked borderline anorexic. Her bones jutted under her skin. Her blond hair was fastened in a ponytail on top of her head, and her skin was pale and washed out. She wore a blue long-sleeved shirt with a W. C. Fields quote that said, "*If at first you don't succeed, try, try again. Then quit. Ain't no use being a damned fool about it.*"

She looked me over, her gaze fastening on my hand in Price's. She lifted her gaze to him, but didn't ask questions. She motioned us to follow her.

"In here."

She led us to a plush living room with white suede furniture, polished wood tables, marble lampstands, and art that probably should have been in a museum. It reeked of money.

She sank down into the middle of one of the couches, folding her legs to sit cross-legged. "Let's get on with his. I want to get home before the storm," she said, cracking her knuckles and rolling her head around on her neck to loosen it.

"You don't live here?" I asked.

She snorted and looked at Price. "Where did you find her? Under a rock?" Then to me, "I wouldn't go dreamwalking with you from my own place. I don't want to be tracked. We'll have to null out of here when we go. You brought nulls, didn't you?" she asked Price.

He nodded and pulled two out of his pocket. These were smaller than the paperweights.

"I get hazard pay, like we agreed, right?"

"Already transferred into your account."

"Then let's get started. Riley, is it? Sit down." She patted the coffee table in front of her.

I hesitated.

"What are you waiting for? Look, we don't have a lot of time. Do you want to do this or not?"

I realized she had almost no eyebrows and her eyelashes were so pale I couldn't see them. With the sharp angles of her face, she looked almost like a Sparkle Dust wraith.

"Riley?"

I wasn't going to look at Price. I forced myself to let go of his hand and went to sit down. My muscles were clenched so tight I could barely move. I slid my hands under my thighs to keep them from shaking.

"Here's how this works," Cass said, leaning toward me, her elbows braced on her knees. "I slide my consciousness into you, then you two go to the building and you pick up trace on someone. I need you to put skin over it. Doesn't matter how weak you are, I'll be able to work with that. I'll make sure they don't see you. I can hold maybe four or five minds at one time, but not for very long, so try to get in and get out fast. All clear?"

Her cloudy blue eyes bored into me. There was a weird intensity to her, like she straddled the line between life and death. I suppose being able to travel through dreams and invade other people's heads on an astral level was kind of like being a ghost.

"Hey. Are you there?" She snapped her fingers in front of my face.

I knocked her hand away. "I'm fine," I snapped. "I get it. Let's get it over with. But you'd damned well better get out of my head when we're done or I'll make you regret it for the rest of your life."

She snorted. "What, would you cry all over me? I'm terrified."

"Cass," Price growled warningly.

"Oh, come *on*. You can't really be into her, can you? She's a scaredy rabbit. Criminy, you could do so much better. Besides, I thought you were into the slick types with platinum hair, designer dresses, and cheekbones that could cut diamonds? This one's a fucking mutt."

"Shut up, Cass. Mind your own business," Price said.

Wow. That's a hell of a defense. Be still my beating heart. I might just faint with all the outpourings of adoration. I hope he didn't break a nail with all that fury and blustering.

"You're quite the bitch," I observed. "Been awhile since you got laid?" I frowned, pasting a concerned look on my face. "Oh, I'm sorry. Maybe you're the world's oldest virgin. Though as hot as you are, what with the whole just-about-to-be-a-corpse look, I can't believe you don't have men hammering down the doors to get in your pants."

Her eyes narrowed. "For your information, I don't go for men."

"Then it's no wonder you're so hard up. Women have higher standards. We won't just go screwing any old piece of white trash that wanders in."

Price whistled and gave a dusty chuckle.

I glared at him. "What's so funny? I mean, you screwed a mutt. You ought to be mortified. What's next? Sheep?"

Cass burst out laughing. Price went brick red, but I turned around so I didn't have to look at him.

"Now that we've established that neither of us are any sort of prize, can we get on with it?" My anger had helped tamp down my fear. I wanted to get on with this possession before I panicked again.

"I'm beginning to see why Price likes you," Cass said, her eyes crinkling as she smiled.

It was infectious. I grinned back. "He doesn't like me," I said. "He's just stuck with me for a while."

She held out her hand, and I took it before I could bolt for the hills.

"He looks like he's enjoying the ride," she said with a waggle of her brows, then got down to business "Don't pull back. I'll let go when the connection is good and strong." Her fingers squeezed hard around mine. She was stronger than she looked.

I knew what to expect, or at least I thought I did. Dreamers approached their victims like something at the edges of your vision. They sneak up while you aren't looking and nose around until they find a crack in your mind and slip in. Everyone has cracks. Most people have big gaping holes. They'll be so focused on something, maybe the sick baby or a difficult boss or the trip they're planning to the Bahamas, that they don't notice that someone is sneaking into their heads. I've heard it's easier to go in when a person is awake than when they're asleep because that tight focus an awake mind has will open up unprotected windows all over the place. When you're asleep, apparently you're more guarded, more aware.

That's what I thought was coming, but Cass came at me like a bullet. I felt her drive through my defenses like they weren't there. I instantly shoved back and fought her grip on my hand. Her fingers clamped tighter, and Price grabbed my shoulders from behind, holding me in place.

I shook my head back and forth and pulled at her fingers with my other hand. The pressure continued, shoving in deeper and deeper, down into the heart of everything that made me *me*. I tried to fling up barriers. Doors slammed in my mind. She brushed past them.

Panic shrilled inside me, and I began to twist and kick.

"Fuck! Hold her! I'm almost there," Cass yelled.

Another surge, and suddenly she was there, at my center.

"Easy now," she said. "You're okay. All I'm going to do is go with you. I'm inside, but I'm separate."

I heard the words in my ears and inside my head, both. I opened my mouth to say something, but nothing came out. I started to shiver as my body reacted to the invasion. The tremors turned to shudders, and it felt like I was having a seizure.

Price sat down on the couch and pulled me onto his lap, holding me tight to his chest as he stroked my back.

"It's okay, Riley. You're okay. You've got to relax. Let it be. I've got you. No one is going to hurt you."

"Give her this."

The hard edge of a glass pressed against my lips. I took a drink and promptly spit it back out. The stuff was disgusting, like licorice-flavored syrup. Price put it to my lips again, but I shoved it away.

"Are you trying to poison me? Get that foul crap away from me."

"It's all I can find," Cass said. "You should drink it." She tsked. "The owners are going to hate the stains you've left on the couch and carpet."

The shudders were starting to subside. "I'm okay," I said, pushing my hair out of my face.

"Sorry about that. I guess I should have used more finesse. Most people don't react that strongly," Cass said, sitting back down on the couch. She took the glass from Price, sipped, and then stuck out her tongue and made a face. "That is truly horrible. People pay money for this stuff? I'd rather drink rubbing alcohol."

"Me, too," I said, my voice raspy. "I'd take some water, though."

"Sure. Be right back."

She set the glass on the end table and left. Price pushed me back, holding my upper arms. He was scowling.

"Are you okay?"

"I'm conscious and I don't seem to be bleeding. What more could a girl ask for?"

I was still sitting in his lap. I wanted to bury my face in his chest and let him hold me. Instead, I swung my legs down to the floor and stood up. I felt Cass in my head. My vision had gone slightly double and my head ached.

She returned and offered me a glass of water. I guzzled it.

"You two had better get on with this. Riley's fighting me and sooner or later she'll either have a stroke or pass out."

"You didn't mention that could happen," Price accused.

"It doesn't usually, but she's got some odd stuff in her mind. It's like a dreamer set up protections. Complicated ones."

"What?" Someone had been in my mind? "I've never had anybody in my head before."

"Sorry to be the bearer of bad news, but you have. A long time ago. Everything they did is integrated." She winced. "It hurts to be in your head. I'm not sure how long I can last. Like I said, you two ought to hurry."

I felt like I'd been hit by a train. I didn't know how to react. *Someone had been fucking around in my mind.* How? Why? When? My brain seemed to go nova. Suddenly I couldn't see or feel my arms or legs. The shakes came back, only it felt more like seizures.

"Riley. Look at me. Riley!"

Price grabbed my shoulders and gave me a little shake. I blinked and stared up at him. He slid his hands up to cup my face, bending so that his nose nearly touched mine. He locked his eyes on mine, not letting me look away.

"Listen to me, baby. I know this is a lot to take in and seriously scary. You'll have to deal with it, but right now, you need to pull it together and focus. Can you do that?"

I gave a jerky nod as the dizziness and tremors receded. What other choice did I have?

"Good." He pressed his lips hard against mine. "It's going to be okay. I promise."

Like he could keep that promise. Besides, I had thought I was okay, but apparently I've been fooling myself. I really have been brain damaged, apparently for a long time.

I felt like someone had just told me I had incurable cancer. Only someone had deliberately given me this cancer. I didn't even know if I was really me or some dreamer construct. Like one of those movies about a robot who doesn't even know she's a robot until she cuts herself open and finds gears and wires.

I'm a robot. What was I programmed for? I remembered that old movie where Cold War sleeper agents got a phone call and suddenly the soccer mom turned into an assassin, totally controlled by someone else. What if I was a walking time bomb like that?

My mouth went dry. I'd suddenly become a danger to my family and everyone else I cared about. I almost laughed. Like I hadn't become that the moment the Tyet became interested in me.

Anger finally woke up in my belly. Steel ran down my spine. My jaw jutted as I straightened. Fuck that. I wasn't going to be someone's tool.

When this was over, if I was still alive, I was going find out what had been done to me. When I did, I was going to rip it out of my head and I was going to find who'd done it and make them pay.

Chapter 16

CASS FOLLOWED us to the door. The ache in my head wasn't getting any better. She eyed me sympathetically. "I could get rid of the double vision for you, but I'd have to go deeper. I'm not entirely sure you could live with it."

"I'll be fine," I said.

She looked at Price. "Don't forget, no more than four or five bad guys at a time. Better to keep it to fewer if you can. Hurry up. Sooner I'm out of Riley's head the better. Oh, and one more thing, no more romantic crap. Remember when you kiss her, you're kissing me, too. I don't need more reasons to go to therapy."

"No promises," he said, grabbing my hand again.

We went back up the block. I held onto him tightly. The dizziness was getting worse by the minute, and if I didn't have him to lean on, I'd probably fall on my face. I scuffed my feet so I didn't have to pay as much attention to what they were doing.

"Tell me how you're doing," Price ordered as we crossed a street. "If this is going to be too much for you, we need to stop now."

That made me laugh. "Define 'too much.'" I shook my head and instantly regretted it. "Anyhow, it doesn't matter. If I don't do this, where would that leave Josh?" I winced. Even I could hear that my voice was fraying as my mind rebelled against Cass's invasion. I was winning Price's case for him. Not that he could stop me. I doubted Cass would give him a refund, and I wasn't turning back, not now that I'd come this far.

He stopped short and swung me around to face him. "Screw Josh. He got himself into this mess without any help, and he's a selfish bastard for dragging you into it. He's not worth your life, Riley. No one is."

I blinked at him, trying to figure out which of his eyes were real and which were the double-vision pair. "Isn't that your job? To put your life on the line for people? I mean the cop one, not the one where you do dirty work for the Tyet."

Saaahmackdown! Cass said in my head. The word vibrated through my skull, sending aching ripples down my spine. *Oops, sorry. But there's more to you than I thought.*

He jerked his head back like I'd hit him. His expression went flat. "My job is to hunt down bad guys. Not to die."

"What do you do when you're the bad guy?" I waved the question away. "Never mind. It's none of my business. You do what you have to do. But I get the picture. You aren't planning on dying for me. Message received."

He swore and looked up as if hoping a patience fairy might show up and dump a load on him. She won't. She never does.

"That's not what I meant. You already got yourself shot for Josh. This isn't your fight. You know Taylor would tell you to back off and leave it alone before you get yourself killed."

"Probably," I conceded.

You got shot? Holy crap! Sorry I called you rabbity. You got guts, girl.

I winced. "Can't you just be quiet?"

Oh, right. My bad. Zipping my lips.

Price's fingers dug into my arms. He looked like he was going to strangle me. I swear his hair was starting to smoke.

"You want me to be quiet?" he demanded roughly, giving me a little shake.

Damn, but that hurt. My head felt like it was about to pop.

"I won't be quiet. Not so you can commit suicide by Tyet. Promise me that you aren't going to take unnecessary risks. If you see signs of trouble, I want you to run. Do you understand? Run."

I put my hands flat on his chest to push myself free. He didn't let go.

"First of all, I was telling Cass to be quiet, though you can feel free to do the same. Second, you don't get to tell me what to do, and third, I'm already up to my armpits in trouble. *You* are trouble. *You* are the Tyet."

A thought occurred to me. I cocked my head curiously and leaned away. "Or is that it? You're worried about what happens to you when they figure out you've been helping me?"

His teeth bared in a snarl. "I know what happens. I'll be gutted and put through a meat grinder and buried in a coffee can. That isn't the issue. It isn't about them," he said, dropping his hands and striding away. He stood with his back to me, his hands on his hips.

"So what is it about?" I was pretty sure that there was something important happening here. I was also thinking I'd like to sit down on a snowbank if this was going to go on much longer. I glanced around, looking for a good spot. I was too distracted to noticed he'd spun back around, but suddenly I found myself hauled flat up against his chest.

"It's about you," he rasped. "It's about us."

"Us?" I echoed. "There's an *us*?"

"God, I hope so," he growled and kissed me.

My mouth opened under his. It wasn't a gentle kiss. It wasn't even friendly. It was primitive and demanding. His teeth ground against my lips. He devoured me, his lips and tongue melding with mine, like he was dying and I was the only thing that could save him. Sparks spiraled through me. My blood fizzed and my bones went liquid. I caught his head in my hands and stood on tiptoe, slanting my head to give him more access. He groaned deep in his belly and tightened his arms around me, his hands sliding over my head, back, and butt like he couldn't get enough of me.

Ew.

Cass. I ignored her.

Far too soon, Price pulled away. I made a sound of protest, my fingers curling into his hair to keep him from going too far. He was panting. So was I. My lips felt swollen and hot. His eyes glittered. He rubbed his knuckles gently over my cheek, then cupped my face. I leaned into his touch. His palm felt cool. He bent and kissed me again, more gently this time. His tongue was warm silk against mine. My head spun. I swear he made me drunk. My heart pounded. When he pulled away again, the world tilted. I felt like I was in a plane that was about to crash. Just at the moment, I was ready to ride it all the way to the ground.

Inside my head, I could feel Cass chortling. It was like running electricity through Jell-O.

Whew! I could use a cigarette. Damn! If I'd known the boy could kiss like that, I might have switched teams and bought a ticket to ride on his merry-go-round.

Despite the pain her words caused, I couldn't help but laugh.

"Cass?"

Price rested his forehead against mine, holding my head between his hands. I leaned against him, unable to stand on my own.

"She's impressed."

"Fuck her."

Yeah, sweetheart. Anytime you want, I'll make you feel better than you ever have in your life.

"She's willing."

His fingers tightened on my head. "I'm taken."

"Oh?" I didn't know what else to say to that. I didn't know if I could believe it. It wasn't possible.

That kiss said I was wrong.

"I don't want anything to happen to you," he murmured.

I snorted softly. "Me either."

Oh how sweet. Pardon me while I fall into a diabetic coma.

"I wish you would. My head is going to crack apart in a minute if you don't stop talking."

Then get yourself straightened out with Clay and get on with it.

Clay. I'd forgotten Price had a first name.

He'd pulled away. He frowned, examining me like I was evidence. All two of him. "What do you mean your head is going to crack apart?"

"Having Cass in my head is not terribly comfortable." I didn't want to talk about her. I wanted to know about this *us* business.

He scraped his teeth over his lower lip. I watched. I must have looked as hungry as he felt because he groaned.

"Don't look at me like that."

"Or what?" I really had no idea. I mean, was he going to toss me down in the snow and yank my clothes off? Or drag me back to his place for a week? Neither sounded bad. Both were better options than walking into a Tyet building looking for a woman who might be in trouble or might be in on Josh's kidnapping.

"I never—" He began and then stopped.

This sounded interesting. My stomach tightened, and bees buzzed in my chest. I lifted a brow. "Never what?"

"I don't—" He broke off again, grimacing and looking down at the ground, all the while holding me like he thought I was going to float away.

"Okay. You don't and you never. I still don't know what you're talking about."

He is very eloquent, don't you think? I've never seen him like this. Weird. Usually he's smooth as glass. He never loses his cool like this. I like it.

I gave an inward roll of my eyes. "Shut up, Cass."

"Definitely zip it, Cass," Price said, lifting his heated gaze to meet mine. "I haven't ever felt this way about anyone." The words came out fast, like if he didn't say it now, he never would.

"Like what?" I wasn't going to jump to any conclusions, even though the bees in my chest had started swirling into a violent swarm. I felt like throwing up. Hope is a painful thing.

"Like I want to kill you and kiss you and not let you out of my sight."

If he didn't look so intense, I might have smiled. I mean, it wasn't exactly a romantic declaration. But clearly it was a tough one for him to make. I'm not much better telling people how I feel. I'm that girl in fifth grade who'd punch a boy if I liked him.

"Okay," I said.

It wasn't the response he was looking for. His hands clenched in my hair.

"That's it?"

"You want to kill me, kiss me, and stalk me. I'm not sure what to say to that."

He gave a harsh bark of laughter.

Oh God! You two suck at this! I totally need some popcorn.

I winced.

"Shut up, Cass," he said, reading my expression correctly. "All right, I guess I wasn't all that clear. I think, no, I *know*, there's something between us. Something powerful. It scares the shit out of me. I've never felt anything like this before. It's crazy. Impossible. It's happening way too fast. I've been telling myself to back off, it isn't real. But all I do is think about you and worry when you're out of sight that you're going to do something ridiculously brave and stupid. I know you're not telling me everything, and I'm terrified whatever it is is going to get you killed. I won't be able to do a damned thing to help you, and it's going to gut me when that happens."

The words tumbled out in a froth of heat and emotion. I could only stare mutely as the words sank in. Was he saying that he loved me? The idea was . . . staggering. I opened my mouth and then shut it, my mind blank.

Uh, this is where you declare your undying love and we move along to the risking your lives part, Cass prodded.

"It's okay," Price said, tension digging grooves around his mouth as my silence got longer. "I'd think I was nuts too. Plus I'm Tyet, and that makes me your enemy, not your friend, as you've pointed out before. If I need to give you some space to process, I will."

He loosened his hands and made to step back. I grabbed his forearms, holding him in place. Words clogged in my throat. I didn't even know what to say. *Yes* was the word that kept trying to work itself out of the tangle, but yes to what? He hadn't asked any questions.

He went still and waited. His gaze was fixed on me. I felt like a deer facing down a mountain lion.

"Don't play with me, Riley," he whispered.

That about tore me in half. This man, this iron-hard warrior, was pleading with me. It seemed like a surreal dream. I was in way over my head, and I didn't care. I'd never experienced any feelings like this before. I'd fallen in love with him, but I'd never imagined he'd fall for me. I'd never imagined telling him how I felt. The words stuck sideways in my throat, but I couldn't say nothing. The fear lining his face demanded that I do something to end it.

I stepped forward until I could feel his breath on my cheeks and smell the spicy tang of his cologne.

"You are important to me," I said.

Oh my God, tell me you didn't just go there! Talk about a sniveling cop-out. You take the cake, sister. I'm back to thinking you're a coward rabbit again.

"Important?" Price's brows winged down, his look withering.

Cass was right. It *was* a cop-out. Don't judge. I don't have a lot of practice baring my soul or giving romantic declarations of love.

I would have looked away like the coward Cass thought me, but I couldn't break the lock of his gaze.

"I'm pretty sure I've fallen in love with you," I said baldly and then went hot with mortification. My face went tomato red, too, which meant my skin was clashing with my hair. I must've been gorgeous.

He clasped my face again, his thumbs rubbing over my lips. I melted. He swallowed, his throat jerking. "Do you mean it?" he asked, his voice full of gravel.

"It is beyond stupid, but yes," I said, my brain short-circuiting.

It's about time. Can we get on with the show already? Your head hurts, remember? I'm beginning to go a little cross-eyed, too. Besides, we get this done and you can go molest each other all you want.

I barely heard Cass. I was too busy watching Price. A slow smile curved his lips. He looked relieved, and then revoltingly smug. He pulled me in for another kiss. It took my breath away. His lips and tongue were slow and worshipful. I wanted to knock him down and pull off his clothes right then and there.

I pressed my hands against his chest and stepped back.

"I don't know how long Cass can stay with me. We have to go."

He took a long breath and let it go slowly. "Right." He took my hand again as if he couldn't stop himself, and started to walk, then looked down at me.

"This doesn't change anything for you, does it? You're not going to pull back on this at all."

I shook my head. "I can't."

He looked ahead and nodded, the shadows making his face look like carved marble. "And the rest? Will you tell me what you're hiding?"

Would I trust him that much?

Did I have a choice?

I did. I could say no. I nodded. "When we get a chance to talk alone."

I couldn't help but wonder if I was about to make the biggest mistake of my life. His hand was warm around mine, and I wasn't sure I cared anymore about the risk I was taking. I was ready to pay the cost for spending time with him, even if I ended up dead.

I guess no matter how a person tries to avoid it, they end up being stupid sometimes.

Chapter 17

"WE NEED TO GET close to the building without sparking suspicion," Price said as we came within sight of the high-rise. A security guard stood in front. As soon as we came into view, he noticed us.

"I think it's too late for that."

"Laugh," Price ordered.

"What?"

"Act like we're on our way somewhere, and we're having fun getting there."

Oh. I let out a weak laugh.

"You can do better than that." He put his arm around me and gave a deep belly laugh.

I shoved against him and backed up a few steps. "This is really insane."

"Effective though." He grabbed my hand and scooped up some snow in the other, threatening me with it.

I squealed and twisted to get away. He let me, and I started running. He chased me—slowly. We passed the high-rise and out of sight of the front guard. He'd given up watching us.

"Keep it up," Price said as I dropped to a walk. "Let me catch you at the alley entrance."

I started running again, and he grabbed me around the waist as I hit the back entry drive. I pretended to fight, making shrieking noises. He pulled me around and kissed me fast before pushing me back a few steps into the alley.

"This is a short cut. I promise," he said, loud enough to be heard by the rear guard.

"Right. Like that last shortcut. I am not falling for that again." I said, playing along. I started toward him as if to pass.

He scooped up another handful of snow, cocking his arm back. "Don't make me have to use this. I swear. It's just across the way. Cutting through the alley will save us a block or two. It's worth it."

I walked backward as he pressed forward. "Bully!" I turned around and looked for the security guard in the shack. She was in the doorway, watching us intently. There'd been a shift change since we'd been through, obviously.

"I can ask her," I called to Price over my shoulder and pointed at the guard. "She'll know for sure."

"You don't trust me?" he asked plaintively.

"You're a man. You wouldn't admit you were lost even it meant freezing to death, which I'm going to be doing soon."

When you get close enough, you can either put bare skin over her trace, or you can touch her, Cass said. *I'll do the rest.*

Price hurried to catch up with me, slinging an arm around my shoulder. "Fine. But when she tells you I'm right, I expect a huge apology. And a massage." He waggled his brows at me.

Right about then, we arrived at the guard booth. She looked relaxed, if a bit annoyed. She was definitely not concerned that we were trouble. "Hi," I said, opening to the trace. The guard's was a shiny mint green. "Sorry to bug you, but we're looking for a shortcut to the Preston place. My aunt and uncle are there, and we're supposed to meet them." I hoped she wasn't so familiar with the owners of houses in the neighborhood that she recognized the Preston's didn't exist.

"Sorry," she said, adjusting her hat down lower. "Never heard of 'em."

"Oh, really," I said smugly, looking at Price. "They don't live right over there?" I pointed vaguely. "How is it possible? The king of shortcuts says they do."

The guard gave a little chuckle and looked at Price. Her gaze stuck there as he gave her a dazzling smile. Yeah, he's that good looking. I chose that moment to let my scarf slide off my neck, and I bent to retrieve it. I reached into the trace dimension and grabbed her trace in my gloved hand. I twisted a loop into it, then pushed up my sleeve and wrapped it around my wrist.

Holy shit, Cass whispered. *How did you do that?*

Do your thing, was my only answer.

A second later the guard's eyes unfocused, and she wandered back inside her booth.

She won't remember you were ever here. Better that way since you're both nulled up.

I relayed the information to Price. He nodded and went into the booth. "What kind of security cameras are there? Does the guard know?"

Nothing. It's guaranteed privacy for all who live here. This is a LOT higher end than we expected. Shit. The first floor has a null field set up—no active magic permitted there whatsoever. There's a small army of guards because of that. I wouldn't be able to handle all of them, but it doesn't matter. You're going to lose me once you cross into the null field. This is never going to work.

I repeated the info, feeling a lot like a radio speaker. My stomach went hollow as I processed the news.

You're sure it's a null field and not a binding ring? I asked. If active magic was forbidden on the first floor, it made sense. Binding rings allowed magic to function inside the ring. You just couldn't take active magic across. A null field kept you from doing any magic inside its boundary.

I'm sure.

"I'll get us through the null field without losing Cass," I said aloud.

Price twisted and looked at me. "How?"

I gave a little shrug. "Magic." He wanted to know what I hadn't told him—well, this was one of those things. "We need to find access to one of the nulls in the field. They'll be linked. If I can lay a hand on one, I should be able to shut the whole field down." And wire me up. I'd practically be a walking lightning bolt.

He continued to look at me a long moment, then turned to scan the parking garage. "All right," he said. "Let's do this."

I followed him to the bank of elevators in the center. Behind them, a staircase led up into the building. The garage was blessedly empty except for us. Not entirely surprising, given the weather. I deepened my connection to the trace.

I could feel the null field above me. I tipped my head back, eyes closed, letting the magic flow over my senses. It was good work. It had probably taken five or six tracers working together to create it. Each would set up nulls that focused inward. They would be set in the foundation or walls, overlapping coverage to create the field. Then a control null would be set in place, and the rest would be connected to it. The last was critical, because with various tracers building the field, the control would keep the various fluctuations and differences between them from tearing the entire field apart.

That made it easier for me to destroy, since the field would have a number of weak spots, just based on the multiple makers, and so would the control. I just needed to find a crack and apply a little magical crowbar action. Nothing to it.

Well, except for the release of magic would give us away unless I siphoned it off, which would fry me like an egg if I couldn't ground it into something. The nulls I carried wouldn't hold that much power. I needed something bigger.

Pass some to me. I can use it to deal with the guards.

Can you hear everything I think?

Pretty much. Don't worry though; I'm no rat.

Just knowing about me makes you a target, I warned Cass.

Seriously? You're worrying about me? I thought you'd be worried I wouldn't keep your secrets.

Seriously? I echoed. *I seem to have fallen in love with a Tyet man; I'm about to walk into a Tyet house to find out where my almost-brother-in-law is being held captive; and then after that, I'll have to go try to rescue him from yet another Tyet stronghold. As threats go, you're way down the list.*

I could feel Cass chortle.

Okay, I get your point. All the same, I won't rat you out.

I won't hold you to it if you're tortured. But if you sell me out for money I will hunt you down.

You're seriously cynical, she said, sounding offended. *Can't I just have your back?*

Why would you?

I don't have a lot of friends. Remember, I don't belong to the Tyet either. You may be one of the few people who understand the knife edge.

I gave an inward shrug, a tacit thank-you. I could tell she knew I didn't believe her. Or rather, I believed she probably meant what she said now, but she had no reason to protect me, and when push came to shove, I might be a handy poker chip to play.

"They'll be guarding the stairs," Price said, having walked around the island of elevators and stairwell. "They'll have sensors on the doors so they know someone is coming up." He started toward the back wall. "But somewhere, there should be an electronics control room."

I followed him, having nothing better to do and no idea how to be helpful until he got me within working distance of the control null. He found a big conduit running along the upper part of the wall and followed it until it dropped down though the floor.

"Dead end," I said.

"Not quite," he said. "Over here."

He went down a little farther, and there was a plate of steel set into the floor. It was marked off by yellow hash marks so no one would park there. Next to it was a loading dock and a set of industrial elevators. A little ways down were double doors labeled Housekeeping and Maintenance in red block letters. A couple of green trash cans on rollers stood outside, along with three empty laundry carts.

"This is the electronic control room," he said, walking around the steel plate.

"How do you get in?" I asked doubtfully. There was no sign of any hinges or a handle.

"Give me a minute." He scouted the walls and finally went up to the corner where the loading ramp met the main dock. A ramp against the wall gave elevator access to the rolling garbages and laundry carts.

Price squatted and put his hand up under the ramp. Something creaked and then the steel plate on the floor popped up with a sound like soft-blowing air. He returned and put his toe under it and levered it higher, lifting it with his hands the rest of the way. The steel plate turned into a small roof held up by four steel posts. Below, a yellow ladderlike stairway was revealed. Lights revealed a small area with a lot of wires and meters.

"Impressive," I said.

"A lot of on-the-job training," he said with a grin. "Wait here." He disappeared down the ladder.

Since waiting involved feeling terribly exposed, I retreated to the shadows against the wall. It seemed to take forever, but Price emerged again in about four minutes. He stepped back onto the concrete and grabbed the welded handles of the steel roof/floor plate and dragged it back down. He stepped on it to seal it back into place.

He looked around. "Riley?"

"Right here," I said emerging out of the shadows.

"It's done. There shouldn't be any stairwell alarms."

"Let's go, then."

I still hadn't figured out what to channel the power into when I broke the null field. I couldn't try to hold it all. I'd cook like a mosquito in a bug zapper.

"What's wrong?" Price asked.

"I need to channel power into something, I can loop some to Cass, but I don't know how much she can handle. I need something glass or metal. Bigger than the marbles I carry or those paperweights."

"Would a rearview mirror work? Or a hubcap?"

I considered. "Maybe. I'd like something heavier, more substantial."

He nodded and chewed his bottom lip. "I've got it," he said and started going around to the various cars to see if they opened. Finally, one did. He popped its trunk and dug around inside before closing it and returning to me. He held out a tire iron. "How's this?"

I took it, hefting it in my hand. The steel was solid. "It could work."

He narrowed his gaze at me. "Could?"

I shrugged. "It all depends on what I find when I get there. Just don't stand too close to me when I get to work. I may go up like a firework."

"How reassuring," he said, his face icy. "What do I do if that happens?"

"I don't know. Go inside and tell them you caught me trying to break in. I doubt I'll be in much shape to care."

He grabbed me by the shoulders. "I hope to hell that's a joke," he growled. His eyes could have cut diamonds.

"Sort of." Not really.

"Let's go. We'll figure out another plan." He started to push me back toward the garage entrance.

It had already been nearly three days since Josh was taken. He was alive, but I didn't know how long he'd last. I wasn't about to waste more time trying to figure out a new plan. I dug my feet in. "I can do this. Really."

His jaw jutted. "So help me, if you hurt yourself, I'll—"

He broke off and swore, his hands clinching like he wanted to punch something. I thought he might hit the hood of a car, but he refrained. He would have set off the alarm.

So what's he going to do to stop you hurting yourself? Kick your ass? Break your legs? Seems counterproductive.

I snorted inwardly. Maybe he'd tie me up and tickle me unmercifully.

That could be interesting. I might stick around for something like that, Cass said.

"You aren't invited," I said out loud.

"To what?" Price's voice was a whip snap. He was taut as a wire.

"My punishment," I said. "Cass seems to think she'd like to be there."

Against his will the corner of his mouth twitched up. "I don't think so."

"Exactly what I thought." I smiled sweetly at him as I pushed past him to the door. Hopefully he wouldn't notice that I'd only said I *could* do it, not that I wouldn't get hurt.

He wedged ahead of me, pulling it open a crack and peering inside. He'd drawn his gun and carried it up at eye level. I clenched the tire iron in my fist.

The stairwell was brightly lit. Price blocked my entrance until he was satisfied there was no danger. He jogged to the base of the stairs, scanning upward along the barrel of his gun. He kept it raised as he climbed with quiet steps. I hung back a ways, figuring he'd need room to maneuver if we ran into trouble.

He stopped on the second-floor landing. Trace crisscrossed the floor in a spangle of colorful ribbons. More than a few were gray and fading. Where there was Tyet, there was death. A fire door blocked the stairs going up. A pair of double doors closed off the lobby floor. On either side, the walls glimmered like the moon on midnight water. A thick weaving of the same intricate spellwork matted the doors.

My chest tightened as I examined the loops and whorls. On the one hand, this was a pretty simple operation: drain the magic off the nulls into the tire iron. On the other hand, simple didn't mean easy. Seeing what I was up against, I knew the tire iron wasn't going to hold all the magic in the nulls, especially since they were probably renewed monthly, if not weekly. Cass wouldn't be able to hold enough to make a difference. If she tried to take the magic I was going to need to dump, she'd burn out like a lightbulb.

Let's not do that, she said dryly. *Still, you could pick up the trace in the stairwell, and I could see about fixing the guards with magic you channel to me. The boost would be helpful, and I'd be ready to use it up as you fed it to me if I had targets in my sights.*

I was willing to try it. I bent and gathered all the ribbons. There were a lot of them, but no more substantial than a laser beam. I could hold them easily between my thumb and forefinger. I pulled up my sleeve and twisted them around my wrist.

Shit. How do you do that?

I just do. Brace yourself. I'm going to get started.

My nerves were itchy. I was sure that we'd be discovered at any moment. I shook off my rising unease and went to the doors. The web of magic crossing them completed the circuit of nulls.

I pressed my hands flat against the doors without reaching into the trace dimension to touch the web. Then I moved my hands in small circles up and down. If the control was inside the room and not on the periphery, this could get harder. I was counting on the fact that setting it within the interior of the circle rather than in line with the other nulls was so much harder that the original tracers couldn't or wouldn't have bothered.

A feeling like pinpricks ran through my palms. I followed the feeling down to the floor. There it was. Right under the doors and below the concrete. I wanted to be able to actually touch the stone, but I'd have to make do. It would take longer is all, though that in itself would help keep me from going up in flames. The main thing was time. We didn't have much. Cass couldn't stay with me forever. Hell, I couldn't tolerate her presence a whole lot longer. My head felt like someone had driven a railroad spike through my ear, and my double vision was getting blurrier. The power here was enough to keep me busy for hours. I was going to have to speed things up, which meant taking some risks.

I pulled all my nulls out of my pockets and set them on the floor. The marbles wanted to roll. I put them on my gloves so that they didn't touch. Beside them I set the tire iron. I sank down cross-legged in front of them and sideways to the door so I could touch the space right above the null control. I'd channel what I could into the nulls after I filled up the tire iron. I suddenly remembered my baton and my gun. I pulled both out. I shucked the magazine and the bullet out of the chamber. Raw magic and gunpowder didn't mix well.

I flexed my fingers and pushed my hair out of my face. I looked at Price, who'd taken up a watchful stance between the two doorways where he had a clear shot at anyone who might chance to come through. He face was taut. He radiated threat. Like a wolf standing guard over his territory. Inwardly, I cringed. He wasn't going to be happy with the next bit.

"It could get hot in here," I told him. "You'll want to get out if it gets too bad. You don't want to crisp up into a French fry."

He scowled. "Explain."

"When I drain the magic out of the nulls, I'm going to have to let it come fast, before we get caught. Once I start draining, I'll have to bind the magic into these." I gestured at the paltry collection in front of me. "I have to form and bind it as I go, otherwise it will spill over and cook us." I didn't point out that if I was too slow, the flow from the nulls would do the same. "You should be prepared to get out of here."

His gaze held mine, and I shivered at the look in his eyes. It wasn't just the anger. It was the stark fear beneath. Not for him—for me.

Suddenly his eyes shuttered, turning remote.

"You said you could do this," he said harshly. "Then do it. Don't fuck it up."

"I know, because then you'd have to punish me. I wouldn't want that, now would I?"

I set the fingers of my right hand over the null control and touched the fingers of my left to the tire iron. I closed my eyes and pushed out with my senses. The null control was like a ball of yarn, all wrapped in colored threads of magic. I touched it gently, learning its structure.

I began to find the strands connecting it to the other nulls. They twisted together with filaments from the control and wrapped and wove around each other, creating a tight knot. If there was a specific pattern to it, I couldn't see it. It looked more like the various nulls had been added at random and then the tracer creating the control had just used a lot of magic to duct tape it all together. It would be easy enough to dismantle, but between the magic in the nulls and that in the control stone, there was a lot more to channel off than I'd expected.

"I'm going to need more magic sinks. Give me any coins you have," I said to Price, hardly aware of him.

There was a moment of silence, then jingling and metallic clicking as he set some on the ground before me.

"Any glass you have, too. Or stone."

There was silence and then some noises and a heavier click as he set his gun down along with something else.

"Keep the gun," I said. "It won't be any use after I get done with it and we don't want to be defenseless."

I didn't hear what he might have said. I started unraveling the magic.

It flowed up my arm like hot syrup and spread through my chest and down my other arm into the tire iron. I shaped it. The easiest thing to make was a basic trace null. I shaped my intent and added more and more magic, picking apart the strands as slowly as I could, hoping to keep the flow down.

The tire iron couldn't hold any more magic. I moved to my gun. Magic likes solid objects. I couldn't separate the parts in my head, so I just treated it as a whole. It's why it wouldn't work as a gun again.

It was full all too soon, and I still had a lot of the null wall and the control stone left to siphon off. I poured magic into the rest of my nulls and then my baton and my knife. I had been leaching a little off to Cass and now fed her more.

Whoa! Slow down. Shit. But oh my heaven. This is the best high I've ever had. Keep it coming, sister. Just slower.

I could feel her doing things through the trace, but I ignored it. Next I worked on Price's coins. Three quarters, two nickels, and a penny. He also had a watch, a pocket knife, and a pair of clippers.

I filled them until they fairly crackled. By this time most of the field was depleted, but I still had the control and no receptacles left.

My brain scrambled for a solution. Magic sluiced into me, but now it had nowhere to go. I felt the pressure building, and sweat beaded on my forehead and ran down my spine. I put my hands on the concrete floor, but I didn't have the skill or focus to shape magic into that size of an object—pretty much the entire building. I needed something smaller.

Price couldn't run and fetch me something fast enough to help.

"You should go," I said. I think I said it. The rushing in my ears made it hard to know. My skin began to blister, and blue and yellow arcs of magic flickered across my skin. *Think*, I told myself. *There's a way out of this. What is it?*

Then I got an idea. It could work, if I didn't snap my hold on the control null's magic.

I twisted up onto my knees, then straightened my legs, all the while hunching over to maintain my touch on the floor. A sledgehammer pounded between my eyes, and all I could see was a kaleidoscope of colors. I held my breath. Next came the potentially deadly part. I inched back toward the stairs. Heat flared around me as my link with the control null wavered and thinned. It was like trying to shape lightning.

I pushed out, reaching deeper into the trace dimension, grasping the control flow with invisible hands.

It hurt.

Worse than hurt. It felt like hundreds of drills were screwing through my bones and teeth. I was crying. My skin blistered from the increasing heat cascading through me.

Keep it together, Riley. Almost there. You can do it. Don't stop. You're strong enough for this. Just hold on.

Cass kept up a running patter in my head. I held onto it like a lifeline. I was aware that Price was beside me saying something. I couldn't hear him.

Another step.

One more.

I reached out with my left hand, searching for the railing. It would hold all the rest of the magic. Price's cool hand closed firmly on mine. I gasped. His touch hurt like hell. He guided me.

Another step.

My fingers hooked over the round rail. I dropped to my knees, pouring magic into the steel pipe. I could barely focus. My head was going to explode like a marshmallow in a microwave. I forced myself to concentrate on what I needed to shape the new null. The framework formed and collapsed. I clenched my body, and willed the null to hold. *Hold, dammit!*

I don't know how much longer it was before the last bits of magic trickled into the rail. My entire world became that flow and the raking pain of the magic. At last it ceased, and I tied it off. My hand went boneless and I fell over onto my side. Instantly Price pulled me up against his chest, stroking my head.

I was a wet rag. So were my clothes. I probably smelled like the inside of a boy's locker room. I was still panting and wishing I could go roll in the snow to cool off.

"Riley? Baby, are you okay?"

"Sure," I croaked. After all, nobody died, least of all me. That made me pretty okay, all things considered.

Cass? Did you get the guards handled?

You're good to go.

I repeated the message through sandpaper lips. My eyes were gritty. I felt like a dried-out husk. "We don't have a lot of time before someone figures out the nulls are gone."

Price pulled me to my feet. I gripped his jacket with rubber fingers. My whole body was rubber. My head was six times its usual size, and pinballs careened around inside. I swayed. He steadied me.

"Can you walk?"

"Sure."

I let go of him and took a step. The walls swam around me. Ugly gray-green vomit-colored walls. There must have been a sale on paint the day they picked it out. I reached out to balance myself against the wall. Price caught me around the waist before I could.

"How can I help you?" he said.

"I could use some water. Maybe something to eat."

"Let's get up to Shana Darlington's apartment. She's bound to have anything you want."

"I'm soaked. I hope she's got clothes I can wear. You know, ever since I met you, I can't seem to keep my own clothes on. Why is that?"

Yes, why is that? Cass smirked from inside my head.

Price ignored me. "Let me pick everything up." He pushed me against the wall and gathered everything up. He pocketed some, putting the rest in my pockets. He gave me my gun.

"It's useless," I said. "Paperweight now."

He exchanged it for the tire iron. I held it loosely, which was about as hard a grip as I could manage.

"Put your hand on my waist," he ordered.

I grabbed his waistband, glad of something to hold on to. He opened one of the doors, and we stepped into a lobby area. It was ridiculously quiet inside, like a library. A front desk faced the elevator doors. It was staffed by a middle-aged woman with sun-streaked hair. A security guard stood out in front of the desk. Two others flanked the stairwell and another stood around the other side near the front entrance.

Thanks to Cass, none of them looked at us.

"Which floor?" Price asked.

Let me check. Fifth, Cass said after a slight moment. *Apartment 550.*

"Fifth," I parroted. "Apartment 550."

"Elevator," Price said, pulling me over and punching a button. It chimed open in a matter of seconds. We went inside. For once I didn't feel like a cat trying to escape a bathtub. I was too tired to be claustrophobic. The doors closed, and we lifted up. That didn't help my spinning head. I turned and grabbed the flat railing and leaned my head against the wall. It was deliciously cool.

"Riley?"

"I'm fine."

"Yeah, you look it."

He sounded pissed. Maybe he'd spank me later. I smiled to myself. I might like that.

The elevator stopped, and the doors dinged as they slid open. Price leaned out, glancing up and down the hallway. It was empty. He grabbed my hand and pulled me after him. We went left. The doors were far between. There could only have been three or four apartments on any level.

"Can you pick up her trace in the hallway?" Price asked as we came up on Apartment 550. The door was a polished wood with an inset of beveled glass that showed nothing within.

I opened myself to the trace. After draining the null field, it hurt. A lot. Like being in a clothes dryer with a billion needles. I gritted my teeth and shook my head. "Nothing. At all. For anybody. Talk about hypercautious."

"Tell me you don't null your way through your front door," Price mocked.

"I have a good reason."

"Everybody has a good reason. All right. I'm going to get us inside. Soon as you can, grab her trace. Cass? I want her to spill her guts. I'll guide our talk with questions, but make her willing to give everything up."

Dizziness caught me, and I pulled out of the trace.

Girlfriend, you need to sit down.

I know.

I'll work my magic fast. She'll vomit everything.

I repeated Cass's message to Price. I swayed, and the floor rose and fell like the deck of a ship.

Price took me by the shoulders.

"Can you do this?"

"Yes." Maybe. Probably.

How reassuring, Cass said.

I cracked a lopsided grin. I must have looked like I was losing it, because Price nudged me up against the wall.

"Wait here," he said.

"How are you going to get in?"

"Don't worry. She'll let me in," he said.

Oh, right. Cop. Badge. The ultimate lockpick.

He hesitated, his hands clenching on my shoulders. He looked uncharacteristically nervous.

"What's wrong?"

"I know her—Shana Darlington."

I blinked. "What?"

"She was a job. Touray sent me in to get close to her." He chewed his lip. "I was her fiancé."

Questions pinballed off the swelter of emotions erupting in my brain. "Fiancé? You? Why?" I don't know if I was asking why he'd been her fiancé or why Touray sent him to get close to her. I don't even know which I wanted the answer to more. The big ones I didn't dare ask—had he cared about her? Did he still?

He glanced at the door and back at me. "The stuff in Josh's safe. They're—" He broke off and grimaced. "I'll have to explain later. Just . . . trust me. Please."

He didn't wait for my answer. Not that I had one. I was reeling from the double-punch news that he knew Shana Darlington—he was her ex-fiancé for fuck's sake—and that he knew about the magical artifacts we'd retrieved from Josh's office.

I was still trying to process the news when Price knuckled the door. He waited five seconds, then knocked again. The latch clicked, and the door swung open, quietly, with no fuss or fanfare.

"It's about time you found me, Clay. I'd almost given up on you. I've missed you more than I can ever say. I've positively *ached* to be with you."

I turned my head in time to see a beautiful woman with waist-length mahogany hair slide her arms around Price's neck and kiss him, and not just a quick smack on the cheek or lips. She was checking his tonsils. I'd like to say it was against his will, but as far as I could tell, he was giving as good as he was getting.

Chapter 18

I'D LIKE TO SAY that I clocked them both with my baton. Truth was, I was too wasted from destroying the null wall to do more than blink ferociously at them. As they kept on sucking face, I really wished I hadn't nulled my gun. I could have at least let go a couple of shots into the ceiling to break them up.

Finally Price lifted his head. "We have to talk, Shana," he said. That's when he finally looked at me.

His face was expressionless, but his eyes were turbulent with emotion. I tried not to look as jealous as I felt. He'd said she was a job. I was doing my best to believe it, despite the kiss.

He really looked like he enjoyed it.

"Who's your friend, Clay?" Shana curled her arm through Price's and leaned into him, her breasts plumping up against his bicep.

I wanted to throw up. Preferably on her.

She was beautiful. Her skin was olive, complementing high cheekbones, a straight nose, and perfect lips. She wore a chunky gold necklace and a big diamond ring on her left ring finger. Had Price given it to her? It matched the little one in her nose. She smelled of an exotic, rich perfume.

"This is Riley," Price said, reaching out to take my elbow and pull me into the apartment.

He disentangled himself from Shana and guided me to a chair. He pushed me down onto the cushy seat, giving me a questioning look. I opened to the trace. Her teal ribbon looped everywhere. I plucked it up into my hand and squeezed. Not that she'd notice. She was excited and triumphant. Like she'd won a prize.

Cass?

Got her.

I nodded the okay to Price.

"What's going on, Shana?" Price demanded, turning to face the other woman. "Where have you been? Why are you hiding out? Your parents are going out of their minds."

She fluttered her lashes at him—seriously, she did—and sank gracefully down onto the black leather couch. A zebra skin covered the back of it. Poor beast.

"Oh, Clay, I had no choice. You have to know that by now. I wanted to tell you. I *told* them you'd want to join us. They didn't believe me. I'm so glad they changed their minds and sent you to me. I've missed you so much!" She held out her hands to him. Her long fingernails were painted shell pink. More diamonds twinkled from them. "Lover, you must know I didn't mean it when I broke things off. You know how I feel about you."

Price ignored her. "Who did you join?"

Her face blanked and her mouth trembled.

Someone's tampered with her. They booby-trapped her head. She'll go nuts if I'm not careful. Have Price play along with her fairy tale. It'll help me get her to open up without breaking her.

Lovely. I stood up, figuring I could kill two birds with one stone. I'd interrupt their moment before Shana's head exploded, and I'd find the kitchen. I thought I might literally be dying of thirst. "I hope you don't mind," I told Shana, hoping she did mind, "I need something to drink. Got anything to eat?" I gave Price a pointed look and went in search of the kitchen.

I shuffled through the dining room with its gaudy chandelier and spindly French furniture and into the kitchen. The refrigerator took up a wall. Half of it was a big freezer, the other half a refrigerator. It was ridiculous. If Shana knew how to boil water, I'd be stunned.

I started opening cupboards, searching for a cup. I found what I was looking for in a cabinet left of the fridge.

"Riley?"

There was a wealth of concern in the way Price said my name. He stood in the wide entry as if uncertain whether he should come closer or not. After all, the knives were within my reach on the counter. I took my glass to the sink. I dropped the tire iron on the granite. The stone didn't crack. Too bad. I filled my glass, leaving the water running. I drank four glasses in quick succession before I could even think of slowing down.

"Where's your fiancée?" I asked finally, feeling the liquid seeping into my parched tissues.

"Riley," he said roughly. "I told you—"

I interrupted before he could say anything that might set Shana off. She was hovering just behind him. "You should sort this out with her. Remember what Cass said about letting her know that you care and that you haven't given up on her."

I flicked a look at him, then to her. She had a faint faraway look. Cass's handiwork was my bet. "I'll be fine. You got any peanut butter?" I asked her and didn't wait for her reply before I started foraging in the cupboards.

"Who's Cass?" Shana asked.

"My sister," I said blithely. "Her fiancé kicked her to the curb, too. She and Price here have been sharing the misery."

"Sharing?" Shana glared at him. "You're seeing someone else?"

"What if I am?" he drawled, but he seemed to have gotten the message. "You're the one who broke it off with me. Why shouldn't I see another woman?" He took her back to the living room, frowning over his shoulder at me. I ignored him and continued to search for food.

I decided that Shana didn't really eat. She did drink coffee, and like me, loaded with cream, as both were readily available. She had some ice cream in the freezer, and a variety of delivery boxes in the refrigerator. Thai, Italian, Chinese, and more. I checked a Thai container and made a face. It was covered with green fuzz and smelled like a sewer. I put it back.

I resorted to eating the ice cream. I hauled myself and the carton of chocolate espresso ice cream back into the living room, hoping that Price had discovered where Josh was.

He hasn't. Cass sounded almost as exhausted as I was. *I am tired*, she admitted in response to my thought. *I'm getting close to breaking through the booby trap on Shana's mind. Hold on just few more minutes.*

I didn't bother telling her I didn't have anything else to do. I sat back in the easy chair. Price was back on the couch with Shana in his lap. He looked at me when I came in, then back at her, as if she was the most important person in his world.

I'll admit that I'd have preferred torturing the information out of the woman with boiling oil and sharp sticks rather than watching her rubbing herself all over Price.

I forced myself to ignore the way she stroked her hand over his chest, and the way his arm curved around her waist. I tried to focus on the conversation. All the same, I couldn't bring myself to close my eyes. I needed to see them.

"So you said you got recruited a little over eighteen months ago," he said. "Before we met. The pay was spectacular, and what did they want you to do?"

"I was told that the FBI was investigating all the banks and investment firms in Diamond City. I was supposed to review the books for my bank and make sure everything in our system was spotless. There had to be one bank that could survive the audit. All the deposits and withdrawals had to be accurate and above board with clean transactions based on solid paper trails from stocks, bonds, real estate, and other investments. I had to create unbreakable trails for shell corporations so they could funnel all their funds out of the other banks, out of the country, and then back as clean money into the new shell companies. All done quietly and clean as a whistle.

"That money had to look like it had been sitting there awhile. That way, when the feds moved in and the banks got probed, their money would still be liquid. I had to create a few nonthreatening problems that wouldn't shut down the bank. My job was to make the tampering easy to overlook. No bank is clean. I couldn't make it spotless, but nothing too dirty. If I did as they asked, I would receive a stipend of one percent of all funds passed through me, plus a bunch of perks, like this apartment. Discretion was fundamental. I couldn't tell you anything, because, well, we weren't playing for the same team."

"If the banks were probed and taken over by the feds because the money laundering was systemic, the Diamond City economy would drop into the sewer," Price mused aloud. "Real estate, bonds, businesses—everyone would be on the hook. It would ripple out into the international stock markets."

"Creating opportunity in the market, if you know the collapse is coming. I assume the consortium I'm working for has taken a lot of short positions," Shana confirmed. "If they filtered the orders through a broad enough spectrum of investment firms and shell companies, the SEC wouldn't notice what they were doing. It also puts them in a position to take over the SD trade."

I had no idea what they were talking about. I didn't do investing. I barely had a savings account, and since it wasn't with Shana's bank, apparently I wouldn't have it long if I didn't do a fast withdrawal. I could imagine the chaos though. If the FBI froze all the bank assets, tons of businesses wouldn't survive. They couldn't pay their bills. There'd be mass layoffs, and nobody would be buying anything or paying debts. I wondered how it would affect the mines. If they had to close up, that would be a disaster of epic proportions. The diamond dole would dry up and so would all the thousands upon thousands of jobs that grew out of mining. What it would do to the national economy, I couldn't begin to guess.

As for the drug trade . . . whoever had the money could basically buy up control of all the operations, or at least buy an army to steal the operations.

"So why did you disappear without a word?"

Shana's words were beginning to come faster. She'd slid back over onto the couch and sat stiffly, like her body didn't really belong to her. She stared at Price as if she'd do anything for him.

She would, Cass said. *She really has a thing for him. So I pulled the fatally desperate need to be loyal to her bosses over onto him. I've got to cement it a little more, but in a minute she'll beg to tell him all her secrets. It still might trigger a breakdown, but it's the best I can do at this point.*

Cass seemed utterly delighted by her accomplishment. I was pleased to be making progress, especially if we could get some news on Josh, but at the same time, my stomach revolted at the way she could manipulate Shana's mind.

"I realized that someone besides me and the contractors I'd hired was nosing around. He was really good, but he couldn't hide his access from the fine-toothed comb I was using on the system. He was picking up on what I was doing."

"That doesn't explain why you broke it off with me and disappeared. Why did you?"

"My bosses didn't like me getting so close to you. I told them you loved me and that you'd come around. But they didn't want you to stop me, so . . ." Her hands locked together, and she pressed them to her chest. "I didn't want to do it. You have to believe me, Clay." She turned and pressed closed to him. "I had to do it. You were starting to ask questions. If you had found out what was going on, they'd have killed you. I just couldn't let them. I had to break it off to protect you."

"Who, Shana? Who are you working for?"

That's the moment that the lightbulb went on over my head and I realized questioning Shana wasn't just about getting Josh back. It probably wasn't even mostly about getting Josh back. Price was working, I thought, feeling utterly stupid for not recognizing it earlier. His Tyet boss, Gregg Touray, told him to get close to her. Touray must've picked up on what she was doing and sent Price to investigate. Just because she'd vanished, didn't mean the job was over. In fact, he'd been out to find her before Josh even disappeared.

I was too tired to be irritated, though I probably had a right to be. On the other hand, it's not like I didn't know he worked for the Tyet. Sure, he hadn't told me Shana had been a job until ten minutes ago, but it's not like I'd told him my life story either.

All I knew was that before he kissed me again, he was going to have to rinse his mouth out with bleach.

"Cass?"

I jerked back to the moment. Price was holding Shana by the shoulders. She was twitching, and her head lolled and flopped to the side.

There's nothing I can do. If I had more time . . . She's done for.

I repeated Cass's message to Price. Shana spasmed and slumped, her body going slack. Price lowered her down to the couch.

"Is she dead?" I asked.

Her brain is, Cass said, sounding thready and thin. *She's toast. You two need to get out of there. I'm not going to be able to help much longer.*

"She's breathing," Price said. "What the hell happened to her?"

"Cass says they messed with her head. Made her uber loyal. It was impossible for her to say who she was working for. Cass tried to divert the loyalty onto you so she could talk, but it didn't work."

Does that about cover it? I asked Cass.

Pretty much. Except the part where you need to get the fuck out of there before I can't help you anymore.

"She says we need to hurry."

Amazingly, I sounded perfectly normal, especially given that Cass was in my head and Shana's meltdown terrified me. Somebody had been in my head. What had they done to me? Was I a ticking time bomb?

Suddenly, I needed to get out of the building and get Cass out of my head. I tossed aside the ice-cream carton and stood. "I'm done. I want to go."

I started for the door.

"You said you needed a change of shirt," Price said.

"I'll live without it."

He grabbed my elbow, pulling me back around. I could hear Shana's uneasy breathing. One of her feet hung off the edge of the couch. Her platform stiletto had fallen off. My stomach twisted, and I stared instead at Price's throat.

"Riley? Talk to me." He sounded angry.

"I want to go," I said, barely able to unclench my teeth. "This was a total bust. I'm not sure she ever knew anything about Josh. Not that you asked. Now I'm back to square one."

I wasn't actually angry at him. Or maybe I was a little bit. He hadn't asked about Josh, after all. But more than anything, I needed to get away from this place. I felt like the walls were collapsing in on me.

Easy, Cass said. *Don't freak out.*

Her voice only reminded me of Shana. I twisted out of Price's grip and strode to the door.

"Riley, wait."

"You wait," I said unreasonably. "I'm leaving."

"What is the matter with you?"

"I don't know. Maybe the fact that your fiancée was just turned into a vegetable. Maybe the fact that whoever did that may be doing the same to Josh right now. Maybe it's the fact that you work for people who not only could do the same thing, but probably would. Maybe it's the fact that you know what those damned things are Josh found and you didn't tell me."

Fury, frustration, and a certain level of hurt overwhelmed me. "Maybe it's the fact that my mother was murdered and cops like you didn't do a damned thing to find the killers. Tyet killers, I might add. Maybe it's the fact that assholes like the Tyet kidnap kids and their mothers and no one but me ever rescues them!"

The words poured out of me, my voice rising. On some level I knew I was just mentally and emotionally exhausted and Price was a convenient target for my confusion and frustration. Having Cass in my brain had ignited a visceral fear that I was rapidly losing control of. In a word, I was a mess. A nuclear mess and rapidly melting down.

"You need a different shirt at least," Price said, ignoring my hysterics, though his eyes glittered and his face was livid. "I don't want you to end up with hypothermia. Stay here."

"Better see if she's got any aspirin, too. My head's got a mariachi band inside it."

He nodded and disappeared.

Riley? Cass ventured.

Not now, I said. *Please. Just—not now.*

She subsided.

A minute later Price returned and handed me a purple sweater. I pulled off my jacket and fought with my bulletproof vest. He came to my rescue, loosening it and pulling it off my head.

I peeled off my sweat-soaked shirt and pulled the sweater over my head. It fit snugly and the turtleneck choked me, but it was better than what I had been wearing. My bra was still damp, but there wasn't much I could do about that.

I slid the vest back on and tightened the straps without Price's help. Good thing I didn't need it, as he'd vanished. I knotted the wet shirt around my hips and slid my jacket on.

I found him in a little office area beyond the dining room. It contained a writing desk and a couple of uncomfortable-looking wingback chairs. Several of the desk drawers were open, and Price was rifling through stacks of papers.

"Find anything?"

"Not really."

"Then let's go," I said.

I didn't wait for him to turn around or answer.

"There's aspirin by the sink in the kitchen."

I stopped and downed several tablets and retrieved the tire iron. Price watched me, then followed me to the door. I reached for the handle and practically lunged into the hallway. I gasped. I hadn't realized I'd been holding my breath. I hurried down to the elevator.

I'd just punched the DOWN button when something icy cold hit my neck.

"What the hell?" I jerked around, raising the tire iron without even thinking about it. I hadn't paid much attention to the fact that taking the null wall down had destroyed the tab, but apparently Price had and decided to replace it. "Again?"

Before I could swing the iron, Price grabbed the hand holding it. I shoved against his chest with my other hand. I'd forgotten he was wearing the bulletproof vest. It was like hitting a house.

"Listen to me, Riley," he said, and the elevator dinged. He gave an aggravated sigh and let go of me, pushing me inside. He punched the button for the garage, then stood blocking the door, arms crossed, feet set wide.

"Why should I listen to you exactly?" I rubbed the spot where he'd tabbed me. It still felt cold. "Come to think of it, I've finished my job for you. You wanted to find Nader, and you got the bonus of finding your fiancée or your mark or whatever the hell she was. That makes us even. Now take the fucking tab off and let me go."

"Screw that."

I didn't even see him move. One minute he was four feet away and the next he'd picked me up and mashed me up against the wall. He overwhelmed me with his scent and touch and taste. I practically went blind as I opened my mouth to his kiss. It was desperate, like he wanted to claim me and win me over at the same time.

His arms wrapped my back like steel bands. My legs dangled a couple inches off the floor, and I clamped them around his hips. He made a delicious sound, raw and desperate. Heat jetted through me. In the back of my head where I wasn't totally giving in to the moment, I wondered if it was real. It's crazy how much I wanted it to be. I was so in over my head.

The bell chimed our arrival in the basement garage. Price lifted his head. He was panting, and his arms tightened on me. My lips felt swollen, and I had beard burn on my chin and cheeks. I licked my lips, and he sucked in a breath.

"We should go," I rasped, letting my legs drop back down.

He didn't let go at once. He rested his forehead on my shoulder, letting me slide down to stand on my feet.

"Price?" I relaxed my chokehold on his neck and pushed against his shoulders. "We can't stay here."

He lifted his head, and I was snared by the savagery of his gaze. I couldn't look away.

"Riley, whatever you think you know, whatever happens, remember this—you can trust me. I won't let you down."

He didn't give me a chance to ask him what he meant. He stepped back and picked up the tire iron from the floor and handed it to me. I didn't remember dropping it. He grabbed my hand, and we made a beeline for exit.

Get out of sight as quick as you can. If you're seen, they'll wonder where you came from so suddenly.

I relayed Cass's message. We jogged up the alley to the corner and turned away from the high-rise quickly getting out of sight. Price hauled me around another corner so that we couldn't be seen from any of the windows.

That's it. I'm out. I'll be asleep for the next week. Good luck. And Riley, for what it's worth, Price is a good guy. He doesn't break promises.

Thanks for your help, Cass.

Grab hold of something. This is going to hurt. Sorry about that. Fast and quick will be better for both of us.

With that, she pulled out of my head. Thorns ripped at my mind. My vision hazed black. I grabbed my head and started to fall down. Price caught me. I made a whining sound as the ache in my head went nuclear. My thoughts whirled like confetti in my head.

I don't remember the next few minutes very much. I threw up. That tasted great. Finally I started being able to string coherent thoughts together, and the pain in my head subsided faster than I thought it could. I was able to stand up on my own again.

I grabbed a handful of snow and tried to clean my mouth out. It didn't work so well, but it was better than nothing.

After making sure I was going to live, Price grabbed my hand. He led me back to the snowmobile, which remained undiscovered. Thank goodness for small favors. I made him check to make sure that the artifacts were still in the seat compartment, and I opened myself up to the trace to check on Josh. He was still alive. I climbed on my seat and took a deep breath. Josh might be alive, but I had no idea where he was or how to rescue him.

"Josh is alive. What now?" I asked, certain Price had a plan. I was also pretty sure I was going to hate it, but at the moment, I was too tired to care.

"Touray is expecting me to turn you in before dark." He glanced up at the heavy clouds.

Flakes of snow were starting to drift lazily through the air. We had maybe an hour until I was late for my own funeral. Not that I thought Touray was going to kill me, but it was a fate as bad as death. I was so tangled in that thought that I almost didn't hear Price's next words.

"Let's get it done."

I could only stare. "What?"

He grabbed my hands. "It's the only play we have left. If anybody knows about Josh, it's Gregg. I won't let him hurt you. I promise."

"You can't promise that." My voice was hoarse. "He's not going to listen to you."

"Yes, I can, and yes, he will. I have something he wants more than he'll ever want you."

"The artifacts?" I still didn't know what exactly they were. Clearly Price knew a lot more on that front than I did. "What are they?"

He shook his head. "There's no time to explain. He will want those. I won't lie. But that's not what he really wants."

I frowned, trying to collect my scattered thought. "What is it?"

The corner of his mouth twisted in bitter smile. "Me. He'll want me."

I didn't know how to react to that. Was he serious? "What do you mean? He already has you."

Again that smile that wasn't a smile. "Maybe I'm not as bought and paid for as you like to think I am. And for the record, I wasn't a cop when your mother was murdered. Had I been, I'd have found her killers."

I'd hurt him by doubting his professional integrity. Never mind that he really did work for the Tyet, he took pride in being a good cop. Which he was.

I rubbed my hands over my face, trying to sort through what he was telling me. "You'd trade my safety for . . . what? What does he want of you?"

"It's not just you. It's Josh, too. As for what he wants from me, let me worry about that."

I shook my head. "No. I can't let you do it." Whatever *it* was.

"Nobody asked you."

"You're suggesting that you'll sell your soul to Touray in exchange for my safety and information on Josh. How is that possibly not my business? What makes you think I'd ever let you trade yourself for me?" Fear ignited anger in my chest, lending my voice strength.

He gave me withering look. "We all choose what sacrifices to make. You're putting yourself out there for your sister and Josh. Hell, you've been doing it for years for those kidnap victims, haven't you? Maybe you've inspired me to leave behind my corrupt ways."

"Price—" I started to protest.

"I'm done arguing," he said, chopping one hand through the air between us. "All I need to know is if you trust me to get this done. Do you?"

Did I? I'd spent my whole life running from the Tyet. They were, without exception, evil and dangerous. Price was different. Though he was definitely dangerous, he wasn't evil. He had a powerful sense of honor, duty, and even loyalty. Of course, he'd served in Touray's organization for a long time, and apparently they were decently close. Could he turn off his honor, duty, and loyalty to Touray so easily? I believed he wanted to, at least right now. But when he was face-to-face with an old friend, a boss—could he say no?

I didn't have a choice. I had the nuclear-option null in my pocket. A quarter that would shut down magic for fifty or sixty yards around me, at least. I'd bolstered it when I took down the null wall, so it might be a broader radius. It wouldn't get me out of handcuffs, but the Tyet probably relied more on magic to imprison people. After all, locks could be picked and most tracers couldn't make nulls powerful enough to escape. They'd probably assume I was no more than the hack I pretended to be, unless Price told his boss otherwise. Would he?

Not that any of it really mattered. I couldn't think of any other way to get to Josh. At least not before he died, or before the haunters drove him insane, if they hadn't done that already. I'd been avoiding thinking of that possibility. It didn't bear thinking about. Stomach clenching, I nodded.

"You might try to look like you believe it," he said mockingly.

"I'm trying."

He looked like he wanted to say something else, but just nodded. "Fair enough. Let's go."

"What do we do after you show up with me in tow?"

Price climbed on the snowmobile in front of me. He twisted to look back at me. The black shadow of his beard hollowed out his cheeks and sharpened the edges of his jawline. "I don't know," he said in answer to my question.

"That's comforting."

"A lot depends on what Gregg knows. He might even be the one who took Josh."

"Wouldn't he have told you?"

He laughed dryly. "I told you, I'm not as bought and paid for as you've been thinking. He trusts me, but within limits."

Price twisted away and started the engine, ending our conversation. He pulled out onto the street, but I hardly noticed the bite of the wind on my cheeks or the cold that teased my eyes to tears.

I had assumed that Josh had been taken by the same people Shana was working for. It seemed likely, because Josh had been poking into Shana's bank system. But what if someone else had him? Someone interested in the artifacts and not the bank fraud? I wondered again what they could be. Was I a fool for taking them to Touray? Not that I could hide them. After all, Price wasn't going to let me out of his sight.

Price had a point: going to Touray might finally get us answers. What I'd do with them if he didn't let me go was a problem I had no solution for. I'd cross that bridge when it collapsed.

I tightened my hold on Price's waist and leaned my forehead against his back. There was so much more going on than I understood. At the heart of it were those three magical trinkets Josh had stashed in his safe, along with the vial of blood. I wonder what he'd say if he knew I was about to hand-deliver them to one of the major players in the Tyet; one of the people whose names were written on the baggies. I'm betting whatever he said wouldn't have been any too friendly.

"Then he should have told me what the hell was going on," I muttered into the wind.

I wondered how Taylor was and if she and my brothers had managed to get out of town. I snorted at myself. As if. She wasn't going to leave as long as Josh was missing and I was hanging out with a Tyet enforcer. She would at least be holed up in one of the family safe houses.

I straightened. No. She wouldn't have gone to any of them. My sister the pilot would be at the hangar, waiting for me, waiting to fly me and Josh out of Diamond City. My brothers might be with her. No, they would be. They'd never leave without me. Josh would be a bonus. Family did for family. They had my back and my trust. Since Josh owned Taylor's heart, he was family, too. If I doubted what I was about to do, that settled it.

I glanced up at the clouds. Taylor had two helicopters. She'd fly us out in a blizzard if she had to. All I had to do was get to the hangar.

There it was. I had a way to freedom. I didn't have a plan or any idea what would happen next, or any way to get to the hangar, but if I could find Josh and get away from everybody hunting us, then we might have a chance.

Those were some awful big *ifs*. And the biggest one was Price. *If* I could trust him.

Chapter 19

PRICE DROVE US down through Midtown and into Downtown. He headed to the north side, away from the diner and precinct, but still a good twenty minutes or more from my house. Thanks to the truck elevator that dropped down from the rim right into the middle of the district, the area was warty with warehouses and distribution terminals. The elevator was a miracle of engineering and magic, its massive metal skeleton clinging to the cliffs like a huge spider. Up to fifty trucks at a time on five different platforms could come in, dump loads, and get lifted back out with little fuss. Most everything that people used came through the Downtown warehouse district, from food to electronics to sex toys.

As soon as we drove in, the gray daylight vanished, the warehouses turning the streets into dark urban canyons. The falling snow thickened. Price drove almost all the way to the caldera wall before turning along a cross street and parking in front of a massive brick warehouse. Faded black-on-white paint along one side said something about the best apples on the planet, and there was a blue-green blob that might have been a picture of the earth. Other than that, there were no other signs I could see that said who owned the building or what it was used for. Tall roll-up doors marched down one side, with a couple of smaller steel doors near where we parked. There didn't appear to be any windows until the fifth floor and up.

I made myself get off the snowmobile, and Price did the same. I woodenly opened the compartment under the seat and took out the burlap. Was I really doing this? It was *such* a bad idea. Yet I couldn't think of anything even slightly better.

"I thought you might show up here."

I started and spun at the sound of a woman's voice. Price thrust me behind him, his gun appearing in his hand like it had always been there. Special Agent Sandra Arnow stood a few feet away, dressed in black snow gear with a yellow FBI stenciled over the left breast. Behind her was another agent. He looked like he was about to go to war. He wore a helmet and a black military-style uniform with a flak jacket and a rifle that looked like it could also launch grenades. Maybe tear-gas canisters. I doubted grenades were common issue for the FBI, even in a Tyet battleground like Diamond City.

The barrel of his gun was trained on Price.

"Lower your weapon, Detective," Arnow ordered.

He didn't have a choice that I could see. I was relieved when he obeyed. "What are you doing here?"

"A little of this, a little of that." Arnow smiled, and it made me shiver. Her skin was so pale it was almost translucent. "I hoped I might have a word with Miss Hollis." Her chill gaze met mine. "In private, if I may."

"I'm not going anywhere with you," I said. She'd probably drag me off somewhere to be questioned or held for jaywalking. I didn't trust her.

"Very well. I understand you and Detective Price retrieved some evidence from Joshua Reist's office."

"I don't know what you're talking about."

Her expression hardened. "Come now, Miss Hollis. Your fingerprints were all over the office and the inside of the floor safe."

"I didn't say I wasn't there. I said I didn't have evidence."

"I'm afraid I must determine that," she said. Her gaze flicked to the burlap bag I held. Her pupils were tiny. "Is that what you found?"

"No."

"It's mine," Price said at the same time.

She looked at me. "It would be in your best interests to help me. You are aware that Detective Price has ties to the Touray organization and that this warehouse is owned by Gregg Touray?"

"Do you have a point?" I asked.

"Touray is the head of one of the largest Tyet consortiums in Diamond City. He is a dangerous man and it's quite possible he is responsible for Joshua Reist's kidnapping."

"Then at least I'll know where he is," I said. I didn't like her. If she'd been a doctor, she'd have worked on corpses. The living would be too scared to let her near them. "It's not like you've done anything to find him."

It was a guess; the flicker of anger in her eyes told me I'd hit the target. "Certainly you may discover that," she agreed. "However, you won't live long enough to tell anyone. There's one other piece of information that Detective Price may have overlooked telling you. He is Gregg Touray's half-brother."

I hadn't been expecting that. The news exploded in my brain. I couldn't move or speak. Arnow smiled triumphantly, while Price said nothing. His sapphire gaze bound me. I couldn't look away.

"Clearly you can see the danger of continuing inside. If you come with me, I will make sure that you are protected."

I broke away from Price's hypnotic look. "Like you protected Josh? Wasn't he working for you?"

Bright red knotted in her cheeks. "How do you know about that?"

"You set him up on the front lines of your investigation and where is he now? As far as I can tell, you're either incompetent or you don't give a shit about the people working for you. Either way, I don't see how I can possibly trust you."

"But you can trust a man who's walking you into a Tyet stronghold? Right into the hands of his brother? What did he do? Get you into bed and talk sweet about what a good guy he is and how he's your knight in shining armor? You can't be that stupid."

"If it's a choice between you and him, I choose him," I said, and even though I could feel terror winding thorny branches around my lungs, I refused to back down. Nothing pertinent had changed. Josh was missing, and Touray might know how to find him. Whether Price was playing me—I hadn't been entirely sure before, and now I had more doubts. I'd do anything for family. It would surprise me if Price wasn't the same. He had that kind of loyalty. It was one of the things I admired about him. Only now it could get me killed. On the other hand, if actions speak louder than words, he'd proven himself to me, and Special Agent Sandra Arnow had demonstrated that she'd wad me up like used toilet paper and flush me.

"Let's go," I said to Price and started blindly in the direction of the warehouse.

He fell in beside me, grasping my elbow. "Riley—"

"Let's just do this," I said, cutting him off. "You do what you have to do. You don't have to be responsible for me."

I fingered the nulls in my pocket. I still had the quarter that would shut down magic use. With it and some luck, I could create an escape. I'm not saying I was counting Price out, but I had to consider the likelihood that no matter how he might feel about me, he'd put family first.

"Dammit, Riley!" He stopped, pulling me around to face him. "I'd have told you if I didn't think you'd take it the wrong way."

"How could I possibly take it the wrong way?" I asked, feeling weirdly numb. Inside I could feel the seeds of hysteria breaking open. He was worried I'd take the news that he was Gregg Touray's brother the wrong way? What was the right way? Should I throw a parade? Buy him a cake?

"I told you I'd keep you safe and get you out of here, and I will. Believe it."

My cheeks were stiff as I smiled. "I wonder if you're lying to me or yourself."

He stared down at me a long moment. I couldn't see his eyes. They were lost in shadows. He pulled off his glove and put his hand on one side of my face, rubbing my lips with his thumb.

"I'll keep you safe," he said.

I wondered if he had any idea how worried he sounded.

"Just keep an open mind, okay?"

Before I could ask what the hell that meant, he put his hand around the back of my head and pressed an icy kiss to my lips. I wonder what Very Special Snowflake Agent Arnow made of that. The kiss was done almost before it started. Price grabbed my hand and towed me off toward the closest door. The door opened before we got there. A man and a woman stepped out. I shifted gears and started to run. Price's hand clamped on mine, stopping me.

"What are you doing?" he hissed at me. "Arnow's watching. We don't want her in this."

"That bitch is the one who shot me at Josh's office." I fought against his grip, but he didn't let go. Instead he turned back to the man and woman.

"We're here to see Gregg," he said.

"He's waiting," the woman said with a hard glance at me and then Price. "You shouldn't have run from us before."

"You shouldn't have been shooting at us, Amy," he said caustically. "I wasn't going stick around and get killed just to find out who was chasing us."

Amy? All of sudden the ground seemed to be moving under my feet. He knew her? By name?

"You weren't supposed to be there and that one ran." Amy flicked her fingers at me. "Didn't see you until too late." She shrugged. "It's not like anybody died."

"It was pretty damned close," Price snapped. His savage expression made her swallow convulsively, but she didn't say anything.

Reality began to seep in. Price was turning me over to the man who'd had me shot. I stared helplessly, frozen by shock and horror. When he dragged me up the steps into the building, I followed dazedly. Baldy—Amy's partner in crime—and Amy followed. Both were armed, though their guns were holstered. They were wearing active magic. Probably some sort of shield, or maybe a null. I couldn't tell.

We stepped into a gray room. Industrial vinyl tiles covered the floor and there were a couple of steel desks, a coffeemaker, and computer screens linked to a bunch of cameras around the exterior of the building. Front and center on one of the screens was the snowmobile. Arnow and her companion were nowhere to be seen.

Amy and Baldy had seen Price kiss me.

Realization hit me. He'd already known. He knew this place. He'd kissed me to make a statement. My brain was starting to melt as I ping-ponged from emotion to emotion.

I'll keep you safe. That's what he'd said. That's when I finally realized that I wasn't just looking to get out of here with my life and freedom intact, not to mention Josh. I wanted some sort of proof that Price really cared about me. I needed proof that his feelings weren't just part of some Tyet game. Call me paranoid if you want, but he'd made Shana fall in love with him. He'd made her believe he was the love of her life. Look at her now. The funny thing is that I wasn't expecting some great moment of ultimate sacrifice. I definitely wasn't expecting him to side with me over his brother. I just wanted—needed—to know I wasn't in this emotional maelstrom alone. The fact was that I'd fallen completely in love with him. I'd forgive him for turning me over to his brother, if only I knew he loved me too.

Stupid? Undoubtedly. But don't love and idiocy go hand in hand? Two branches of the same tree?

"I'll take that," Baldy said, pulling the tire iron out of my hand before I could protest. He went to grab the sack, but Price took it instead.

After that, Baldy and Amy Oakley led us along a warren of hallways until we got to a bank of elevators. We passed armed men and women with hard faces guarding doors or patrolling the hallways. We got on an elevator, and our two escorts followed. Baldy hit the twelfth floor button, and we launched upward.

The elevator chimed arrival, and the doors slid open. We stepped out into a cavernous space. The floors were copper-colored concrete, and there were more windows than walls. The space was mostly empty but for a polished wood conference table and some folding chairs, and a couple of square silver birdcage-looking things that dangled from the ceilings. Most of the light came from spotlights overhead. Gloom crowded in through the windows.

At the far end of the room several white-painted doors blended into white walls. The whole place looked faceless and bland. I bet blood cleaned right up off the floors.

Price walked in and looked around. "Where's Gregg?"

"He wants her secured first," said Amy Oakley. "Lock her down."

Price gave an impatient shrug and waved me to follow him. I went. Lamb to the slaughter.

On the other side of the conference table a square was cut out of the floor. It was about a foot deep and ten feet across. One of the cage-things hung above. It clearly lowered into grooves cut around the edge of the square. Silver lined the bottom of the grooves. More ribboned through the concrete, I was sure. Buttons in a panel on the side of the conference table controlled the lowering and lifting mechanism.

"Get in," Price said. "Nothing's going to happen to you." His expression was taut.

"I want to search her first," said Baldy.

I glared at him. "Touch me, and I'll kick you in the balls." I wasn't going to let him grope me.

"You think you have a choice?"

He stepped up in front of me. He was broad-shouldered and topped me by a couple inches. But if he was hoping to cow me, he failed. I glared back up at him, letting my baton slide out of my sleeve into my hand.

"Your breath stinks on ice," I said. "You should probably get that checked if you ever want to get laid. A dog would be disgusted, and they eat shit."

He blotched red and started to swing a punch at me. I was already in gear, ducking and punching him in the balls, even as I snapped my baton to full length. I whirled around, ready to crack it over his collarbone. Before I could, Price grabbed Baldy's fist and held him.

"Touch her, and I'll gut you," he said in a tone like he was admiring the weather. Baldy blanched, and the woman put her hand on her gun.

Price shoved Baldy away. "Riley, empty your pockets. Remove your jacket as well."

"She ought to strip down to nothing," the woman groused. "It's protocol."

"The cage is designed for far stronger abilities than hers," Price said. "You know that as well as I do, Amy. So shut up."

"Is that an order, *sir*?"

Price turned his death glare on her. "If that's what you need it to be, yes."

I guess that's the bonus of being the boss's brother. All three of them turned to watch me. I set the baton on the table and pulled all the junk out of my pockets, turning them inside out. I added my jacket to the pile.

"The vest too," Baldy said.

I looked at Price, and he nodded. My fingers shook when I peeled back the Velcro. I hadn't realized how much I'd been counting on its protection, especially here in the same room as the person who'd shot me once. I didn't think Amy or Baldy would hesitate to do it again. They were probably just waiting for an opportunity.

"Boots," Amy said, and she smiled.

I didn't see that I had a choice. Price didn't argue the point. I unlaced them and toed them off.

"Get into the pit," Price said when I was through.

I bit the inside of my cheeks, tasting blood, and complied. I barely had both feet flat when the cage started dropping. Baldy had his fingers on the button.

Amy had tossed the tire iron onto the table and now guided the cage into the grooves before releasing the hook on top. She wrapped her fingers around one of the four gargoyle faces decorating the top corners of the cage. I felt magic flare and hum into a field around me. The nulls focused inward, contained by the silver of the cage walls. It was powerful. At least as strong as the null wall I'd torn down. Only now I was on the inside, making it impossible for me to perform magic.

Well, theoretically. If I could summon more magic than the nulls could smother, then I could do something, provided I had anything left to give. My quarter was a magic eater. It was designed to absorb magic and feed itself. So any power use would make it stronger. But once activated, that feedback loop would burn up the nulling spell pretty quick. I'd never been able to really stabilize it. I'd have anywhere from ten or fifteen minutes to an hour, depending on how much magic it had to absorb.

None of which mattered now, since I didn't have any nulls but those on my skin. Neither was any more use than the items on the table, since I couldn't activate them unless and until I killed the cage's magic.

That brought me smack up against the fact that I was now helpless inside a cage, a prisoner of one of the leaders of the Tyet. Maybe the same person who'd tortured and kidnapped Josh. My stomach lurched, and I kept my teeth clenched, though my mouth filled with bile. I would *not* show Amy Oakley and Baldy how scared I was.

"Get Gregg," Price said, though it was impossible to tell who he was talking to, except he sure as hell wasn't talking to me.

I wrapped my arms around my waist, digging my fingers into my sides. I paced the edges of my prison. I couldn't look at Price. A hot, hard knot tightened in my stomach. I shivered, despite the warmth of the room. Pressure rose inside me—to scream, to suck down the nulls and let the magic loose in a volcanic blast. I didn't know if I could. I didn't know if I would survive. Probably not. *Better to go down fighting.* The thought whispered through me, echoing in my brain. The air suddenly seemed too thin, too hot. I started to pant.

"Breathe slow," Price said. "You're about to hyperventilate. You'll pass out."

He said it in the same utterly detached tone he might have used to tell me that my fly was down.

"Go to hell," I muttered through my clamped teeth. Just at the moment, I wished I'd never met him. I hated being at someone else's mercy. I hated that I'd let him talk me into this mess. I was pissed as fuck that I couldn't summon enough anger to hate *him*. Or the faith to trust him completely. I was left in a no man's land as gray and empty as the room we were in.

I didn't want to pass out, though, so I silently counted five on the inhale and five on the exhale. Baldy had gone to fetch the boss. Amy leaned on the edge of the conference table while Price stood nearby.

"Never figured you for going soft," she said.

"Soft?" His brows rose.

"Keeping her alive. Shit, kissing on her like a lovesick orangutan. You've gone all marshmallow."

His eyelids dropped, and he looked almost sleepy. "Any particular reason I should have killed her?"

"She's a loose end. Shoulda put a bullet in her head. Sloppy. I mean, screw her if you have to, but take out the trash when you're done."

Price smiled. Sharks and crocodiles had nothing on him. He looked like he would carve out her liver and eat it right in front of her. Amy paled but didn't look away.

"You are very free with the lives of my assets," he observed.

His assets?

Amy swallowed hard, but didn't back down. "*Your* assets? You answer to Gregg, remember? Besides, she's worthless. A hack tracer. We know everything there is to know about her."

"Do you?" he said. "And yet you still want to kill her?"

That caught the other woman up. Her thick brows wrinkled. "What do you mean?"

"You said you know everything there is to know about her. If that's true, then either you're supremely stupid or—" He broke off and shook his head. "No, the only option is that you're stupid."

She swiveled to look at me. I turned my back on her. What was Price doing?

"Why don't you enlighten me?"

"I don't think so. Run along and do some homework and see if you can figure it out for yourself."

"I'm not leaving you alone with her."

Price pulled out a chair and sat down, kicking his legs out and crossing them at the ankle. "Why not? She's worthless, right?"

"I don't trust you." Amy spit the words like poisoned darts.

The humor drained from his expression until he looked like he was carved from steel. His eyes glittered. "You don't trust me," he repeated without any inflection.

I didn't understand what was going on, but Amy went white as paper and her hands trembled at her sides.

"That's right," she rasped. "You're acting weird. Not yourself. Maybe a dreamer's got ahold of you."

His lips thinned. "A dreamer? If you think that, maybe you should put a gun on me. After all, you never know what I might be capable of doing."

"Don't tempt me," Amy snarled.

"Anytime," he taunted.

"Enough, you two," came another voice.

I started, jerking back around. Gregg Touray had entered quietly and was already halfway across the room. I'd seen him on the news and in the papers. Baldy remained just inside one of the white doors.

It never ceases to surprise me how utterly normal the leaders of the Tyet seem. Like a guy in the grocery line or getting money at the ATM.

Gregg Touray was dark like Price, but his hair was clipped short and his eyes were a dark brown instead of sapphire blue. His face was heavier, more square, and he wasn't as lean. Where Price was a panther, Touray was more like a bear.

He was wearing a black shirt and black jeans, with a thick silver bracelet on his left wrist. He joined Price and Amy. He ignored the woman, reaching down to pull Price to his feet.

The two men hugged. Touray thumped Price on the back in his enthusiasm.

"Clay! I was starting to think you'd run into trouble." He pulled back, smiling widely.

Price smiled back with genuine affection. "A little. Nothing I couldn't handle." He sobered. "We need to talk. Alone. But before that—did anyone mention that you've got an FBI strike force outside?"

Touray's eyes narrowed. "Bowman?" he said, swiveling to look at Baldy.

Baldy straightened to attention and glared at Price. "It's bullshit. The snow's started again. There's nothing out there."

"Special Agent Sandra Arnow confronted us in the parking lot on security camera. She had a SWAT team agent with her. Tell me you aren't so blind that you didn't see that."

Baldy looked startled. "We didn't see anybody else but you and her." He jerked his head at me.

Touray scowled. "You and Amy get everybody into place. Now." His voice cracked like a whip. At the same time, he reached under the table. Small blinking red lights around the doors and elevator popped to life in a silent alarm.

Bowman trotted for the elevator. Amy hesitated. "Are you sure? He's—" She broke off without finishing, flicking a look at Price.

"I'm what?" Price asked. He stared stonily at her. "Don't imagine you can hammer a wedge between us."

"Just because you're blood doesn't mean you won't betray him," she shot back, then looked at Touray. "I know he's your half-brother, but he's not acting right. You shouldn't be alone with him. You can't trust him."

"Go, Amy," Gregg said. "Never again presume to comment on my brother's loyalty. I trust no one more. He will never betray me; he doesn't know how."

She glared at Price, her lips pinching white, and then she followed Bowman to the elevators and stepped inside.

When they were gone, he turned to look at me. "Let's make this quick. Is this the tracer Amy shot?"

"Riley Hollis," Price said.

"Hello, Miss Hollis," Touray said.

He looked like he expected an answer. I said nothing. What could I say? Hey, nice cage you've got here. Calling him names didn't seem like a great idea either. He might decide to punish me with a little bit of torture.

Touray waited a minute and shrugged, turning back to Price. "Sorry about the cage. Amy and Bowman were adamant that I not be left exposed."

"I wouldn't let anything happen to you," Price said.

"I'd like to think so, but despite what I said to Amy, the jury's still out on that," Touray said, then motioned back to the chairs. "Sit down. You're right. We need to talk. "

"What about the FBI?"

"Nothing I can do until they attack. It will take them awhile to get through the shield wards, depending on the talents they've managed to recruit. I expect we don't have anything to worry about for a few hours at least. Let's get down to business. Start with what you've been up to. Have you gone off the reservation?"

I could feel menace gathering in the corners of the room as the two men stared at each other. Price didn't seem at all intimidated. I, on the other hand, was wishing I was anywhere else, and not just because I was in a Tyet cage. This confrontation could end very badly.

"I want to know what's going on with Joshua Reist," Price said.

Touray sat back, tapping his fingers on the wood. I thought he might ask who Josh was, but he didn't. The obvious conclusion was that he was behind the kidnapping.

"Why do you want to know?"

Price tapped his fingers on the table. "Maybe I'm tired of you keeping secrets from me."

"That's always been your choice, not mine. You never wanted to know too much; you always wanted to keep things simple."

"Nothing has ever been simple."

Touray smiled. "I told you that you'd get sick of straddling the fence one day. Are you going to tell me why you suddenly need clarity?"

"Are you going to explain what's going on?" Price shot back, his temper rising.

"Where is this coming from?" Touray asked suddenly. "What has changed?"

He turned to look at me for a long moment. I stared back. He stood up and came to stand outside the cage. I tilted my head back so that I could see his face. Lines fanned out from his eyes, making him look older than he was. I'd been wrong about the color of his eyes. They weren't brown, they were black and full of demons I never wanted to meet. His gaze settled on me with a weight that made me want to sink to the floor. I stiffened my legs. I wasn't going to be intimidated. At least, I wasn't going to let him know he intimidated me.

Though I could see the resemblance between the two brothers, Touray was as different from Price as the sun was from the moon. He burned with a violent, bleak energy. Regrets swirled around him like a cloak. He wore black because even if he changed colors, the shadows would cling to him.

I could feel the magic boiling inside him. He was a traveller, and a powerful one at that. He could take himself anywhere. If he was strong enough, he could take stuff with him, maybe even living things. He could send things places and steal them without ever walking into a room. The ultimate magician. Now you see it, now you don't.

"Who is she, Clay?"

He turned away from me. I might as well have been a statue. I breathed in, my lungs aching. I didn't know I'd been holding my breath. I'd thought Price was dangerous, and he was. But Touray—he was something else altogether. I could see more clearly, now, the differences between them. As if putting Price next to this monster sharpened everything I knew about him. Price clung to a certain code—a sense of honor and justice—that permeated all he did. He wanted to be a good man; he wanted to be respected for being good.

Touray was a survivor. He didn't care about being good, or having honor or respect. If he had to do terrible things in the name of his goals, he would. Price wanted to know those goals were worthy of his sacrifice; he worried about it. Touray didn't bother worrying about anything like morals or right and wrong. He did what he had to do. If he had to kill me, if he had to cut me open and dig around in my brain to get answers, he'd do it without hesitation. He might feel sorry about it, but he wouldn't let that stop him. He wouldn't let his brother stop him.

He scared the living shit out of me.

"I told you. Riley Hollis. Private tracer."

Price's voice made me start.

Touray sat down again. I wished he was on the other side of the table. Better yet, the other side of the room. He rested his elbows on the armrests of the chair and steepled his fingers, watching his brother. "You said you didn't want any more secrets."

Price smoothed his hands over his thighs, clearly wrestling with something. He scraped his teeth over his bottom lip and nodded. "I want to know about Joshua Reist. If you've got him, I want to return him to his family and I want Riley to walk out of here with no questions, no strings."

His brother eyed him speculatively. "Do you now? Why would I do that? Providing I could, of course."

"Because I'm willing to give you what you want in exchange."

Touray's brows rose, and his face blanked in total shock. I doubted that happened to him often.

"You mean that?"

The eagerness in his voice made me wonder why he wanted Price so very much. He had no magic. Sure he was a good cop, and he had a lot of skills, but Touray sounded hungry for him, out of proportion for what Price had to offer. Unless it was just knowing he had someone in his organization who was absolutely and completely loyal to him. Blood will tell, as they say.

"So long as Riley stays safe and we get Josh back, if you have him," Price said, a muscle in his jaw twitching.

A moment later he started talking. He told his half-brother about hiring me, and Josh's kidnapping, and searching Josh's office.

Touray interrupted. "Why her? Why not use an in-house tracer?"

Price scraped his fingers through his hair. "Something about this smelled. Next thing I know, I was being tailed. I wanted someone unexpected, someone unlikely to already be paid off. The night I hired Riley, my tail cornered us. We almost didn't get away."

"They shot at us. He blew them to bits," I added, deciding I was tired of not having any voice in this conversation. I was also tired of being afraid. "I should be getting hazard pay."

Both men looked at me. Price's gaze lingered, but I refused to look at him. I might break. If the eyes were the windows to the soul, he'd know how hard I'd fallen for him. I didn't think I ever wanted him to know. We both had baggage, to say the least, and his was about to get a lot more heavy as he stepped deeper into his brother's organization. For me, I reminded myself. He's doing it for me. My chest swelled with the force of my feelings, even as hopelessness and anger engulfed me. I'd found a man I could love—I did love—and moment by moment, he was slipping away from me. I was letting him slip away from me. I couldn't see any other choice.

At my revelation, Touray's expression turned vicious and cruel. "Why didn't you tell me?" Touray demanded. Something colder than rage twisted around his words.

"Wasn't worth worrying you about," Price said.

"No one touches you," Touray said flatly, slapping his hand on the table. "Ever."

"Doesn't work that way," Price said. "Especially if I come on board. I will be your right hand and your weapon. And by the way, I *can* take care of myself. I'm pretty good at it."

"I know you can, but I don't give a fuck. You're half my heart—my family. Anybody who comes after you earns himself a mountain of pain before they die."

He meant it, too. I could see him making a mental note to make sure that he found out who was behind the attack. Price gave a little shrug as if there was no arguing with that, as clearly there wasn't.

"Maybe you should tell your drones that before they shoot at us then," I muttered.

"What?"

He twisted to look at me, and I wished I'd kept my mouth shut. But in for a penny . . .

"What did you say?" he demanded when I didn't speak.

I peeled my tongue from the roof of my mouth. "You should tell your drones not to shoot at your brother if you don't like it when he gets hurt."

"Amy shot at *you*?" he asked Price, ignoring me.

"She shot Riley," Price said.

"Dumb luck. You were blocking the door," I said.

Price flashed me a heated look that said *shut up*. I don't know why I was pushing it. Did I really want Amy to die? Touray wouldn't hesitate to kill her. I knew that all the way down to my toes. Then again, I was pretty damned sure she'd known exactly what she was doing and the consequences for it. What if she had shot Price and not me? I wouldn't have been able to carry him out. He might have died.

That pissed me off. Something I had in common with Touray.

"It is what it is," I said to Price.

He flinched. He knew I wasn't talking just about Amy, but the fact that whatever was between us was doomed before we were ever born. He was Tyet and I was not. We couldn't seem to stop keeping secrets or lying to each other. Even now I didn't fully trust him, even as I was watching him sacrifice for me. That made me a monster, I was sure. At the very least, I was despicable.

His brother followed the exchange, and realization flickered across his expression and his shoulders seemed to settle under a heavy weight. That's when I knew that no matter what he said, no matter if he let me go, I wasn't going to survive to my next birthday. I would not be allowed to come between him and his brother.

Chapter 20

"WHAT HAPPENED after that?" Touray asked Price as if he hadn't just decided I was going to die. I wondered if I'd be killed before or after he did Amy?

I have to admit that I wasn't that heartbroken that she was going to die, too.

Price explained how I'd used the blood null, how he'd healed me, and that we'd opened up the contents of Josh's safe. He made it all sound so impersonal.

"This is what we found inside," he said, pushing the burlap bag toward his brother.

Touray eyed it a moment and then untied the sack and pulled everything out. He read the baggies one by one and set them aside, read the letter to me and Josh's sheet of notes, and then laid the tin cylinder, the wood box, and the brass wing nut-looking thing in front of the notes along with the pouch containing the vial of blood.

"Careful. I used nulls to absorb the protective spells, but I don't know if they reactivated when I closed them up again," Price said.

"I'll be right back."

Touray stood and strode away and out through the doors.

"You need to shut up," Price said to me as soon as his brother was gone. "Let me handle this."

"I don't want you handling anything for me," I said.

"Riley, you have to trust me. I promise, I won't let anything happen to you."

I laughed bitterly. "You're blind. Your brother is going to kill me. He's decided."

"You're imagining things."

I lifted my brow. "Am I? You're probably right. I'm such a silly little girl. What do I know about anything? After all, I was born yesterday on a turnip truck and fell right off. That's how I ended up in love with such a fucking liar. So delighted to meet your brother, by the way. Hell of a detail to leave out when you were talking me into coming here." I was irritated, but not nearly as mad as I sounded. I just needed emotional distance.

Anger gave that to me and kept me from crying.

He slammed a fist onto the table, his face livid. "Just shut up," he gritted through his teeth.

"Or what? You'll lock me up in a cage? *Oops!* Too late. You could always have Amy shoot me again."

"I wonder if Gregg has any duct tape around here," Price muttered, flinging himself back in his chair and rubbing his eyes. His knuckles were already bruising where he'd smashed them against the table.

His brother chose that moment to return, carrying a big amethyst crystal. It was a single spar about eighteen inches tall. He set it on the table and activated it, then picked up the tin cylinder with the weird turquoise thing inside. He unscrewed the lid and emptied the cylinder into his hand. The amethyst crystal lit up inside. So the protections renewed themselves. That was significantly difficult magic.

I crossed to the other side of the cage to watch more closely.

Touray turned the object in his hand.

"Do you recognize it?" Price asked. "Is it one of the Kensington artifacts?"

Touray hesitated and then gave a short nod. "I believe so." Boyish wonder colored his voice. He put the piece back in the cylinder and reached for the wood box.

"Careful with that one. It's got a mind of its own," Price warned.

I kind of hoped the metal device inside would run itself into Touray's throat and choke him, but I doubted I'd get that lucky.

He slid open the box and the glow inside the amethyst spar doubled in strength.

"Don't touch it," Price advised as Touray started to pick it up. "It's got a thing for blood."

His brother glanced up at him and then back down at the metal piece nestled in the box. Finally he set it aside and took up the wing nut.

"No box for this one?" he mused, turning it.

"It was in a glass bulb," Price said. "I had to break it."

"Did you keep the shards?"

"They're in the trash at my house."

"I'll want them."

"You got it."

A new tension filled Touray. His fingers shook as he opened the pouch and took out the vial. His eyes closed, and his hand contracted into a fist around it. "Thank God," he muttered.

That's when all the windows exploded. Either Touray's wards weren't all they were cracked up to be, or the FBI had some kick-ass talents on their side. Maybe both.

Glass spun like razors through the air. I dropped to the bottom of the cage, holding my arms over my head and tucking my face against my thighs.

Shards pelted me. Several cut my neck, hands, and back. My ears rang. Blood trickled from my nose.

As the sound of falling glass died, I heard Price shout my name.

"Riley!"

He ran to the cage, dropping down so he could see me better. He reached for me. I pushed gingerly up to my feet. Glass cut through my soles, and I swore, bending and sweeping clear a place for me to stand.

"Are you okay?" He had little slices all over his cheeks and nose. It looked like he'd managed to cover his eyes with his arm, saving them from damage. His jeans were hashed with cuts that were rapidly blotching red.

"I'm still breathing," I said, trying to figure out if anything really important had been cut. Cold billowed into the room. I was grateful for the chill.

He looked me up and down, then turned to check on his brother, who shimmered in his seat and then became solid. Touray was unhurt. He must have travelled when the explosion hit. Lucky bastard.

Muffled shouts sounded outside and then more explosions. The building shook and moaned. Touray swore and stood. He started gathering up the items from Josh's safe and stuffing them back into the sack.

"How the hell did they get through security that fast?" Price demanded.

Touray shoved the sack at him. "Take these out of here. They are worth your life. Hell, they are worth the lives of everybody in the city. Get them out of here, hide them, and don't let anybody else get ahold of them." The words hammered like bullets. "Go through the tunnels."

Price wasn't paying any attention to his brother. He was hitting the cage controls on the table. My little prison didn't budge. He smashed them with his fist, then swung around and kicked the cage hard, trying to knock it off its moorings. The resulting sound jangled through the space. "I'm not leaving without Riley. I promised her I'd look after her."

"Clay!" Touray grabbed Price's arm and yanked him around and jammed the sack into his chest. Price grabbed it before it could fall. "That wasn't a request. That was an order. Get the fuck out before they get ahold of this stuff. The FBI couldn't get through my walls without help. They waited until you walked in with it and came for it. It was a trap all along."

"I want Riley safe," Price said, his face murderous. "That's not a request, either."

"I'll take care of her," Touray said after a slight hesitation. "I promise."

My heart stopped beating as Price considered. It stopped altogether when he nodded. He took the artifacts and grabbed his jacket off the table, glass sprinkling to the floor, then jogged down to the white doors and left. He never once looked at me.

Touray scanned me up and down like I was defective. I wanted to squirm, but the bottom of the cage was too full of glass. I'd already cut my feet. He had told Price he would take care of me, but I'd watched enough movies to know that probably meant he was going to kill me.

I heard *pops* and canisters thudded down through the empty windows. I was blinded by strobe flashes. A metallic mustard smell spread through the room followed by white smoke. Almost instantly, my nose began to itch and my eyes began to water.

"Cover your nose and mouth," Touray ordered, pulling off his shirt and tying it over the lower half of his face.

I grabbed for my shirt still knotted around my waist and tied it into a mask.

"Don't rub your eyes. It only makes it worse." He came closer, squatting down so he could look me in the eyes. "I've got no way to get you out. The attack on the building activated the fail-safes and locked the cage down. The cages are designed not to react to outside nulls. You're going to be safest inside. I'll come back for you as soon as I can."

In the meantime, I could starve to death, or die of thirst, if I didn't get shot first. That is, if I believed he'd come back for me, which I didn't. Not to mention he might get dead before he could fetch me.

That left me with no choice. I didn't let myself think about the consequences. None of that would matter anyhow if I didn't survive.

I stretched out my arms and pressed my palms against the sides of the cage. I opened myself to the trace. The magic of the cage nulls was elegantly crafted. It layered around me like overlapping scales. I had no time to admire it or to take it down carefully or safely. Instead I plunged my hands into it. My fingers curled into claws, and I raked downward, ripping the magic.

It was suicidal and impossible and I did it anyway.

The woven spells tore apart and sent a blast outward. Touray flew back over the table. The ceiling and the walls rattled. The floor rumbled and bucked. Magic whipped through me like scorpion tails. I caught what I could, pulling it into me, but most of it spun wildly out of control. Glass spun through the air in a hurricane. It was all I could do to keep myself in the eye of the maelstrom.

When the storm of magic relented, I dropped to the floor. My teeth clashed together, and the taste of blood filled my mouth. I flopped like a fish, my hands, head, and heels banging against the floor. My eyes burned, and so did my forehead. Tears fogged my vision, and my lungs and the inside of my nose felt like I'd sucked in hot coals. Snot bubbled from my nostrils, and drool ran from the corners of my mouth. The shirt protecting my face was gone. Shards of glass sliced my face and scalp and through my clothing.

I don't know how much time passed before I regained control of myself. A few seconds, maybe a minute. I had no time to gather myself or think. All I knew was that I needed to get up and get out of my prison.

I stood. The floor of the cage was swept clean. Small miracles. I whined as my cuts flared with pain. I couldn't see. I couldn't breathe. Bits of glass clunked to the ground as it fell from my clothes and hair. I felt like I was drowning, and the stench of the gas overwhelmed everything. My heart pounded loud in my ears. I heard gunshots. I grabbed the cage and shoved on it, screaming in fear and pain. I don't know if I made a sound.

The nulls were destroyed. The cage didn't move. I shoved again, putting all my weight into it. My arms collapsed like rubber. I tried again, locking my elbows and driving my weight against my hands. Nothing. I started to sit, planning to kick with my legs. Suddenly Touray was there. He grabbed the bars, the muscles of his massive arms bulging. I heard a grating sound, and the cage scraped across the stone floor as he lifted it, exposing a small gap for me to escape. I ducked under and wriggled up on the other side.

He snatched my wrist, one hand pressed hard against his nose and mouth. The shirt he'd tied over his face had vanished. His skin was blistered, his eyes and nose running. A couple of knots swelled purple on his forehead and temple, and his skin was hashed with cuts. His left eye was swollen nearly shut.

He dragged me after him like a caveman dragging off his kill.

"Wait," I said, pulling back. I might as well have been playing tug-of-war with an elephant. I let my knees collapse and dropped to the floor, becoming dead weight. What were a few dozen more glass cuts, anyway?

Touray whirled to pick me up and stopped when I splayed my hand out in front of me.

"Are you insane?" he demanded, his voice thick and hoarse. "We have to get out of here. They'll be on us any minute."

I didn't reply. I stood and returned to the table and found my boots had fallen to the other side. I shoved my feet inside. The glass that was still stuck in my feet cut deeper. I bit back my whimpers.

"Let's go," Touray said, reaching for me again.

I pushed him aside and scrabbled my hands frantically across the table. The marble nulls had disappeared. I found the quarter and clawed it into my hand. Touray clamped my wrist in a death grip and dragged me away. My feet tangled in the tire iron, and I snatched it up.

Every step was agony. A forest fire roared in my chest. I coughed and wheezed, and my mouth wouldn't stop drooling. My eyes felt like they were swimming in acid. My head spun. I could only see shadows and suggestions of light. A porcupine exploded its spines into my lungs. Blood dripped from I don't know how many dozens of cuts.

A door opened, and Touray thrust me through as he slammed the door behind us. The air was cleaner. I gasped, but my lungs had forgotten how to use air.

He snatched my wrist again and pulled me through several rooms. In the last, magic buzzed across my skin as he activated a spell. A desk pivoted, exposing a trapdoor. Touray lifted it.

"Down," he ordered.

I had no choice. I shoved the tire iron into my waistband at the small of my back and sat down. I was leaving behind a lot of blood, but there was nothing I could do about it.

I swung my legs into the dark hole and caught my toes on the ladder within. I lowered myself as fast as I could. My hands and feet screamed agony. The insides of my boots were slick and wet, and my arms felt dead. I reached the bottom and stumbled back to let Touray down. I started coughing then. Each cough ripped through my chest. It felt like someone was pulling my lungs out by the roots.

Halfway down the ladder, Touray stopped and reached up, pulling the desk back into place and sealing us in total darkness. I heard him drop to the floor and fumble with something, then light blossomed from a couple of sconces on the walls.

We were in some kind of storage hallway. Shelves filled with plastic tubs and boxes lined the walls.

"This way," he said and headed up the corridor.

The ceiling was low, and he had to stoop. The top of my head had maybe an inch clearance. Ducting and electrical conduits ran along the ceiling, increasing the danger of giving myself a serious headache. Like I didn't already have one. Like my whole body didn't feel like raw meat.

The walls narrowed until only one person could pass. I shuffled along, my feet sliding back and forth inside my boots as glass cut deeper into my flesh. The tears that ran like rivers down my cheeks and neck were as much from the pain as from the gas.

Touray took a sharp turn and another, and I found myself walking into what looked like a monk's cell. It contained a twin bed, a dresser, a wood chair, and a small bathroom, with one door leading in and another leading into another room.

"Get in the shower," he said. "Scrub off the chemicals as much as you can. I'll get some clothes."

"Better get some tweezers and Band-Aids, too," I said, my voice thick with snot that didn't seem to want to stop oozing out of my head. "Boxes of them."

"I'll be back in a few minutes. You don't have long," he said and vanished out the door.

I set the tire iron and the quarter on the dresser before sitting on the bed to pull off my boots. My feet were hamburger. I did my best to pull out the glass, flinging the shards onto the pillow, leaving crimson smudges and drips on the brilliant white. I only got a few pieces. The rest were too deep or slippery. After that, I stripped off my pants, bra, and underwear, and more glass fell to the floor. I went to shower, leaving a path of bloody footprints across the floor. I turned the shower spigot on, and the water came out instantly hot. Nice. I stepped into it and gasped as water hit my wounds. I clenched my fists, waiting for the pain to grow tolerable. It didn't. Touray would be back any minute. I didn't want him to help me shower. I grabbed a washcloth from the linens rolled up in a stainless steel basket attached to the wall above the toilet and beside the shower.

I had my choice of a bar of soap or a liquid dispenser. I used the liquid, lathering the washcloth and dabbing myself as vigorously as I could stand. My skin burned, but the steam felt good on my eyes, nose, and mouth. Even my tormented lungs seemed to welcome it. I took mouthfuls of water and swished them around my mouth and spit them out.

When I was done with my skin, I scrubbed my hair with the shampoo in the stall. It smelled like strawberries. I tried to imagine Touray or Price with strawberry-smelling hair. I giggled. Hysterics, I know. Nothing funny about my situation. All the same, I was still laughing and coughing in between laughs when I stepped out of the shower.

I wrapped a towel around myself and dropped two hand towels on the floor for my feet. I scuffed back into the little room. Touray was waiting for me. He'd already showered as well. He was wearing pretty much a clone of what he'd been wearing before. The only evidence that he'd been hurt were the slightly pink hash marks from the cuts and two rosy spots on his head where the lumps had been. His eye was no longer swollen or bloodshot. The bastard had used one of those heal-alls. Where was mine?

Apparently he didn't think I was worth it. Waiting on the bed was a pair of jeans, one of his black shirts, some socks, an oversized red plastic first-aid box, and a bottle of rubbing alcohol.

I saw it and blew out a breath. That was going to be unpleasant. Maybe that was his point.

I didn't bother with modesty or even talking to him. I dropped my towel and turned to let him clean up the cuts on my body. He picked out more shards of glass and bandaged what needed it. When he was finished with everything but my feet, I put on the shirt, sans bra. It was covered in tear-gas chemicals. I did put on my underwear, since it hadn't been exposed to the gas, and then slid on the jeans. They were loose, but not so bad I was in danger of wearing them around my ankles the first time I took a step.

"We keep some extra clothes around in case," he said in answer to the question that must have been loud on my face. The jeans were definitely not his. "Sit down. Let's see your feet."

I plopped into the chair and propped my heels up on the bed. He swore softly.

"This is going to sting," he warned in a supreme understatement. "I have to be fast, so I won't be gentle. I'd use a heal-all, but someone could track us with that. The nulls upstairs should slow them down, but not if we give them a beacon."

"You used one on yourself," I pointed out.

He nodded. "I travelled out of here to do it. Traveling's too fast to track."

He'd travelled out, and he'd come back. For me. Because Price had asked him to keep me safe? Or because I was too valuable an asset to let die?

I was pretty sure I knew the answer.

"Do what you have to do," I said. I sounded like I'd swallowed razor blades. I felt like it too.

He took the pair of tweezers and began on my feet, probing with his fingers to help find the shards. My stomach lurched, and heat streaked through me. I curled my fingers around the edges of the chair and held on, forcing myself not to kick and scream.

Almost ten minutes later, he straightened. "That's all I can do for now. This next bit will hurt a bit."

Like digging around in my flesh for glass hadn't hurt? I just nodded. I couldn't unlock my teeth to speak.

He'd dabbed the cuts on the rest of my body with cotton balls and alcohol. Now he took the lid off the bottle and poured the liquid over my feet. I moaned. I'd rather have walked over hot coals.

"Can you hold these in place?" he asked me as he pressed gauze pads against one foot. I bent and held them as he wrapped blue flextape around them. He did the same to the next foot. Next he deftly eased the socks over his handiwork. He picked up one of the towels I'd been walking on and cleaned the blood out of the inside of my boots, handing me one at a time.

I put them on, lacing them loosely as I bit dents into my lower lip.

Touray put his hand under my elbow to help me up and steady me. I wanted to shake him off, but I'd likely have fallen on my butt. I collected my tire iron and the quarter from the top of the dresser and went with him to the door.

"What now?" I asked.

He gave me an admiring look, like I surprised him. Yeah, I was tougher than I looked.

"A loose end. Then we get out before we get killed."

He led the way out the door, and I followed.

"What sort of loose end?"

"How is it I've never heard of you?" he asked, ignoring my question entirely. "You broke the nulls on my cage. I should have heard of someone who could do something that powerful."

Two could play that game. "What makes that stuff so important? Why would the FBI even care?"

It's really tough holding a conversation when you're walking on ground meat and the rest of you feels like it was just doused in acid, inside and out. My nose and eyes were still running, though not nearly as bad now. My lungs were starting to ease, but I couldn't have taken a deep breath to save my life.

He glanced back at me, a searching look. I shivered. He didn't say anything more.

That one look made me keenly aware of my predicament. I was lost. If the building was on fire and I had to get out on my own, I'd be toast.

Touray led me to another ladder space. This time it was hidden behind a set of shelves. They swung open and the steel ladder was bolted to the wall inside the shallow niche. Clearly he'd anticipated the need for escape routes. In his line of work, I'd have had dozens.

"Go ahead," he said. "Hurry. We haven't much time."

"How do you know?" I asked, shoving the tire iron into my waistband again. I stepped onto the rungs. My feet were on fire.

"If my people don't hit the fail-safe soon, the building will self-destruct."

"Self-destruct? How long do we have?"

"It depends on how deeply they've encroached. Once I hit the alarm, the system activated. There are several points of no return." I could hear a grim sort of satisfaction in his voice. "Once an enemy crosses into one of those areas, then the destruct is immediately triggered and the building is vaporized."

If I could have been more afraid, I would have been. As it was, I had hit my limit. "How very James Bond of you," I muttered. One bright note was that if I was going to die, hopefully Amy and Special Bitch Sandra Arnow were going to go with me. We could play poker in hell together. I must have said it aloud.

His dry laugh caught me by surprise. "I'm beginning to see what Clay sees in you."

Somehow that didn't warm the cockles of my heart. I clambered downward. He mounted the ladder above me and pulled the door shut. Dim lights popped on as it did. I heard a click as he locked it. I looked down between my feet. I couldn't see how far down it was. The lights only lit a few feet below me. I stepped down and another bulb woke below.

"Quiet now," he whispered as we dropped lower. "We don't want to be heard."

I began to hear noises now. More explosions and gunshots. The building shivered and groaned. Shouts. Pockets of silences. I couldn't make out what anyone said. I wondered how close somebody was to triggering the self-destruct.

I placed my feet carefully. They felt huge, like they didn't really belong to me. But of course they did, because they sent streaks of serrated pain up through my chest with every step. The bad news was I couldn't feel anything but them. The good news was that I couldn't feel anything but them. Their flames swallowed my entire body, eating the petty hurts from my other wounds.

Because I had no choice, I kept descending the ladder until the noises faded to distant thumps and crackles. I was pretty sure we were underground. My arms and legs shook, and my hands were slick on the metal rungs.

"Hold up now," Touray said.

I stopped, locking my knees and sliding my arm around the rung and holding onto it with my wrist, supporting some of my body weight to give my feet a break. I leaned my forehead into the metal and concentrated on not letting go.

"Looks like it's clear," he said.

I lifted my head. He'd slid back a small panel in the wall and now snicked it closed.

"Behind you is a latch. Pull and twist and the door will open."

I kept my arm crooked around the ladder and twisted my body. My feet slipped. I kicked wildly, snatching at the ladder with my free hand. One of my feet slid through, and I banged my shin. I made an animal sound, high and screechy. There's a point where the agony becomes too much to keep inside and all you can do is let it out.

"Shhhh!" came Touray's entirely unsympathetic response.

"Bite me," I muttered and finally got a foot back on a rung. I turned and fumbled for the latch. Grabbing it, I pulled and twisted. A panel popped away and I shoved it open.

The dim light from the shaft did little to illuminate the interior of the room. I didn't know how I was going to get myself off the ladder and inside.

A black shadow dropped as Touray grabbed a bar above the door and swung himself through. He turned and reached for me.

"I've got you," he said.

I sort of hop-leaned into him, clutching his shoulders as he put his arms around me and lifted me through. He set me on the ground by the wall, and I promptly slid down to my butt. He shut the door and flipped a switch on. Fluorescent lights flickered to life. We were in what appeared to be a maintenance closet. He stuck his hand down to help me up.

"Let's go. No time to rest."

I put my hand in his, and he heaved me up, catching me around the waist to steady me.

"Tell me about you and Clay," he said as he pulled us out into yet another featureless corridor.

"The sex is phenomenal."

He made a strangled sound.

"What? Not what you were looking to find out?"

He gave me a sour look. "No."

"You already know he hired me to do a trace." I wasn't going to give him anything easy. He might be helping me at the moment, but he still scared the shit out of me. He was a wolf, and I was a rabbit dinner.

"My brother has never challenged me over a woman before," he said.

"What does that have to do with me?"

"He ignored my orders in order to protect you. He has never done that before."

"I didn't see him ignoring you," I retorted. "He was damned quick to run off when you told him to."

"Only when I told him I would keep you safe."

"*This* is safe?"

"We are under attack," he said. Silence fell between us. A moment later he broke it, his voice grim. "I hold few things sacred. My brother means everything to me. He wants you safe, therefore I will keep you safe. Or at least you will be alive and reasonably whole."

"Uh-huh. I saw that look you gave me in the cage. You plan to kill me."

"I considered it. But then I promised my brother I'd keep you safe. Now I am honor bound to protect you."

"Until it works in your favor not to."

He flashed me a startling and totally unapologetic grin. It was like watching the beast turn into a gorgeous prince. I swallowed, not immune. I almost didn't hear what he said.

"Not even then."

I made myself focus. "Uh-huh. If I buy that, I suppose you want to sell me some oceanfront property in Wyoming, too? Maybe a bridge in New York?"

His arm tightened around my waist. "How did you break the nulls on the cage?" he asked abruptly.

"How do you travel?" I countered. "I just did it."

"I had the best tracers working weeks to create those nulls. *I* couldn't have broken out."

I shrugged. Let him put two and two together. I wasn't going to do it for him.

"What else can you do?" he asked, and something in his voice made my skin itch. It had that underlying greedy tone, reminded me of a druggie looking for his next Sparkle Dust hit.

"I've got mad dish-washing skills," I said, knowing full well he'd just ask Price, and Price would tell him I could pick up dead trace and make blood nulls and whatever else Touray wanted to know. It was only a matter of time. All the same, I didn't feel like doing the legwork work for him.

"Don't try to run from me," he warned suddenly. "You and I have business, I think."

A spike of fear drove through me. "Is that a threat? So much for keeping me safe." I'd lived my first twenty-seven years as a cockroach, hiding in the dark and in the cracks of Diamond City, just to avoid letting a man like this discover me. Now I felt exposed, like I was about to get crushed under someone's boot.

"Not a threat," he said. "But if you don't help me, people you love will surely die."

I stopped and pushed away from him, staring incredulously. "How is that not a threat?"

Those black eyes fixed on me like a shark's eyes. Hungry. No. More like ravenous. I shuddered, wishing I could cockroach under a door and disappear.

"Riley," he started.

A *zing* of fear flittered through me. I'd forgotten he knew my name. Like that mattered, but it was just another thing that gave him a handle on me.

"You've just walked into the first volleys of a war that started years before you were ever born. If the other side has its way, things will change in Diamond City, and not for the better. People will die. A lot of them. People are going to die, anyway, if I can't shut down this war sooner rather than later. To do that, I'll need your help. So maybe it is a threat, but not one I'm making. It's just reality."

I licked my lips, my throat dry. I believed him. "Why me?"

"Because you ripped apart my cage nulls like they were wet paper, and because of this." He dug in his pocket and held up the little vial of blood from Josh's safe. "Because you might be the key to everything."

Chapter 21

THE KEY TO everything?

"What the hell does that mean?"

Noises echoed down the hallway. It was impossible to make out whether someone was ahead of us or behind. He shoved the vial back into his pocket and grabbed my arm, pulling me along.

"No time to explain now," he said in a grim undertone. "Just don't get killed, whatever you do. If you get caught, I'll come get you. Just wait and don't get dead."

"Funny. Your brother said the same damned thing before he brought me to you and locked me up in your cage."

He didn't have any answer to that, or he didn't feel like talking anymore. He dragged me to a crossway and pulled me left. Another crossway and right. We wove back and forth until we came to a steel door blocking the way. It had no handles. A square black panel inset into the wall was the lock. Touray pressed his hand to it. A beam scanned over it, and the door gave off a low moan as bars inside retracted. The heavy slab of steel swung away from us.

Touray shoved me ahead of him, taking a gun from his waistband and smashing the panel with the butt. He pushed the door shut, scanning his palm on the other side. Once again the door moaned as the locking beams slid back into place. Touray didn't wait for them to finish, but drew me along.

The hallway was mint green and smelled of antiseptic, urine, and vomit. It made me think of one of those dive nursing homes that everyone lives in terror of ending up in. We passed six doors and came to a seventh. A window high up was woven through with steel wire. Touray put his hand on the knob and stopped, turning to look at me. He started to say something, then sighed and shook his head. He opened the door, waving me ahead of him.

We stepped into a room the color of dog vomit. It was mostly empty, but for a small bathroom stall with a toilet, a washstand, and a shower. There was also a hospital bed in the middle of the room. On it was a man.

He lay still, staring straight up at the ceiling. His shoulders and legs were strapped down, his wrists bound to the sides of the bed.

I stepped closer, horror putting a fist through my stomach. "Josh?"

His head jerked up to look at me. His blue eyes were sunken and huge. He was almost translucent, and his skin stretched tight over his skull like he hadn't eaten in weeks. The room smelled of piss, vomit, sweat, and bleach.

"Riley?" His voice was hoarse, almost nonexistent. "Riley?" He began to kick and struggle against his bonds. "Riley!"

I ran to his side and grabbed one of his hands. It was like holding dry twigs. "It's okay, Josh. I'm here. You're going to be okay."

His eyes looked wildly around the room as if he couldn't see me. "Kill . . . Don't . . . Taylor . . ."

"Taylor's fine," I said, though I didn't know for certain. I hadn't seen her in days. I looked at Touray.

"What did you do to him?" I didn't know that I'd ever been so angry. I wanted to kill him. If I'd had a gun, I'd have tried to shoot him

He held up his hands. "I found him this way."

"Yeah, right. You broke into his house and *found* him and tortured him."

"No," he said so forcefully I almost believed him. "I'd heard about him. The news spread like fire once the FBI started kicking up a fuss. Rumor was he knew something about the Kensington artifacts. I wanted to hear what he knew, so I tracked him down and took him away from his captors. He'd already been pretty worked over. They put haunters onto him around the clock and—" He grimaced. "They pumped him full of SD. I've been working on detoxing him, but he's in rough shape. He's mostly not been lucid. I tried a heal-all on him, but it had little effect. I planned to get a dreamer in to see if his mind could be repaired, but he's started to shift into a wraith."

Horror froze me in place. I turned to look for the signs. They were there. The opal shine in the eyes, the blue tinge to his tongue, and the translucent skin. I could see the shadows of his bones and arteries in his arms. He was fading. As with Touray's security, there was a point of no return with Sparkle Dust. Once you hit it, you were a walking corpse. There was no recovering. It was just a matter of time before you dropped dead.

I couldn't accept it. I couldn't let myself believe that it might be true. "You're lying."

"I wish I were. This is the kind of thing my enemies do," Touray said, the grooves around his mouth and nose deepening.

"Are you saying you've never done anything like this?" I heard myself say in a cold, distant voice. "Are you saying you wouldn't have done this to him to find out where he hid those artifacts?"

He had the grace to look away. I thought so. All the sides in this war—whatever this war was—were equally horrible.

"I tend to try sugar to convince people to help me," he said. "The others—they prefer fear and pain. It's faster."

I stared down at Josh. He looked panicked. If he still recognized me, I couldn't tell. His head swiveled back and forth, his eyes darting and flicking after images I couldn't see. His pupils were tiny. He screamed and flinched, rolling and twisting and kicking at his restraints.

"What have they done to him?" I whispered, not expecting an answer. I got one anyway.

"He's locked inside a nightmare in his head. They amplified it with SD. I'd hoped he'd get better away from the haunters and the drug. He's had bouts of lucidity, but they are getting fewer and further apart. I'm surprised he even noticed you were here."

He started loosening the restraints. "We can't leave him here. There might be more artifacts out there that he knows about."

How mercenary of him. Not that I expected different. People were no better than pawns to his kind.

As soon as Josh's hands were free, he started swinging at the air, punching and scrabbling. Then he grabbed at his own face and screamed. He clawed furrows in his cheeks before I could grab his arms. He gibbered at me and twisted to bite me.

"Give it to me," he begged, staring at a phantom only he saw. "Please! I have to have it!"

Touray pushed him back down and snapped a pair of handcuffs over his wasted wrists. Next he put a pair of leg shackles on Josh's legs and snapped them to the wrist cuffs. Wearing blue hospital scrubs and wearing the shackles, Josh looked like a dangerous mental patient.

"Is that necessary?" I asked dully. The tear gas had stolen all my tears, or else I would have been crying. I felt hollow. My heart was bruised and bloody. This wild-eyed maniac was not the man I knew. Josh was the dictionary definition of a young urban professional. He wore suits and ties and button-down shirts; his hair was never out of place; he was tidy—if not freakishly clean; I'd bet good money that he ironed his sheets. He never yelled, never even raised his voice. This crazy, delusional man could not be Josh.

Yet it was.

Taylor would be heartbroken.

"It's safer to keep him contained. Can you walk on your own?"

Touray asked me. "I'll have my hands full with him."

I followed them out of the room. Josh continued to twitch and shake, jumping against the wall and then breaking into a shuffling run and crashing to the floor. Touray and I helped him up. Blood ran from his nose.

"Leave it," Touray ordered when I started to go back to his room for a towel to stop it up. "We don't have time."

"You can't keep him," I said as my brain caught up with what was happening. "He's not an animal or a piece of meat for you to take or use as you like. He's a man and he's hurting. My sister loves him. I won't let you have him."

"How will you stop me?" was Touray's quiet question.

Yes, Riley, how will you stop him? I asked myself. "Whatever it takes," I said out loud.

"Perhaps we will bargain for him. Your services for his freedom."

I wondered what Price would think of that offer. Would he think his brother was taking advantage of me? Blackmailing me? Then again, what did it matter what Price thought? All that mattered was that I got Josh safely away. If it came down to tracing for Touray, I'd do it. First I'd try to incapacitate him, preferably with the tire iron.

"We'll see," I said noncommittally.

A booming clang echoed down the hallway from behind us. Something had been rammed against the steel door.

"They've found us," I said unnecessarily. "They must have circumvented your fail-safes."

Josh chose that moment to begin howling. He started into a lurching run. Touray and I jogged to keep up. Neither of us tried to stop him. Speed seemed like a much better idea, though where we were going, I had no clue.

I could barely keep up. My feet were in agony. The inside of my boots squelched with every step as blood leaked through the bandages.

The door clanged again, and then I felt a gust of cool air running past me. "What was that?"

"They broke through. Too damned fast," Touray said grimly.

He pushed Josh around a corner and stopped and turned. He pulled me behind him and hit a button on the wall. A door slid out of the wall into place. Like the other, it was steel. I heard the locking beams slide into the floor and ceiling. Touray pressed his hands against the door, and I felt a hum of magic kick to life. It buzzed over my skin as it rolled away on the other side of the door.

"That should take care of them," he said, and then gave me a sidelong glance. "I am the last fail-safe."

I felt the air shudder and the door whined with a low stress sound. The sounds from beyond the door deafened me and dust puffed through the seams above and under the door. Though we stood on the solid rock of the mountain, it trembled and shuddered as the building on the other side collapsed into rubble.

"What about your own people?" I whispered when the silence returned.

"If the FBI got this far, then my people are dead," he said flatly and motioned for us to leave.

Touray guided us downward. We were in a gently sloping rock tunnel, I realized. The door had marked the end of the building. Touray had sent Price to the tunnels to hide the artifacts. He was somewhere in the mountain ahead of us.

The relief of that knowledge made me want to drop to my knees.

"Why don't you travel us out of here?" I asked Touray.

"Nowhere else safer to go," he said. "Besides, travelling would make Josh's mental difficulties much worse."

"Why?" It's not that I didn't believe him, but he didn't exactly have mine or Josh's best interests at heart.

"Travelling can be confusing for the mind. It can get lost, for lack of a better term."

I frowned. "What do you mean?"

He sighed, nudging Josh to keep moving. "You ask a lot of questions."

"It helps me stay alive."

"Travelling is a little bit like a hallucinogenic drug trip. The mind fractures from the body and travels through a dreamspace. When the body and mind arrive, they are separate and it can be difficult for the two to find each other. When they do—if they do—it can take time for body and mind to adjust. Josh could very well be lost forever."

I stared at him, my mouth falling open. Was he for real? "Is that the truth? Travelling is that dangerous?"

"Not for me," he said. "For passengers, it can be. It's easier if the passenger is unconscious, but right now, that's impossible for Josh. Even if he were to be knocked out, his mind would not quit working. Awake or asleep, he is tortured."

"Fucking bastards," I said, spitting the words.

"You can see why I will do whatever it takes to fight against them. If they win this war, they will own Diamond City and every person within it."

"Sorry, but I don't see how that would be a big change from now," I said. "The Tyet owns the place as it is. All that changes is the management, and as far as I can tell, you're about the same."

He shook his head. "You're wrong. The people who took Josh are greedy for much more."

"What more is there? The Tyet controls the mines and half the businesses in town. What else is there?"

"Power. They want to be gods."

I stared in disbelief. "You're not serious."

"As a heart attack. Those artifacts might just give them the means."

"What do they do?"

"Nobody knows for sure. All we know is that Zachary Kensington created them and united the Tyet during the early days. Supposedly each one corresponds to a primary talent, and when used in concert, they confer godlike powers. It's believed that once the Tyet was united and control established, Kensington hid them so that no one would use them capriciously. Nobody has seen them since, until now.

"Two are still missing. I am hoping Josh can tell me where to find them. I'm not the only one who wants to know. That's why I can't let him be captured again, and why I need to get him to a dreamer before his mind can't be recovered."

I looked at my almost brother-in-law. I barely recognized him. His face worked, the muscles twitching and pulling. It reminded me of the way dogs sometimes have active dreams, all twitchy and jumpy. Only Josh's nightmares weren't going to just end on their own.

"I thought haunters needed to touch their victims," I said. "How come he isn't recovering?"

"I assume it's the Sparkle Dust. The addiction is . . . awful," was Touray's not very helpful response.

I couldn't imagine Josh's torment. I pushed up next to him and put my arm through his, pulling him against me. Maybe touching someone familiar who cared about him would help.

"I'm here, Josh. I'm here. You can escape. You just have to follow my voice."

I kept talking to him, blindly following Touray.

"This way," he said after a while, breaking my concentration.

I hadn't noticed the arched doorway cut into the left-hand wall. Touray went up the steps. Josh followed, but struggled with his shackles.

"This isn't going to work," I said, my heart aching for him. His hands clenched and unclenched. His head hung, swinging ponderously from side to side. I wondered what demons he faced inside his head.

Touray turned and unfastened the leg bindings. Instantly Josh fisted his hands together and lifted them. Instinctively I grabbed him, pushing him sideways against the wall and holding his arms in place.

"Josh! He's a—" I couldn't say "friend." I didn't believe it myself. If Josh heard the lie, there's no way he'd contain himself. "He's not the enemy right now," I said more softly, trying to catch his gaze with mine. "He's helping us. I promise. I'm going to get you home and safe." I didn't care who I had to kill or sacrifice to get him safely back to Taylor. Whatever it was, I'd do it.

Josh seemed to hear me. The glassy look in his eyes faded for a second. His face twisted, and tears rolled down his face. "Riley?" He dropped his arms around me and clamped me in a desperate hug. I hugged him back just as hard. His forehead rested on my shoulder.

"Don't let them take me," he whispered raggedly. "Kill me. *Please.* Just kill me."

My throat closed, and I dug my fingers into his back. "You're going home to Taylor," I promised fervently.

"Come on," Touray urged.

I ducked out from beneath his arms and pressed my palm to his cheek. I hoped to see a flicker that he'd understood what I said, but he'd sunk inward again, his eyes darting back and forth, seeing things I couldn't begin to imagine.

Touray unfastened Josh's cuffs, and I got behind him and put a hand on his back just to let him know I was there. Hopefully he didn't think I was some sort of zombie or a monster out to eat his liver.

The steps went up and up. The ceiling was low enough that I began to feel claustrophobic. Lights lit one by one ahead and faded to black behind us. The doorway had disappeared behind a slow curve.

We spiraled upward for who knows how long. My leg muscles burned and my feet—I can't even begin to say how much they hurt. If it had just been me, I would have sat down and waited for whoever to come kill me and get it over with. But I wasn't going to let Josh down, so I kept pushing. I didn't even think after a while. I couldn't. Every ounce of my being was devoted to taking the next step. Getting shot hadn't hurt this bad.

I don't know how long it was before we reached level ground. Touray didn't pause to let us rest. Probably a good thing. I'd have fallen down, and I wouldn't have been able to get up. *I've fallen and I can't get up!* Like the old lady in the commercial.

I was sweating, and my hair clung to my head and neck. I wiped the moisture away from my eyes. After the tear gas, I didn't need to add salt to the mix. My eyes still felt like they were twice as big as they should be and full of chunks of rock.

"Not far now. There's an equipment storage area and freight elevator up ahead. We'll take it up to the main staging level and grab an SUV," Touray said.

"Then what?" I couldn't help but ask.

"Then we find a dreamer to free Josh's mind."

That was all well and good, but what then? Just because Touray had promised to keep me safe for Price didn't mean he wouldn't lock me up.

For Price. That was irritating. Like I was a prize horse or something. Touray would know better than to use nulls next time he put me in a cage. Plus he wanted to pick Josh's brains. Possibly literally. No, I needed us to get away before he could keep us *safe*.

Easy peasy. Tiny obstacles like the fact that a second massive blizzard in as many days was raging outside, the roads were buried, and Josh was crazier than the Mad Hatter, not to mention that I was barely capable of walking—none of that could stop me. I swallowed. I couldn't let them stop me, anyway. I had to figure out a way.

The storage area was the size of an airplane hangar. Columns of stacked crates and iron bins filled various quadrants of the space, along with forklifts, pallet jacks, and other massive pieces of mining machinery. Lights bloomed along the ceiling, lighting the place up with bright morning light. I squinted and blinked in the sudden glare.

The elevator was more like a massive fenced platform. An enormous shaft was cut up through the mountain to give it passage upward. A breeze swirled down, carrying the scents of snow and diesel fuel. It cooled the sweat on my forehead.

Touray clicked back the latch on one of the gates. Josh followed him aboard, and I came in last. I wrapped both hands around the rail. I hated elevators. Josh prowled back and forth, head bobbing. He was making little gibbering sounds. Touray pulled the gate shut and touched the controls. Instantly we began to rise in the air, magic humming across my skin.

This sort of thing would take a lot of maintenance. He had to have quite an army of talents working for him. I thought about having a regular job. Magic and technology mixed heavily in Diamond City, and a lot of companies and cities paid a ridiculous wage to lure magic users to work for them. If I had a regular job, I'd make a lot more than what I made as a hack tracer. But then again, I'd have to clock in and out at specific times and I'd have a boss breathing down my neck. No, thanks. I liked my life.

My old life. It was over now. If I managed to get away, I was going to have to do a cockroach and hide in the cracks until I could find another place to live and another identity to hide under. I'd have to leave behind all my friends and my family. I sucked in a soft breath. That was a gut punch.

I touched the place where Price had tabbed me. It was still working, but only barely. Tearing apart the cage had sucked most of it dry. Amazing it had any juice left at all. Price must have learned his lesson and hit me with a much stronger tab than the first two. Part of me wanted to fry it. Another insane part wanted to leave it alone so that he could find me.

The elevator shaft closed around us. Lights lit on the rails and in vertical strips on the walls. I watched Josh. There was no danger of him jumping over the edge. There was no room. He prowled, pausing here and there to fight with invisible monsters. As we reached the top of the shaft, he let out a long, low moan and dropped to his knees, covering his head with his hands.

I knelt beside him and pulled him into my arms. He buried his head against my stomach and sobbed. I didn't know what to say or how to soothe him. I just held on for dear life.

"I've got you. I've got you," I repeated over and over, smoothing my hands over his head and back.

Touray paced back and forth. Finally he stopped beside to me. "We have to go." Urgency colored his voice.

I looked at him. "What's wrong?"

He shook his head. "Nothing I can put a finger on. But we should get out of here before . . ."

"Before what?"

"Before we can't leave."

Something in the set of his face and the hard shine of his eyes told me he was truly worried. If he was worried, then I should be flat-out panicked.

I pushed Josh upright and helped him to his feet. He clung to my hand as I turned to nod at Touray.

"Let's go."

We stepped out into a bigger space than before. A parking lot of vehicles stretched out on the right, jammed with everything from big dump trucks for hauling dirt and rock, to little golf-cart sized vehicles for driving in the tunnels. On the left was a big open area with massive gas, diesel, and propane tanks. Behind them was more storage. I couldn't see beyond that.

As we stepped off the platform, I expected the lights to come on. They didn't. Instead the lights on the elevator winked out. We were in absolute darkness.

I clutched Josh's hand tighter. He'd gone silent and now stood stiff and straight. He quivered with tension.

"What's going on? Is this normal?" I asked even though my stomach was turning cartwheels. I was really hoping he'd say yes, this happened all the time. "Maybe the storm knocked out the power?"

"It wouldn't knock out magic," Touray said. "More than the FBI is involved in this raid," he muttered. I don't think he meant for me to hear. Then he said, "What aren't we supposed to see?"

I put my hand in my pocket and wrapped my fingers around the quarter. The tire iron was a comforting weight in the small of my back. Touray had a gun, but Josh didn't have a weapon. I needed to find him one and hope he remembered what to do with it.

"We can't stay here," I pointed out in a whisper.

"I'm going to turn the lights on in one of the vehicles," he said.

"Maybe we should just work our way to the doors in the dark," I said. "If we turn the lights on, they'll know exactly where we are." Whoever *they* were. "Better yet, why don't we just find a vehicle, load up, and get the fuck out of here?"

"We can't. Nothing will roll without shutting down the security field."

I would have complained that doing so was paranoid overkill, but given our situation, it obviously wasn't. "Lead the way," I said. As if I could see and follow him.

He fumbled for my hand. I hesitated and then slipped the quarter into my mouth. I know, germs and gross and all that, but I could still activate it in my mouth, but I couldn't in my pocket. I tucked it between my teeth and cheek and gripped Touray's hand, not letting go of Josh. Touray tugged me after him.

We crossed an open space, and he turned. I bumped into the front fender of a cart before I realized it was there. Josh shuffled after me. He was silent as a gravestone, and his vise-grip on my fingers hurt.

I kept expecting Touray to turn on some lights, but he didn't. Apparently I'd made sense when I said he shouldn't. There should have been a flashlight somewhere, though. Who has an underground warehouse and parking garage without some backup lighting? I started to ask, but thought the better of making noise. My skin itched with the feeling that we weren't alone. I could have been wrong. I mean, I've been wrong a lot in my life. All the same, I really wanted to get the hell out of there. At least in the storm I could lose pursuers, even hauling along Josh. Maybe I could lose Touray, too. And Price?

I shied from thinking about him. It had been dangerous to be involved with him before I knew he was Touray's half-brother. Now it was downright suicidal. I said before I don't like to be stupid, and getting involved with him was about as stupid as I could get. But even so, the idea of not seeing Price again was crushing. Just the thought of it made it hard to breathe.

"Better not think about it then," I whispered to myself. Not quiet enough.

"What?" Touray whispered back.

I didn't have time to answer. Lights blazed, and I was blinded. A null field buzzed up around us. Josh made a screaming sound and dropped my hand to press both palms to his ears. Touray let go of my other hand and drew his gun from his waistband.

I blinked and stood there like an idiot, trying to get my eyes to come back into focus. When they did, the first thing I saw was Price. He lay on his side on the floor fifteen feet away, blood dribbling sideways over his face. More dampened his jeans. A ragged hole revealed red flesh. I couldn't tell if he was still breathing.

Chapter 22

"GOOD EVENING, Gregg. Do drop the gun, if you please." A woman's voice broke sharp through the silence.

I heard her words in the fuzzy distance. My entire body turned to graveyard ice. I couldn't take my eyes off Price. All my attention telescoped down to him. Nothing else existed.

Was he alive?

Seconds ticked past as he lay still as stone and something inside me started to crumble.

His chest heaved as if he struggled against a great weight, then slowly deflated.

I nearly melted to the floor. The world around me tilted out of control. I tipped forward, leaning my hands on my knees as I tried to steady myself. The surge of relief *hurt*. Tears filled my eyes.

In that moment between moments, realizations slammed me like bullets. The first burned right through my heart: I was crazy stupid in love with this difficult, dangerous man, who'd made his much more dangerous brother promise to keep me safe. He'd made his brother choose me. Made his brother choose, because Price had chosen. In that instant, I knew that I didn't care about the secrets he'd been keeping, the fact that he'd locked me in Touray's cage, or that we had no future together. What mattered was him. Alive and whole. A few hours ago, I'd thought what I felt for him meant heartache and jealousy, stomach butterflies and amazing sex. High school stuff. Seeing him unmoving on the floor with a gunshot in his leg and blood streaming across his face, I knew it meant something else altogether, something primal and vicious. At the moment, I'd burn down the world to save his life.

The second realization was that his well-being meant more to me than my own life. How the hell that had happened, I didn't know. I didn't care. It was a cold, hard fact.

Way back in my mind, I heard the echoes of my dad warning me to be careful. I had to protect myself; I had to keep *them* from finding me, from killing me like they'd killed my mother.

My earliest memories were of my dad telling me to keep my head down and not to let anyone know what I could do. He was fanatical. He taught me to fight and to fight dirty. I knew how to shoot a gun by the time I was five. I wondered what he'd think of what I was about to do. Dad never talked about my mom, but when I asked about her, he got this look of such unbearable agony that it looked like even his skin hurt.

Looking down at Price now, I knew that pain. Just like I knew that I was going to use all the skills my dad had taught me and all the magic I had to get him out of there alive. Whatever it took, I was going to do it.

I think my father would have understood. I think everything he'd done had been to prepare me for this day.

I straightened, brushing the echoes away like clinging ghost hands. I wasn't going to play the run-away-and-fight-again-another-day game anymore. Today was fight day. Today was the day I kicked up my own shit-storm and let everybody else go hide for a change.

Time snapped back into focus, and I came back to the present. Josh, Touray, and I stood inside a circle of null-infused steel blocks. The circle was only about twenty feet across, with Price laying just within opposite to us. A short woman with a shiny cap of blond hair stood just outside the circle pointing a gun down at his head. I knew her instantly. Her face graced the masthead of the *Diamond City Journal*, as well as billboards, magazines, and too many other places to name. She was Savannah Morrell, socialite and billionaire. The weapon looked clunky and large in her pale, soft hands, but I had no doubts that she knew what she was doing.

"I mean it Gregg," she said. "Put it down. You don't want your brother to die today, do you?"

If he hadn't bent and set the gun down at his feet just then, I'd have dropped him like a sack of onions.

"Kick it away."

He swiped it forward. It skidded over the stone floor but remained inside the circle.

Morrell scowled. She couldn't cross the null line without deactivating it. "Don't fuck with us, Gregg. We aren't playing games. If you want to leave here alive, you'd better cooperate."

He curled his lip. He looked like he wanted to rip her arms off. Given the chance, I was pretty sure he would. Violence coiled around him. My skin prickled. He was on my side, I reminded myself—for now, anyway. I just had to find a way to get Morrell's gun off Price. Touray wouldn't be able to use his magic, but he wasn't going to need it. Brute strength and rage would be all the weapons he needed.

"Now who's playing games?" he sneered. "You and I both know you're not going to let me leave here alive, Savannah."

She shrugged. She had that liquid dancer's grace I'd always wished for. She was probably in her midforties, but looked a lot younger. The gun she pointed at Price's head didn't waver in the slightest.

"I'd like to work with you, Gregg. That's what this intervention is about." She waved the nose of the gun around at her companions before aiming back down at Price.

I twisted my head to see who else we were up against. Three men stood around the edges of the circle. Just like Morrell, I recognized them from newsstands and TV. Barry Ostrander was to the left of Savannah Morrell. He owned the glitzy hotel where Price had parked his car the night he'd hired me. A binder, Ostrander was a slight man with blond hair that looked artfully messed, and a long, tanned face. I remembered reading that he liked to rock climb and scuba dive. He wore a pair of silver-rimmed glasses. An affection, given that tinkers could fix just about any health problem, unless—

I narrowed my eyes at him. The glasses had to contain some sort of spell. What could he see that the rest of us couldn't? Nothing, at the moment. The null field would block his vision.

Next was a tall, bullnecked man carrying a spare tire around his waist. His hair was shorn close to his domed head, and his face was ruddy. Something about him set my teeth on edge. Maybe it was the dead look in his gray eyes. That was Anderson Briandi. He was a plastic surgeon and a dreamer like Cass. I shuddered as a chill washed over me. I didn't want him even looking at me, much less fucking around in my head.

The last man was dark skinned and entirely bald, with heavy jowls and a smiling face. His ears stuck out like cab doors, and he looked like he never passed a donut shop he didn't visit. Jason Drummond. Despite his happy, doughy look, I knew he was as dangerous as the others. He was a tracer like me. A pretty good one, by all accounts, though I doubted he was as strong as me.

That left Savannah Morrell. She was a maker. A hell of a cast of bad guys, all united against Touray. Or rather, they'd come to bargain with him, Tyet-style. He'd do as they said or Price would die.

Assuming someone like me didn't throw a monkey wrench into their plan.

A reckless smile ghosted over my lips and faded as my attention returned to Price. Blood had begun to pool on the floor beneath his knee. Was he in shock? My gaze flicked to the spreading bruise on this head. Did he have a brain injury? How long could he survive like that?

I glanced at Touray and then at Josh. The latter was mumbling and weaving drunkenly through the circle, his hands alternately waving in the air and slapping at his head. Would he be any help? I had the tire iron and Touray had strength. If Josh grabbed the gun—

He might shoot me. He'd already attacked me once. Or maybe he'd just keep wandering around like a drunk bumblebee. Either way, he'd help distract our captors.

I decided I'd better tune back into what Savannah Morrell was saying. I expected she had a lot more to say. She had the look of a woman who liked the spotlight. As I listened again, I teased the quarter in my cheek with the tip of my tongue. It tasted like blood, metal, and dirt.

". . . want the Kensington artifacts and I want Mr. Reist. I'll leave here today with those, no matter what. The rest is up to you. If you agree to cooperate with us, then you and your brother get to live. If not—" She gave a little shrug, her red lips pursing.

You'll notice she didn't mention me. Her gaze flicked to me and away. Dismissed. I was nobody.

It took me a second to register what Savannah Morrell had just said—she didn't have the artifacts. Price must have hidden them before they attacked him. My mouth started moving before I could even think.

"Touray doesn't know where they are," I said. "Price hid them. If he dies, you won't find them."

"Is that true?" Morrell demanded, her voice a whip crack. She was talking to Touray.

He nodded, his head tipping back defiantly. "So now you've got a problem. Kill him and you can't find the artifacts. Kill me and this disappears forever."

He pulled the vial of blood out of his pocket, holding it between his thumb and his forefinger.

Morrell gasped and paled, if that was even possible for Miss Marble. "Is that—"

"Kensington's blood?" Touray lifted it up to let the light shine on it better. He squinted at it, putting on a show. "That's my guess."

He tossed it and caught it again. Morrell made a squeaking noise, and the others grunted and gasped and swore.

"What are you doing?" Morrell shrieked.

"Reminding you that killing me or my brother isn't going to serve you," Touray said coldly. "If push comes to shove, I will shatter this on the floor and you will never find Kensington's hidden chamber. Is that a risk you want to take?"

"Don't be a fool," Morrell said.

Touray looked at Briandi, Ostrander, and Drummond. "I mean it. If I don't walk out of here with my brother, then I *will* break it. I've got nothing to lose."

Notice how Josh and I weren't included in his equation? That just gave me the warm fuzzies all over. I guess Touray's promise to keep me safe came with an expiration date, and losing Josh was acceptable. Fortunately, I didn't plan to rely on Touray. Much.

"You wouldn't," Briandi said, his voice deep and rumbling. "You want to find that chamber as much as we do."

"More," said Touray. "But I won't find it if I'm dead, so why let you have it?"

"Drop it then," Ostrander said. "Jason is good. He'll trace it."

"He *is* good, isn't he?" Touray said. "But is he good *enough*? You'll only get one shot on the trace. If he can't do it, there's no way you'll ever find it. Kensington's been dead a very long time"

I have to admit, I was getting really curious about what was hidden in Kensington's chamber. It sounded like Drummond could pick up dead trace. That was news to me. I thought I was the only one. Every year, hell, every minute older that trace got, the harder it was to pick up and follow.

"What do we do?" Drummond asked his companions in his feminine voice. "I'm not sure I can pick up trace that old."

"Walk away," Touray suggested. Ordered, really. He had balls. "Now. Walk away and prepare for when I come to kill you."

"Not exactly a reason to let you go," Ostrander commented, but I could tell he was worried. He couldn't stop looking at the vial of blood any more than the rest of them.

"No? Well I'm not inclined to sugarcoat it. You invaded my house, you shot my brother, and you took me prisoner. What did you expect me to do? Send you flowers and chocolates? You get a chance. Maybe you can run far enough and dig a whole deep enough that I don't find you. Or maybe you can raise a big enough army to fight me off. Be warned—if Clay dies, I will make you pay with your pain. I will make you suffer more than you can possibly imagine."

I believed him. I'd heard more than I wanted to about the kinds of things he was capable of. For a second I thought they might fall for it. But then—

"No," Savannah declared. "If you want your brother to survive, then you'll give us that vial and behave. The longer he lies there bleeding, the closer he gets to dying. We'll stay here and watch him breathe his last breath, if you like. If you really love him, you'll save him."

I saw Touray swallowing jerkily and felt the furious swirl of his thoughts. Time for me to step up.

"If you didn't have this null wall, you wouldn't be so cocky," I said. It was all the hint I could give Touray.

His head jerked toward me, but I didn't look at him. He'd seen me take down the nulls on the cage. He had to know I was ready to do *something.*

I didn't wait for a reply. Surprise was our best chance. I clamped the quarter null between my teeth and activated it, hoping it would work the way I'd planned. Testing it hadn't been possible. I meant for it to suck up all the magic in a localized area, then maintain the circumference even on the move. There was no way to deactivate it once set in motion. Absorbing so much magic would burn it out pretty quick, depending on how much work it had to do. It was a good idea in theory. I underestimated reality.

Imagine one of those big parties where they've hung a net up at the ceiling to hold a billion balloons. Suddenly the net vanishes and all the balloons fall on the audience. Now imagine that the balloons are really lead weights and they are all funneling down to one point at ten thousand miles per hour. That's what this was like. All the spells holding magic in the near vicinity simply vanished. The unbound magic sluiced into me. It pounded me in sticky, smothering waves, then pushed inside me, through me, into the null inside my mouth. My body felt like it was being pried apart, tendons and ligaments stretching, muscles separating, bones splintering. I found myself sprawled flat on my back, unable to move and unaware how I'd got there. As I lay there, the quarter continued to drink down the magic as fast as it came.

The lights flickered overhead, and I heard noises echoing from the cavern as magic tore away. More flowed through me than I imagined the quarter could hold. It wasn't long before the flow slowed. I forced myself up. The surprise of my attack wouldn't last long. I had to move.

I yanked the tire iron out of my back pocket and lunged at Savannah. I picked her because she was pointing the gun at Price. I needed her threat to be gone.

She hesitated, distracted by the noise and dying lights. I launched myself over the null line, swinging the tire iron and smashing it into her forearm. A shot exploded and nearly deafened me. The gun clattered to the stone floor. Savannah screamed and staggered back, clutching her arm close, then broke away, running off though the maze of vehicles. One down.

I whirled to find Touray locked together with Briandi. Ostrander hovered in the background. Jason Drummond scuttled forward, going for Touray's discarded gun. I looked down, searching for the one Morrell had dropped. Where was it?

There was no time to look. Drummond stooped. Everything slowed. I heard a fist thud against flesh, and Briandi fell backward a step before launching himself at Touray. Josh yelled something incoherent and ran at Ostrander, driving his shoulder into the other man's stomach. He picked him up and slammed him into the side of a truck. Ostrander dropped senselessly to the ground and Josh fell on top of him, pounding the other man furiously. His arms jerked like pistons. His face pulled into a snarling mask. Ostrander tried to block the blows, but he had no chance against Josh's wild fury. I wondered if Josh even knew who he was fighting, or if it was some monster from the nightmares only he could see.

My attention flicked back to Drummond. He'd swung himself back around, his arm extending, aiming at Touray. I leaped for him, swinging the tire iron over my head. It felt like I was caught in honey. I tripped over one of the steel null blocks and everything whipped into fast-forward. The tire iron went flying, and I staggered forward, crashing into Drummond's side.

"Bitch!"

He grabbed me by the hair and shoved me down. I landed hard on my knees. Pain rattled down my shins and up my thighs. I struggled to get up and found myself looking up the barrel of his gun. The muzzle filled my whole world. I didn't even have time to panic or for my life to flash before my eyes. I flung myself aside as three shots sounded almost simultaneously.

My head hit the stone floor. Gold sparks exploded across my vision, followed by a fall of soot snowflakes. I blinked rapidly, taking stock of my body, stunned that I was still alive. Where had the bullets hit? My head throbbed and so did my knees and shoulder where I'd struck the ground, but the burning pain I'd experienced when I was shot before wasn't there.

How could he have missed? Adrenaline jolted through me, and I scrambled to my feet. Drummond sprawled in front of me, his legs bent awkwardly, his face slack with surprise. Three bloody holes perforated his chest.

For a second I stayed glued to the floor, too stunned to move. Then I spun around, searching for my savior.

I found him on the ground behind me. Price. He lay on his back, holding Savannah Morrell's gun. His sapphire gaze swallowed me. It was like being swept into a whirlpool. I felt myself spinning and careening, sinking down into a maelstrom. My heart thundered against my ribs so hard I thought it would shatter into pieces. His eyes were full of turbulence and desperate undercurrents I didn't understand, but they held both promises and demands. My stomach clenched in anticipation.

Touray knocked into me, and I stumbled aside, losing sight of Price. Shots rang out again and silence fell, broken only by Touray's deep panting breaths and the thud of Josh's fists on Ostrander's flesh.

The man was unconscious, his face unrecognizable. Josh sat astride him, not yet tiring. I called his name. He hesitated, his fists freezing in mid-swing. His knuckles were bloody and swollen.

"Josh," I called again and stepped toward him. "It's over. You can let him go."

He looked sideways at me like a dog protecting a bone, and I barely recognized him for the man I knew. This one was tortured and hard, like he was chiseled from diamonds. He turned away and gripped Ostrander around the neck. Almost gently, he lifted the man's head and knocked it against the floor. Again. And again.

The pulpy crunching sound twisted my stomach, and I swallowed hard. I didn't try to stop him again. I wanted to, but for the first time in my life, I was afraid of him. Mild-mannered, sweet Josh. I was so stupid. It wasn't over for him and wouldn't be until the nightmares in his head stopped and even then—who knew what would be left? I hoped to hell his head could be fixed, because no way was he getting near Taylor again otherwise.

"Clay, are you all right?"

It was hard to see. Lights still functioned fifty feet away, but we were at the center of a dark circle. My eyes adjusted slowly.

Touray knelt down by Price. Anderson Briandi had fled, following Morrell. Just down the row of vehicles, a truck window was shattered and another couple of bullet holes pocked the fender. Price must have gotten a couple shots off at him. I bent to check to see if Drummond was still alive. No pulse.

I stepped away from his body, and the pain of my feet along with all the other bruises swept over me in a black wave. Exhaustion netted my muscles, and I wanted nothing more than to curl up in a ball somewhere and sleep for a year.

No chance of that.

Touray tied a makeshift bandage around Price's leg.

Price grimaced and growled at the pain. "Take it easy."

"We have to stop the bleeding. You've lost a lot of blood. How's your head?"

"I've got a hard head. I'll live."

"Good, because I'm going to need you. We've just gone to war. Come on. We have to get out of here before Savannah and Anderson come back with reinforcements."

Touray helped his brother to his feet. I hung back. After my earlier realization about how much I loved Price, I was turning chicken. A Godzilla-sized chicken. I wanted to run and disappear almost as much as I wanted to wrap myself around him and not let go.

He looked haggard and gray. Blood smeared his face and crusted in his hair.

I'd almost lost him. I was still going to lose him.

No. I forced myself to be honest. I was going to give him away. Or more accurately, I was going to run away. For the first time since I'd fallen in love with him, I asked myself why my gut was still urging me to run, and none of the answers seemed good enough.

"Are you okay?" he asked me, one arm over Touray's shoulder.

Just like before, I fell into his eyes and lost hold of reality. Tides of emotion swirled around me, pulling and pushing. I couldn't get a breath. I was drowning in him, in his demand and the anguish twining around my bones.

When I didn't speak, he scowled and started to say something, but his brother interrupted.

"Can you bring Josh?" he asked me, only it was more like a command. Then to Price, "Are the artifacts safe?"

I didn't listen for the answer. As Price looked away from me to his brother, I could suddenly move. I drew in a long, shaky breath. This was it. This was my chance to run with Josh. I could null our trace with the tire iron. The storm would cover our escape. We could just jump into a vehicle and go. They all had their keys inside.

If I could get Josh to go with me. *If* I could find someone to try to heal him. *If* Touray and Price didn't catch us first. And the biggest *if* of all: *if* I could walk away from Price.

I looked up again to find him watching me. His jaw was knotted and white lines bracketed his mouth. He knew what I was thinking. Expected me to do it, even.

He gave himself to his brother for you. What else do you want?

I caught myself before I could even consider. It didn't matter. Price was never going to betray his brother. I turned away.

Josh was still banging Ostrander's head against the ground, slowly, deliberately. Blood pooled around the prone man's head. I went over and put my hand on Josh's shoulder.

"We need to go," I said firmly, pulling on him. "The others might come back. We need to find someone to help you."

I don't know how much he understood, but he did let go of Ostrander and stood up. His hands were swollen and covered with blood. He wiped them on his pants. I looked away, feeling green.

Touray and Price started up the row of vehicles again. I hobbled after them with Josh in tow. I still couldn't decide what I should do. I'd befriended a lot of people with abilities over the years, but I avoided dreamers. I had too many secrets to lose, and I was terrified they'd sneak into my head without my knowing. The only dreamer I knew was Cass, and it would take time to find her. Price would guess that she'd be my destination and follow. I didn't have a choice. I had to stay with them.

That made me happier than it should have.

Did I really want to pick safety over this amazing thing between Price and me? Even if what we felt only lasted an hour or a day or a week? Was I being a coward?

The answer to that was obvious and not one that I liked thinking about. But now I had to decide if I wanted to stay a coward. Did I want to live a long life of fear? Or did I want to grab what joy I could get and suffer the consequences?

That answer was obvious, too. If I had the courage to follow my heart. At that moment, if my arm hadn't been linked through Josh's, I would have jumped in with both feet and said, fuck it. I'd deal with Touray and whatever else I had to. But the reality of Josh stopped me. He'd been kidnapped and tortured by people like Touray. I could never be one of those people.

I looked at Price leaning heavily on his brother. A salt smile curved my lips. Touray was in for a surprise. Price was never going to be able to do that kind of thing either. He didn't have to tell me he'd stayed out of his brother's business and become a cop in order to do good. He was a tough and dangerous man, and he was a good man. I didn't know how he was going to survive living in that shadow world. He'd have to change it. I wondered if Touray was prepared for that.

Chapter 23

TOURAY HELPED Price into the passenger seat of a one-ton Chevy SUV. I pushed Josh into his seat, bending his arms and legs like a stiff doll until I could buckle his seat belt, more to keep him from freaking out and attacking the rest of us than anything else. I hobbled around to my side and slid into my seat, shutting the door with a long sigh.

"I'm taking you to Maya," Touray said to his brother as he keyed the engine over.

"We need a dreamer for Josh," Price said. "The sooner the better. He's in worse shape than I am."

"He can wait. I want you looked after."

"Go to Cass first. You can travel to fetch Maya."

"Can I? My magic doesn't seem to be working at the moment."

Touray glanced meaningfully over his shoulder at me. I shivered at the greed and speculation in the look. Like he was shopping and had just found a Picasso in a thrift store. Not that he'd be caught dead in a thrift store, but you get the point.

Sometime in the fight I'd swallowed the quarter. It was fast reaching its limits. I shrugged at Touray because I had no idea when it would run out and when he'd get his powers back. They could sort out what they wanted to do. I was just along for the ride at this point.

I leaned my head back against the headrest and closed my eyes. Royal mistake. I instantly became all too aware of my injuries. My entire body throbbed like Yosemite Sam's thumb after Bugs Bunny whacks it with a hammer. Fifty times the size it ought to be and pulsing like a puffer fish on crack.

Touray made a frustrated sound. "Fine. We'll go to Cass. Where is she?"

"Midtown."

"Maya's closer. I'll travel for Cass as soon as I can."

I felt his eyes on me again.

"She won't like that," Price warned.

His voice was a little louder. He'd turned his head to look at me, too. My fingers twitched, and I clenched them together.

"Too damned bad," Touray said. "I'm not wasting time driving in this storm if I don't have to."

They started talking about the attack on the building and how the FBI had come to work with Morrell and the others. Pretty quick I drifted off to sleep. No dreams, thank goodness. Apparently my mind needed to rest as much as my body.

I woke up awhile later. It could have been all of five minutes for all I knew. We were still driving—if you could call it that. We inched along. Snow whirled around us. The headlights showed nothing but a wall of white. I wondered how Touray was even staying on the road. Maybe he'd drive over the edge of the caldera and solve all my problems in one quick plunge.

"Finally," Touray muttered. He started to glow around the edges of his body, and the rest of him thinned so I could see through him. He began to speed up, following some sort of path his magic opened up to him.

The quarter null had sputtered out. That must've been what woke me. I looked at Josh. His head hung like he was asleep, but I could see the gleam of his eyes, and his lips moved.

I closed my eyes again, but sleep wouldn't come again. I'm not sure how long we drove before Touray pulled up and stopped. I looked out the window, but all I saw was snow and darkness. Touray shut off the engine and the lights.

He opened the door and stepped out. The overhead lights blinked on and Josh's head jerked up. His hands were sausages. I wondered if any of the bones in his hand were still whole.

Touray went around to open Price's door and help him out. Cold air and snow gusted inside. A chill splashed over me. I didn't have a coat. Neither did Josh. Touray at least had on long sleeves.

I fumbled open my door and stepped into snow up to my knees. Cold instantly soaked into my feet. The cold felt heavenly on my fiery feet. Getting around the back of the SUV took a few minutes. I was almost too tired to make it. Freezing to death was starting to feel like a pleasant option.

By the time I got to the other side, Touray and Price stood outside the car. Price had his arm over his brother's shoulder, and Touray held him tight around his waist.

"Let's get you inside," Touray said, pulling his brother forward and past me.

I wouldn't lose them. I had their trace to follow. All the same, I wasn't sure I could manage Josh on my own.

"We'll wait for them," Price said.

"She can follow our trace," his brother argued. "Let's get Maya looking at you."

"I can wait," Price said stubbornly.

I unbuckled Josh. He hadn't moved since we stopped. His head still dangled down as he spoke silently to himself.

"Come on, Josh. We're here." I pushed the seat belt out of the way and took his arm to pull him out.

He made a snarling sound and smashed me in the mouth. My lip split, and I tasted blood. I staggered backward, and he leaped on top of me. I landed on my back in deep snow and couldn't move. His knees drove into the pit of my stomach. He punched the side of my head. Pain fractured my skull and snow clogged my eyes and mouth as I twisted to the side, unable to breathe. I tried to push him off, but my arms were buried in the snow.

Another punch, this time on the other side of my mouth. I pushed myself downward, hoping to burrow away. Abruptly his weight was flung away.

"Riley? Riley! Are you all right?"

Price grabbed my shoulders and sat me up. I made a whining sound and pressed my forehead against my knees, trying to breathe away the pain. It didn't work. I took stock of myself. My head whirled, and my face hurt. My ears rang. I couldn't hardly hear anything. I touched my tongue to the cuts in my mouth where my teeth had sliced. I was crying. I couldn't stop. Josh did this to me. *Josh.* I knew it wasn't his fault. I knew it, but the worst of my hurts was the sense of betrayal. Like he should somehow have known me; like I should have been the exception somehow because I'd come for him when no one else had.

What if he'd attacked Taylor?

I wanted to curl up and stay on the ground forever. I wanted to go back home and lock the doors and never come out again. I wanted none of this to ever have happened.

"Riley? Talk to me, baby. Are you okay?"

Price smoothed my hair, and I flinched away. It hurt to be touched.

He swore. "I'm going to kill the mother-fucking bastard."

"Not his fault," I muttered, and the words came out slurred. My lips were too swollen to work properly. "Your fault. You and your brother. All of you Tyet people."

I could feel his recoil. But it was true.

He didn't get a chance to reply. His brother joined us. "Come on. Let's get inside. Maya will take care of her."

He and Price lifted me to my feet. My knees instantly buckled.

Touray swung me up in his arms. "I'll come back for Josh," he told Price.

I shuddered. Touray was built like a Mack truck. I was pretty sure he'd knocked Josh cold. Irrational though it was, that pissed me off. I know Josh had been out of control and attacking me, but Josh's issues were Touray's fault as much as or more than the fault of Savannah Morrell and her friends. Josh had been through hell. Touray could obviously have called in Cass anytime he'd wanted. He didn't. He let Josh suffer. Then Touray clocked Josh and dumped him in the snow. I started to struggle and Touray's arms clamped tight.

"What the hell are you doing?"

"I can walk," I said. Lisped, really. "I don't need your help."

"Yes, you do, so shut up, stay still, and deal with it."

"Or you'll punch me, too?"

"Don't tempt me."

"Gregg," Price growled warningly behind us.

"She's a pain in the ass, Clay."

"I know," Price agreed.

Asshole. *When had that become more endearment than insult?*

I closed my eyes because the snow was getting in my eyes. It fell thickly over me, soaking me to the skin. I didn't have a coat. Cold sank inside me. If I hadn't been so exhausted and hurt, I'd have complained. As it was, I just wanted to sleep and forget.

Things got fuzzy for a while. I stopped paying much attention. I was safe enough for the moment, and there wasn't much that Touray and Price were going to let me do, so I might as well just roll with it. At some point we went inside and warmth surrounded me. I was set down on something soft with a pillow, and I snuggled into it as someone put a blanket over me. I heard a woman's voice and Price and Touray both talking. Arguing, actually, but I didn't pay any attention to what they were saying. I was happy to be ignored.

I woke up quick when someone pulled my boots off. I let out a scream and tried to squirm away.

"Sonovabitch!" Price swore. Then, "I'm going to kill Gregg."

I lay panting with pain as I stared up at a green ceiling. "Why?" I asked.

He loomed into view, his expression twisted with fury. The lump and bruise on his head were gone. "Why didn't you say something about your feet?"

"What was there to say? It's not like anybody could help me."

"You shouldn't have been walking on them!"

"Did I have a choice?" The last came out with a yelp as someone tugged the other boot off.

"Impressive," a woman said, somewhere in the vicinity of my throbbing feet. Her voice was rich and husky, with a Spanish accent. "She couldn't have hurt herself worse if she'd been trying. These are going to take me awhile to mend. Let me have a look at the rest of her, though, and see if anything's more pressing."

A round, dark-haired woman in a blue and yellow Hawaiian print dress came around to nudge Price out of the way. She bent over me, running her fingertips lightly over my forehead.

"Ow," I said, trying to twist away.

"Don't be a baby," she said, her eyes clouding white.

Her magic tickled as it spread over my skin, then began to feel like worms squirming through my flesh. I tried batting her away, but Price grabbed my hands.

"Idiot," he said, and I made the mistake of looking at him.

All those feeling I'd been working so hard to dam up and ignore came crashing back down. My heart thudded rapid fire against my ribs.

"You're okay?" I whispered, needing to hear him confirm what I saw.

"I'm fine. But you—" His mouth twisted, and his throat jerked as he swallowed. "This shouldn't have happened to you. None of it." He let go of one of my hands and started to touch my face, but pulled back. "I'm afraid I'll hurt you."

"Too bad you don't have some of those heal-alls that fixed me before."

"He has me, and I'm much better," came the woman's tart voice—Maya, I supposed. The wormy feeling subsided, thankfully.

I turned to look at her. She was probably in her midforties or early fifties. Her eyes were still white.

"My name is Maya. I'm a medical tinker. You've got loose teeth, a fractured jaw and cheekbone, dozens of bruises, cuts from head to toe, and feet that look like they've been through a meat grinder. You lost a fair bit of blood from all the cuts, and I suppose from that barely healed bullet wound I felt, so you may be dizzy. There's some infection trying to set in, but nothing too hard to fix. Once I work on you, you'll need to eat and drink and rest. You'll want to stay off your feet as much as possible for a week at least."

"Right," I said, like it was anywhere near a possibility.

"She'll do it," Price said with an arrogant smile at me. "I guarantee it."

I raised my eyebrow at him, despite the fact that it hurt like hell. "How do you intend to do that?"

"With duct tape and rope, if I have to. Though I can think of better ways to keep you in bed."

The look he gave me was scorching. My insides melted. My hand tightened on his, and my mind went blank.

"All right, then. This is going to be uncomfortable. Try not to move. I'm going to start at the top and move my way down. Your feet will be hardest. Have you had tinkering before?"

"A couple times. Had a broken arm when I was little. My tonsils when I was ten, and then I got stabbed a few years back."

"Good, then you know what to expect. I'll deaden what I can, but it's still not going to be easy. Hold still, now."

She pulled up a chair beside me and settled her ample body into it. She smelled of curry and cinnamon. She took my hand between hers and heat wrapped it like a glove. Needles sank into my flesh. *Ow.* Then the heat burned away the pain. More of that wormy feeling wriggled up my arm and neck into my head. I took a long breath and let it out slowly. Sweat broke out on my forehead. Next would come the feeling of things nibbling and stitching inside me. There would be sharp pressure, stretching, and squeezing. The worst of it was the feeling of someone working inside of me. It was like being the star of my own personal horror film.

Price still had ahold of my other hand. He sat down on the edge of the bed. "You were stabbed. Who did it?" In an instant, he'd turned back into the Tyet enforcer—cold, ruthless, and brutal. If the guy who'd attacked me was here, he'd be dead on the floor. "How bad did he hurt you?

"Bad enough," I said, remembering. I'd been on a cheating spouse trace. I was reporting to the wife when the husband came home. She was supposed to talk to a lawyer and get the divorce going before she told him anything. Instead, she flipped out at him. Things got out of hand pretty quick, and he'd found himself a butcher knife. The wife locked herself in their bedroom, and he opted to take his fury out on me. I'd started for my car, and he'd stuck a knife in me. He'd been going for my heart, but he hit a rib and got a lung and an artery instead. I nearly died all the same. Luckily, Patti had come with me, and she got me to a tinker in time.

"What happened?"

"I got between an angry wife and a cheating husband." I shifted as a chewing sensation erupted under my scalp and traveled over my skull and into my eyes.

"Easy, now, sweetling," Maya said. "Stay still. This is a bit like surgery, but with magic. Moving about makes things tricky."

I forced myself to remain motionless, even though the sensation was enough to make me want to throw up. Again. I'd been doing that a lot lately. So attractive in a woman. Especially with the vomit breath. Speaking of which, I really could have used a toothbrush.

"What did the police do?" Price asked, still fixed on the subject.

"I didn't report it. Guy probably had the cops in his pocket, anyhow. He's got money and influence."

"Tell me who he is."

"Not a chance," I said, scrunching my face as the activity beneath my skin grew more intense. I could actually hear the gritting sound of bone mending.

"Why not?"

"Not your problem."

"He hurt you. That makes it my problem," Price said, and there was an edge of violence in his voice that raised the hairs on the back of my neck.

"It was a long time ago. I can take care of myself."

"I don't care."

Price stunned me then by bending and pressing a hard kiss against the palm of my hand. "No one touches you. No one hurts you, and gets away with it," he said roughly.

I sighed. "Next you'll be asking about the boy in kindergarten who pulled my hair and the girl in eighth grade who gave me a black eye."

That made him chuckle.

"Where's Josh?"

Price's expression went flat. I'd blamed him for Josh attacking me. I couldn't take it back. The truth sucks sometimes.

"I tied Josh up. Gregg went for Cass. I'm surprised he's not back."

"Stop talking now," Maya ordered. "I can't work on your lower face if you're moving."

I didn't have much to say at the moment, so shutting up wasn't all that hard. I looked up at the ceiling, not wanting to meet the hurt or resentment or whatever else might be in Price's eyes at the moment. Especially not that *whatever else*. I was ready to curl up in his lap like a cat and never leave. Neither did I want to think about what was going to happen next, but I couldn't seem to stop myself.

What was I going to do? Touray would want me to work for him, whether I wanted to or not. Savannah Morrell and Anderson Briandi would be looking for me, too, though whether they would want to use me or just take me out of the picture so Touray couldn't use me was the question. Then there was Price. What exactly did he want? More importantly, what did I want?

My instant kneejerk answer was that I wanted everything to go back to the way it was a week ago, before Price or his brother or the Tyet knew I existed, before Josh had been driven insane, before I'd been stupid enough to fall in love.

But resetting the clock wasn't possible. And in truth, I didn't want to go back. I was tired of hiding *me*, and what I could do. I was tired of scuttling around in the shadows like a cockroach. Until this moment, I hadn't realized how much I resented the secrecy.

All that brought me back to the question, what was I going to do? One thing was certain: I wasn't going to become anybody's puppet, and I wasn't going to let myself get killed. I also wasn't going to let anyone have Josh again. I sighed and closed my eyes. That was a whole lot of what I *wasn't* going to do, but it still begged the question—what exactly was I *going* to do? And just how did Price fit in?

Chapter 24

CASS AND TOURAY returned and disappeared in a room with Josh, while Maya finished tinkering away my wounds. When she was done and had shooed me to the dining room to eat, I still hadn't answered those questions. A doorway led into the kitchen. Maya had been bringing out all kinds of food. Enough to feed an army. I wondered where it all came from. Then I hoped she had enough.

"You're doing it again," Price said.

I sat at an oval table in the dining room and spooned spicy peanut soup from a broad bowl. "What am I doing?" I asked. I was back to being whole and pain free. My body still trembled with the memory of it. I grabbed a piece of bread and dipped it into the soup.

He sat opposite to me. "What are you doing? Thinking. Making plans. Shutting me out. I can hear your brain spinning." His hand curled into a white-knuckled fist on the tablecloth.

I shrugged. "What do you expect? You've got a conflict of interest. I don't see you going up against your brother. I'm alone with here with Josh, I'm unarmed, and I don't know how I'm going to walk out of here free. I'm trying to work out what to do."

"Do I have to?" he murmured.

I scrunched my brow. "Do you have to what?"

"Go up against my brother?"

I went still, hollowness opening up inside me. "What are you suggesting?"

His sapphire gaze locked with mine. "Nothing. Everything. There has to be a way that doesn't pull us apart."

"A way to what?" I asked stupidly, even though I knew exactly what he meant. I realized this was my chance to find out for certain just how far he was willing to go for me.

He made a frustrated sound and shoved his chair back, raking his fingers through his hair. "Be together. Dammit, Riley, there's a lot going on you don't know about."

The hollowness within me grew. "No, I don't know even a fraction of what's going on," I said. "I don't care about any of it, either. What I need to know is if Josh and I can walk away clean if we want to. Can we?"

He hesitated. The truth was in that tiny moment. "You're asking me whether I will choose you or my brother."

I shook my head. "I'm not asking. I don't need to. I just got my answer."

I pushed the soup away and stood. I needed to get away from him. I was back to hurting. Worse than before Maya had tinkered me. This was a crippling pain that made me want to step in front of a train, the sooner the better. Maya wasn't going to be able to help me with this.

"Because I have to take a second to think about it?" he demanded, standing up. "What the hell do you expect from me? This isn't a question of deciding what I'm having for lunch or what color I want to paint my living room. This is my family, my job, and my life."

I shook my head, wrapping my arms around my stomach. "I don't expect anything."

"Bullshit."

He grabbed my shoulders and jerked me close, waiting until I met his angry gaze.

"You expect me to fail you, to screw you over. You refuse to believe I might not be that guy, the one that fails you. You refuse to give me the slightest benefit of the doubt." He shoved me away in disgust. "Why I even—" He broke off, his mouth twisting as he looked up at the ceiling. "Fuck me."

I grabbed ahold of my anger with both hands. It was better than that pain that felt like dying. "Yeah, because it's not like you forced me to work for you by tabbing me, or lied to me about who Shana really is or that Touray is your brother," I said. "Why wouldn't I trust you? Given that someone just like your brother killed my mother and tortured Josh, and the fact that I've spent every day of my life afraid that someone like him might find me and take me, why would I want to know for sure that I was your first choice? That you'd care more about my life than your brother's fight? You left me in that cage so you could hide those damned artifacts and you never looked back. Do you know what he did? He was going to leave me there. I had to break the nulls to get out. So excuse me if I have a couple of trust issues."

His face went scarlet and then paled to marble. He might as well have been made out of the stuff. I could read wary bitterness in his eyes, and lurking beneath it, fear. Fear of losing me? It didn't seem possible.

"It sounds like the only way you'll ever believe in me is if I let you walk out of my life. No games. No strings. Is that the proof you want?" he asked, the words dry and hard as pebbles.

"I want—"

I stopped cold. What the hell *did* I want? But I didn't even have to think about it. The answer was easy: Price. But I wanted him wrapped up in a package that came with freedom and let me choose my own road, not get dragged down someone's else's path because I was in the wrong place at the wrong time. I didn't want to feel badly for severing him from family. There was no pretty package. So, which did I want more? Freedom without strings or Price? Because I couldn't see how I could have both.

My head ached, and my brain felt prickly and swollen. I was too tired to think about this. Too tired to decide whether I wanted chocolate or vanilla ice cream, much less make a decision that would completely change my entire life and endanger my whole family. Okay, the endangering part was a done deal. Everybody I cared about became a target the minute I revealed myself to Touray, much less to the rest of his Tyet buddies. This was about me and Price and what I needed from him.

I put my hands on Price's chest and pushed away. He let me step back a few inches, but didn't let go.

"Tell me, Riley. You told me you love me. I hope to hell that's still true because I love you more than breathing. What can I do to prove that you can trust me short of walking out the door or turning my back on my brother? Tell me what I have to do."

He loved me. The words sent my heart spinning with joy even as despair settled over me. It wasn't enough. It was a Catch-22. I couldn't win for losing. "I wish I knew," I said finally, the words so soft I barely could hear them.

Price heard. He dropped his hands. For a moment he said nothing. "If that's the way you need it, then you've got it."

Instantly I felt cold. There was a finality in his voice that scared me. It pissed me off, too. I know it's absolutely crazy, but as much I needed him to let me safely walk away, I also needed him to fight for me. Clearly I needed to get my head straightened out.

Touray came out of the hallway followed by Cass and Josh. Cass looked almost transparent, her bones sharp beneath her skin. Her eyes were sunken. She gave me a hazy nod. She saw the table and wordlessly sat down, stuffing food in her mouth with both hands.

Maya had fixed Josh's hands and the rest of his injuries though she couldn't reverse the effects of the SD on his body. He stopped in the doorway and stared at me. His eyes were shadowed and bruised looking, but he recognized me.

"I hurt you," he said tonelessly.

"You didn't mean to," I said. I couldn't get a read on how he was feeling or what he was thinking.

He didn't seem to hear. "I could have killed you. I wanted to kill you."

"You didn't know it was me."

He shook his head and looked down, anger and fear rippling across his tight expression. "But I did."

I could only stare. My stomach turned inside out. Price made a guttural noise and started forward. I thrust out my hand to stop him. "Why?" I could barely push the word out. I felt strangled.

"I wanted to be dead."

"You thought *I'd* kill you?" I squeaked, incredulous.

"You should have killed me. I asked you to."

I was back to staring. My mouth hung open. I closed it, then opened it to say something, but words failed me. My brain was blank. "Why?"

The corner of his mouth twisted upward in an acid smile. "You don't know what they did in my head. It was hell. Worse than hell. It was sick and twisted. Your worst nightmares come to life. Then they gave me the SD and made me enjoy it."

"But that's over now," I said. "Cass stopped them. Didn't she? Didn't you?" I turned to her.

"Sure," she said, her mouth full. She swallowed. "Look, I took out all the crap they put in his mind, but that kind of stuff leaves scars. The only way to clear all that out is to wipe his mind all the way back to being a baby. Nobody wants that. Besides, he's got latent ability and the SD addiction is going to ride him. He'll have to fight it all his life."

"Ability?" I looked back at Josh. "What kind?"

"Haunter," he said. His mouth worked, and he bared his teeth. "I'm a fucking haunter."

"Shoulda been a dreamer," Cass said as she spooned soup into her mouth. "Maybe you still could be. But your mind knows haunts now. I could maybe help you. I'd have to go back into your head."

"No!" he said sharply. "No one is getting into my head again." Then more quietly, "Thanks all the same."

She shrugged. "Don't blame you. No matter what, you're going to have to learn some control or you'll risk going nuts again. I can talk you through some of it. Or maybe you should find a haunter to help. Offer's on the table if you need it."

"Thanks, but I don't much care for the company you keep."

Cass's gaze sharpened and turned menacing. I swear the temperature in the room dropped twenty degrees. She pointed the butter knife at Josh.

"Don't forget I know all about you, Sparky. I was in Riley's mind while she was trying to rescue you, while she risked her life—not for the first time—just to find you. Yeah, you've been through a rough time, but you knew what you were up to, and you knew you were deliberately sucking her into this mess, so don't go acting all high and mighty. You might go have a look at yourself in the mirror, first."

With that she stood and looked at Maya, who stood in the kitchen doorway drinking a glass of iced tea.

"Got some vodka? I could use a shot or two."

Maya nodded, and the two disappeared into the kitchen, leaving me alone with Josh, Touray, and Price.

I felt like the world was spinning out of control. The floor kept rising and falling like I was on the deck of a ship. I edged to one of the dining room chairs and gripped the back, steadying myself.

"What now?" I whispered, more to myself than them.

"We're leaving," Price said and took his brother's arm. "Now. Travel us out of here."

"Like hell," Touray said. "I've got questions and these two have at least some of the answers. Besides, you know she's stronger than Drummond. She can use the blood to track Kensington's last steps. She has to be." He looked at me, his brows deeply furrowed. "I'm right, aren't I? You can track dead trace?"

Price cut in before I could answer. "Doesn't matter, Gregg. She's out, unless and until she wants in."

That boggled Touray. Me, too. Both of us stared at Price like he'd grown tentacles out of his ears.

"Not a chance," Touray said finally, when he'd found his voice again. "Look, I know you've got a hard-on for her. Maybe you've even fallen in love with her. But you know what this means. We can't just let her go. Besides, if we don't protect her, Savannah will get her, or somebody else. You don't want that, do you?"

A white line appeared around Price's lips as he pressed them together. "That's a risk she's willing to take," he said. He looked at me, his brows rising. "Isn't that right?"

My throat hurt too much to speak. I gave a little nod. Was he really walking away? Letting me go, just like that? I was torn between swamping relief and utter desolation. He could have fought harder to get me to stay with him.

God I'm a fool and a contrary bitch. I wouldn't have fought for me either. I'd have run for the hills as fast as I could. Which apparently was exactly what Price was doing.

"Clay—" Touray started.

Price whirled to face him. "No," he said. Cold menace turned his words to bullets. "We walk away. None of our people go after Riley or Josh. We pretend they don't even exist."

"I can't do that."

"Then you'll never find the artifacts."

My mouth fell open. I hadn't expected that and neither had Touray. He paled and shock slackened his face. "What are you saying?"

"I'm giving you terms. Josh and Riley walk away clean, or you don't get the three artifacts back. Take your pick."

"You're a son of a bitch," Touray muttered and spots of red appeared in his cheeks. Anger poured off him and thickened the air so it was hard to breathe.

"So are you," Price agreed. "What's it going to be? You'll have three of the artifacts and the vial of blood. That cripples Savannah and anybody else she's working with. You don't really need Riley, or Josh."

If I'd been in a laughing mood, I would have burst into gales. Touray wasn't going to be able to push Price around. Maybe I was right. Maybe Touray's organization was going to have to change to suit Price better. Maybe Price would teach his brother a thing or two about honor and integrity.

"Fine," Touray gave in finally, when Price showed no sign of backing down. "I'll leave them alone." He looked at me, his glittering black eyes pulling at me with questions. He turned back to his brother. "You know you're not doing them any favors. I may keep my hands off, but no one else will. If you care at all about her, you'll let this go. We'll keep her safe. That's better for us all."

I held my breath. What would his answer be? What did I want it to be?

The corners of Price's mouth quirked in a ghost of a smile that faded as quickly as it came. "She'll have to make her own self safe. That's better for her," he said finally.

The words hit me like fists to the gut. He really was walking away. But more than that, he was letting me have myself. It was a gift. It was completely against everything he was. He was a hard man used to protecting the people he cared about. To let me do what I needed to do—whatever that was—said he really did love me. It also meant I might have made the wrong choice.

I stood rooted to the ground as he shoved his hands into his pockets, his chin jutting as he met his brother's angry gaze.

Touray finally gave a quiet sigh. "You've got my word."

Price gave a little nod. "Good."

His brother held out his hand. "Let's go."

I couldn't tear my eyes away from Price. He was leaving. Just like that.

Was I going to let him go without a word?

I told myself to say something, anything, but my tongue was glued to the roof of my mouth. I stood there like an iron statue. A tear slipped out of the corner of one of my eyes and rolled silently down my cheek.

Price pulled a hand out of his pocket and reached to take his brother's. All of a sudden he twisted and strode over to me. He captured my head in his hands and pressed his forehead against mine.

"Crying?" he asked raggedly. "This is what you want. Tell me now if it's not. Because I'd just as soon not grind myself up over nothing."

Grind himself up. Was I really doing this? I closed my eyes and gave a little nod. I couldn't do what I needed to do and be tied to him, to them. "It's what I want. What I need, I think."

"Damn it. Damn you," he whispered without any heat at all. His thumbs rubbed over my cheeks. He lifted his head, and his mask fell away, exposing a turbulent mix of longing, anger, anguish, and despair. "You'll be safe here until the storm is over. Then get out of town."

I shook my head, my hands pressing against his. "I'm not hiding anymore."

His fingers curled into my scalp. "You have to. They'll be hunting you."

"I'll be ready."

"Riley—"

He broke off with a frustrated sound. "I know you want me to stay out of your life, but Savannah Morrell and the others, they won't hold back. What they did to Josh was nothing. You *have* to hide," he pleaded.

He pleaded.

"The genie's out of the bottle," I said. "Sooner or later they'll find me. The only way to keep me and mine safe is to make sure they know better than to screw with me."

"Without my help," he said bitterly.

"For now," I said. "Just . . . for now."

He went still, searching my face. Finally he said, "You know where to find me."

I nodded. "I've got your trace."

He hesitated, then let his fingers relax, though he didn't let go. "Time to be on my way then. I don't suppose you'll listen if I tell you to be careful."

"I always try."

He scraped his lower lip with his teeth and squeezed once more with his fingers and stepped back. Piercing cold hit the back of my neck. I jerked and stared at him. Had he tabbed me? Again?

Price lifted his brows and gave an unapologetic shrug as he backed away to his brother. He knew as well as I did that I could destroy the tab.

Warmth spread through me. Somehow he'd given me exactly what I needed. Room—and trust—to make choices for myself and do things my way, but he'd still made it clear he was staking a claim.

He looked over at Josh, and his expression morphed into stone-cold killer mode. I shivered. "Touch her again, and the last week will seem like a vacation at the beach."

Josh's lip curled. "I've got abilities now. I'm not afraid of you."

"You don't have to be scared. You just have to believe me. I've taken down people with abilities much greater than yours. You're nothing special. So trust me when I tell you that if I hear you've so much as touched Riley wrong, I'll come for you. You'll never see me coming, and you'll regret it for the rest of your very short life."

"Ahem," I said, cutting in. "Josh isn't going to hurt me again, and if he tries, I'll break his legs for him."

I gave my almost brother-in-law a look that said I was absolutely serious. He had the grace to flush.

"As for you—"

"As for me?" Price taunted when I didn't finish.

"Don't let the door hit you in the ass on the way out."

He gave a little bow. "As you wish." He dropped his hand onto Touray's shoulder, and opal light spiraled around them. A second later they were gone.

I stared at the empty spot a long moment, my chest tightening into a knot. He wasn't coming back, and this was what I wanted. I wondered if I would believe it if I kept telling that to myself. I turned to find Cass and Maya watching me from the kitchen doorway. Maya's face looked sorrowful, her dark eyes moist. Cass held a bottle of vodka and several shot glasses. She set them on the table and filled them up, then handed them around.

"Here's to love," she said with a wink at me.

I blushed.

"To joy and healing," Maya offered.

Josh looked down at his glass and then at me. He raised it slightly. "To family. And revenge."

I lifted my glass, considering a moment. "To getting out alive."

"I don't know what you've been up to in the last few hours," Cass said, filling the glasses again. "But I have a feeling that last one is going to be quite a trick."

"Thanks to my sister's boyfriend here, I walked into the middle of a Tyet war," I said, swallowing the shot then holding out the glass for a refill.

Josh started to say something, and I waved him silent. I doubted he was going to apologize, and I didn't need to hear any more about him wanting me dead. The new Josh didn't seem to know how to say sorry. Not that it mattered. I wouldn't do anything differently, except maybe not get shot. And definitely not let him use me for a punching bag.

"Turns out I've got skills they want, so they are going to be coming after me. Hard and fast. Even if Touray keeps his word, I'll be busy." My lips twisted. Busy was an understatement. I'd be fighting for my life. "But I'm tired of running and hiding, so I'm going to turn it around."

"How?" asked Josh and Cass at the same time. Maya just settled into a chair and watched me. She was one of Touray's tinkers. Anything I said would get back to him. Guaranteed.

I considered my words. "All my life I've been protecting myself, living in the shadows, just like my dad taught me. He had my whole family helping to protect me. I made nulls and hid behind them. It was a good life, a safe life."

I looked around at the others. "Everybody's scared of binders, makers, dreamers, and travellers, not to mention all the secondary abilities. Get on their bad side and they'll come after you. But us tracers—we're just bloodhounds. We can find you and we can hide you, but there's no reason to fear us."

I swallowed my drink. Liquid courage.

"To answer your question about how I'm going to turn it around," I said with a lot more bravado than I actually felt, "the Tyet is going to find out that trace magic is just as dangerous as any other. I'm going to teach them to fear tracers, to fear me. I'm going to make sure they think hard before coming after me or mine ever again."

When I was done, I was going to find Price and hope to hell he still wanted me. Gods and devils willing, I'd live happily ever after.

I just had to survive until then.

The End.

An Excerpt from Diana Pharaoh Francis' *The Cipher*

(The Crosspointe Chronicles)

SOME DAYS DESERVED to be drowned at birth and everyone sent back to bed with a hot brandy, a box of chocolates, and a warm, energetic companion. Today was without question one of those days.

The cutter lurched over the chop, shimmying from side to side in a stomach-twisting quadrille. Rain pebbled the deck and sails. Water sheeted across the bow and swirled around Lucy's feet, too great a flood for the scuppers to handle. Her socks were soaked and she could hardly feel her toes. She ought to have had her boots majicked against the weather like her cloak, but that was a bit more majick than she could take.

Cold eeled deep inside Lucy. Her insides quaked with the penetrating chill and her muscles clenched against it. She tightened her arms around her stomach, wishing she'd eaten a better breakfast and thinking longingly of her forgotten flask of tea.

A few minutes later she heard a shouted "Heave to!" Sailors scrambled up the shrouds to reef the handful of bellied sails. The men at the poles dug sharply into the churning water as the cutter heeled to starboard.

"Sorry, ma'am! Weather's too heavy. Can't take you all the way in to shore. We'd be swamped or bilged. Gotta put you ashore on the arm."

The mate didn't wait for her response, which was just as well. She ground out a string of epithets. She had plenty in store. She'd grown up on the docks among people who lived too close to the edge of life to be bothered with hoity-toity manners. Or any manners at all. She rubbed her cold fingers over her cheeks and pressed them against her mouth to stop the torrent. She was on duty. She had the reputation of the customs office to think about, not to mention her own. She didn't need witnesses to her fears, which were entirely irrational. Knowing that did not settle her stomach or loosen the tension that shook her hands.

The deck dropped and the cutter yawed sickeningly to the side. Lucy gasped and grappled a bench for balance, her feet sliding. The sailors shouted and clung desperately to the rigging. The boat rolled to the other side. She sucked in a harsh breath, bracing against the wall, her legs spread wide. The wash of black waves sounded hungry and loud above the rush of the wind. Clamping down on the whimpers crowding her throat, she bit her lips together until she tasted blood. She jeered silently at herself, hoping everybody was too busy to notice her landlubber fear.

She straightened with an effort, clinging to the back of the bench. The cutter righted itself again and continued its lurching way. Lucy's gaze flicked to the strand of wards glimmering like green pearls beyond the mouth of the harbor. The Pale. Their glow didn't quiet her nausea. Just because in four hundred years the fence of tide and storm wards had never failed to keep sylveth out of the harbor, it didn't mean that today couldn't be different. And Lucy didn't want to be in the water when it happened. Not that the cutter offered safety against sylveth. Nothing did.

She shivered and her throat jerked as she swallowed. She'd seen for herself what raw sylveth could do. She closed her eyes against the memory. But she couldn't halt it any more than she could stop the storm.

The day had been fine, the black sands sparkling in the sunlight, the air redolent with spring. Ten-year-old Lucy and her family were on a picnic during one of their few summer retreats. Robert had been teasing her again. She stalked off, leaving all three of her brothers in peals of laughter. She didn't know how far she walked. She only remembered coming around a jut and stumbling over something soft and sticky.

She had stared at it for long moments, unable to decipher what it was she was looking at. Then a hollow sound slowly filled her ears. Grains trickled past as she stood, unable to tear herself away, recognition creeping over her with insect feet.

It was sylveth spawn, born of majick. Whether it had originally been human or animal or something else entirely, there was no way to tell.

Its skin was cratered and spongy, its gray expanse dotted with weeping protuberances. A ten-foot tentacle with orange suckers all along its length protruded from one side of its jellied mass. On top was a turgid frill, fanning across the surface like tree fungus. It smelled like rotting potatoes, burnt fish and hot butter. The entire length of the creature jerked and twitched as if something inside were trying to escape. More ghastly than anything Lucy could have dreamed of—it was breathing. It might once have been a piece of ship debris, a horse, or even something as prosaic as a laundry tub. Or a sailor who'd fallen prey to a sylveth tide.

In its raw, unaltered form, sylveth wormed through the Inland Sea in silvery skeins of destructive majick. Whatever it touched it changed, and rarely for the good. The Pale was the only thing that kept Crosspointe safe from its warping. But the sylveth sent regular reminders to wash up on the beaches so that no one ever forgot the danger lurking in the sea.

When she could convince her legs to respond, Lucy had run. Ever since that day, she hated sylveth, even the worked sylveth that the majicars promised was safe enough to handle. If it wasn't, they said, the Pale would never let it through. But there were centuries of gossip and rumor that argued otherwise. About babies turning into giant insects and tearing apart a herd of cows, about houses walking off with the families inside, about rugs transforming into rabid flying creatures and hunting farmers in their fields. Fireside tales to frighten children. Everybody knew it. Almost everybody. Lucy's gut refused to believe it. Not that what she thought made any difference. Worked sylveth was the most valuable commodity Crosspointe had to export; it was one entire leg of the three-legged stool making up Crosspointe's economy. Being in customs guaranteed she not only had to be near it but she had to handle it.

Lucy fingered the pendant hidden under her clothing. Even if she hadn't been a customs inspector, she was a Rampling—and loyal down to the toenails. Before she was three minutes old, the crown majicars had put a sylveth cipher around her neck. Every Rampling got one, made of the strongest protective majick available. A shield, a badge, a brand, a collar—it couldn't be removed, not by anyone, not even her. The only thing worse than the pendant against her skin was letting anyone else see it.

Her hand dropped to her side. In Crosspointe, it wasn't the sylveth you had to be afraid of; it was the spells that were attached to them. She eyed the frothing waves. She hated sylveth. But somehow, unbelievably, stupidly, she still craved . . .

She didn't dare finish the thought.

THE CREW ROWED closer to the quay, singing a rhythmic chantey in time to their strokes. The cutter bucked and pitched. Lucy watched as a seaman climbed nimbly up on the rail. He stood swaying, a line caught in his fist. The prow swung toward the quay and he tipped forward in a headlong fall. Lucy caught her breath. But the fall turned into a graceful leap. He landed easily, spinning about to snub the mooring line around a waiting bollard. As the rowers heaved against the waves, the seaman hauled in the slack.

At last the cutter jolted against the tarred hawser bumpers. The gate rail was lifted away and a plank tossed down over the last few feet. Seamen lashed it into place, though it bounced and slid loosely on the quayside.

The tide was going out, making it an uphill climb from the deck. Waves broke over the gangplank and the cutter heaved away from the quay. Lucy considered the narrow bridge skeptically. It might hold a half-grown child, but she was bigger than that. Looking at the narrow bridge, she felt more like a well-grown horse.

"Hurry! Can't hold here long!"

Lucy grimaced. She should have stayed in bed. The wind and rain slapped her face. Beneath the slender bridge, the water churned like black ink. On the other side, the seaman waited, holding out a blunt, rough hand. Two quick steps was all she had to take.

She took a firm hold on her satchel, refusing to look down. She cautiously slid her foot out on the slick wood. As she did, the cutter yawed wide. She slipped, falling hard to one knee. The captain caught her under the arm, helping her up.

"We'll get you a safety line!" he shouted.

"Never mind!" Lucy hollered over the wind, shrugging him off. She lifted the strap of her satchel over her shoulder and thrust herself onto the gangplank. It shimmied and drooped. Her bruised knee buckled as fire flared up her thigh. She flung herself upward at the seaman, snatching at his outstretched hand. He caught her fingers, his callused grip powerful. For a moment Lucy's feet dangled over the water and then he swung her easily up to safety. Unmindful of her dignity, she stumbled and grappled a piling, her body quivering.

He didn't wait for thanks, but released the mooring line and sprang back aboard. The gangplank was hauled in and the cutter shoved off.

Lucy pushed herself upright, hunching into the wind and shuffling toward the harbor terminal. Her cloak fluttered up and spume fountained across the walkway, soaking her uniform surcoat and trousers. She swore again, thinking longingly of her bed.

She passed a host of vessels crowding the slips lining the quay. They were mostly cutters, tugs, and lighters in the employ of the harbor or customs. They pitched from side to side, the lanterns hanging from the riggings winking like frenzied fireflies. A group of sailors trudged past Lucy, laughing and jostling one another. They moved in that rolling gait so typical of seamen, hardly seeming aware of the storm.

Inside the anonymity of her hood, Lucy snarled at them for their calm indifference. But then, sailors spent most of their lives beyond the Pale. What was a storm compared to that?

Lucy stumbled, her throat closing. Fools.

She worked her way up the quay to the harbormaster's terminal. Stern-faced Hornets in charcoal uniforms trimmed in saffron and emerald guarded the entry. Lucy paused long enough to show her customs badge. They nodded and waved her on.

She hesitated, turning to gaze out through the mouth of the harbor. Merstone Island rose out of the ebony water like a sleepy ghost. Beyond were the vast black waters of the Inland Sea. She had a lot of friends out there. Her chest tightened. She did her best to avoid thinking about them, else she'd chew her fingers to bits with constant worry. But in a gale like this . . .

Unwillingly, she thought of Jordan. His ship ought to be coming in soon—she'd expected him more than a sennight ago. She frowned, her jaw jutting out in defiance against her sudden fear. He was an excellent captain. Few were better. He'd been sailing since he was a boy. He was too careful, too cunning to be caught by sylveth or any of the other dangers the Inland Sea had to throw at the ships that dared its depths.

She tried to make herself believe it. But even the most brilliant captain didn't have a chance when the sea unleashed its fury. Braken's fury. Lightning flashed, sending jagged spears of white light across the entire sky. Her eyes closed against the knife-bright glare. Hard on its heels, thunder cracked. The air shook with the angry concussion. Lucy swallowed hard. And the sea god was pissed.

Acknowledgments

This book has been a true labor of love for me, and I have very high hopes that readers (you!) will love it as much as I do. I want to thank the people who helped me bring it to the page. First, to Lucienne Diver for her faith and hard work for so many years. Second, to Debra Dixon for taking on this book and for her wonderful insight in editing. Third, to Sue Bolich and Devon Monk, who gave me amazing feedback and helped make *Trace of Magic* so much better. Fourth, to Tony, who gives me the support I need to write and stay sane in trying moments. Fifth, to Q-ball and Syd, whose hugs make everything all right again. And finally, to all of you who spend your money and time on my words, thank you, thank you, thank you.

About the Author

Diana Pharaoh Francis is the acclaimed author of a dozen novels of fantasy and urban fantasy. Her books have been nominated for the Mary Roberts Rinehart Award and *RT Magazine's* Best Urban Fantasy. *Trace of Magic* is the first book in a new urban fantasy series.

Visit her at dianapfrancis.com and find her on Facebook.

CPSIA information can be obtained
at www.ICGtesting.com
Printed in the USA
LVHW102141261022
731683LV00025B/574